DARK CITIES

Edited by **CHRISTOPHER GOLDEN**

TITAN BOOKS

DARK CITIES
Hardback edition ISBN: 9781785655791
US paperback edition ISBN: 9781785652660
UK paperback edition ISBN: 9781785655807
E-book edition ISBN: 9781785652677

Published by Titan Books
A division of Titan Publishing Group Ltd
144 Southwark Street, London SE1 0UP

First edition: May 2017
2 4 6 8 10 9 7 5 3 1

A CIP catalogue record for this title is available from the British Library.

Printed and bound in Great Britain by CPI Group (UK) Ltd.

DARK CITIES

CONTENTS

DARK CITIES

An Introduction by
CHRISTOPHER GOLDEN

In the opening years of the 1990s, I had an office on the 39th floor of the building at 1515 Broadway in Manhattan. My office window overlooked Times Square. On the wall just behind my computer I tacked a small piece of paper bearing a quote from the novel *Dead Lines* by horror legends John Skipp and Craig Spector.

> *New York is the City that eats its young,*
> *with high-rise teeth and pavement tongue.*
> *I came.*
> *I saw.*
> *I was digested.*

I loved working in Manhattan, but at twenty-two, I didn't have the courage to live there. It's one of the major regrets of my life and sometimes I wonder just what the hell I was afraid of. (Sure, part of it was the staggering cost of living in the city, but I know it wasn't just that. The city intimidated me.) Still, I managed to do my share of exploring, have my share of late nights and subway rides and wandering into the wrong streets, the strange little blocks far downtown that don't follow the strict order of their uptown counterparts.

Since those years, I've wandered other cities and gotten lost in cobblestoned labyrinths that look as if they haven't changed in centuries, and I've messed up directions and found myself on a dead-end street bookended by boarded-up crack dens in the most dangerous neighborhood in the city. There are so many cities I love, from Boston to Vienna, London to New York, L.A. to Paris. But just because I love them, that doesn't mean they don't make me a little nervous sometimes.

On a recent conference panel, a half dozen writers discussed where they felt more afraid, in the city or in rural areas. (Strangely, the suburbs never came up, though so much of modern horror has taken place in small towns.) While I understood the fear of walking in the forest alone—listening for the wolves or mountain lions that must be following your every step—I confessed that I find more potential terror in the thought of walking the streets and alleys of a large city in the small hours of the morning, when everyone with good intentions is either fast asleep or working third shift. The wolves that hunt people on the streets of some dark city are the ones that haunt me, even if those wolves are only shadows themselves.

As trend-waves crash onto the shores of publishing— zombies, dystopian fiction, contagion—I've turned more and more toward the kinds of horror stories I've always loved best, intimate and personal, rooted in love or loneliness or abandonment. I also gravitate toward folklore, both ancient and modern. When I start thinking along such lines, searching for great stories to read on whatever subject has me fired up at the moment, my desire for such stories leads to a simple conclusion: don't just seek out such stories, make them happen.

When I reached out to the extraordinary list of authors you will find within—from massive *New York Times* bestsellers to some of the most acclaimed literary writers in the genre—the response was overwhelming. These writers share my fears and are inspired by their own. In the following pages, each will explore the horrors they've found in the city's shadows, whether those shadows be in the lonely corners of an uncaring city or inside their own hearts.

Come, now. Turn the page. Enter the darkest of cities.

THE DOGS

by

SCOTT SMITH

Her real name wasn't Rose—that was just what she used when she met guys on Craigslist: Rose or Rosa or Rosemary or even Rosaline (but mostly Rose). She'd always liked names that came from flowers. When she was six, she'd had a set of dolls, four of them, dressed like little cowgirls, and she'd named them Rose, Daisy, Petunia, and Tulip. Rose had been her favorite, though, the one she'd slept with every night.

There was a way you could phrase your post on Craigslist so it was clear what you wanted—or what you were offering—without being too explicit. Rose's go-to headline was: "Gorgeous Young Girl Searching For Generous Older Gent." She didn't think of herself as a prostitute because she never took money from the men. Or only one time, with that Egyptian guy, and then just because it would've felt awkward to refuse it—the wad of bills he'd slid into her jacket pocket as they kissed goodbye at the door. It was a thick wad, but mostly tens and fives (even a couple of singles), so it seemed like it ought to have been more than it actually turned out to be. Rose ended up feeling disappointed when she finally had a chance to count it, in a bathroom stall at Penn Station, waiting to board the 8:37 AM train back to her mother's house. She hadn't eaten, and she was coming down from whatever the pink pills were that she and the Egyptian had taken together, so her hands were shaking, and she kept dropping the bills onto the bathroom's dirty floor, kept dropping them and picking them up, and each time she did this she lost count and needed to start all over again. She never managed to arrive at a consistent number—it was one hundred and twelve dollars, or maybe one hundred and seventeen—a weird number either way, and small enough to make Rose feel cheap and whorish rather than classy like she'd hoped.

Money was never the point. It was the sense of adventure, the feeling of power, and the thrill of the places where the men took her, places Rose never would've been able to go on her own—expensive restaurants, clubs, and hotels... even their own apartments sometimes. Rose spent a night in a penthouse once, overlooking the East River, with a Christmas tree on the terrace. The guy she was with turned on the tree's little white lights for her. Rose wanted to take a photo with her phone, but the guy wouldn't let her. He was worried she'd post the picture online somewhere, and that his wife might see it. The wife was in Anguilla with the children, who were out of school for the holidays.

Rose lived at her mother's house, in New Jersey, an hour's train ride west of Penn Station. She had a room in the basement. This wasn't as depressing as it might sound. Rose had her own shower and toilet down there, her own entrance; the only reason she ever needed to venture upstairs was if she wanted to use the kitchen—which she didn't, mostly. She had a mini-fridge beside her bed, and a hot plate she never used, and there was a pizza place a short walk down the road, so who needed a kitchen? Rose was nineteen, but believed she looked older. She'd bought a fake Ohio driver's license online two years ago; it listed her age as twenty-three, and no bouncer or bartender had ever questioned it. Rose had gotten her

GED the previous summer, and then had taken a few classes in dental hygiene before dropping out (she told anyone who asked that she planned to go back, but she didn't really believe it). Now she worked part-time at a beauty salon in downtown Dunellen, massaging shampoo into the scalps of elderly women and sweeping up the cut hair. On the first of every month, she paid her mother seventy-five dollars cash for the room in the basement (her mother called this "a symbolic gesture").

Her mother didn't know about her Craigslist dates. Rose would tell her she was going to spend the night in the city with friends—with Holly or Carrie—and this always covered things. Her mother didn't know that Holly had moved with her boyfriend to Buffalo, or that Carrie had gotten mono and then hepatitis and then some sort of intestinal disorder, and now she was living in Alabama with a Pentecostal aunt and uncle, who were trying to cure her with prayer (so Rose didn't really have anyone left in her life you could properly call a friend).

Enough people had told Rose she was pretty in the past decade that she'd come to believe it, too. She was self-conscious about her teeth (she had a slight overbite; if she wasn't careful, it could make her lisp), and she wished her hair had more body to it, and always in the back of her mind was the comment a boy had made in tenth grade (that she had a rabbity, white-trash aura about her), but generally Rose could keep all of this at bay, and feel almost beautiful—especially at night, especially if she'd been drinking. Long blond hair, blue eyes, skinny hips, softball-sized breasts: sometimes on Craigslist she'd describe herself as "a young Britney," and no one she'd met had ever challenged her on this.

* * *

He said his name was Patrick, but he didn't seem like a Patrick to Rose. In Rose's mind, "Patrick" implied an Irish look—tall and fair-haired and blue-eyed, rather than short and dark and fidgety, the latter quality so pronounced in this case that Rose thought maybe he'd fortified himself for the date with a bump or two of coke. She didn't care what his real name was. Most of the men she met were lying about one thing or another, just like her—names were the least of it. He took her to dinner at a sushi place in the Meat Packing district, and then escorted her across the street to a bar where it was too loud to talk. They ended up making out for five minutes in the little hallway that led to the bathrooms, and when she refused to follow him into the men's room, Patrick told her he wanted to take her home.

He'd said he was thirty, but Rose guessed he must be closer to forty, if not already safely across the line. She thought he probably wore glasses in his normal life, because his eyes had a blurred, watery look when he talked to her, as if he couldn't quite bring her into focus. His face was round, and slightly flushed, like the baby angels she'd seen in old paintings. Rose was certain she'd known the name for these creatures once, but she couldn't remember it now—sometimes this would happen to her. Right after they'd sat down for dinner, he'd announced that he was a lawyer, and Rose had no reason to doubt him, but if he was saying it merely to impress her, he was aiming in the wrong direction.

He kissed her again in the cab uptown, his mouth tasting of sushi and sake, and then he cupped her breasts in his hands, first the right, then the left, giving each a gentle squeeze: Rose had a brief memory of her mother, in the produce section at Safeway, testing oranges for ripeness. She was half-splayed across Patrick's lap, and she could feel his erection through his pants—the bulk and heat of it. When she pressed down with her leg, Patrick groaned, then bit her ear.

His apartment was on the Upper West Side, somewhere beyond Lincoln Center, but before the Apple Store, a prewar building, with no doorman. The elevator was tiny, almost phone booth size—they rode it to the seventh floor—and then there was a long, dimly lit hallway, a door with three separate locks. The door was dark gray, and had two black numbers painted at eye level: 78. Patrick looked nervous suddenly. He undid the first lock, dropped his keys, undid the second lock, dropped the keys again. Rose was accustomed to this by now, the terror some men appeared to feel when there was no longer any question of what was about to happen. It always seemed odd to her, since this was precisely the moment when she began to feel most calm: no one needed to think anymore, they were in the chute, all of the necessary decisions had already been made, and now gravity could take command. Other people's anxiety had a way of unsettling Rose—as if it were contagious—and she felt an urge to soothe Patrick. She lifted her hand to caress the nape of his neck; she was close enough to feel that buzzy sensation another person's skin can radiate an instant before you touch it, when the barking began. Rose jumped at the sound, then laughed, and the final lock was undone, and the door was swinging open, and there they were: three dogs, one big and black and shaggy, one small and white and fluffy, and the last of them lean and brown with a white patch over its eye, like the hero in a children's picture book.

Rose managed only a brief impression of the apartment. It had a dorm room feel: linoleum on the floor, a glimpse of what appeared to be a plastic lawn chair through the archway to the darkened living room. There was a flurry of panting and licking from the dogs, along with much wagging of tails, and some leaping and yapping by the fluffy white one, and then Patrick was leading Rose across the little entranceway, kicking off his shoes, dragging his shirt over his head, pulling her down the hall to the bedroom. He pushed her onto the bed, and started to undo his belt, while all three dogs watched from the doorway. The dogs stayed there while she and Patrick fucked; every time Rose glanced in their direction, she saw them staring. Rose was too drunk to enjoy the sex—it felt hazy and faraway, and the bed kept threatening to start spinning—but none of this was Patrick's fault. He was surprisingly gentlemanly in his efforts; he seemed to want her pleasure almost as much as he desired his own, and Rose was grateful for this—grateful, too, for the glass of water he fetched afterward, grateful for what felt to her like clean sheets, and grateful most of all that Patrick showed no appetite for post-coital conversation. Sometimes guys wanted to talk. In Rose's experience, it was never a good idea.

The last thing Patrick said to her was the dogs' names.

Jack was the taut, brown, intelligent-looking fellow with the patch over his eye—a mix of whippet and Lab.

Zeus was the big, black, shaggy one… a Bernese mountain dog.

Millie was the tiny, fluffy, white one: a Bichon Frise, which Patrick assured Rose meant French bitch.

"For real?" Rose asked.

Patrick laughed, and something about the sound jarred loose the word she'd been searching for earlier. It just popped into her mind—sometimes that could happen, too.

Cherub.

A moment later, with the lights still on, they were both asleep.

* * *

"The most difficult part is right here: believing this is happening. If you can manage that, you can manage everything."

Rose was still half-asleep when she heard the voice—a male

voice, calmer than Patrick's, deep and slow. There was an air of authority to the words, of command; Rose sensed it was the slowness that accounted for this quality (one further tap of the brakes, and the voice would've slipped into a drawl). She opened her eyes. Patrick wasn't in the room—she could hear the shower running. Jack, the tan dog with the eye patch, was sitting beside the bed, staring at her, and she knew without a moment's doubt that it was his voice she was hearing.

"He'll come back from the shower in another minute, and he'll suggest you have sex again. He'll pressure you to try on a pair of handcuffs. Then he's going to kill you."

Rose lifted her head from the pillow. She could still feel the alcohol from last night, a sloshing sensation inside her brain, as if she might spill out of herself were she to move too quickly. Zeus, the big black dog, was lying on the floor by the closet. Millie, the little white one, was on the armchair by the window. They were both watching her.

Jack's voice continued: "Other girls have decided this was a dream. I hope you won't make the same mistake."

Over on the chair, Millie began to wag her tail. Rose's clothes were scattered across the floor. She was thinking about how much effort it would take to pick them up and pull them on, and how unpleasant it would be to rush out of the apartment without washing her face or emptying her bladder or rinsing her mouth, when she heard the shower shut off.

Jack walked toward the armchair, his nails making a clicking sound on the linoleum. There was a square of sunlight beneath the window, and he lay down in its center. He didn't move his mouth when he spoke—it wasn't like that. Rose just heard the words inside her head, and she knew they were his. "The knife is in the night table drawer," he said. "All you need to do is get there first."

Then he shut his eyes. So did Zeus and Millie. From one second to the next, the three dogs went from staring at her to what looked like the deepest sort of sleep. Then Patrick was in the doorway, smiling down at her, naked, rubbing his hair with a towel. His penis was edging its way toward an erection, both stiff and floppy all at once. "Wanna try something fun?" he asked. He moved toward the closet, without waiting for a reply.

Rose was about to tell him that she'd just had the weirdest dream, that his dog was speaking to her in it, telling her that—

But then Patrick turned from the closet, his penis all the way erect now, a deep purple. He was moving toward her, holding a pair of handcuffs, bending to reach for her wrist.

She lunged for the night table, and all three dogs began to bark.

* * *

Afterward—maybe an hour, maybe two, Rose wouldn't have been able to say for certain—she was sitting on a bench, five or six blocks away, on the edge of Riverside Park. The panic was starting to ease now, but this didn't mean she was feeling calm, not remotely. Numb would be the better description, though even this adjective would imply a degree of equanimity that was completely lacking. It was more like the absence of sensation that comes with extreme cold, as frostbite starts to set in: Rose knew there was a lot going on inside her head, but it had reached a point of extremity beyond which she could no longer feel anything specific, just a generalized, deeply subterranean hum of distress.

It was early April, and the wind off the river retained a wintry bite, but the trees didn't seem to mind: they were beginning to bud. Nannies pushed strollers; squirrels made darting forays across the still-not-quite-green grass. Rose's nose was running. She didn't know if it was the wind or an early bout of allergies or maybe just some physiological response to what had happened—to what she'd done. Could terror cause your nose to run? She kept wiping the snot on her sleeve, her leg jiggling with leftover adrenaline, while she tried to decide what she ought to do.

She'd gotten the drawer open, and there was indeed a knife inside, a large knife, the kind a soldier might carry in a sheath on his ankle, though there wasn't any sheath for this one, just the knife, its blade forged from some sort of black metal, its grip feeling slightly sticky in Rose's hand. The next few moments might not have unfolded so easily for her had it not been for the dogs. All three were leaping and barking, and in the midst of this tumult, Zeus made contact with enough force to knock Patrick off balance. Rose wasn't trying to stab him in any particular place; she was just swinging the blade, and the dogs were leaping, and Patrick was rushing toward her—stumbling, really, and then falling—and that was how the blade ended up piercing his throat, sinking deep, all the way to the hilt. Patrick dropped to the bed, and the knife came out of his body with a sucking sound, like a stick yanked from a muddy yard, and there was blood everywhere, an immense amount of it, fountaining upward, hitting the wall beside the bed and splattering to the floor with a lawn-sprinkler sound, and Patrick was gurgling and frothing and trying impotently to rise, and Rose dropped the knife, gathered up her clothes, and ran from the room. Her arms and face and chest were covered with blood. At first, she'd feared it might be hers, but when she washed it off in the kitchen sink, she couldn't find any wounds, and finally she decided it all had to be Patrick's. Standing at the sink, still naked, searching for a towel to dry her body, there was a moment when she thought she was going to call 911. It seemed like the obvious path, and if there'd been a landline in the apartment, she might've gone ahead and dialed the number—it would've been so easy, just three quick taps of her finger, and then other people would be making the decisions for her. But there wasn't a landline, and Rose's phone was still in her purse, and her purse was still in the bedroom, which was where Patrick was, along with the three dogs, so Rose found a tablecloth to dry herself, and she crouched to pee into a drinking glass, and emptied the glass into the sink, and then she was shivering, so she pulled on her clothes, and suddenly it seemed like maybe the easiest thing to do was leave, just leave, walk across the little entranceway to the front door, undo its three locks, and flee.

Sitting on the park bench, Rose tried to imagine what she must look like to the people passing by. It was a shock to realize she probably seemed perfectly fine; it made the whole situation feel that much stranger. A horrifying, desperate thing had happened to her, and none of these strangers who saw Rose here, sitting in the sun, wiping her nose on her sleeve, jiggling her leg, none of them would ever be able to guess.

Not one. Not ever.

She'd made mistakes. Jesus fucking Christ: it appalled her to think how many.

If she were still planning to call 911 (and she was, wasn't she?), she should never have left the apartment—she shouldn't even have left the room, shouldn't have washed herself at the kitchen sink, shouldn't have pulled on her clothes. She should've scrambled for her cell phone, should've called for an ambulance right there, standing beside the bed, bent over Patrick, balling up the sheet and pressing it against the jagged wound in his throat.

Jesus, Jesus, Jesus. She'd fucked this up.

Now, when she dialed 911, the police would want to know why she'd left, why she'd waited so long to call. And what was she supposed to tell them, anyway? That she'd stabbed a near stranger in the throat because his dog had warned her the guy was planning to kill her? How well was this story going to play for her? Rose didn't have any wounds, not even a bruise—Patrick hadn't managed to touch her.

And the *dog*... well, she had to think through that part of the morning's events, didn't she? It had seemed so obvious when she was there in the room, half-awake, hearing his voice.

But now?

Oh, for fuck's sake. She'd had one of those weird early morning dreams, hadn't she? She'd mistaken it for real, and she'd killed a guy.

But what about the handcuffs? And how had she known there was a knife in that drawer? And *why* was there a knife in that drawer?

Rose thought of Doctor Dolittle. She thought of Son of Sam. Neither model seemed especially helpful.

She'd left her purse in the apartment. Her phone. Her wallet. And that was just the easy stuff. There would be fingerprints. Hair. Saliva. Vaginal fluid. Tiny flakes of dead skin. There would be other stuff, too—there had to be—stuff she'd probably never be able to think of.

Rose had no idea what she was going to do, but one thing seemed unavoidable: she needed to go back.

* * *

The street door was locked.

Rose hadn't thought of this, and it made her angry with herself—there was so much she wasn't thinking of, so much she was getting wrong. She tried the knob; she pushed at the door with her shoulder. There was a buzzer system, with buttons for the different apartments. In movies, people were always using this sort of thing to gain illicit access to buildings. They'd push a button, claim to be a UPS deliveryman, and some too-trusting tenant would buzz them in. Rose didn't think this strategy would work for her, but she also didn't think she had much to lose in trying: she started with the top floor, pressed the button, waited long enough to realize there wasn't going to be a response, then tried the next apartment down the line. She was on her fifth button before she got an answer. What sounded like a very old man's voice said: "Hello…?"

Rose put her mouth up against the speaker: "UPS."

There was a long pause—too long, it seemed to Rose—maybe there was a camera? Or maybe the old man was coming downstairs to sign for the supposed package? Or maybe he'd seen all of those movies Rose had seen, and he was calling the police right now, so she'd have one more inexplicable thing to explain to them when they finally showed up? Or maybe—

The door buzzed, and she jumped forward, pushing it open.

The building had fifteen stories. Rose got into the elevator and pressed buttons for the ninth, tenth, eleventh, twelfth, and fourteenth floors. That way, if the old man had stepped out into the hallway and was watching the elevator, he wouldn't know which floor Rose was going to. She rode to nine, then crept along the hall to the stairs, and tiptoed back down to the seventh floor.

Apartment 78. The gray door, with its three (not locked) locks.

Rose felt an impulse to ring the bell (which she resisted), and then—once she'd pushed open the door and stepped into the apartment—she had an even stronger urge to call out Patrick's name (which she also resisted). From the entranceway, you could see into the kitchen. The tablecloth Rose had used as a towel lay in a damp mound on the linoleum in front of the refrigerator. To the right of the kitchen, a short hallway led to the bedroom. Beyond the bedroom, the hallway turned to the left—Rose assumed this must be where the bathroom was.

She made her way to the bedroom. Part of her was hoping that none of it had happened—that it had all been a dream, not just the talking dog: everything. Patrick would still be asleep in the bed, or else awake now, drinking coffee, wondering where Rose had run off to so abruptly, and why. The sight of the bloody sheets cured Rose of this fantasy: the blood on the wall above the bed, the blood pooling on the floor. There was no sign of Patrick, so Rose assumed he must've slipped off the mattress, that he must be sprawled on the floor now, hidden by the bed's bulk. But when she edged her way into the room, angling toward the armchair by the window, where her purse awaited her, and inside her purse, her cell phone, and through the magic of the cell phone, the police… when she cleared the foot of bed and forced herself to look, there was more blood, there was the knife lying in the center of that blood, and there were paw prints—dozens of them—around the margins of the mess, but there was no Patrick.

He must've crawled under the bed as he bled himself out. It gave Rose a shivery feeling to imagine this.

She crouched, bent to peer into the darkness. Down low like that, just an inch or two above the puddle, the raw-steak smell of the blood hit Rose with extra vigor, and for an instant she thought she might vomit. The sensation passed as quickly as it came. She could see nothing under the bed but dust bunnies and clumps of shed dog hair.

Which meant… Patrick was alive?

Such an outcome seemed impossible to Rose, but even as she thought this, she was stepping into the pool of blood, and reaching for the knife. It was the purest sort of reflex, fear-driven, from the base of her spine. Part of her was saying:

Couldn't this be a good thing? And another part—the stronger part, the part that had never intended to call 911, that had known all along the only way through this was to bury what needed to be buried, and run away from the rest—*that* part was shaking its head, and saying: *No, no, no, no, no...*

Rose didn't see any blood on the linoleum in the hallway, and this puzzled her. She couldn't imagine how Patrick had been able to escape the bedroom—crawling or staggering— without leaving some sort of trail behind. Then she reached the bathroom, and came upon Millie. The hallway was dim, and Rose's first impression was of a soccer-ball sized clot of white fur, tensely vibrating. It took her a moment to realize that Millie was licking the floor, with a frenzied aura of purpose. The dog swung its tiny body toward Rose; she stared up at her for a half-second, her muzzle stained dark-red. Then she pivoted away, lowered her head to the floor again and resumed her licking, audibly panting with the effort. Beyond her, Rose could see that the linoleum was smeared with blood. The trail led to a shut door at the end of the hall, fifteen feet past the bathroom.

Rose could hear something making a shuffling sound on the other side of the door, and... was that a grunt? She took a step forward, and called out: "Patrick?"

The sound stopped.

"Patrick...?"

Jack seemed to materialize from the center of the door. Rose flinched, almost dropped the knife. Then she realized there was a swinging panel cut into the wood—a dog door. Jack had pushed his way through it, and he was standing there now, in the dim light, his front paws in the hall, his back paws still on the other side of the door. His muzzle, like Millie's, was stained with blood. There was a strong odor coming from the room; Rose couldn't identify it—all she knew was that it was unpleasant. Jack stared at her. She could feel him looking at her face, then at the knife in her hand, then back at her face. She heard his voice in her head again. "Why don't you go wait in the kitchen? Get yourself something to drink. I'll be out in a minute, and we can talk this through."

And then, without waiting for Rose to respond, he ducked back through the tiny door.

* * *

The strangest part wasn't that the dog could speak. It was that —while it was happening, at least—Rose didn't find it strange at all.

The first thing Jack said when he came into the kitchen was: "Would you mind freshening the water in the bowl?"

There was a dog bowl sitting on a mat beside the refrigerator, half-full of water. Rose took it to the sink, rinsed it out, refilled it, and set it back on the mat. Then she sat in her chair again and watched Jack lap at the water. When he was finished, he lay down beside the bowl, facing her. He'd managed to clean most of the blood from his muzzle, and Rose was thankful for this. She'd found a Diet Coke in the otherwise almost completely empty refrigerator, and she sat clutching the can in her hands, feeling grateful for the chill against her palms—there was something soothing about the sensation, something grounding. She'd been sitting here for the past five minutes, waiting for the dog to appear, and wishing that she'd never posted her ad on Craigslist, wishing this, and then wishing it again, and then again, which was a pointless expenditure of energy, she knew, and a stupid thing to waste a wish on.

"Where do you live?" Jack asked.

"In New Jersey," Rose said.

"With roommates?"

Rose shook her head. "At my mother's. In her basement."

"That's good," Jack said. "That's very good. So moving in here won't be a problem?"

Rose just stared at him. *I'm talking to a dog*, she thought. *I killed a man, and now I'm talking to his dog.* She felt exhausted suddenly, and dizzy to the point of nausea. She thought she was about to faint, so she bent forward and placed her head between her knees. It helped, but not a lot.

Jack made a noise—it sounded like a sigh. "I know this is probably quite confusing for you, but if we can just focus on the basics, I'm confident you'll soon find your bearings."

"How do you know how to speak?" Rose asked, without raising her head.

Jack ignored the question. "It might feel uncomfortable for you to acknowledge this, but you're not really in a position of power here. And the sooner you come to grips with that fact, the sooner we'll sort everything out. There's a body in the back room. A body with a knife wound to the throat. Your fingerprints are on the knife. Are you with me this far?"

Rose could feel the dog watching her, waiting for her to lift her head and look at him. She didn't move.

Jack seemed to take her silence as an affirmation. "Would you like to know what would happen if you were to run away? Zeus and Millie and I would eventually get hungry. We'd start to bark and whimper and howl, and soon enough one of the neighbors would call the landlord, and the landlord would call the police, and the door would be broken down. And the body would be found. And the knife. And your fingerprints. And inside the back room? Other bodies. I think you'd be startled to learn how many. Now, you could certainly try to tell the police: 'I didn't kill those girls. Daniel did.' But then they'll ask how you came to know this. And you'll say that his dog—"

Rose lifted her head from her lap. "Who's Daniel?"

"The young man you stabbed in the throat."

"He said his name was Patrick."

"What did you tell him your name was?"

Rose dropped her head back between her knees.

"You're a Jersey girl," Jack said. "Isn't this what you've always dreamed of? A Manhattan apartment?"

"How can you talk?" Rose asked again.

Once more Jack ignored the question. "You don't have to worry about the body. Zeus and I are taking care of it. Millie will handle the blood on the floor and walls—I think you'll be surprised at how clean she can get things with that tiny tongue of hers. The mattress and pillows are lined with plastic—Millie will lick them as good as new. It's really only the sheets that are ever a problem. Daniel used to tie them up in a Hefty bag—double bag it. There's a chute beside the elevator; it leads straight down to the building's incinerator. Just drop the bags in, and it will be like he never even existed."

Rose lifted her head again. "What about his family? His friends?"

"Daniel was a guy who spent the past seven months luring young women to his apartment, so that he could handcuff them to his bed, and kill them. Does that sound like someone with a close-knit social network?"

Rose was silent. She was thinking about all the people Daniel must've come into contact with as he moved through his days: his boss, his—

Jack seemed to guess her chain of thought: "He worked at a copy shop in midtown. They'll call once, maybe twice. When they don't get an answer, they'll hire someone new. In three weeks, they'll have forgotten Daniel's name."

"He said he was a lawyer."

Rose wouldn't have guessed a dog could smile, but that was what Jack did now. Not with his lips, of course—it was just an upward slant of his tail, a tilt of his head, and the way his ears lifted slightly—but it communicated the same amusement that a smile would have. It was a funny thing to see a dog do—almost more extraordinary than his talking. "You'll find new sheets in the hall closet," he said. "Daniel bought them in bulk. The keys are on a hook by the door, along with the leashes. Zeus and I usually like to go out first thing in the morning—around eight or so. Millie sleeps late; she goes out around noon, and then again together with me at six PM—that's when you'll take us to the dog run, over by the river. The last walk is for Zeus and Millie, around midnight. How does that sound?"

Rose shook her head. "I can't—"

"Of course you can. You don't have a choice."

Jack got up and walked over to Rose. He rested his head on her knee. He could talk, but he was still a dog. He looked up at her with that adorable white patch over his eye, and gave a slow wag of his tail. Rose's hand lifted toward him, reflexively; she only stopped herself from petting him at the last instant. Jack offered her another one of his smiles. "I know it must be a lot to absorb. We're asking you to change your whole life. But consider this: maybe it will be a change for the better. There's a bankcard on the table by the front door. The code is six-three-eight-four. I don't know what the exact balance is at the moment, but it should be enough to live on for quite some time, if you're frugal. You could take a course or two, if you liked. Lay the groundwork for a career. You'd have the freedom to do that, living here. It can be a win-win situation, if you only embrace it with the right attitude."

Rose tried to imagine the life he was proposing. Four walks a day with the dogs. A bankcard that wasn't hers. Resuming her dental hygiene studies. Nights spent sleeping in the bed where she'd killed Patrick. Or Daniel, rather. And where Daniel had killed some as-yet-unknowable number of young women. Whose bones, Rose assumed, must be lying in the back room, picked clean by the—

"What should we call you?" Jack asked.

"Rose." She spoke without thinking, and she realized as soon as she'd said the word that it implied a degree of consent.

"You can't imagine how tired we were of him, Rose."

"Who?"

"Daniel. The cologne… did you smell the cologne? We asked him to stop with it—again and again, we asked. But he wouldn't listen. And Millie, well—you'll see what I mean soon enough—Millie can be difficult in her way. But Daniel had no patience with her. He started to lock her in the hall closet for long periods, and we couldn't accept that sort of behavior, could we? So we decided to find a replacement. And as soon as you walked through the door, we were certain you were the one. You have a kind smile. Has anyone ever told you this? And you smell nice. Do you eat bacon, Rose? Because there's a bacon-y smell to your skin. We all noticed it, right from the start."

Rose stared down at the dog. Her hand kept wanting to touch his head, and finally she surrendered to the temptation. She scratched him behind the ears. Jack shut his eyes with pleasure. "How can you talk?" she asked again.

"It's something with the apartment. Out on the street, we're just like any other dogs."

"But your vocabulary? The phrases you use? Like 'win-win'? How do you know that?'

It wasn't just smiling; Jack could shrug too—a lift of his shoulder, a downward tilt of his head. He did it now. "We watch a lot of TV."

"The others can talk, too?"

"Zeus doesn't like to. But he can, if he wants."

"And Millie?"

"You'll see. She likes it maybe a little too much."

Rose could still call the police. She could walk back to the bedroom, fetch her cell phone, and dial 911. She considered doing this for a few seconds, and then found herself thinking about the bankcard Jack had mentioned. It was difficult to keep from wondering how much money might be in the account.

"One step at a time," Jack said. "That's always the easiest way, isn't it? Start with the sheets. Bag them, throw them out. Then take Zeus and me for a quick walk. By the time we get back, Millie will have cleaned the mattress. You can put fresh sheets on the bed. And then, well, you'll see. It will start to feel like home in no time."

* * *

There was still a lot of blood on the bedroom floor, so Rose spent the first night on the couch in the little family room, just off the kitchen. She kept waking and staring into the darkness, at the shadowy skeleton of the plastic lawn chair across the room, at the TV hanging on the wall, and the empty bookshelf beside it, and wondering where she was—wondering and then remembering, not just where she was, but what had happened. In the morning, her back hurt from the couch's lumpy cushions, and she showered until her fingertips started to wrinkle, and she thought: *I can't do this, I'm going home, I don't care what happens.* But when she climbed out of the shower, Jack was sitting on the mat beside the tub, and Zeus was in the hallway, pacing back and forth, and she realized that they needed to go outside for their morning walk, so she dressed, and leashed the two dogs, and took them around the block. And then she was hungry, but there wasn't any food in the apartment, and she only had four dollars in her wallet, so she took the bankcard from the table beside the front door, and went to the bank on the corner, and punched in six-three-eight-four at the ATM. The card had a woman's name on it: Tabitha O'Rourke. Rose didn't want to wonder too long who this woman might be, or how Jack had come to know the PIN for her account, which had a balance of... *whoa*... just over nineteen thousand dollars.

Rose withdrew twenty dollars, then immediately thought better of this sum, reinserted the bankcard, and took out two hundred more. She bought some groceries at Fairway and carried them back to the apartment. She made a grilled cheese sandwich, and ate an apple, and took Millie out, and then she came back and sat on the couch with Jack at her feet, and it wasn't that bad, really, not at all. And Rose thought to herself: *Okay, maybe one more night.*

Jack looked up at her from his place on the rug, and he did that thing that was just like a smile.

The next day, Rose took a train out to New Jersey and brought back a suitcase's worth of clothes. She left a note for her mother on the kitchen table, saying she was going to be in the city for a while, dog-sitting for a friend. She spent the evening cleaning the kitchen, and then she used the bankcard to withdraw another hundred dollars, and she bought more food and filled the fridge with it.

A week passed.

Millie finished licking up all the blood in the bedroom— Jack was right; she did a remarkable job—and Rose took to sleeping there. It wasn't nearly as creepy to spend the night in the bed as she'd feared, and the mattress was much more comfortable than the couch's misshapen cushions.

Jack and Millie liked to watch TV in the evening. Rose

would sit on the couch with the two dogs, one on either side. Jack often dozed, only half-attending to the screen, but Millie watched with a tense alertness that Rose found a little unsettling. Zeus never took part in these evenings. He spent most of his time hidden in the rear room. He would emerge for his two walks every day, and then trot back down the hallway as soon as they returned, squeezing his big body through the swinging panel that had been cut into the door. All three of the dogs slept in the back room. Rose assumed there still must be some meat left on Daniel's body, and that this was what the dogs were sustaining themselves on, because Jack would prod her to refresh the water bowl, but he hadn't asked her to buy them any food yet. She kept waiting for him to do this.

One morning, Rose woke early, just before dawn, with a full bladder, and after she used the toilet, she crept down the hall to the rear room, and crouched in front of the door, and quietly pushed open the wooden panel, and tried to peek inside. The room was very dim—there didn't appear to be a window—and she could sense more than see the three dogs. It was hard to tell what else was inside the room. There was that smell again: a not-good smell. Rose had a vague sense of tumbled objects—bones, she supposed, though she couldn't be certain—and then she heard the beginning of a growl, low and threatening, as much vibration as actual sound, and she dropped the panel back into place, and retreated quickly to her bedroom.

Rose assumed it must've been Zeus who'd done the growling, because Zeus didn't appear to like her very much. He had a sullen and aloof demeanor; perhaps it was just Rose's impression, but he seemed to make a conscious effort to avoid her gaze. Millie was the opposite—it was difficult to get away from her. And, unlike Zeus, she talked. Jesus, how she talked: she never seemed to shut up. Her days were a continuous outpouring of substance-less chatter. She had obsessions, and she shared them liberally. There were TV shows she'd seen over the years, repetitively, and now she liked to recount their plotlines, complete not only with long excerpts of dialogue, but also with Millie's elaborate analyses of their characters' actions. *Friday Night Lights. The Brady Bunch. Melrose Place* (the original— Rose made the mistake of mentioning the remake, and the next seven hours were consumed by Millie's criticisms of it). *As the World Turns. Sex and the City. The Flintstones. Seinfeld. Gilligan's Island.* The list appeared to be endless. Rose wouldn't have thought it would be possible to fill entire days talking about this sort of thing, but apparently it was quite easy. She took to carrying her iPod around the house, to block out Millie's voice.

And Jack? Jack was her favorite.

In the mornings, before Millie was awake, and with Zeus still hiding in the back room, Rose and Jack would have the apartment to themselves. Jack would curl up on the couch beside Rose while she drank her first cup of coffee, or he'd lie on the mat beside the tub while she showered, or he'd sit on the still unmade bed and watch as she dressed. He called her "Girl." As in: "You need a new pair of tennis shoes, Girl. Those are completely worn out." Or: "You realize what time it is, Girl? Aren't you going to be late?" Or: "Let Millie choose the channel, Girl." Outside the apartment, walking around the neighborhood, he was just a normal dog. But what a beauty! With his lean, muscular frame, his silky coat, and that white patch over his eye… people would turn to watch them pass. They called out to Rose: "Gorgeous dog!" And whenever this happened—almost every afternoon, in other words—Rose would wish that it was just her and Jack living together in New York, that there was no Zeus, and no Millie, and no back room full of bones. She'd wish, too, that Jack couldn't talk, and that she hadn't stabbed Daniel, and that she didn't have to lie awake at night and wonder what had happened to Tabitha O'Rourke. But what she'd wish more than anything else—what she'd wish, and then wish again, and then wish once more, three times for luck—was that her life didn't feel so much like a bomb, ticking its way down toward *boom*.

One morning, in the shower, she thought of something that she probably should've considered much earlier. "What about the rent?" she asked.

Jack was in his usual spot, on the mat beside the tub, licking his paws clean. "What about it?"

"Don't I need to pay it?"

"It's deducted from the bank every month—automatically."

Rose wiped the water from her eyes, stuck her head out from behind the shower curtain, and peered down at the dog. There was a lot of money in Tabitha O'Rourke's account, but not so much that a New York rent wouldn't rapidly erode its balance. "From the same account as the bankcard?"

It wasn't just smiling and shrugging; Jack knew how to shake his head, too. This particular gesture he managed just like a human would. He did it now. "A different one."

"Daniel's?"

Another shake of that bony skull: "It belongs to someone who lived here before Daniel."

Rose ducked her head back behind the curtain, immersed it under the showerhead's torrent of warm water. She didn't ask: *Who?* Because then, when she'd received an answer, she'd need to ask: *What happened to her?* And Rose didn't want to ask that question.

There was something pleasantly narcotizing about her daily routine in the apartment. She woke just after seven, and made herself a cup of coffee, and showered, and dressed, and took Jack and Zeus for their morning walk. Then she ate breakfast, and ran whatever errands needed to be run, and came back around noon to take Millie for her first walk of the day. Sometimes, if the weather was nice, she'd sit on a bench alongside the park, with Millie in her lap—enjoying the silence that came from being outside the mysterious domain of the apartment, and wondering if the words still filled Millie's tiny head even as they sat there in such blissful quiet, if the dog was sifting through the hundred and fifty episodes of *The Twilight Zone* that she'd memorized, or analyzing the strengths and weaknesses of the various guest stars who'd appeared on *Fantasy Island* over the years. Then it was home for lunch, and sometimes a nap, or sometimes—when Rose was feeling ambitious—a yoga class at the tiny gym just down the block. At six PM, she took Jack and Millie to the dog park. This was her favorite part of the day. She'd throw a tennis ball for Jack, and Jack would fetch the ball, then drop it at her feet, and wait for her to throw it again, and again, and again, his body quivering with pleasure in this activity, again, and again, and again, until Rose's shoulder began to ache with the exertion. That was when things could feel almost normal to Rose, at dusk in the dog park, with the ball bouncing down the gentle incline toward the river, and Jack sprinting away in pursuit.

At some point, of course, the money was going to run out.

At some point, Rose would have to deal with the back room. She'd need to break down the door. She'd need to think of a way to dispose of the piled bones.

Mostly, though, Rose did her best not to think too far beyond the present moment. This was what Jack advised her to do. He assured her it was how Buddhists lived—and quite happily, too. Rose liked to believe she was getting pretty good at it.

After the dog park, she'd fix dinner, do the dishes, retire with

Jack and Millie to the living room for the nightly dose of TV. Then she'd take Millie and Zeus out for their midnight walk, and brush her teeth, and wash her face, and pull on her pajamas, and climb into bed. As easily as that another day was done.

And another.

And another

Sitting on a bench at the dog run one evening, Rose thought of what Jack had said that first morning: *It can be a win-win situation, if you only embrace it with the right attitude.* She'd finished with the ball throwing for the evening; Jack was lying at her feet, panting from his exercise. Millie was perched on the bench beside her, watching the other dogs play. This was in the middle of May, and the air smelled heavy with pollen. Rose shut her eyes, breathed deep: *win-win.*

* * *

It was only a day or two later, a little after midnight, that Jack said: "Just a heads-up? Your rent's due tomorrow."

Rose was in the bathroom, brushing her teeth. She leaned, spit the toothpaste into the sink, twisted off the water, then turned to look at Jack. He was sitting in the bathroom doorway. "I thought it was withdrawn from the bank account," she said.

"Not the apartment's rent. *Your* rent. As a subletter."

"I have to pay rent?"

"Nothing in life comes for free, Girl."

Rose considered that for a moment, then shook the water from her toothbrush, set it in the glass beside the faucet. "How much?"

"It's not about money."

"It's not?"

Jack shook his head. "It's about keeping us fed—Millie and Zeus and me."

Rose turned the water back on, waited for it to get warm enough for her to wash her face. "You want me to buy some dog food?"

"We want you to bring someone home with you."

Rose was bending toward the sink, cupping water in her hands, but she stopped at this, pivoted to look at Jack again. She knew what he meant, but she didn't want to know, and this desire was strong enough so that, for a moment at least, it almost felt as if she actually *didn't* know. "I don't understand."

Jack gave her his exactly-like-a-smile thing, with his tail and head and ears. "Yes, you do," he said.

Then he stood and walked off down the hall. She heard the dog door creak as he nudged it open and vanished into the rear room for the night.

* * *

In the morning, sitting on the couch, drinking the day's first, pre-shower, pre-walk cup of coffee, she told Jack she wasn't going to do it—not now, not ever.

"You're acting as if you have a choice here," Jack said. "This situation would unfold so much more smoothly, if you accepted that you don't."

"It's not that I won't do it," Rose said, hating the hesitancy in her voice, how it made her sound as if she were attempting to negotiate, rather than issuing an ultimatum, which was her intention. "It's that I can't."

"You've already done it once."

"That was self-defense. That was panic. That was—"

"Exactly. Think how much easier it will be now. When you know what you're doing."

"I'll cook you whatever you want. Chicken. Steak. Fish. Do you like—"

"Remember when you asked how we can talk? And I said it was the apartment? That was only half the answer. It's also what we eat. What we've been fed."

"So stop fucking talking! Eat normal food and become a normal dog. Would that be such a terrible thing? What's so great about speaking, anyway?"

"You bring someone home. You have sex with this person. And then you kill them. That's your rent."

"I have *sex* with them?"

Jack nodded.

"Why do I need to have sex with them?"

"It tenderizes the meat."

"You're kidding, right? This is some sort of joke?"

"There's a ticking clock here, Girl. Just so you're warned."

"Meaning?"

"You won't like Zeus when he's hungry."

Rose had finished her coffee by now. She stood up, started for the kitchen. "Fuck Zeus," she said, as she left the room. "Fuck Millie. And fuck you. I'm not going to do it."

She meant this, too. Or at least she thought she did. Because Jack was right: Rose still believed she had a choice in the matter. She brought home two packages of chicken breasts that afternoon, three cans of cream of chicken soup, a bag of potatoes, a bundle of carrots, an onion, and some bouillon cubes, and she spent the evening making her mother's chicken stew. She ladled out a dish of it and set it down beside the dog's water bowl.

Let them smell it, she thought. *Let them taste it.*

But the dogs ignored her offering. By the following afternoon, the stew was starting to have an odd, jelly-like appearance, so she threw it out, and washed the dish, and ladled in a fresh serving, and placed this beside their water.

She'd cooked enough to get through four days of this ritual, and when the stew ran out, she bought two sirloin steaks. She grilled one and set it on a plate beside their water, and when the dogs ignored this, too, she took the second steak out of the fridge and set it down uncooked, and on the seventh day, when they'd ignored this, too, she ordered Szechuan beef from a Chinese restaurant, and tried that. She could sense they were hungry—they were growing short-tempered and listless. Jack had stopped chasing the ball when they went to the dog park; one of the other owners even asked Rose if there was something wrong with him. She was certain she just had to persist, that eventually they'd relent. They'd begin to eat, and once they began, it would be difficult for them to stop. Rose didn't know how long it would take for them to lose their ability to talk, but once they did, she could force open the door to the rear room and clean out the bones. And once she'd cleaned out the bones, she could leave the apartment—she could go back to her old life. She'd have to figure out what to do about the dogs, of course, but this shouldn't be that difficult. She could take Zeus and Millie to the pound, and maybe keep Jack for herself, bring him with her back to—

She was at the kitchen sink, washing her dinner plates, when she heard a noise behind her, and she turned to find Zeus entering the kitchen. He shuffled toward the bowl of Szechuan beef, and Rose felt her heart rate jump—the throb of blood in her veins, urgent and hopeful. She watched Zeus sniff the bowl. He turned and looked at her.

"Go on," she said. "Try it."

Zeus gave the bowl a sharp smack with his paw, sending it skittering to the far side of the kitchen, the Szechuan beef spilling over the linoleum.

"Bad dog…!" Rose shouted. "Bad dog…!"

Zeus crouched, began to empty his bladder, staring at Rose the entire time. Then he turned and walked slowly out of the kitchen, an immense puddle of urine spreading across the floor behind him, mixing with the spilled food. Jack was watching from the doorway. "You're a week late now, Girl," he said. "Which means you'll have to pay a penalty."

Rose ignored him. She grabbed a roll of paper towels, began to sop up the mess. Did Jack really think that Zeus peeing in the kitchen was such a terrible thing? That it would pressure her into bringing a stranger home for them to eat? A stranger she'd need to fuck first, to "tenderize" his "meat?" Because if that was what he really thought… well, he had another thing coming.

* * *

But that wasn't what Jack thought—not at all, as it turned out.

* * *

It happened later that night. Much later.

Rose was asleep. She was lying on her stomach. The room was dark, and someone was on top of her, holding her down. Someone else was roughly yanking at her underwear. Rose was waking up—not slowly, but all at once—and the person on top of her wasn't a person, it was Zeus, and the person yanking at her underwear wasn't a person, it was Millie, and Jack was there, too, standing beside the bed, watching, and she heard a voice, but it wasn't Jack's and it wasn't Millie's, and she knew it had to be Zeus's, a deep, angry voice, that said: "You bitch. You fucking bitch."

Millie got Rose's underwear down, and Zeus was thrusting at her—growling and thrusting—no, that wasn't it, that wasn't it at all, he wasn't thrusting *at* her… he was thrusting *into* her.

Rose screamed.

"You bitch," Zeus said. "You fucking bitch."

He kept saying these words, over and over, in rhythm with his thrusts. This went on for a full minute, maybe two, an excruciatingly long stretch of time, and finally Rose felt the dog come inside her. Then he leaned down, growling again, and bit her left shoulder. He clamped into her with his teeth and he twisted and tugged, and twisted and tugged, and then he tore a hunk of flesh from her body.

Rose was still screaming.

Her right arm was trapped under her torso, but she was swinging with the left one, trying to land a blow, flailing, open-handed, and then something grabbed at her, arresting the arm's motion. There was a snapping sound, like a branch breaking. This last part happened so quickly that it was finished before Rose could even register the full horror: Jack had caught her hand in his mouth… Jack had bitten off her pinkie. The pain took a long moment to arrive. Rose was fumbling for the lamp, turning it on, blood running down her back from the wound on her shoulder, blood spigotting from her hand, Zeus's semen spilling out between her legs.

Oh my god oh my god oh my god…

Jack and Zeus had already vanished from the room. Only Millie remained, scurrying about on the floor beside the bed, frantically licking at the spilt blood.

* * *

Rose sat for three hours in the Mount Sinai Emergency Room (a towel wrapped around her hand, another towel clamped to her shoulder) before a nurse finally called her name. She was led into an examination room, told to take off her clothes and put on one of those hospital robes that tie in the back, and then she waited for another forty-five minutes before a tired-looking

Indian woman entered. This woman introduced herself as Dr. Cheema. She started to set out a collection of medical supplies on a metal tray, and she asked Rose what had happened.

"I was attacked by a dog. Three, actually."

Dr. Cheema pursed her lips and clucked her tongue, but didn't seem especially interested or impressed. "Do you know if they've been vaccinated for rabies?"

"I think so."

"Can you find out for certain?"

"I can ask them."

"The owners?"

Rose thought to herself: *No, the dogs.* But she didn't say these words; she just nodded.

Dr. Cheema picked up a syringe, inserted it into a small ampule, pulled back on the plunger. "Okay, then. Shall we start with your hand?"

If the doctor had probed even a little further, Rose believed she would've told her everything. She would've told her about the apartment, and Daniel—she would've even tried to explain the talking-dogs part of the story. She didn't care; she was past caring. But Dr. Cheema didn't probe. She focused on Rose's wounds, flushing them clean, stitching them up. The shadows under the doctor's eyes were so dark they looked like tattoos, and Rose could sense her fighting a repetitive impulse to yawn—the involuntary inhalation, the stiffening of her body, the clenching of her jaw. It was six in the morning, and a man was shouting somewhere down the hall, telling someone to fuck off, to get their fucking hands off him, shouting this— screaming, really—and then suddenly falling silent. Rose didn't want to picture what was happening—not to the man, and not to herself, either. Dr. Cheema was standing behind her, willing her body not to yawn, and she'd injected something into Rose's shoulder so that Rose no longer felt any pain, just a tugging sensation each time the doctor stapled another suture across the wound. Rose was given a bottle of antibiotics, a bottle of painkillers, and a slip of paper with a surgeon's name on it: Dr. Thomas Hawthorne. She was supposed to call this man later that day and make an appointment so that Dr. Hawthorne could address the damage to Rose's hand, which looked like a paw now—a polar bear's paw—encased in its white wrapping.

They sent her home.

Rose didn't have enough money with her for another cab, so she dry-swallowed two of the painkillers and started walking west, into Central Park. The sun had risen, and the joggers were out. Rose tried to imagine what life must be like for these people, up early before work, pulling on their brightly colored outfits, tying the laces on their shoes, heading out into the dawn, the sweat rising on their skin, the shower afterward, the healthy breakfast, and then onward into the well-oiled machinery of their days. Even at the best of times, Rose could feel an aversion to people like this. But now, with Zeus's semen still leaking out of her, dampening her underwear, with the pain in her hand and shoulder both there and not there (the pills were keeping it at bay, but Rose could feel how weak they were, how quickly they'd fade from her system, and how restive the pain was, waiting for its moment), with her sense of fatigue like a companion, limping along at her side, leaning more and more heavily upon her with every step, what she felt for these strangers running past was something closer to hatred. She would never be like them. She would never even know people like them. She thought of the young men who showed up at shopping malls with loaded rifles, and she believed she understood why.

Her hand was beginning to throb. At some point very soon

it was going to become unbearable. And yet Rose would have to find a way to bear it, because that was what it meant to be alive. She wasn't going to return to the apartment. Her body decided this before her mind: she realized she was walking south through the park, rather than west. Rose didn't have money for a train ticket, but this didn't matter. She could get on the train and then, when the conductor came to punch her ticket, she could pretend to have lost her wallet. She knew that if she looked distressed enough—*and what could be easier today?*—the conductor would end up comforting instead of scolding her. She'd have to get off the train in Newark, but then she could just catch the next one coming through, and repeat the pantomime. And so on, station by station, all the way home. It would take a lot longer to reach her destination, but she'd get there in the end. She'd done this once before, a year ago, after she'd been pickpocketed, dancing at Cielo. When she got to the Dunellen stop, she could call her mother collect from the station's payphone, and beg her to come and pick her up. If she cried—*and what could be easier today?*—she was certain she could get her mother to do it.

And then?

She supposed it would all play out exactly as Jack had originally threatened. The dogs would bark and whimper and howl until a neighbor took notice. The neighbor would call the landlord. The landlord would contact the police. The police would break down the door—not just the door to the apartment, but also the door to the rear room. They'd find the bones there, and the apartment would become a crime scene. Neighbors would describe Rose to the police; the techs would find her fingerprints, her DNA. Rose didn't know how long all of this would take, but she knew it wouldn't be long enough to count as a respite. Soon enough, she'd be in a jail cell. But she didn't care; she'd been past caring in the Emergency Room, and now she was even past the point of not caring, past the point of thinking at all—she was just walking, with her fatigue shuffling along beside her, and her hand throbbing in rhythm with her heart, and her underwear like a damp hand fondling her groin.

She was near the Reservoir when the first dog lunged at her. It was a little terrier mix, twenty pounds of clenched muscle on the taut end of a leash, growling and barking and snapping its jaws as Rose moved by, the owner staring in surprise, saying: "JoJo! Stop it! What's gotten into you?"

And then, just a little further down the path, a black Lab, carrying a tennis ball in its mouth, loping along with a happy-go-lucky air; the dog dropped the ball, and leapt toward Rose as she drew near, growling and slathering and pawing at the dirt, and its owner had the same startled reaction as the terrier's, straining to hold the Lab back, saying: "Ichabod! What the fuck…?"

A third dog, then a fourth, then three chihuahuas on the same leash, all of them straining toward Rose in a state of fury, teeth bared, and Rose realized in a muddy sort of way what must be happening. If she was right—and she was certain she was—then the park was the wrong place for her to be, the wrong place entirely. After all Rose had been through, she wouldn't have thought she had the energy to run, but she was scared, so adrenaline was in the fuel mix, and run she did: east now, toward the Metropolitan Museum, toward Fifth Avenue. If she could just get to the exit, if she could just—

She heard a man shout: "Bo…!"

And then she heard the barking—deeper than the Labrador's barking, and the terrier's, and the chihuahuas'—deep enough to force Rose to glance back over her shoulder. Bo was a pit bull. He was fifteen yards away, sprinting toward her, his leash bouncing along behind him in the dirt. He'd broken free of his owner's grip.

"Bo…!"

The owner was running, too, but the owner was overweight and out of shape, and still forty yards away.

"Bo…!"

Bo hit Rose in the chest with both front paws, knocking her onto her back. She was trying to push him away, but he was far too strong.

"Bo…!"

Rose felt the dog's breath for an instant, the damp heat of it against her face, and then he had his jaws around her throat, pressing her downward, cutting off her air. *I'll go back,* she thought, screaming the words inside her head. Somehow, she knew this was the key that would free her: *I'll go back! I'll go back! I'll go back!*

Instantly, Bo let her go.

The owner was there—panting, flushed, sweaty. "I'm so sorry. I'm so sorry." He grabbed Bo's leash, gave it an angry, belated tug, his hands visibly shaking. The dog was cowering, hunch-shouldered. A crowd had gathered, a little clot of wide-eyed bystanders, staring at Rose, at Bo, at Bo's owner, who kept giving those angry tugs to Bo's leash: "He's never… Jesus… I'm so sorry… Are you—?"

But Rose was on her feet now. She was in motion again, and she didn't look back when Bo's owner called after her. She was running with her wounded hand cradled protectively against her chest—running west, running for the apartment.

* * *

The dogs were sleeping in the back room when Rose returned. She took a hot bath, scrubbing one-handed at her vagina, her wounded hand tied up in a plastic bag, to keep the bandages dry. After her bath, she swallowed another of the painkillers and dropped into a drug-heavy sleep on the couch. The sun reached the living room window in the early afternoon, and it fell on Rose with enough vigor to rouse her into a murky half-consciousness. She thought to herself: *Maybe I can kill them.* She wasn't confident she could manage it with the knife—especially not when it came to Zeus. But what about a gun? Shouldn't she be able to buy a pistol somewhere? Take a train outside the city, get off in one of those small, NRA-friendly towns upstate, find a—

"You realize we can sense what you're thinking, right?"

Rose lifted her head. Jack was lying under the window, watching her.

"If there were a way to avoid doing what you need to do, don't you think Daniel would've thought of it?"

Rose lowered her head back onto the couch's cushion, shut her eyes. She might've slept some more then, or maybe not—it was hard to tell—but Jack's voice kept coming, and either she was dreaming it, or it was real. Some part of Rose's mind was struggling to decide if it mattered which was true, dream or reality; a little engine inside her brain was assiduously chipping away at this question, but somehow never managing to reach a conclusion. Dream or reality, Jack was offering Rose arguments she could use, if arguments were what she needed.

"Would you kill a cow for us? Because that's what you did when you put those steaks down on the floor. There was a dead cow in the pipeline that led to that particular moment, and you bore some responsibility for it, didn't you? And if that's okay, doesn't it seem like it should be okay to *actually* kill the cow—with your own hands? Not only okay, but maybe also more honest? And if it's okay to kill that cow with your own hands, why isn't it okay to kill a human? Doesn't that seem like a slightly self-serving moral scale you folks have developed for yourselves?

And can you understand how from *our* perspective—Millie's and Zeus's and mine—there's no difference whatsoever?"

Rose could smell urine, and she realized she hadn't taken the dogs out since the previous evening. Now the day was slipping away from her, the sunlight shifting slowly across the floor, then departing altogether. Without the sun, the room grew chilly. Rose thought of moving to the bedroom, burrowing under the covers, but this would necessitate finding sufficient energy to rise and walk, and she worried her legs might not cooperate in such an endeavor, so she just rolled over instead, pressing her body up against the back of the couch, feeling as if she were about to start shivering, but then not shivering, not yet.

"We saved your life. Have you factored that into the equation? If we hadn't warned you, Daniel would've cut your throat. And now? When it's time to pay us back? Look how you're acting. You're a week late, Girl. A week and a day. You don't see a problem with this?"

There was a noise behind her, a creak in the floor, and she rolled over to find Zeus standing beside the couch, his huge shaggy head only a few inches from her face. Rose tried to tell herself this part was definitely a dream, but she could smell the big dog's breath—a rotten-tooth heaviness in the air—and was that really the sort of detail that occurred in a dream? She stared at the dog, waiting to see what he was going to do, and feeling too weak to thwart whatever it might be; then the floor creaked again, and Zeus turned and walked from the room, taking his smell with him.

"Think of someone hateful. That usually helps with the first one. Someone you'd *like* to stab."

Rose was hungry. She had to pee. Her hand felt as if a great weight were lying upon it: an immense slab of steel, vibrating slightly.

"Come on, Girl. Everyone hates someone."

A terribly cold slab of steel—or maybe terribly hot? Rose couldn't decide which; she knew only that it was one extreme or another. And not vibrating: it was bouncing. Or no, not bouncing either: it was *hammering*. Her painkillers were in her purse, and her purse was on the far side of the room. She stared at it, trying to will it closer, but it didn't work.

"If you can't think of someone hateful, think of someone weak."

The room was dark when Rose finally forced herself into a sitting position. It was almost eight o'clock. From sitting to standing, from standing to walking—each transition posed its own challenges. She brought her purse into the kitchen and filled a glass of water at the tap and drank the water, swallowing another painkiller in the process. She was only supposed to have one pill every twelve hours, and this was already her fourth. She supposed it was probably a bad idea, but she also knew this wasn't the worst thing happening in her life right now. She wished it were.

If she didn't do anything to stop them, the dogs were going to attack her again that night. Rose was certain of this.

She ate a peanut butter sandwich and drank a glass of milk and changed her clothes, and by the time she left the apartment, a little after nine, she had something almost like a plan in mind—or no, maybe not a plan, but a destination at least, which felt like the next best thing.

* * *

Rose had gone through a six-month stretch, just after she turned eighteen, when she'd thought she might like girls as much as boys. While exploring this question, she'd stumbled into an on-again, off-again entanglement with a friend of hers named Rhonda. And it was Rhonda who had first taken her to a lesbian bar called the Cubbyhole, down in the village.

Even without her wounded hand, Rose had worried about bringing a guy home. She wasn't strong—she was skinny, and physically timid—and the idea of engaging in a life-or-death struggle with a man filled her with dread. She'd have the knife, of course, and she'd have the element of surprise, but it still didn't seem like enough to guarantee success. So her plan, if you could call it that, was to sit in the Cubbyhole, and hope a woman would decide to pick her up—a petite woman, preferably—the smaller, the better.

If you can't think of someone hateful, think of someone weak.

Rose sat on a stool at the bar, sipping a tequila-and-soda, which started out seeming like a brilliant choice, but then began to feel more and more misguided with every sip, and twenty-five minutes passed in a slow drip, and she thought to herself: *This isn't going to work.* She'd go back to the apartment unaccompanied, and Zeus would rape her again, and Jack would bite off another finger, and Millie would scurry about on the bedroom floor, licking up the blood, and Dr. Cheema would stare at her with those tired eyes and purse her lips and cluck her tongue and stitch her back up again, and Bo would be waiting in the park—

"Is this stool taken?"

The baited hook, the cast line, the long, drowsy wait… and then that sudden thrill when the fish strikes.

Her name was Amber. She was too tall, too lean, too fit—a beautiful girl, in her early twenties, with a full mouth, and green eyes, and red hair down to the middle of her back. She was dressed in jeans, cowboy boots, a sky blue hoodie. She had a tiny stud in her nose—it looked like a diamond—and Rose had to will herself consciously not to stare at it.

When Amber asked about her bandaged hand, Rose told

her she'd caught it in a car door. Amber winced and leaned forward to touch Rose's wrist. "You poor thing," she said, and she was looking at Rose, *truly* looking. Rose tried to remember the last time someone had offered her this gift. The doctor hadn't looked at her, not really, and her Craigslist dates had never ventured it, and her mother—

"Another round?" the bartender asked.

Rose didn't resist when Amber offered to pay. She twisted on her stool to get a better look at this stranger. Amber's hair wasn't just red, it was thick and curly; maybe it had something to do with the painkillers and the tequila, but Rose wanted to touch it, wanted to take big handfuls of it and press them against her face. The two of them held eyes for a long moment, and then Amber started to laugh. "You're an odd one, aren't you?" she asked.

Rose took a swallow from her drink, draining half of it, and then she leaned forward and kissed Amber, and Amber didn't flinch: Amber kissed her back. Her mouth tasted of cinnamon. Rose buried her un-bandaged hand into that luscious red hair; she grabbed a fistful and held on tight, feeling lonely and frightened and sad. She never would've imagined herself to be a terrible person, but it turned out that she was, because just look at the unforgivable thing she was about to do. This girl wasn't hateful. And she probably wasn't weak. But she was kind—and Rose despised herself for sensing that this might be enough.

She pulled away from the kiss, leaned to whisper into Amber's ear: "Will you come home with me?"

* * *

The gray door, the three locks, the panting, whimpering dogs...

"Holy shit," Amber said. "Look at these guys! You didn't tell me you had dogs. I *love* dogs." She crouched to pet them, bending to let Millie lick her face.

"Oh, Girl," Jack said. "She's perfect. We knew you'd come through."

Rose remembered Daniel, his sense of urgency that night, his nerves, the way he'd hurried her down the hallway to the bedroom, just like she was hurrying Amber now, kicking free of her shoes, pulling off her clothes, tumbling the girl onto the bed. Amber laughed: "Easy there, hustler."

It wasn't just her mouth that tasted of cinnamon; her skin did, too. Her vagina was freshly waxed, and for a moment Rose couldn't stop herself from thinking of the dolls she'd owned as a child, the hairless fold between the legs. She was drunk, and overmedicated, and she only half-knew what she was attempting—just enough to be certain that she was being too rough, and too fast, doing everything to Amber that she'd hated when guys had done it to her, and Amber kept grabbing her hand and trying to guide her, and Millie was right beside the bed, panting and pacing, and saying: "Fuck her! Fuck her good! Use your mouth!"

"Is she okay?" Amber asked.

Rose stopped what she was doing, lifted her head: "What do you mean?"

"That panting and pacing. Is she hungry? That's what my sister's dog does when she's really hungry."

Rose heard Jack give a little laugh. He and Zeus were in the doorway to the room, watching. "She's all right," Rose said. "She's always like that."

"Stop talking!" Millie's voice had taken on a pleading, whining quality inside Rose's head. "Keep fucking. Fuck the bitch! Fuck her good!"

Afterward, once Amber had come, maybe for real, and Rose had done her best to fake it, and they were lying there in each other's arms, Rose arrived at a decision: she couldn't do it—she *wouldn't* do it. Her hand had stopped hurting for a bit, but now it was making up for this dereliction with a compensatory vengeance. Rose plucked the pill bottle off the night table, took another painkiller.

"What are those?" Amber asked.

"Oxy," Rose said. "For the pain." And she held out the bottle. "*Mi casa, su casa.*"

Amber laughed again—she had a pretty laugh. "I *knew* I liked you." She presented her palm, and Rose tapped a pill into it.

This had been part of Rose's almost-a-plan, which she was now certain—or nearly certain—she couldn't (wouldn't) follow through on.

They turned out the light.

Rose counted to sixty in her head, and then she told Amber that she needed to use the bathroom. This, too, had been part of the plan that she couldn't (wouldn't) follow through on: she would go to the bathroom and wait for the girl to fall asleep, and when she came back, she'd quietly ease open the night table drawer, lift out the knife, and do what needed to be done.

Rose tiptoed from the darkened room and headed down the hall. Millie followed her, panting ever more heavily: "Where are you going? Get the knife! Stab her! Cut her up!"

Rose shut the bathroom door on the little dog. She sat on the closed lid of the toilet and tried not to feel the pain in her hand, tried not to feel anything at all, in fact, thinking *couldn't* and *wouldn't*, and *can't* and *won't*. At some point, she began to lose track of time. Her head kept dipping—she'd drunk too much tequila, swallowed too many pills. It seemed as if she must've waited long enough by now: Amber ought to be asleep. Not that this mattered, of course (because of *couldn't* and *wouldn't*, because of *can't* and *won't*).

Rose pulled open the door, stepped quietly into the hall.

Millie was gone; she'd returned to the bedroom. The light was on in there again, and Amber—inexplicably—was still wide-awake, sitting against the headboard, staring at Rose, who stood in the doorway, hesitating. Millie was dozing in the armchair. Zeus was asleep at the base of the bed. Jack was beside him, his head on his paws, his eyes shut. It was odd: the dogs were never all asleep—not out here, at least, away from the back room, especially not Zeus.

Thinking this, Rose knew what was about to happen.

She should've turned and sprinted for the door. It was all reflex from this point on, though, and Rose's reflexes had never been the best part of her.

The dogs began to bark even before she was in motion.

She was running for the bedside drawer.

But Amber—kind, green-eyed Amber, with her long red curls, her cinnamon-flavored skin, her Barbie doll vagina—Amber, that lovely girl… she got there first.

IN STONE

by

TIM LEBBON

Several weeks following the death of a close friend, I started walking alone at night. I was having trouble sleeping, and I think it was a way of trying to reclaim that time for myself. Instead of lying in the darkness remembering Nigel, feeling regret that we'd let the time between meetings stretch further each year, I took to the streets. There was nothing worse than staring at the ceiling and seeing all the bad parts of my life mapped there in cracks, spider webs and the trails of a paint brush. I thought perhaps walking in the dark might help me really think.

On the fifth night of wandering the streets, I saw the woman.

I was close to the centre of town. It was raining, and the few working streetlights cast speckled, splashed patterns across the pavement, giving the impression that nothing was still in the silent night. Over the past hour I'd seen several people. One was a night worker—a nurse or fireman, perhaps—hurrying along the street wearing a backpack and with a definite destination in mind. A couple were youths, so drunk that they could barely walk or talk. One was a homeless woman I'd seen before. Two dogs accompanied her like shadows, and she muttered to herself too quietly for me to hear.

They all saw me. The worker veered around me slightly, the

youths muttered and giggled, and the homeless woman's dogs paused and sniffed in my direction.

But the new woman didn't look or act like everyone else. At three or four in the morning, anyone left out in the streets wanted to be alone. Closeness was avoided, and other than perhaps a curt nod, no contact was made. It was as if darkness brought out mysteries and hidden stories in people and made them solid, and that suited me just fine. I wasn't out there to speak to anyone else; I was attempting to talk to myself.

There was something about her that immediately caught my attention. Walking in a world of her own, she followed no obvious route through the heavy rain, moving back and forth across the silent main street, sometimes walking on the sidewalk and sometimes the road. The weather did not appear to concern her. Even though it was summer, the rain was cool and the night cooler, but she walked without a coat or jacket of any kind. She wore loose trousers and a vest top, and I really shouldn't have followed her.

But Nigel told me to. It was his voice I heard in my head saying, *Wonder what she's up to?* He had always been curious and interested in other people, the one most likely to get chatting to strangers if we went for a drink. Last time I'd seen him he'd been more garrulous than ever, and I wondered if that was a way of hiding his deeper problems and fears. He could say so much, but still didn't know how to ask for help.

The woman drifted from the main street to a narrower road between shops, and I followed. I held back a little—I had no wish to frighten or trouble her—but tried to make sure I kept her in sight. The rain was falling heavier now, and I had to throw up my hood to shield my eyes and face. The side street was not lit. Rain blanketed the night, making everything even darker and giving a constant shimmer to reality. Her movements were nebulous and fluid, slipping in and out of the darkness like a porpoise dancing through waves.

To my left and right, large spaces opened up. These were the service yards of big shops, covered delivery and storage areas that I barely noticed if walking these streets during the day. Now, they were pitch black burrows where anything might exist, and I was pleased when the woman passed them by.

As she neared a smaller street, she paused. I also stopped, tucking in close to a wall. I suddenly felt uncomfortable following her. I was no threat, but no one else would believe that. If people saw me stalking the woman, they might think the worst. If she saw me, I might frighten her.

I was about to turn and walk back the way I'd come when something gave me pause.

The street ahead was a place I knew well, home to a series of smaller, independent shops, a couple of nice pubs, and a few restaurants. Nigel and I had eaten and drunk there, and I'd walked that way more times than I could recall. In the stormy night, it glowed with reflected neon from shop windows. A rush of memories washed over me, and I gasped.

The woman seemed to hear. She tilted her head slightly, then walked out into this narrower road. I followed. I had the sudden sense that I was witnessing something secret. I felt like an intruder, emerging from my safe, warm home to stroll dark streets I knew nothing about.

During the day, this place was a bustling centre of commerce and fun. Now it was a whole new world.

By the time I moved out onto the street, the woman had paused beside a series of bronze sculptures on plinths. They'd been placed fifteen years before as part of the millennium celebrations, and I hardly ever noticed them. Seeing them at night, flowing with water that shimmered and reflected weak light, gave them a strange form of life.

The woman was staring past the sculptures and into the mouth of a narrow alley. I knew the place. It was a dead-end passageway between a fast-food joint and a newsagent's. I'd stumbled down there once years ago, drunk, a young woman holding onto my arm as if I could be more stable than her. I had vague memories of what we'd done. Shambolic, clumsy sex amongst split bags of refuse and broken bottles did not make me particularly proud, and I'd only ever spoken of that moment with Nigel.

As I wondered what her interest might be in that grubby place, and just what it was about her that troubled me, she began to take off her clothes.

I caught my breath and pulled back around the corner. I felt unaccountably guilty witnessing the woman's shedding of clothing, even though she was doing it in the middle of the street. Her shoes came off first, then her vest and trousers. Naked, she stretched her arms to the air and let the rain run across her body. She might have been beautiful.

Rain flowed into my eyes. I wiped them and looked again. There was something wrong.

The woman was moving past the bronze statues and heading towards the entrance to the alley. Her motion seemed strange. She drifted rather than walked, limbs swinging slightly out of time, her movements not quite human. Her pale skin grew darker. Her hair became a more solid cap around her head. She slowed before the alley—hesitant, or relishing the moment—then stepped into its shadows.

As she passed out of sight, I had the very real sense that she was no longer there.

I ran into the night.

* * *

"And you ran all the way home?"

"Yeah."

"Dude. You. Running."

I laughed. "Who'd have thunk it?"

Ashley licked her finger and used it to pick up cake crumbs from her plate. Finger still in her mouth, she caught my attention and raised an eyebrow. I rolled my eyes. Ash had been my best friend since we were both babies, and although I couldn't help but acknowledge her beauty, I'd never been drawn to her in that way.

"Still not sleeping?" she asked.

"No. Not well at all."

"Hence the walking at night."

I nodded.

"You're very, very weird."

We both sipped at our coffees, comfortable in our silence. The cafe around was filled with conversation and soft music, merging into a background noise that kept our own chat private.

"Maybe she was a prostitute."

"No."

"You're sure?"

I nodded.

"So you'd recognise one?" She had that cheeky glint in her eyes, and I couldn't help but smile. Ashley called herself shallow, but I knew that wasn't true at all. She was simply someone who knew how to regulate her depths. She'd been a levelling force in my life forever, and never more than since Nigel stepped from that ledge.

"It's only around the corner," I said. "Will you come with me?"

"And search for the mysterious vanishing woman? You bet!"

We left the cafe. It had stopped raining and the town was

alive with lunchtime buzz. Ash and I met for lunch at least once each week, working within ten minutes of each other making it easy. I dreaded her leaving to work elsewhere. She'd mentioned it once or twice, and I knew that she'd had a couple of interviews. It was only a matter of time. Ash was not someone that life held back, and the world was calling.

"It will get easier," she said, hooking her arm through mine as we walked.

"Yeah, I know."

"Wish I'd known him better."

I nodded. Felt a lump in my throat and swallowed it down. "Me too."

As we approached the place where I'd seen the woman earlier that morning, I heard the cheerful shouts and laughter of a group of school kids. They were maybe nine or ten, posing around the bronze statues as teachers took photos. They probably shouldn't have been up on the plinths, but no one would tell them to get down. Who would intrude on such excitement and joy?

I headed past the statues and children, aiming for the alley between the newsagent's and the fast-food joint, which was doing a busy trade. People queued out the door. A young woman emerged from the alley, wearing an apron with the takeaway's name emblazoned across the front. She offered us a quick smile, then pushed past the queue and back into the shop. I felt a release of tension from my shoulders, a relaxing in my gut. Ash must have felt it too.

"See?" she said. "No gruesome murders."

I turned to her and nodded, and then something caught my eye. A litter bin stood beside a bench close to the statues, and splayed across its lip was a dirtied white vest.

"Oh," I said. I blinked, remembering the woman lifting the vest up over her head.

"What?" Ash asked.

I pointed at the vest. "Why wouldn't she dress again afterwards?" After what, I did not say, or even wish to consider. She must have walked home naked. If she had walked home at all.

I headed for the alley, and Ash came with me. It smelled of piss. No surprise there. But it also smelled of rain, fresh and sharp, even though it had stopped raining before I'd finished running home eight hours before."

"Delightful," Ash said. She stepped over a pool of vomit on the ground.

It was unremarkable, a narrow alley with a dead end thirty feet in, dirty rendered wall on one side, old bare brick on the other. A couple of metal doorways were set into the walls, without handles and looking as if they'd been locked for decades. There were a few black bin bags, one of them split and gnawed at by night creatures—cats, rats, foxes. A pile of dog crap held a smeared shoe print. A dead rat festered against the blank end wall.

"She didn't come out again," I said.

"Not while you were watching."

"But her clothes."

Ash shrugged.

I walked the length of the alley, fearing what I might see, eager to make sure there was nothing there. I shifted a couple of rubbish bags with my foot, releasing a foul stink that made me gag.

"Jesus, what a wonderful smell you've found!" Ash said.

I covered my mouth with the collar of my coat and went in deeper, shoving bags aside with my feet. Old wrappers spilled, slick with rotting food. Things crawled in there, dark and wet, reminding me of the nude woman flowing with rainwater, silvery, flexing and shifting like something inhuman. I bent down to look closer and saw a nest of slugs, leaving trails like slow echoes and pulsing like something's insides.

"Weird," Ash said. She was looking at a spread of brickwork close to the ground, a few feet from the end of the alley. I went to her and stood close, our coats brushing. She grabbed my hand.

"What?"

"Don't know," she said. She shivered. "Let's go."

"Hang on." I crouched, leaning in closer, trying not to block out precious light so that I could see what she'd seen.

"Come on. Let's go."

"What *is* that?" I asked. But neither of us could answer.

The bricks were old and crumbling, covered with black moss, joints clotted with decades of filth. This wall had never seen sunlight, and perpetual shadow had driven darkness into the brick faces and the mortar in between. Across a spread of brickwork, something protruded. It looked like a swathe of dark pink pustules, solid-looking rather than soft, dry and dusty even though the brickwork around them was damp. I reached out to touch, but Ash grabbed my arm.

"What if it's poisonous?" she asked.

"It's just the bricks," I said. "Frost-blown, maybe. They've deformed over time." I reached out again, but didn't quite touch. Something held me back. Something about the shape of the feature, the way it swept up from the ground and spanned several courses of bricks.

It looked like an arm reaching from the ground, embedded in the wall and only just protruding. At its end, a clenched fist of brickwork protruded more than elsewhere, cracked and threatening to disintegrate at any moment.

I wondered what that fist might hold.

Ash grabbed my coat and pulled me upright, shoving me

before her along the alley and back into the street. "It should be cleaned," she said. But she didn't enter the fast-food shop or the newsagent's to share this opinion with them. Instead, she headed back to work.

I stood there for a while looking at the discarded clothing in the litter bin. It was slowly being buried beneath lunchtime refuse—coffee cups, crisp bags, sandwich wrappers. Soon it would be completely out of sight. Forgotten.

I wondered where the woman had gone.

* * *

"I'm sorry," Ash said. She'd called me after work, on the way to her boyfriend's place.

"For what?" I was in the park, beyond which lay the old terraced house where I lived. It was raining again, and a few umbrellas and coats hid anonymous people as they took various paths home.

"I just… that place at lunchtime felt a bit odd. Didn't it?"

"Yeah." But I couldn't quite verbalise how the alley had felt strange. *Like somewhere else*, I might have said. The idea crossed my mind that I'd seen a ghost, but I had never believed in them. I was a rationalist, an atheist, and until Nigel's death I'd been happy and comfortable with that. Since he'd taken his own life, I had been struggling. Not for him, because he was gone now, flickering out from a wonderful, expansive consciousness to nothing in the space of a pavement impact. But for me. All that was left of Nigel was in my mind, and the minds of those who loved him. That didn't seem much to leave behind.

I thought of those weird shapes across the rotting brickwork, blown clay in the shape of a rising, clasping arm and hand.

"Max says hi."

"Hi, Max."

"See you soon. And don't go wandering tonight. Weather forecast is awful, and you need sleep."

"Damn right. Bottle of wine, then bed, like a good boy."

"Good boy." Ash hung up, leaving me alone in the park with the rain, and the puddles, and the memory of a time me, Nigel and a few others came here to play football when we were kids. I thought I heard his laugh. But it was someone else, and I started walking again before whoever was laughing caught up with me.

* * *

Wind roared around my house and made the roof creak, rain hammered against the closed windows, and next door's dog barked, waiting for them to come home. I tried to sleep for a while, but failed miserably. The brief buzz I'd had from the bottle of wine was gone, melted away into the darkness of my bedroom. I lay awake for a while staring into the shadows.

Then I got up, dressed, slipped on my raincoat that was still wet from walking home from work, and went out into the night.

It was almost two in the morning.

I walked into the city. I lived in a suburb, but it was only fifteen minutes through the park, past the hospital and into town. All that time I saw no other pedestrians, and only a few cars. Some of them were police vehicles, and one slowed when it passed me, a pale face peering from the window obscured and made fluid by rain impacting the glass. I stared back, hiding nothing. The car moved on.

I was heading along the main street, intending to visit that alley again. There had been something strange about the woman, but I found that I was not afraid. I had no idea why. Maybe it had been Ash's strange, repulsed reaction to that feature on the wall, and my realisation that I was less troubled than her.

The weather was atrocious. Wind howled along the town's main thoroughfares like a beast unleashed, revelling in the fact that there was no one there to view its nighttime cavortings. It whistled through the slats of fixed benches, rattled shutters on jewellers' shops, and flung litter into piles in doorways and against wet walls. Rain lashed almost horizontally, spiking into my face and against my front, the coat hardly any barrier at all.

I leaned into the wind and rain, working my way through the town, and the night was alive around me.

I saw a few people. It was earlier than I usually chose to walk, and a couple of the later clubs had only kicked out an hour or so before. A few drunks huddled against the weather and tried to remember where they lived. Some were in pairs, more alone. I also saw the homeless woman with the dogs. The hounds looked my way, but I don't think they growled, or if they did the wind carried the sound away. Maybe they were growing used to me.

There's a part of town where five roads converge. People call it a square, though it isn't really. It's disordered and accidental, the same as most people who pass through from midnight onwards. That night it was a wilder place, and as I approached along the main street I had to stop and stare. The square seemed primeval. Great cliffs of brick, stone and glass rose up on all sides, channelling torrents of wind and rain that met in the middle as if in battle. A tornado of litter and rain twisted back and forth, throwing off its contents and sucking more in. The sound was staggering, the effect intimidating. I could see shop windows flexing beneath the onslaught, as if the buildings themselves were breathing great, slow, considered breaths.

I stood there for a while just watching, and then as if carried like shreds of refuse on the storm, memories of Nigel came in.

We cross the square, arms around each other's shoulders.

It's a Saturday afternoon and we've been in the pub all day, ostensibly to watch a big rugby match, though neither of us is really into sport. The atmosphere was electric, the pub a sea of shirts of two colours, good-natured banter fuelled by beer turning into hearty singing, and much friendly mockery of the losing team. It's been refreshing and upbeat, and Nigel has said that tribal warfare has never been so much fun. We're going to buy food. We head down one of the narrower streets—

—and Nigel reels from the blow, staggering back into a doorway as the big, thick thug storms after him. I've never been so afraid in my life. But that's Nigel getting picked on for no reason. We simply walked the wrong way and met the wrong nutter. He's drunk, that's obvious, and though I'm not one to judge by first appearances, he looks like he likes a fight.

He launches another punch at Nigel, then I'm piling into the bastard from behind, shoving him forward as hard as I can into the shop window. Glass cracks. He half-turns to glare at me, murder in his eyes and blood running from a cut in his forehead. Nigel lands a punch on his nose, a pile-driving crunch that we'll talk about for years to come—

—we're following two girls who have been smiling at us all afternoon. We're too old to stay at home, too young to hit the pubs, so town is our afternoon playground, and today feels special. Nigel is the good-looking one, and both girls have been eyeing him. I've become used to playing second fiddle to my friend.

I sighed, and my breath was lost to the storm like so many memories. His death still hit me like this, and I wasn't sure I'd ever grow used to it.

Buffeted by high winds, soaked to the skin, I decided to make my way home.

The shape started across the square just as I took my first

step. It was a man, perhaps late fifties, long grey hair swirling around his head and coat flapping in the wind. Yet none of his movements seemed quite right. His hair moved a little too slowly, like flexing wire on a stop motion mannequin instead of real hair. His coat seemed to shift and wave in slow motion. He paced across the square with a definite destination in mind.

He looked just like the woman I'd seen the night before. Out of place, removed from his turbulent surroundings, walking his own path through a city that seemed unable to contain him.

I followed.

Walking across the square, emerging from the shelter of the buildings, I submitted myself to the full force of the storm. It was as if with every step I took, the storm focussed all of its attention on me, driving along streets and roads and smashing together at that violent junction. I staggered left and right, arms spread for balance, the hood of my coat alternately filling with wind and acting like a sail, then flattening against my scalp like a second skin. I forged on, head down, thinking of Arctic explorers fighting against harsh gales to reach their goal. Rain stung my face. I could hardly see anything, squinting at the ground just ahead of me to see where I was going. I crossed the paved area, then a road, and then finally I felt the storm lessen as I neared another building. Hugging myself to its shelter, I looked ahead and saw the man. He was barely visible, a hundred metres ahead and already passing into the night. Winds whipped around him. Rain hammered down, dancing swirls in weak streetlights.

Between one blink and the next, the man was gone.

I strode ahead, moving fast to try and catch up. The storm screamed at me, threatening or warning. I paid no heed. I needed to see the man again, follow him, try to talk with him. I walked back and forth along the street, passing closed shops and cafes, and saw nothing. I ventured into doorways in case he had fallen and was hidden beneath piles of wind-blown litter. When I faced a narrow arcade, I pressed against the metal grille securing its entrance and tried to see deeper.

The night seemed even darker in there, and more still. The shadows were heavy. Watching, I also felt watched.

I took a couple of steps back. My breath was stolen by the wind. Glass smashed in the distance. A car alarm erupted somewhere out of sight, and part of a large advertising hoarding bounced along the road towards the square, shedding parts of itself as it went.

Even if the arcade was not locked up, I would not have wanted to go that way.

I hurried back through the square and started towards home. I saw a couple of other people, and they avoided me as surely as I avoided them.

I slept for three hours that night, naked and cold in my bed with wet clothes piled beside me. Dawn woke me. The man haunted my dreams even as I lay in bed awake, still walking, grey hair and coat shifting to some force other than the storm.

* * *

Morning brought relative calm. As I ate breakfast I watched the news, and saw that the storm had wreaked havoc across the country. Damage was in the millions. Miraculously, no one had died.

I chewed cereal that tasted like cardboard and thought about that.

No one had died.

It was a Saturday, and as I followed my previous night's route into town, the streets soon started to bustle with cheerful shoppers, gangs of kids laughing and joking, and people all with somewhere to go.

I had somewhere to go as well. The square was a very different place from just a few hours before, full of people and life, none of them aware of the shattering storm that had existed there so recently. The storm was a dangerous animal, come and gone again, and it had visited with almost no one knowing.

Across the square and along the street where the man had disappeared, I expected to see his discarded coat slowly being buried in a litter bin or draped over the back of a bench. There was nothing.

The arcade was open. Home to a cafe, a clothes shop, a candle shop and a second-hand bookseller, it wasn't somewhere I ventured frequently. In daylight, it looked less threatening. I stepped inside. A waft of perfumed air hit me from the candle shop, followed by the scent of frying bacon. It felt safe and warm.

I tripped, stumbled, almost fell, and a youth reached out and grabbed my arm to stop me hitting the ground.

"You all right, mate?"

"Yes," I said, startled. "Thanks."

"No worries. They should fix that." He nodded vaguely at my feet then went on his way, headphones in and thumb stroking his phone.

I looked down. The mosaic floor covering was humped as if pushed up by something from below. Yellow paint had been sprayed across the area some time ago, either a warning to beware or an indication of somewhere that needed to be fixed. No one had fixed it. The paint was faded and chipped, worn away by thousands of feet.

"Hey!" I called after the kid. "You know what happened here?" But he had his headphones in and was already leaving the arcade.

I frowned and moved sideways, shifting my perspective of the raised area. The mosaic tiles weren't only pushed up a little from below, forming the dangerous swelling that I'd tripped on. There was something in their clay shapes.

It looked like a face.

I gasped, closed my eyes, turned away and leaned against a wall. When I opened my eyes again I was looking through a window at an old man sitting inside the cafe, nursing a mug of tea. He stared at me, and past me, then looked down at his phone.

I glanced down at the ground again.

It *might* have been a face. The curve of one cheek, forehead, the hollow of an eye socket, and splayed out behind it was a flow of irregularities in the old tiles that resembled long, grey hair.

"Oh, God," I said. I wanted to grab someone and ask them if they saw what I saw. But if they didn't, what then? What could I say, ask, believe?

I took a photo of the raised area then hurried away, because there was someone I could ask. Ash was my leveller. She would hear me out.

* * *

As it turned out, Ash had already phoned that morning and left a message on my landline.

"Hey. Give me a call. Got some news."

I made some coffee first. Every step towards home had calmed my panic, and I was feeling more and more foolish over what I thought I'd seen. As I waited for the coffee to brew, every second that passed seemed to bring me closer to normality once more. Looking at my phone helped. The photo I'd taken showed nothing amiss, other than a slightly misshapen area in the arcade floor. However I viewed it, whether I zoomed in or not, there was no face.

But that's right, I thought. *Because it's daytime. They only come out at night.*

The idea came from nowhere, and was chilling.

The phone rang as I was pouring coffee. I jumped and spilled some, cursed, snapped up the phone.

"Hey, it's me," Ash said. "Fancy a coffee?"

"I just made one."

"Right. Can I come over?"

"Er… why?" It wasn't often that Ash and I saw each other on the weekends. She was usually doing stuff with Max, and I was busy with the football club, or meeting friends, or travelling down to Devon to visit my family. Dad would grumble and talk about politics. Mum would ask if I'd met a nice girl yet.

"Max and I are moving away. I got that job in Wales. I heard yesterday."

"Oh. Wow."

"You okay?"

"Yeah, sure. Of course. Delighted for you!"

Ash was silent for a while. "You go walking last night?"

"No." Once uttered, I couldn't take back the lie. I wasn't sure why. Maybe because Ash had already started to move away, and to include her in my troubles would be selfish. She'd wanted this for a long time. That didn't mean I had to be happy, but I could still be pleased for her.

"So I can come over, tell you all about it?"

"Come on over."

"I'll bring cake."

"You know me so well."

* * *

"The city eats people," she said. She took a bite of cake as if to illustrate the fact. "We're communal animals, but we're not meant to be somewhere with so many other people. Why do you think places like London feel so impersonal? Live in a small village, a hamlet, know almost everyone there, that's when you're happiest. Here... it's like we've created a monster and we're feeding it every day."

Her comments hit me hard. They sounded like her trying to defend her decision to leave for somewhere more rural, and that wasn't like Ash—she was always headstrong and positive. Maybe she was worried about me.

"You think that's why Nigel did what he did?"

Ash raised her eyebrows, as if she'd never even considered it.

"I think Nigel was a sensitive soul. Life was too much for him, and living in the city didn't help at all. But no, he had his own real problems, only aggravated by being here. What I mean is... people disappear. One day they're here, the next they're gone, and it's as if they've vanished into nothing. Know what I mean? The city eats them, spits nothing out, and eventually they're just forgotten."

"That's pretty depressing."

"I don't want to disappear," she said.

"You never could. You're too... wonderful." I grinned, bashful at the compliment. But she saw how serious I was, because she didn't take the piss.

"You should leave too." She tapped her engagement ring against her mug.

"I'm... not sure I could."

"Really? You love this place so much?"

I shook my head. No, I didn't love the city at all. I just couldn't imagine anywhere else feeling like home.

We chatted some more, then talked about her leaving party which she'd be throwing in a couple of weeks' time. She wanted me to DJ there. I said I was honoured, and I'd only do it if I could throw in some AC/DC. She hated them, but relented.

As she finished her cake I thought of the city eating people, and the outline of a face in broken tiles, and the bubbled surface of blown bricks in the shape of an arm with a clenched fist.

* * *

Now that I had an idea of what to look for, I saw the city in a whole new light.

That Sunday afternoon I walked. There were plenty of people around because many of the shops remained open, and the place felt relatively safe. But as time passed by, and I saw more, that sense of safety began to evaporate.

By the end of the afternoon I felt like a meal in the jaws of a beast.

I saw distortion in an old swimming pool's caged-over window, and if I looked at just the right angle I could make out the shadow of a naked torso in the imperfect glass.

At the base of an old hotel's side wall, where access chutes into the basement had been concreted over, two knotted protuberances might have been hands with fingers broken off. Clasping for air forever, the stumpy remains of digits pointing accusingly at everyone left alive.

The stepped marble plinth of a war memorial had been damaged by vehicle impacts and the effects of frost, but there was another imperfection in its structure that became obvious to me now. The curve of a back, ribs plain to those who could see, one shoulder blade arched as if the buried subject were swimming against its solid surroundings.

Finally I decided to go to the place where Nigel had died. I had only been there once since his death, and facing the reality of the scene had been too disturbing. Now, there was more I had to see.

I would go at night. I dreaded what I might find.

* * *

It was three in the morning, and the homeless woman was there with her dogs once more. The creatures glanced at me, then as I started to approach they pulled on their leashes, one whining, the other snarling.

"I haven't got anything!" the woman said. The fear in her voice was awful.

"I'm no harm," I said. "I just want to—"

"What are you doing here at three in the morning, then?" she snapped.

"What are you?"

She didn't answer this. Instead, she tugged on the leads and settled her dogs. We were outside a pub, long-since closed for the night, and she leaned against some handrailing that delineated its outdoor smoking area.

"I'm walking because someone I know died," I said. "A friend. And I want to know…" *Whether the city took him*, I wanted to say, but I wasn't sure how that might sound. "I'm going to see…"

"Plenty wrong with the city at night," the woman said. "During the day, people keep it alive. Probably best you go home."

"But I've seen you before. You're always walking."

"I know where not to go."

"How?"

"Experience." She muttered something under her breath. I couldn't see her face properly, and I didn't want to go any closer in case that looked threatening. Perhaps she was talking to her dogs.

"I'm going to the old station building," I said. I hoped that might encourage some comment, positive or negative.

"Hmm."

"Should I?" I asked.

I saw her silhouette shrug. "You should just go home." She started walking away and the dogs followed. When I tried to trail after her the animals turned and growled, both of them this time. I slowed, then stopped.

"Why?" I asked, expecting no reply.

"Make a habit of this and the city will notice you." Then she was gone, keeping to the middle of the street and avoiding the deep shadows beside buildings.

The night was quiet and still, no storms, no rain, and on the way through town I saw several other walkers. I wasn't sure who or what they were. I did not follow them. I was also careful to keep my distance, partly because they scared me, but also because they deserved their privacy and peace.

I carried on towards the old station building. It was six storeys high, converted into an office block a decade before, and Nigel had worked in an advertising agency on the second floor. That morning he'd taken the stairs, walked past the door exiting the staircase into his studio, and continued to the top. The maintenance door into the plant room on the roof should have been locked, but he'd planned his morning enough to make sure he had a key.

Once out on the roof, no one knew what he had seen, said or done. There was no note. Three people in the street below had seen him step up onto the parapet. Without hesitation he had walked out into nothing.

Where he'd hit the ground there was a raised planting bed at the refurbished building's entrance. He'd struck its wall, breaking his back. I went there now, a torch in my hand, dread in my heart.

At every moment I expected to see Nigel walking somewhere ahead of me. The echo of a man taken by the city and clasped to its dark, concrete heart, out of place and no longer of this world. But I was alone.

I searched for half an hour—the brick paved area around

the entrance, the planter wall, the soil and shrubs of the planter itself. But I found no sign of Nigel. As every minute passed by my sense of apprehension lifted some more.

He's not here. The city didn't get him. It didn't eat him.

People had seen him jump, and perhaps that made a difference. He hadn't died alone with only the cold concrete for company. His body hadn't lain there for hours or days afterwards, night crawling across him, darkness coalescing around him. Even dead, Nigel had remained in the human world, because his suicide was born of it.

Though still sad at his death, I felt relieved that he had escaped something worse.

My mood buoyed, I started for home as dawn peered across the built-up skyline. Yet something was different. The skyline I saw looked slightly out of skew, as if new buildings had risen during the night and others had been taken down. The silence remained, broken only by cautious footsteps echoing from unknown walls. Occasional strangers avoided each other's glances. But there was now something else that I had never noticed before. In the silence that hung over the city, a terrible intelligence held its breath.

As I reached home, I feared that the city had noticed me at last.

THE WAY SHE IS WITH STRANGERS

by

HELEN MARSHALL

It was only after the papers were signed, the dissolution of the marriage arranged and witnessed, that Mercy Dwyer finally moved to the city. She had never lived in a city before. She had known only the sleepy village of Hindmoor Green in which she'd been raised, a place where no street needed a name because there were few enough that they could be recognized, like children: everyone knew what they were, everyone knew where they went, no question as to their identity had ever been raised and for all she expected from now until Judgement Day none ever would be. Hindmoor Green had been comprised of a small circle of buildings clustered around a post office, a one-pump petrol station, and the local pub. Beyond the village boundaries was the hazy sameness of rolling hills and ancient woodland. There were fields too, and pastures; but all of it was so similar that if you looked in one direction, you saw exactly the same view as if you had looked in the other entirely.

There was a legend, she had heard, that the universe had been created and destroyed three times: each time it had been built smaller than the last. Mercy believed it. Hindmoor Green was the smallest version of the universe she could imagine. It was complete. She knew its borders, and she respected them. But the city was, to her surprise, much, much smaller. To herself she called it New Manchester or sometimes New New Manchester. It was claustrophobic, folded up like a paper bird, wing touching breastbone touching foot touching beak. Once she dropped a penny from a bridge. She watched it flutter through the sky, turning end over end, winking. It crashed through her skylight, three miles to the north. She found it on the kitchen table like a gift, nestled amongst ribbons of scattered glass. She knew it by the date, by the tiny indent in the Queen's chin her thumb had scratched. She didn't wonder at this. She wondered only about the inevitable suicides. Every city had them. Bridges were portals not just to the next city over but to the next world. But what happened to the bodies? Were there families who woke to startled guests at the breakfast table? Mercy liked to imagine these unexpected meetings, how the children in their school clothes would welcome the visitor with joy or exasperation, cream or sugar with the coffee, eggs on toast. How much could be healed with such simple accommodations?

It was a kind thought, and Mercy thought it because she was a kind person. She had a kind face. In her childhood she had smiled often, and there were lines because of it now. Not deep lines, more like shallow cuts or old scar tissue. But it made people trust her immediately. The first time someone stopped her in the street she was a bit frightened. It was only that day she had moved into the townhouse terrace, and she was still learning her way. But it was a woman and her child, foreigners clearly, just as she was. The woman had sad eyes, sensible shoes, and a smell like wood smoke. She wanted to know how to reach a particular street. "I'm sorry," Mercy told her, "really, I don't know. I've only just arrived myself." The silence after this seemed to last an eternity. Mercy felt her heart breaking. She wanted to help. The boy was soft-looking, his flesh hadn't sharpened into adulthood yet. He turned away from Mercy and stared down the street. It was getting dark, but the lamps hadn't come on yet. The darkness pressed the cobblestones flat. She shivered. The boy was shivering too though he hadn't noticed yet. "That way," said Mercy, guessing desperately. The mother gave her a look—grateful but anxious. "Thank you," she whispered. Then she tugged at the boy's hand. They set off into the gloom.

* * *

Mercy had a daughter named Comfort who came to stay with her on weekends. Comfort was a sweet girl, eight years old, but almost nearly very grown up. She took the train from Hindmoor Green to the city by herself with no one but the conductor to watch out for her. Mercy had feared for her daughter the first time she made this trip alone, but lo and behold, when the train had pulled into the station, there was Comfort exactly where she should be. She was always full of questions after the trip. Mercy didn't know many of the answers. Mostly she made things up. "How many stars are there in the sky?" Comfort would ask her. "Only twelve," she would say, "but the sky is a mirror maze so it seems like there are many more."

Mercy had loved her husband, but they had married very early. She had been seventeen, he had been twenty. She didn't remember what the rush was. It hadn't been Comfort. Comfort came later. When Mercy looked back on the early months of her engagement to Noah, she remembered the warm glow she had felt in the pit of her stomach, a furnace fueling the engine of her days. In Hindmoor Green he had seemed larger than life: always laughing, big hands, square palms. But they hadn't really known each other. Had they moved too quickly? Her parents said so. "Build the foundation," they said, "test it, make it perfect. Don't put all your weight onto something that may not hold." But she had never lived like that. She knew all things had a crack at the heart of them. They would fall apart eventually. This had never scared her, not even as a child, when someone—a teacher—had first explained what death was. She had known death was inside her already, she hadn't needed someone to tell her. The only houses she feared were the ones that were built to stand forever. Those she did not trust. She loved the houses of snails and sea creatures. They grew or were discarded. She lived her life by the same principles. When things with Noah fell apart, she knew how to pull herself from the wreckage. How to start over. She built her life up again, but smaller this time, less expansive, less willing to admit visitors.

"Is this my bedroom?" Comfort asked the first time she saw the townhouse terrace. "Is this where I shall play?" Mercy allowed that it was. Later there were other questions: "How far is it from your room to mine? Why do the stairs make that sound when I stomp on them? What shall we keep in the cellar?" In a fit of exasperation, Mercy said: "Bodies," and she blinked twice afterward in surprise. It was an accident really, she hadn't meant to say that. But one of the city's builders had told her a story in the pub, and it stuck with her. "This building? What it is, right, is a boneyard, this and every other," he said, spitting on the ground. His eyes were glazed with alcohol. His breath shone. He sniffed his palm, scowled, then whispered into her ear: "The foreman's dead corrupt. He takes the money for it, gets a heavy bag, about so big, wrapped like so. Bodies. They put them in the foundation. For luck, maybe. Or to seal up the cracks. Me? I dig the hole." Mercy hadn't been able to sleep after she heard that. When she walked to the shop where she worked, she couldn't look at the builders. She couldn't look at the buildings. She was afraid that Comfort wouldn't be able to sleep either. But Comfort slept through the night like a darling. She didn't stir once. In the morning she wanted to make mudcastles in the back garden. She filled her orange plastic bucket with dirt, and upended it gleefully. "Can I bury you, Mummy?" she asked. "Not today, pet. Maybe tomorrow."

* * *

Mercy glimpsed the woman and her boy sometimes. They stared at her from the reflections in glass panels of certain buildings. When she saw them, she would turn quickly, whether away or towards she didn't know. She resolved to do better in the future. So she bought maps of the city. Just a few at first, then more and more until her house was filled with them. Comfort draped them from strings. She built enormous mansions from them. Mercy would find herself crawling through tunnels bridged by paper folds. The hallway lights glowed behind onionskin levees. Streets swirled around her like fingerprints, the snaking lines of the canals. She touched them, and whispered their names. She didn't know why someone would want to go to one place more than another. They seemed equally strange to her, equally inhospitable. But she had promised herself she wouldn't lead anyone astray, not if she could help it.

In autumn, the night rain crawled like a stream of black ants down the window. When winter came, an unexpected snowfall made the faucets drip. Water snaked over the counter and seeped into the warren that Comfort had constructed, left the sodden paper hanging like old towels. Now it felt as if Mercy were crawling through seaweed. The tunnels could have been on the bottom of the ocean. The builder told her, afterwards, that it hadn't been the snows. Something had crawled into the pipes and died there. It had created a blockage. Still, the ink ran. It painted her fingers, her cheeks. It was as if the city was sealing itself onto her. But she didn't mind. She was learning.

There were foreigners everywhere, and they all came to

her: shy, distraught, eager, afraid. Mercy learned their gestures. "How far now…? Which is the way…?" She came to measure distance in five languages, and then six, and then she learned that she didn't need words at all for what she wanted to tell them. The ones who asked her knew the way already. The city was printed on them as well, only they couldn't see it. Not yet. But she could. She felt the tracery of lines glowing beneath their skin like thin, blue veins. She only needed to help them remember. And that, she learned, required very little: a kind smile, shy look, her hand touching theirs.

* * *

"Are you happy then?" the builder asked her. It was Wednesday. They were sitting at the pub, him leaning against the bar with a pint of bitter and her balanced on a stool, not talking to him, not listening to him. He was a big man, his body seemed to be stacked from successive layers. He reminded her of the mudcastles that Comfort built, only in reverse. "You look happy," he said, spreading his fingers. "You look dead happy." The question caught Mercy like a hammer blow between the dull eyes of a bull. She thought about the range of possible answers: "I make do" and "No more than anyone else" and was afraid to admit the truth: she *was* happy. It was easier with things as they were, with her tiny world, with her daughter present but not permanent, her husband regretful but never angry.

"If you're willing," Noah would say to her as he slipped into their narrow bed together, him already pressed against her. Afterwards, his mouth would tickle her ear: "How I love you," he would tell her, "my bright star, my darling." She could not imagine that all he ever wanted was her: slim-waisted, flat-chested, almost boyish in the coarseness of her hair. But Noah loved her. She saw it in the way he longed to sink himself into her so deeply that direction would reverse itself, like a tidal flow, and he would come back to himself: but complete this time. She could not tell him that she felt incomplete. She was not capable of holding that much love, of returning it unspoilt. It slipped out of her like water through a drain. Now there was a quiet space in the middle of the day when nothing was required of her. It was during these hours she took to the streets, looking for the strangers. Hoping they would stop her. "You could take me home," Mercy said to the thick-handed man beside her. She imagined him crawling through the tunnels that Comfort had made, on his hands and knees, surrounded by the smell of creeping damp. "Nah," he said. "A happy woman is no woman for me."

When Mercy left the bar it was on tottering feet. She felt unwell. She couldn't see the stars. The city blotted them out. There were towers where there used to be stars, and clouds, and a dull glow of silver from the streetlights, atoms of light bouncing between cloud and sodden sidewalk. But the stars. She had owned a telescope when she was younger. She loved the fierce red of Mars, gleaming like desert rock or a newly minted penny. She had read recently about the moon of Mars, Phobos: named for fear, son of Venus and Mars. She had read that tidal forces were ripping the moon apart. Its lifespan was now predicted to be 40 million years, a long time, no doubt, but finite. It was not forever. Above Mercy, the moon was shredding itself, its center a pile of rubble, shallow stress grooves lining its skin. She would be long dead by the time it fell apart, but it made her sad anyway, and strangely frightened, to think about what was happening. It was all invisible anyway, out beyond the lambent atmosphere, but it was happening and it was terrible. Like a premonition. "You should have come home with me," she whispered into the darkness. "See, I'm sad and I'm tired and I'm frightened. Just like you are."

In the distance she heard the sound of glass bursting. The terrible fraying of metal. She did not stop. She did not turn around. Three days later she learned the builder had been struck down in the street. It was an accident. She did not go to the funeral. The papers did not mention where he was buried.

* * *

Two weeks later, Mercy saw the builder. He was standing at an intersection of Potato Wharf and Liverpool Road with a dazed expression on his face. His jaw hung slightly slack, as if death had loosed the muscles that had formerly hinged it together. Normally Comfort was anxious, almost shy, when they walked the streets together. The city, she had been told, was different than Hindmoor Green, more dangerous. She would dog Mercy's footsteps, fitting comfortably into the space her shadow carved in the sunlight. But today she was eager. She had skipped on ahead, never once glancing back to be sure Mercy was following.

When Mercy saw that awful figure slouched against the terracotta facing of an old canal warehouse, she reached for her daughter. But Comfort had already passed beyond the range of potential interception. "Are you drunk?" she exclaimed, a mixture of delight and skepticism. Indeed, he smelled of something faintly boozy, dark and yeasty-sweet. But the builder did not speak to her daughter. His eyes raked upwards, met Mercy's, and a sharp spark of light leaped up into the pupils. "Please," he said desperately, "I don't know the way." Mercy's tongue was thick, it plugged the cave of her mouth like a rockslide. "Come with me now," she said. "Let me show you." His hand was clammy but unexpectedly warm. She squeezed it gently.

* * *

In Hindmoor Green, they burned the bodies of the dead. The ashes rose in a feathered bloom from the chimney of the crematorium and resettled upon the fields with the softness of snow. The dead became dust: comfortable, comforting, a velvet veil over sacred things, objects too precious for daily handling. The dead inhabited lungs, they etched themselves under fingernails. The dead were lifted gently from the inner canthus of the eye by tongue or tears. They did not come back. It was different in the city, Mercy realized. Perhaps it was that the buildings were settled too deeply, perhaps their towers soared too high. The city was small, yes, but it was expanding, colonizing those parts of heaven and earth that had since been left vacant. When Mercy took the hand of a stranger, she was never certain of where they had come from and where they were truly going.

Her own first train journey from Hindmoor Green had been a revelation. She had never imagined the size of the country she lived in, the glow of white chalk in the hillsides, the copper and tan waters of the ship canal snaking inland from the sea. There was terror too, yes, the sense of hurtling into the unknown like a silver arrow, but mostly it was the joy that Mercy remembered afterward. How her eyes devoured the sight of the men disembarking onto the platform in their crisp suits, briefcases in hand, slouched children, dainty women in sensible shoes, used to the journey. She did not know what the city would look like, and the tallness of the buildings was a shock. How could such things exist? Distantly she had always imagined the sky as a thin blue film but these things revealed that as a lie: they gave it depth, they were a measure stick for its enormity. She had not known what she would do when she arrived, only that she was empty, and the city would imprint some kind of shape upon her. She wondered if it was the same for the dead man. He had been a builder after all. He had known the city better, more intimately, than she ever would.

But it was the memory of the dead mother and her child that hurt Mercy the most. She had not known what to tell them, had not properly understood their questions. She had pointed blindly, and they had followed her directions. But where had she sent them? Once she had believed that one place was as good as another, but she was learning differently now. When she looked at the strangers she could tell: some of them were going to good places. There was a brightness in their eyes, a calmness, a sense that things would be easier when they got wherever they were going. But for others there was only exhaustion, an aching look that spoke of the miles behind and the miles ahead. When she woke from dreams of those two, she would go to her daughter's bedroom and crawl into the narrow bed. Mercy had always thought her daughter was exactly as she was named: a comfort, somehow extraneous to Mercy's existence, a delight, to be sure, but unnecessary, nothing to seal the gaps. But when she breathed in the smell of the sheets, which she refused to launder until the day before Comfort arrived, she knew this was not the case at all. Comfort had become her center, the smallest, purest part of her. The foundation stone of her entire life.

* * *

Now it was Friday morning. Mercy had walked to the train station to meet her daughter. Her eyes skimmed the eyes of those she passed, careful not to linger too long. Today was not a day she would give over to the strangers. Today would belong to Comfort. It was her birthday. In the kitchen sat a little sunken cake clothed in nets of sugar and glazed orange slices. Mercy had eaten the ones that hadn't set properly so that only the best remained.

The train arrived. The doors flung out a stream of people,

men clutching briefcases, women clutching the hands of their children, children clutching at whatever caught their eye as they passed: sunshine on the rails, pigeons, flutters of paper. Mercy waited. She had become more at ease with the crowds. She knew they would part, and there would be Comfort looking sleepy and sensible and not at all uncertain of where she was. But as the platform cleared, Comfort did not emerge. A worm of panic crawled into Mercy's heart. This had never happened before. She went to the platform attendant. He spoke in a slow drawl, "Perhaps she's on the next train, Mum."

Comfort wasn't on the next train. Nor the one after that. Nor the one after that. Mercy's hands were shaking now. Noah had left her at the station in Hindmoor Green. He had kissed her on the cheek. He had watched her climb the stairs. Mercy spoke to the station master, a close-shaven man with weepy blue eyes. He was apologetic. He was baffled. He would do everything in his power to find out what had happened. Then there were the police, sure it had been a misunderstanding, a mistake. "Did you have problems with your daughter?" they asked. "Was she unhappy?" Mercy let them talk. At home, she remembered, was a labyrinth of old paper and a cake with perfect slivers of orange. They would dissolve on her tongue like snowflakes if she let them.

* * *

There was a comradery among the dead, Comfort discovered. She awakened in their city, a city of twisted glass lit by a warm, flaxen glow whose source she couldn't see. The dead crowded around her. She knew they were dead immediately because they had no smell. When she kissed their cheeks, they had no taste. The dead insisted on touching her, on hugging her close to their chests. It reminded her of past birthday parties when her father's family, a large and noisy crew, would descend upon her home to pinch her cheeks and exclaim over her height. It was not an unpleasant feeling. Comfort asked them questions, and they answered immediately. There was a joyfulness to their speech, even if it was strange to her. They remembered what it was like when they first arrived. They were frightened too. "I'm not frightened," she told them, and she realized this was true. She was happy. She felt as if she had stumbled upon some marvelous secret, and, in many ways, she had.

Time lost its urgency. She was unhooked from its rhythms. She watched it flow past her the way one might sit on the banks of a river, watching the passage of boats. She grew older. She fell in love. She married. She had a daughter of her own. She named her Solace, for her mother. Solace Dwyer. Time passed. Comfort believed once that time would have no meaning after death, but this turned out not to be the case at all. To exist, she learned, was to be in time. But time was not the problem in the city of the dead. Space was the problem. The city was shrinking, moment by moment. Comfort could see the horizon approaching with the height and mass of a standing wave. Soon it would topple and pin her in place. She knew this. The dead stood together. They had lost their joyfulness. They smelled of nothing, they tasted of nothing, but even so, it was very bad. Perhaps it was the fear. The dead had learned to fear what was coming. She clutched her daughter's hand.

There was a story Comfort's father told her about a man named Jacob. She did not miss her father. She did not, if she was honest, remember her father. But she remembered the story. Jacob was favored by God. He was the father of many children. One night God sent him a dream. He dreamed of angels going up and down the sky on a vast ladder. Comfort imagined this would be how she would leave the city of the dead. But the way out of the city of the dead, Comfort discovered, was nothing like that at all. You couldn't leave by regular methods. The city had no borders, or rather, its borders were turned in upon themselves. Walk as far as you could in one direction and at some point you would find yourself retracing your footsteps. There was only one way to leave. The city had a crack at the center of it. The road through the crack was very long, so long it seemed impossible. Comfort tugged at her daughter. They would begin at once.

They walked. Their shadows fell behind, always. Sometimes Comfort imagined dragging them like a weight. There were others walking too, but conversation was difficult to keep up. Although the dead couldn't feel pain, they could still feel despair: the slow enclosing of hope. This did not break Comfort. For her despair was only a sort of pressurization. Her hope, made smaller, had become harder, sharper. Eventually she found herself in another city. It too was made of spires of glass, but these were frightening rather than familiar. "Where are we, Mum?" her daughter asked. But the glass confused her senses. It reminded her of how birds must feel when they see lights in the windows of tall towers and think they are the stars.

* * *

There was no news for Mercy in the days that followed. The loss of Comfort was a crack that ran down the center of her life. She felt as if it had cleaved time in two, before and after. Noah came to stay with her. The first night he slept in Comfort's room, which made Mercy inexpressibly angry. She did not want him to have that. He was covering over one of the only things that remained of her daughter with his own male smell. At breakfast, she hurled a teacup at the wall. It broke into three pieces. Noah swept these up without comment. He cradled her in his arms.

She fought him bitterly, but his arms were exactly as she had remembered them, strong, those hard square palms like shovels patting down the earth. He kissed her, and she let him do it. The second night he slept in her bed. He did not touch her, but she could feel him lying alongside her, taking up space that used to belong to her. He snored gently. She turned her back to him, but the heat of his limbs snaked over her anyway.

For a time Mercy became a shut-in. She was afraid to leave the house. She kept imagining the look on Comfort's face if she returned to find her mother missing. Noah folded up the maps. Her living room became a living room again, ordinary, thick with dust in the corners where she had not bothered to look. In Hindmoor Green, she might have discovered a piece of Comfort tucked away there, but in the city she knew the dust was simply dust. Comfort had been buried elsewhere, in a basement, perhaps, or the foundations of the new bank: her tiny bones curdling in cement. Mercy did not like the dust. She was appalled by the open space of her living room. She had become so used to following the paths that Comfort made: here, along the sofa, two feet, three feet, then over the chair, then a rest, perhaps, under the old oak table whose tablecloth formed a perfect shelter. But Noah set it right. The chairs were placed neatly where they ought to be so the two of them could sit together over a breakfast of eggs on toast, coffee with sugar or cream. Simple kindnesses to help her cope.

And just like that Mercy realized it was not that she didn't love Noah. She did. She loved his kindness, the hot snort of his breath as he slept, the sound of his footsteps on the stairs. It was just that she had traveled so far in one direction that she hated the feeling of having returned home, just like that, just that easily. So one morning, while he was sleeping, she levered herself from beneath him, put on her winter coat, and left. She did not know where she was going. Mercy took to the streets, circling the waterfront piazzas, and following, apparently at will, the paths that lined the canals. There was a smell in the air, something heavy and brooding. She knew the streets by name though many she had never visited before: Market Street, Bridge Street, Oldham Road, Stockport Road, New Street. They were what they were. They said what they were, where they were going. Nothing else in her life had ever been so straightforward.

She did not know what she expected to see until all at once, she did know, because there was Comfort. She looked older than Mercy remembered, taller. She had cut her hair at some point, and now it hung short and feathery beneath her ears. There were lines on her face. She clutched the hand of a tiny girl, three years old. "Comfort," she cried, "please!" But the look her daughter gave her was uncertain, confused, exhausted. There was no recognition. "Sorry," she muttered. Her voice was deeper now too, robbed of its sing-song quality. "I seem to have lost the way. How many streets are there in the city?" she asked. "Only twelve," Mercy said, "but the glass is like a mirror here so it seems like there are many more." They stared at each other like strangers. But then the girl smiled. Her lips were soft and delicate, she had her grandfather's chin, her grandfather's blunt nose. "Where do they lead?" the girl asked. Mercy touched the girl's hand. It was cold and clammy, but Mercy could feel the pulse of something—new life—beneath her skin. It stretched the fabric of her, but she did not crack. She felt her heart expanding, she felt herself growing larger. She had anchored herself so firmly in heartache, and now the heartache was dissolving like sugar on the tongue. The touch was all she needed. Calmness washed over her. "I don't know," Mercy said, "I've never known, not for certain. But come with me, both of you. Let me take you home."

WE'LL ALWAYS HAVE PARIS

by

M.R. CAREY

I will take the trouble to set this out for you, because I feel it's important that you understand. I must ask you to listen and to refrain from raising questions while I speak. I believe the most pertinent issues between us will be very clearly explained in the course of my story. If at the end of it you still find yourself puzzled, unclear as to why you are about to die, then in that respect and that respect alone you will have good reason to reproach me.

* * *

In the 14th arrondissement of the city, close to the Brooklyn Bridge and the Alhambra, there is or used to be (it is hard to be categorical) a patisserie whose terrace looks out directly onto the Seine. It had been my custom ever since I found the place to have a breakfast croissant there, watching the lazily ambling waters of the river while the particulars of the cases on which I was currently working flowed through my brain with a similar lack of haste or direction. This ritual had afforded me many valuable insights, and I had come to rely on it more and more in these recent times of turbulence and irreplaceable loss.

So naturally, this was where the latest body had been found.

I was summoned to the Rue Asseline at 6.00am on a morning in October—this October just passed, which was neither mild nor merciful. You remember it, yes? The chill of winter was already in the air despite the warming smell of baking *Viennoiseries* carried on the westerly wind. The cafés had not opened at that hour but they were already preparing for the early morning onslaught.

The corpse was lying at the edge of the pavement, one arm stretched out into the road. He looked as though he had met his demise in the act of hailing a cab. He was formally dressed, in a black tuxedo whose satin edgings had lost their lustre forever, stained as they were with their late owner's cerebral matter. His skull was not only smashed, it was also seriously truncated. Monsieur Crâne, very evidently, had struck again.

The Irishman, Sergeant Riordan, was there before me and was scraping at the dead man's fingernails, where presumably there was something of value to be found. An assailant's blood and tissue, perhaps, or the rare earth of some specific and identifiable quarter of the city. I don't care much for Riordan's irreverent manner but I admire his stubborn perfectionism and his dedication to duty. When the dead rose and became the undead he fought indefatigably in the city's defence. It was said that he had put a bullet in the head of his own wife when she clawed her way out of the body bag and tried to eat their only child. Afterwards he had carried her corpse three miles to lay her down in the mass grave in the Jardin du Luxembourg along with all the other *zombis*. Respect must be paid to such a man.

A young woman, her hair wet as if she had just stepped out of the shower, was standing beside him. She was taking photographs of the crime scene. Not of the body, but of the buildings round about. Curious, I thought. She was curious herself. Her pale blue eyes and ash blonde hair, the extreme pallor of her skin seemed to belong to another place and time. She might have been one of the city's marble statues come to life. Or she might have been one of the *zombi* revenants, but there were no revenants now. We had won that war, at a cost— to each and all of us—almost too high to reckon.

I took up a station immediately behind Riordan, leaning against the wall of an adjacent building. I was resigned to a long wait. The Irish detective's methods are exhaustive, and exhausting. "So," I said to pass the time, "do you have any ideas as to the cause of death?"

The woman—apparently Riordan's partner or assistant— looked around as I spoke, her gaze taking me in from toe to crown. Her stare allowed the possibility that I might be, or become, interesting. It explicitly did not go any further than that.

"You're a very funny man, Inspector Philemon," Riordan murmured. "It's a struggle to restrain my merriment with you making such jocular observations."

The woman walked across to the edge of the pavement and took a series of photographs of a small dog that had wandered up to join us. It stared into her lens with a long-suffering patience, as though it was used to such impertinences. "Is the dog a suspect?" I asked Riordan.

He looked around at the woman, at the animal, and gave a little snort that conveyed no information at all.

The woman took my picture next. The magnificent frontage of the Hotel Belle Époque provided a very photogenic backdrop, but I doubt it did anything to offset the shadows under my eyes or the rumpled, lived-in state of my clothes.

Riordan straightened. He was looking similarly lived-in, to be honest. Both of us had been on this case more or less continuously since it had first broken more than a month before, and we were far from the only ones. The body of a young woman, a streetwalker, had been found lying in the middle of the Champs-Élysées. In swerving around her the cars had made hundreds of concentric ruts in the autumn mud, roughly circular but tapered at either end: a yoni mark, as though in deference to her profession.

The top of her head had been removed. There was nothing above the bridge of her nose. The resulting damage, however, had none of the neatness of an incision. It had not been done with a scalpel or a bone saw. It was more in the nature of a crush injury, as though someone had pounded the woman's head repeatedly with a hammer until the resulting mass of pulped flesh and bone fragments could be scraped away. What was left of the skull and the head bore the typical signs of crushing: the bone fragmented along parallel lines of stress, and pulled free of the muscles in the same vertical plane. Striated trauma artefacts extended all the way down into the shoulders and upper back.

Monsieur Crâne had left his calling card. He was to do so again a further twelve times in the following weeks. Today's corpse brought the overall total up to fourteen, and still we were no closer to an arrest, or even to establishing a suspect.

We were still recovering, of course, from the great war between the living and the dead. Perhaps on some level we could not help but see the victims as potential enemies. Certainly we carried our scars from that war, every one of us. We were the walking wounded, emotionally and psychologically depleted. The world we lived and moved in seemed drained of colour. It was almost as though that high tide of death had left us beached and we were only waiting for another wave to carry us away.

There were, of course, more prosaic problems with the investigation. Logistical ones. The victims were bafflingly diverse. The first, a prostitute who must have been attacked in the course of her nightly work—an occupational hazard, one might have thought. But the second body to appear was a Japanese commodities broker well known on Wall Street, and the third was a respectable lady who ran a cantina on Juarez Hill. Back to the gutter for victim number four, a homeless drunk. And so, and so, and so. Perhaps there was no scalpel involved, but Monsieur Crâne's needle pricked the fabric of society at every level and pulled it into a tight, unlovely gather.

I took these musings to the establishment I mentioned earlier, the *Café Moche* on Fifth and Taylor, just off Unterdenlinden, and stirred them into lethargic activity with a double espresso. I ordered a croissant too, but left it untouched. I considered lacing the coffee with brandy, a great specific both against the weather and against unpleasant thoughts, but it was still very early in the day. I usually endured my stations of the cross without anaesthetic until the middle of the afternoon. Otherwise I would have been drunk all the time. To make a continuing investment in what was left of my life and work required me, occasionally, to be sober.

But the waiter, Sam, must have seen the temptation cross my mind. "You want a slug of something hard in that, Phil?" he shouted from the bar.

I shook my head. "Not unless you have the Koh-i-Noor diamond ready to hand."

He laughed—a loud and raucous sound. "Still on order. I'll let you know."

"I'll take a brandy, though, if you're offering," said the young woman from the crime scene. She slid into the seat opposite me and shot me a cold smile. "Lutetia. Lutetia Lumière. In case you're wondering, you're very pleased to meet me."

I looked around for Riordan. He was not on the premises.

"You seem to have misplaced your partner, Madame detective," I observed. "Should I telephone the precinct and ask them to conduct a search?"

The woman—Lumière? A good name for a photographer,

I supposed—ignored the question. She pushed some photos across the table at me. I pushed them back, which caused her to twist her very expressive lips into a warning frown. "I need you to look at these," she said. "They're part of my inquiry."

"But not of mine," I pointed out mildly. "The Sûreté and the Garda are not collaborating on this case. I'm sure Sergeant Riordan would be quite homicidally distressed to know you were canvassing the details of his investigation with an officer of a rival organisation."

Lumière grinned. "Sergeant Riordan can keep his investigation. I'm talking about mine. And I don't work for the Garda."

"Then why…?" I began, but she stopped me with a raised finger. She was still smiling, but there was something hard and sharp glinting from underneath it like broken glass in a flower bed.

"Hey. Excuse me. I said I don't work for the Garda. I also don't work for the Sûreté or the Policeini or the Aktionsstyrke or the Kogu-Keisatsu. I'm strictly freelance, Inspector. Which is why I'm sitting here talking to you now, under the possibly mistaken impression that you actually give a shit about all these dead people we keep tripping over. If I'm wrong, I'll just move right along."

It was an impressive speech, though it was slightly undercut by the arrival at that precise moment of her brandy, delivered by Sam with a wink and a smirk. I knew very well what had put that leer on his face. We had fought together, the two of us, and killed together those who were already unarguably dead. He was misinterpreting this meeting as a romantic liaison and he was pleased on my behalf. He was an optimist, and looked out continually for signs of a thaw in my perpetual winter. And I continually disappointed him.

Lumière thanked him for the brandy, then turned the

searchlight of her attention back to me. "Okay," she said. "Let's start at the beginning. What do we have?"

I raised an eyebrow. "Assuming, for the sake of argument, that there is a composite entity that could reasonably be called *we*, what *we* have is fourteen bodies killed at various places around the city in a one-month period. Nothing to tie the suspects together, and nothing for that matter to link the murders themselves apart from the manner of death, which in all cases is severe crush injury to the head."

Lumière shook her head sternly. "Sloppy, sloppy, sloppy," she said. "Three times over, for the three things you left out. If we're going to work together I'm going to need you to be a little more forensic."

I considered what might be added to my summary. The alternative would have been to get up and walk away, which I wasn't inclined to do since I had been there first. "All the killings were at night," I offered. "At least, the bodies were found in the morning in the vast majority of cases."

"Good. What else?"

"The crush injuries aren't the only consistency in the evidence. In all cases the crime scene was surprisingly clean. There was blood and cerebral tissue to be found, and some bone fragments, but far less than one would expect from such an extreme physical trauma. Oh, and some of the bodies also bear lacerations to their lower legs and ankles, as though they were bitten, *ante-mortem*, by a large animal."

"And that's two. Finally?"

I shrugged irritably, taking another sip of my coffee. "I don't know. You tell me."

"Accelerating pace, Inspector. The intervals between the killings have been getting shorter. These last two were on successive nights."

This was true. I had shied away from saying it because I was trying not to think about it. It meant that tonight would almost certainly yield a new horror which I would have to face come tomorrow morning. I had had enough of such sights. Possibly I had had too much. On a day like this it was hard to shake the feeling that I was nearing some psychological terminus at a reckless and irrevocable velocity.

"So that is what *we* have," I summed up, with brittle emphasis. "What we don't have is anything in the way of witness testimony, any fingerprints or physical clues left at any of the scenes, or any clinical evidence that might help to identify a suspect. Therefore, after one month and fourteen bodies, *we* are still very much where we were at the outset. Which is to say, desultorily masturbating while the world goes to Hell."

I would not have used such a crude analogy if the woman had not insulted my professionalism. But Lumière didn't seem shocked or taken aback. She drained half of her brandy in one gulp, rolling it around her mouth before she swallowed. "When I masturbate, Inspector," she said, "it's never desultory. Look out of the window."

I took a glance. The fog had settled in thickly, conclusively deciding the uneven struggle between afternoon and evening. "It's foul," I agreed.

"Not my point," said Lumière. "Now look at your plate."

I glanced down at my uneaten croissant. "Perhaps I was not so hungry as…" I said. The sentence remained unfinished as the pale woman lashed out, as quick as a snake. I was suddenly lying on the floor of the café with my own blood welling up thick and cloying in my mouth.

She stood over me, holding the stem of her broken brandy glass. Her face was calm and perhaps a little solicitous. "I'm sorry about that," she said. "But the liquor will sterilise the cut.

And if it needs a stitch or two, I've got a kit right here in my pocket. Get up, Inspector."

I did so, but I drew my Chamelot-Delvigne as I rose, and by the time I was on my feet again I had it pointed at her face. The café's other patrons had mostly remained seated, but were watching us warily. A debacle like this one could turn serious very quickly. Sam was watching too. He had picked up the stout shillelagh he kept behind the bar, but seeing that I had the situation in hand he made no move to deploy it.

"You're under arrest," I told Lumière coldly. "For assaulting a police officer."

She seemed unperturbed. "Tell me again about your croissant," she invited me.

"What?" I demanded. "What in the world are you…?"

Once again I faltered into silence, although this time not because of an incised wound. It had been morning when I came into the café. That was why I had ordered a croissant. Now it was evening. The day had passed in the space between two breaths.

"*Merde alors!*" I exclaimed.

Lumière laughed. "I know, right? It gets easier to see through the bullshit, trust me, but the first time you pretty much have to be in severe pain. I got my hand slammed in a revolving door. Blessing in disguise, although I fucked and blinded like a longshoreman at the time. All these things are tied together, Inspector. I can show you how. Are you up for this?"

I hesitated, but only for a heartbeat—and mostly because her idiom had left me a little confused. "Up for, *c'est quoi*?"

"Ready. Motivated. Inclined to pursue a specific course of action."

"Yes," I assured her. "I am very much up for this."

She took me first back to the site of the latest murder. There was no fog now. We had opened the door of the café to find the street cold, clear and lamplit. "I tried three times with that Irishman," she told me as we walked through the frigid dusk. "Smacked him in the mouth, bit him, and stabbed his hand with a letter opener. He couldn't see it. So I thought I'd try you. Glad I did."

"You weren't tempted to work alone?" I asked her. "If you're still walking around loose after doing all those things to Mr Riordan you must be a woman of formidable talents."

"Thank you, Inspector Philemon. But this is much too big for me to handle on my own. Probably too big for the both of us together but hey, misery loves company."

My own misery did not. I almost said as much, but she slowed and stopped. We had come to the exact corner, the place where the dead man had been lying when I first arrived on the scene that morning (or an hour ago, for both of those statements seemed correct). There was no body to be seen now. The liveried doorman in front of the hotel stood with his hands clasped at his back, his fastidious sneer making any crime here seem not just impossible but *déclassé*.

"You said earlier," Lumière reminded me, "that there was no physical evidence left at the crime scenes. I think there is, but people are missing it for the same reason they miss all this messed-up time-shifting."

I looked around, but at first could see nothing.

"Try chewing your lip," Lumière suggested. "The torn bit. Stick your tongue in the wound to make it smart."

I felt no inclination to do that, and it wasn't necessary. Just grimacing so that the wound cracked open again was enough. I winced in pain, and at the same moment saw what I had failed to see before.

"The hotel!" I said, pointing. "I think… I'm almost sure…"

Wordlessly the pale woman handed me one of the photos she had tried to show me in the café. It was a photo of me that morning, standing exactly where I was standing now. To my left, a brass sign announced with many Romanesque flourishes that this was the Hotel Belle Époque.

Now it stated in stiffly serifed copperplate that it was the Waldorf Astoria.

"That… that isn't possible!" I whispered.

"And eighty-minute days are?" Lumière's tone was sardonic, even flippant, but there was tension in her face. She held out the rest of the photos for me to take.

I leafed through them with shaking hands. I easily recognised the common theme. Each of them showed one of the scenes where a body had been found. Each of them ignored the body and concentrated on the physical landmarks in its vicinity. A street sign, an awning, in one case the elegant neo-classical façade of the Bundesbank.

Looking at them made my head ache. I sensed in each case that a substitution had been made similar to that which I had just witnessed. Tverskaya Street had once been the Boulevard Saint Germain. The Hafiz Mustafa was formerly the Patisserie LaRochelle.

"What is happening?" I demanded. "What does all this mean?"

"I have no idea," Lumière said sourly. "All I know is that the murders are accompanied by these inexplicable phenomena. These transformations. And that most people walk right past them without even slowing down. They're completely unaware that anything has changed."

A memory struck me, coming out of nowhere. "This morning," I said. "Your hair was soaking, though the weather was dry."

Lumière nodded approvingly. "Very good, Inspector," she

said. "You're getting the hang of this. A block away it was raining. I walked through it to get to the crime scene. The weather changes, as well as the buildings and the time of day. And as my last exhibit, suppose I were to ask you the name of this city? The one in which you've been living for—I would suppose—the last several years."

"I was born here," I told her. "Right here in—"

I had to struggle to finish the sentence. The word just wouldn't come. I twisted my lips to form the opening consonant, fought to push the breath out of my throat.

"Almost there," Lumière encouraged. Or did she mock me?

"Paris!" I yelled like a lost soul. "I was born in Paris!"

Lumière clutched my shoulders, her eyes shining. I was wrong, there was no mockery here. "Oh, nicely done!" she said. "Excellent! This was Paris once. But it takes an exceptional man to remember that. I knew as soon as I heard your voice, Inspector, that you wouldn't let me down!"

I took no comfort from these words. Indeed it is hard to describe the anguish and rage I felt right then. I thought I was inured to sorrow, that it had become my element, but this new pain cut through the dullness of my despair like a scalpel. Paris was my home, my second mother, and she had been taken from me in the way a sneak-thief takes your wallet, *en passant*, leaving you none the wiser. I almost wept. I almost screamed.

Lumière put a hand on my shoulder. "Bear up," she told me, with gruff compassion. "There's work to be done."

I shook my head, meaning both that I would survive the blow and that I did not believe her. "What work?" I asked her, when I trusted myself to speak. "What can anyone do against this?"

"You're a cop investigating a murder. So I humbly suggest that you investigate. I've given you pretty much everything I've got. Now it's your turn. Maybe you can see something I haven't. Something that will let us come at this from another angle."

I was about to say that I had nothing. It would have been true only an hour before. But I realised, with a startling suddenness, that it was no longer true. Lumière's photographs had given me a fresh perspective on things I had thought I already knew. A kind of parallax. And from this novel position novel vistas were abruptly visible.

"We must go to the precinct house," I told Lumière. "I need to access my files."

We rode on a trolley car whose route, according to the sign painted on its side, ran along Van Ness and Market Street. Upon reading those words, alien geography stirred obliquely in my mind. We got out at the Boulevard Raspail, however, and it looked—praise God!—the same as always. We walked past the statue of Napoleon, eclipsed now by the huge memorial to the dead and undead of our recent war. Grieving citizens had heaped the steps leading up to the memorial (two men facing each other over an open coffin) with bundles of cut flowers or in some cases bare branches.

I stopped to pay my respects. I did this nightly, seeming to leave behind each time a larger piece of my soul.

"Did you fight, Inspector?" Lumière asked me.

I shrugged the question away. "Of course. Everyone fought who could. I would have given my life to keep the city from succumbing to that plague."

Lumière nodded and asked no more.

It was late. Or rather it seemed late. When we arrived at the precinct house there was no clerk on duty at the desk. We rode up in the rickety elevator, whose creaks have always seemed to me to be the complaints of an unhappy poltergeist. Normally I find that reflection amusing: just then it filled with foreboding those few hollows in my mind that were not already too full to take any more.

"So this is where you work," Lumière said, walking beside me down the rows of empty desks. "It's charming."

"It's an office," I replied brusquely, in no mood for badinage. "A place of work. It's not required to be charming. Only functional."

When we reached my desk I took off my jacket and the shoulder holster beneath it, hanging both on the back of my chair.

I pushed armloads of open files off my desk onto the floor. Each of them represented a stranger's life and some measurable part of my own, but right then they were unwelcome distractions. I unfolded the map on which I had plotted the current epidemic of murders, as a doctor might plot the spread of some actual epidemic. I added both today's and yesterday's to the tally, and then stood back to study the map at a distance.

"Is there something I should be seeing?" Lumière asked me.

"There is a pattern," I said. "There was already the suggestion of one, but with these two latest atrocities it stands out much more clearly."

Lumière leaned over the map, glaring at it in deep concentration. "There's no pattern," she said. "The placing of the bodies seems almost random. The Marais. Bloomsbury. Greenwich Village…"

My pride was a little restored at this proof that there were some things I saw more clearly than she did. "It's not random at all. We can join all the crime scenes with a single line, thus." I did it as she watched. "They are all, as you see, on the circumference of what one might loosely describe as a circle. Not a single body has been found within that circle. I am taking it for granted, of course, that the bodies are found some distance from where the victims were actually killed."

"Hence the lack of physical evidence."

"Exactly. So. The place where all these poor souls met their end must be somewhere within our circle," my hand hovered over the map, "and probably close to its centre. The murderer may well have thought that he was placing the bodies at random. Certainly he chose a random direction in which to walk after each killing. But he walked for more or less the same length of time, the same distance—so keen to keep his location secret that he was impelled always to stay on a straight line that led away from it."

I took a ruler from the desk drawer. "It might be possible, therefore," I said, "to use those same lines to track him backwards to his source. If we were to connect the dots through the centre, rather than around the periphery, we might be able to discern the centre of this atrocious web. The place where the spider sits."

"Do it!" Lumière urged me.

It was a rough and ready form of divination, at best. I took the northernmost and southernmost points and drew a line between them. Then I did the same for their nearest neighbours, and so on, going clockwise around the edge of the circle. Fourteen murders produced seven straight lines. There was no common centre, but it was close. Very close. All seven lines passed through the Rue Garancière, most of them within a hundred yards or so of the point where it is crossed by the Palatine. Something about that location pricked my memory in a way that was far from pleasant.

Lumière was staring at my face. "What?" she demanded.

I tapped the map. "There was a murder at exactly this point," I murmured. "Or at least, a possible murder. The body was never found. Only blood. A great deal of it. The man who called us said that there had been a body. That of a woman. But she was gone by the time we arrived. He said he had recognised her as one Sylvia Astor, a student of literature at the Sorbonne. I arrested and held him for a time, thinking that he might have killed and abducted the woman himself, but he knew no more than he had told us. And Sylvia Astor was not seen again."

Lumière's fixed stare still interrogated me. I shrugged, for I had nothing more to add. "This was before Monsieur Crâne began his reign of terror, of course. That has somewhat monopolised our attention since."

"How long before?"

"Five, perhaps six days." I held up my hand, for she seemed about to break in. "Yes, Lumière, I know. The timing is perfect for Mademoiselle Astor to have been the first victim. And the place of her death, if indeed she was killed, was here. Here at the confluence of these lines, at the very centre of the web."

"The Church of St. Sulpice."

I nodded. "There is a stairwell at the side of the building, leading up from the crypt. The blood was pooled on the steps. If the woman had been attacked down there and then had tried— wounded, bleeding—to find her way back up to the street, that would match what I saw."

Lumière's face was cold and hard. Once again she reminded me of a statue. "Is that enough evidence to call in a manhunt?" she demanded.

"More than enough," I assured her. "I will put it on my superintendent's desk as soon as he arrives tomorrow."

"I don't want to wait that long."

"No?" I confess I was not surprised. I felt the same impatience myself. "What should we do then? I suppose I could call on him at his home, and ask him to swear out a warrant tonight."

"Or we could go there right now, and make the arrest ourselves."

I pondered this invitation for several moments. It held

some appeal. Clearly, however, I must not go to St. Sulpice without leaving some record of my discovery. I found a scrap of paper and quickly scribbled down a message, a letter to Superintendent Faber explaining the discoveries we had made and what we now proposed to do. I took it to his desk, found an envelope and addressed it to him.

Lumière was at my shoulder the whole time, full of urgency. "Let's go, Philemon. You know there's going to be another murder tonight."

I hesitated, uncertain of where the letter would be the most likely to be seen. Finally Lumière snatched it from my hand and tucked it under the arm of the winged Victory statue of which the superintendent is so inordinately proud. "I said let's go," she repeated. Her voice had a grating edge to it and her eyes were dark. There was something personal at stake for her in this, clearly. Well, so there was for me also. I was desperate to see the face of the killer who was murdering not just my city's inhabitants but—however insane it sounded—my city herself.

The trolley car or the Métro would have taken us to St. Sulpice, but Lumière set off at a brisk walk, almost a run. It seemed the urgency of our business and the agitation of her spirits would not allow her to wait. I fell in beside her.

"When we get there," I told her, "you should wait out on the street. It's unwise for both of us to go inside." She made no answer to this, but only speeded up her stride.

It was now well past midnight, if such terms retained any of their meaning. The streets were all but empty. Here a demi-mondaine staggered home from some sordid tryst, tottering on dysfunctionally high heels. There a homeless drunk sorted through the rubbish behind a trattoria in hope of finding either a late supper or an early breakfast. Nobody accosted us, or even seemed to see us.

The church's frontage, that breathtaking arcade with its towers and doubled array of columns, was completely dark. It had been closed by order of the city some years earlier, after a fire had all but destroyed it. It looked most unwelcoming. If a building could be said to have an aspect, the aspect of this one was solitary and introspective.

I approached the main doors, Above our heads, in faded black paint, was the legend that had been added to the façade in the days following the revolution. *Le Peuple Francais Reconnoit L'Etre Suprême Et L'Immortalité de L'Âme.* It is good to be explicit about such things. A thick chain had been threaded through the handles of the doors and secured with a heavy padlock. There was no getting in that way.

"The crypt," I said, "is to the—" Lumière did not wait on my words, or my pointing finger. She led the way around the building to the north side, where a flight of marble steps led down into profound darkness. By the time I reached the top of the steps she was already at the bottom, invisible to me. Her voice floated back up to me. "There's a door!"

I followed, taking the steps with care. Even so I almost tripped and fell when I reached the bottom, the sudden levelling of the terrain deceiving and unbalancing me. I groped around until I felt the outline of the door Lumière had described. It stood open. From beyond it came a whiff of immemorial dust and damp.

Had I searched the crypt on the day when Sylvia Astor's body was found? I could no longer remember. Too many other bodies had intervened.

"Over here," Lumière's voice said from the pitch dark.

"I can't see you," I told her.

"Follow the sound of my voice."

I drew my service revolver and advanced. One step, a second, then a third. My skin was prickling, wanting to recoil from a touch it had not yet felt. There might be a murderer in this room with us. Monsieur Crâne, with his inexorable hammer and his burning madness.

"To the left," said Lumière.

I turned and moved in the direction of her voice.

I had gone perhaps two steps further when something bit down on my leg just above the ankle, all the way to the bone. The shock was almost as terrible as the pain. I screamed aloud, and fell to the stone floor, clutching at my injured leg. A band of thick metal had closed on it. Or rather two half-bands, for there were hinges or brackets at either end.

As I wrestled in vain with the trap, an electric torch clicked on a few feet away from me. Its beam was pointed directly at me so I could see almost nothing beyond it: only the vague outline of a shape that had to be Lumière.

"Sorry about that," she said.

I took aim with my revolver and fired it repeatedly. The forlorn click of the hammer striking an empty chamber sounded with each stroke of my finger on the trigger.

"Emptied it," Lumière said. "Back at the precinct. While you were writing this." She set the torch down, and an envelope right beside it. The envelope bore Superintendent Faber's name, in my own hand.

She sat down facing me, almost close enough to touch. But the leg-trap, I saw by her torch's light, was secured by a chain that was embedded somehow in the floor of this wide, low-ceilinged room. My freedom of movement was not very much.

"I hate to lie," Lumière said. "Especially to a man like you. A native. It goes against the grain. And since there's no need for it now, let me tell you that my name, when I was alive, was Sylvia Astor."

I must have groaned or cried out at this. Certainly I felt a movement of despair. We had fought so hard, so bitterly, to scour our city of the *zombis*, and now they were back.

"It's not as you think," Lumière assured me quickly. "Let me explain. You deserve that, at least."

What she told me was simple enough, and terrible enough. The undead had indeed been defeated, and eradicated. But their infected bodies had been laid in mass graves hastily dug in the city's many parks. The gardens of the Luxembourg Palace, the Champ de Mars, the woods of Boulogne.

The infection had continued to spread, unseen. It sank into the soil.

"The city got sick," Lumière said. "With the *zombi* sickness. It forgot what it was. It thought it was other cities of which it had heard or dreamed. Fantastic places with names like New York. London. Lima. Dublin. Some of the undead had been tourists. Perhaps the city could not tell their memories from its own.

"And it hungered, with the *zombi* hunger. It ate me first, after I committed suicide on the steps of this church. It drank from me and clutched me to its heart. I became its servant. Willingly. My memories of my old life were gone. I was reborn in that moment, a part of something very old, very strong and very beautiful."

Lutetia, I thought. The Roman name for Paris. And my city has always been called the City of Light, which is what *lumière* means.

"I procure the bodies, for the city to eat," the pale woman went on. "But I'm very careful. I have to get to know them first. Only native Parisians will do. Only those who can remember the city as it used to be. That way, when it assimilates your cerebral tissue it takes your memories too and is able to claim back some portions of itself." She smiled sadly. "I showed you the photos out of sequence, Inspector. I hope this will console you. The changes… they're going the other way. Paris is remembering. With each death, each feeding, as she eats the brains of her *citoyens*, she heals. Recovers some of her lost memories."

"But the hotel," I objected. It was hard to think through the pain, but I wanted very much to understand. "The Belle Époque. It changed into a building from New York."

"Well that was me cheating," Lumière said. She actually blushed, which produced a strange effect on those bleached-bone cheeks. "The building didn't change at all. I just took down the old plaque and put up a new one. I paid the doorman ten francs to look the other way. I needed you to believe me, and to believe me you had to see with your own eyes. Or think you had seen."

She reached into the darkness beyond the torch's beam and retrieved, from somewhere, a sturdy hammer whose head was foul with blood and brains. "I use this," she said. "Mostly it's enough. The leg trap is for those who are biggest and most dangerous. To hold them still while I strike.

"I smash the skulls and pulp the brains. The brains are the part that matters, of course, and a semi-liquefied state seems to be best from the point of view of absorption. I scrape them up, take them away in a bucket or a picnic hamper and sow them in the parks and gardens where the *zombis* were buried. Apply the medicine to the site of the infection, as it were. *Je sème à tout vent*, like a good daughter of the Republic."

She paused, and regarded me. After a long moment she reached out to touch the back of my hand. "I really am sorry," she said softly. "You're wrong when you say that everyone fought against the *zombis*. A lot of people just ran and hid. I hate to take someone like you, who did his duty and never asked for thanks.

But your memories are very vivid. You still speak French, which almost nobody else does. You eat croissants. You have a hip flask which I would bet good money is full of cognac. You're just too tasty, Inspector Philemon."

"That is not an accusation I've ever had to defend myself against," I answered her. Lumière laughed, but her face was sad.

"It's all right," I told her. And it was almost true, although I was afraid that having my brains bashed in would hurt. "Do what you have to do, Lutetia. I like the sound of being part of… what was it you said?"

"Something old and strong and beautiful. But I don't know if it will be the same for you, Philemon. The city drank my life-blood. Absorbed me. But it didn't devour me." She tapped her temple. "There's still a brain in here."

I considered this fine distinction, fascinated.

"Then let it absorb me too," I suggested at last. "And I'll help you find new subjects. The two of us together will be able to accomplish twice as much."

Lumière seemed taken aback. "You'd do that? As a policeman you're pledged to protect and serve."

"To protect and serve the city. That was both the letter of my oath and its spirit."

Silence again. Lumière bowed her head and knelt in complete stillness for what felt like a very long time.

Then she looked up, and abruptly smiled. "She says yes," she told me. "We're going to be partners."

She gathered me into her arms, which were as hard and cold as funerary monuments. Something woke inside me, and opened. I did not recognise it at first, because it had been so long since I experienced it.

It was joy.

* * *

So now, you see, I have given you—in telling you my story—the most circumstantial explanation of your fate. You say you are not French, but your accent is good and your grasp of idiom very convincing. You certainly have very recent and very vivid memories of the city.

I look forward to sharing them.

GOOD NIGHT, PRISON KINGS

by

CHERIE PRIEST

Holly crossed and uncrossed her legs at the knee, like her grandma always said she ought to. She cleared her throat, fiddled with her bracelet, and watched the man across the desk as he scanned the paperclipped contents of a manila folder. His salt-and-pepper eyebrows rose and fell as he read, but she couldn't tell if he was impressed or confused. Maybe he was interested, or maybe he was going through the motions.

"It says here, you were a real estate agent."

"That's true, but I let my license lapse in 2007." She laughed awkwardly, and tugged at the bangle on her arm. "The recession culled the field like crazy."

"I'm sure it did," he murmured noncommittally. Without looking up.

"After that, I went into business for myself. Internet consulting. Helping companies with their product content, that kind of thing. But I had to walk away when… when there was no one else to look after my grandmother."

Finally, he graced her with eye contact. "How many siblings do you have? How many cousins?"

"There are nine of us, all together. Me and my brother, and seven… or eight…" she stumbled over the count. Suddenly, and for no good reason, she wasn't sure. But no, she'd said it right the first time. "I have one brother, and seven cousins."

"But *you* were the one tasked with caring for her. And for your great-aunt, as well?"

"Everyone else was… they had families of their own, is all. Or else they weren't up to it, for whatever reason. I'm the oldest, anyway. It was fine. I left my business, and went to work at the courthouse. It gave me more stability. Good health insurance. Steady hours. And I'm not totally alone; my brother helps out, when I'm at work."

"You support him, too?"

"He mostly earns his keep, looking after the ladies." Another vaguely inappropriate chuckle escaped before she could stop it. "That's what we call Grandma and her sister, my great-aunt Jean: 'the ladies.' Like they wear hats, or take tea, you know. But they don't… they don't do either of those things."

The man closed the folder and put it down, then folded his hands on top of it. "Your grandparents raised you. All nine of you."

"Not exactly, but kind of. It was complicated, and crowded. But it wasn't bad, not usually. Grandpa was a preacher. He traveled, sometimes. My mom and my aunts took turns on childcare duty, rotating in and out of school, in and out of the house." She wasn't sure why she was telling him this. "But Grandpa died, a handful of years ago. Not long after that, we realized Grandma was slipping."

"You were already here, in the city."

Holly nodded. "It made sense for me to take care of them. But this isn't about that, is it?"

He shrugged. "It's hard to say. Is your brother equipped to take over? Now that you're gone?"

She faltered. "I… I had a brother." She stared down at the closed folder on the desk, like it might tell her something, if she could open it.

"No, no. Stay with me, dear. You have a brother."

"We were the preacher's kids." She stared at the folder. "Preacher's grandkids, whatever. Everyone always says preachers' kids are the worst… nine little troublemaking PKs. But we weren't that bad. Not really. Not most of us." Holly drew up short. "Except for… except for those two." Even here, she didn't want to say their names. No, she couldn't say them.

Gently, he drew her attention around again. "But lately, you've been working at the courthouse, filing records, and the like."

She swallowed. It did nothing to soothe her raw, dry throat. Her head hurt. She stopped playing with her jewelry and wrapped her arms around herself. "That's right." What were their names? Those two stray cousins. She picked at the empty place in her memory, but found only coldness there. A barb, hard as an icicle.

She couldn't take her eyes off the folder. "May I?" She gestured toward it.

"Of course. It's yours, after all."

She collected it. Opened it. Scanned the laundry list of facts. It was a resume in a single, large paragraph. No, that's not what it was, at all. "This is an obituary."

"Yes, dear." He was kindly, but cool. Perfectly professional. Whatever his job was, he'd been doing it for a very long time.

She whispered, "What is this?"

He leaned forward, removed his glasses, and rubbed them fingerprint-free on the hem of his sweater. He put them back on. "This is an opportunity."

"Am I still in the city?" she asked. She wasn't confused. She wasn't even surprised.

"You're still in *a* city."

"What does that mean?"

"This is where everyone comes, when there's unfinished business."

She frowned. "Doesn't everyone have unfinished business? By the time they have one of these?" She held up the folder, the obituary.

"No. Not like yours."

"What's different about mine?"

"Yours is broken. This is where you come to fix it."

Her throat closed tight. She opened the folder again and read the last line, the one that said she'd fallen, and hit her head. It said that she'd frozen to death in the snow. "I am angry," she admitted. The words barely squeaked free. "Can you help?"

Again he was so kind, so calm. He sat back in his chair. "I can tell you this much: you should do what you've always done. Go where you've always gone. Find your way back to the end, and decide what you wish to do about it—but do it quickly. Your time here is limited."

Holly did not understand. "Okay," she said. "Okay." She took the folder under her arm, pulled her coat around her shoulders, and left the office. Outside on the street, she stood on the sidewalk and said, "Okay," again, in case it would make any difference, to herself or anyone else. "Okay," she exhaled the word with its own white puff of chilly air.

She remembered the way home, more or less. The ladies were at home, one comfortably baffled, one grumpy and none too mobile. Holly didn't have her own room, but she had her own couch and it was an easier sleep than any dorm room bed or futon she'd ever had.

She could go home. She had to start somewhere.

The city was made of twilight and ashes, with midnight-sharp shadows lining up like soldiers between the buildings. They stood sentinel in the alleys, inscrutable and faceless. The skyscrapers buffered the places in-between, and when Holly looked up, she couldn't see their tops. All of them disappeared into that gray-dark cloudland overhead, their details all lost, or scrubbed clean.

She usually took a bus home from work. The thought blipped through her head like a reflex—not a memory, but a force of habit.

A bus appeared. It must be the right one; it was the only one, and it was unmarked. Even the sides were free of advertisements, and graffiti. Maybe it wasn't the right bus. She got on board anyway, walking past the driver and reaching out to pay her fare before remembering that she didn't have any money.

The driver ignored her. Or else he couldn't see her? Holly didn't know how being dead worked, except that now she was in a city that was both familiar and unfamiliar, remembering and forgetting things that should've been certain.

The bus was empty, except for a man in a suit. The man was soaking wet, staring straight ahead with a briefcase on his lap. Holly thought he must've been dead too. She walked past him, and he made no move, no deliberate sound. Only the soft drip, drip, drip of water sliding from his clothes and onto the floor.

She sat down in the back. The bus lurched forward, and rolled silently through the haze that blurred everything on the other side of the windows. She opened the folder, and read her obituary over and over again, milking every word for any ounce of extra meaning.

The prose style was formal and refined, so her brother probably didn't write it. Maybe her mother did. Maybe someone just shoved all these details into the lap of some poor editor at the newspaper, and said, "Here, make some sense out of this. She was alive for thirty-eight years, and now she isn't. These are some of the things that happened in the meantime."

The obituary didn't tell her anything she didn't already know, but it reminded her of a few things she no longer remembered. Her father was dead, but he'd been dead for years. Would she run into him, here in the city? The man at the office said her time here was limited. Was everyone's?

Grandpa was dead, too. And who else? The obituary didn't say. No one else of importance, then, if it didn't make the papers.

The bus stopped, and it stayed stopped until she stood up and left. She hadn't pulled the cord, but this was the right place. Everyone was waiting for her, or at least the driver and the wet man up front. They were waiting for her. Waiting for something.

She took the handrail and the three steep steps down to the sidewalk. The door closed behind her with a hydraulic whoosh… the only noise she'd heard from the bus at all… and she was alone outside the walkup she'd called home for the last three years. "Or however long," she muttered, pushing the door open like there wasn't a callbox, and who needed a key, anyway? She pushed. It opened.

The interior hall was just as it always had been—floor to ceiling with period details that could be called charming, if they weren't so dirty. Micro-tile designs, mostly intact on the floors. High ceilings and dusty fixtures that halfway worked. Doors pointed in arches that deco had borrowed and streamlined from gothic.

If there were voices behind those doors… living, breathing people who talked and fought and laughed… Holly couldn't hear them. Everything was far away, on the other side of that miasma outside—the one that wasn't made up of smoke, smog, or mist.

The stairs were the same. Watch the handrail for splinters. The apartment door was the same, only now there weren't any numbers on it. It was the right one, though. She knew it when she turned the knob and let herself inside.

Eau de old lady.

Funeral flowers in perfume bottles, the contents gone yellow and pungent. Lilies and gardenias, and the sharp sourness of crushed pills, the eucalyptus lies of ointment. Old books and newspapers. Tea left steeping too long. Decaf coffee from a packet.

Grandma was sitting on the couch, the one she always called a davenport. "It's a shame to see you, dear."

Holly mustered a smile, and raised it half-mast. "What a weird thing to say to your granddaughter."

"They told me you died in the snow. An accident."

"Mary, who are you talking to?" Aunt Jean was there, too. When Holly squinted, she could see the younger, fatter woman perched in the La-Z-Boy, clutching the TV remote. She was shouting. She always shouted, because Grandma's hearing had gone to shit long before her mind did, and she never liked wearing her hearing aids.

"I'm talking to Holly."

"Whatever makes you happy, then."

"Grandma…" She blinked, in case her eyes were wet. They should've been. She should've been crying, but somehow she wasn't. Did anybody cry here? Was that a thing that ghosts could do? "It wasn't an accident."

"I know."

"Do you know what happened?"

"I have my guesses. They think I don't know, see. They think I haven't heard, about those boys and what they did. Seven pretty kittens… and two prison kings."

"Pretty kittens Or piglet kissers. That's what you called us."

She nodded solemnly, and said the same thing she'd said a thousand times, when the cousins were small. "Letters can mean anything. They don't have to hurt."

"I love you, Grandma. I should've said it more."

"You said it every night."

Holly stopped smiling. She didn't feel like it, anymore. "Still."

Aunt Jean butted in, like always. "Mary, I'm gonna ask you one more time…"

"Settle down. She's leaving."

Yes, she was. Backing away, because there wasn't anything here that could help her. Grandma knew about the boys, about the terrible cousins whose names she dare not think aloud, lest they appear. They lived with their mother, in part of the city where no one wanted to go, because it wasn't nice anymore. It was one of those last addresses people ever have, before they give up and live out of their cars.

(The boys couldn't live just anywhere, not anymore. The law got that much right.)

You could get there by car, or you could get there by a combination of bus and walking. You wouldn't want to go there, but if you had to, that's how you'd do it.

Holly had a car. She didn't know where it was, but it was usually parked under the building, in the garage. She took the service elevator down, and yes, it was in her spot. She couldn't read the license plate and she couldn't find her keys, but the door opened when she pulled the handle. She climbed inside, and put the manila folder on the passenger seat.

The engine turned over, and she pressed the button on the visor clippie that would open the garage's wide, rolling door to let her outside.

On the way to Aunt Patty's place she thought about the proper kernels and perfect kites, because those were nicer things that started with PK. Not *preacher's kids*, spoken with a sneer. Not the built-in curiosity about what bad thing they'd do next, or what embarrassment they would be, for whichever church where Grandpa worked.

Seven pretty kittens out of nine.

So Grandma knew about the other two, despite everyone's best efforts to keep her in the dark. It should've been easy to keep her in the dark. She was more than half deaf, and teetering on the edge of Alzheimer's.

But somehow she must've seen, or picked up the truth from things spoken too loud, too close. She might've caught some bit about making bail, or raising money for better lawyers. It was even possible that late at night, on her tiny grandma feet, she tiptoed throughout the house, opening drawers and turning on laptops. She liked the Internet. She liked seeing pictures of the great-grandkids. She wouldn't like finding the links that no one wanted her to see, or the frantic emails between the seven pretty kittens who did their best to protect her.

What could you do, against cunning like hers?

What would Grandpa have done? That's what everyone wanted to know, when word first got out about the brothers. *Thank God Grandpa is gone, or this would've taken him.* That's what everyone said. *Thank God he isn't here to see this.*

It was hard to say what he might've done. Some of the seven PKs remembered his guns. Would he have marched right over there, and shot them both dead? Would he have fallen right over, succumbing to heart attack number four? Unless Holly could find him, there in the city, no one was ever likely to know. So instead she said the same prayer the other six said—thank God, yes. *Thank God that the third attack took him.*

The more she thought about it, the angrier it made her. She shouldn't thank God or anybody else for taking him sooner, rather than later. That shouldn't be the silver lining. Grandma being out of it, as far as anybody else knew—that wasn't a silver lining, either. Even if she didn't know whatever it was she knew.

Fuck those boys, and their terrible habits. Fuck them both, and fuck their mother too—for all the excuses she made, and all the crocodile tears she cried. Fuck her for stealing what was left of the money.

Something whispered to her, *No.*

She almost panicked, almost hit the brakes.

No. Not that, either.

Holly kept driving. "Grandpa?" she asked. She hoped so. She reached for the hope that it might be him, then swallowed it all down. Ghosts don't haunt the dead, she was pretty sure of that much. But she talked to him anyway, as she paused at stoplights, and checked the street signs, even though she couldn't read them through the fog.

"Last time I saw you, we were sitting on the couch watching football. It was Sunday, and your team was winning." She stopped for a school bus. Traffic on all sides froze, and unfroze when the stop sign retracted, and the bus moved on. "Then you looked at the front door, and I watched you watch something… your eyes tracked from the door to the dining room, and into the kitchen. Then you watched… whatever you were watching… as it headed back out the door. So I asked you, what were you looking at? And you didn't answer. You looked at me with your eyes as big as I'd ever seen them, and you asked me who that man was—the one in the black hat. You said he was carrying a Bible."

She was almost there. Aunt Patty's place was up on the right, a basement flat with bars on the small windows that stuck up far enough to catch a few drops of light for a few hours every afternoon.

"I wonder if it was the same man as the one I talked to in the office. He didn't have a Bible, though. Or a hat."

Holly got out of the car and left it running at the curb. (If it had ever been running at all.) She shouldn't have found a parking space so quickly, but things were different in this version of this city. She understood that now. Or she understood it better than she had at first.

There was a light on, burning in one of the windows where the boys shared a bedroom. The light flickered. A television? It shouldn't be a computer. They weren't supposed to have computers anymore; it was part of the plea deal.

Rage welled up, harder and hotter than any tears she'd ever cried. The anger burned so white she could hardly breathe, until she remembered that she didn't *need* to breathe. That made it easier, to keep walking without running or screaming—to open the door like she lived there, and let herself inside past Aunt Patty, who was fat like Aunt Jean, and she would've been just as bitter if she hadn't been so goddamn self-righteous. Aunt Patty wasn't supposed to have a computer, either. Not while the boys were under her roof. She was sitting at the dining room table and checking the Internet on a smartphone, reading some conspiracy website. It assured her that she was persecuted, and that she was afraid of all the right things, all the right people.

Holly swept down on her, and struck her aunt's hand as hard as she could. The blow was fast, and it came unseen. It came hard. It threw the phone across the room, where it lodged in the wall's chipping plaster like a butter knife in a loaf of bread.

Aunt Patty didn't speak. She didn't move. She stared at the phone, and she breathed as fast as a rabbit.

"I'm dead," Holly told her. "I'm dead, and I hate you." She didn't know if Aunt Patty heard her, but she wanted to be heard, so she shouted it: "I'm dead, and I hate you!"

Aunt Patty flinched. Her face went tight with goosebumps.

Holly leaned in closer, until her mouth was near enough to bite her aunt's ear. "Everything is your fault, too." She backed away, went to the kitchen—it was on the other side of the dingy, cluttered room. She opened a cabinet, found some glasses, and began throwing them. They shattered on the floor, and against Aunt Patty's chair.

Patty still didn't move. Holly didn't care if she did. She didn't care if she couldn't. She kicked the back of the woman's chair with all the force she could rally; she dug her foot in, like she could shove it all the way up Aunt Patty's miserable ass. The chair rattled and toppled, taking her aunt with it.

She didn't watch it fall. "I'm not here for you. Maybe I should be, but."

Down the short hall with only three doors—a bathroom, two bedrooms—Holly stormed, gathering up the city's weird, smoke-like fog alongside her. It poured through the cracks in the foundation, the missing insulation between the windows and their casings... she called it all inside, and pulled it into her hands. She squeezed it, crushed it, and pushed it forward to blast open the bedroom door that belonged to the two PKs whose names she couldn't remember. Only their faces. Only their crimes. Only the fallout.

They were in there, because where else would they be? *If they'd ever had anything better to do, then none of this would've ever happened, now would it?* The other voice, the one she talked to, in case it was her grandfather—it was too soft, too far in the back of her head. Did it want her to stop? Or was it just along for the ride?

The two prison kings blinked at her, two pale and eyeless cave fish confronted with the dawn. They saw something, but it might not have been Holly. She hoped it was something more fitting, something like a naked child with fear in its eyes and blood dripping down its legs. She hoped it was a little boy with his hair yanked back and his mouth hanging open while the camera flash went *snap snap snap.*

The brothers were separated by enough years that they should've been more different in appearance. There should've been more to distinguish them than their height, but there wasn't. They both looked like their father, long out of the picture, not that it would've mattered.

No. Not quite.

The taller of the two had jumped a crooked retreat, and he stood with his back to the window, flat against it. Everyone had always said how much he looked like Grandpa. Everyone had always said it, because it was always true. A spitting image, though she'd never seen it before. He wasn't a spitting image of the grandfather who'd been old for as long as Holly had ever known him, but a carbon copy of the younger man—thick from years of manual labor before he'd taken to the seminary. A bespectacled man, bald before thirty. The taller brother was the younger of the two, and he was twenty-seven. What was left of his hair was yellow and vanishing.

Holly balked.

She waited for the quiet voice to tell her what to do, but it didn't.

There was nowhere for any of her surprise or pain to go, so she used it to fuel the anger that burned her up, feeding it into that furnace. "You did this!" she screamed at them, not knowing if they could hear her. She screamed it again, at the screen they shared between them. They had a computer, yes. Their parole officer must've missed it, but they were only playing some first-person shooter with Nazis in it. This time. Last time it'd been worse, and the investigation had gone on for two years. That's how long it'd taken to go all the way down that rabbit hole of karmic sludge and anguish.

She'd never been clear on the particulars. There were plea deals, and problems with the evidence, and outright incompetence with the forensic IT department. But here the prison kings were, having dodged any real time behind bars. They got away with it—like they'd gotten away with everything, relatively consequence free, for their entire goddamn lives.

But Jesus, she'd forgotten how much the tall one looked like Grandpa in the old pictures. The ones where he was grinning in black and white, smiling under the weight of feed sacks, tied up in bundles.

She hated the tall one for his face.

She reached for the beds and upended them, one and then the other. She threw them across the room and broke the iron rods off the frames while the boys yelled and hollered, begging for help that wasn't going to come from anyone except their mother, and she was useless. The only power she'd ever had was raising sociopaths. She couldn't bring them up, and save them, too.

The computer screen was flat and cold and it shattered when she touched it—so she picked up the pieces and threw them like she'd thrown the phone, like knives at a target. Most of the shards landed in the mattresses, and the curtains. Some of them hit the floor.

The boys pulled up their twin-sized mattresses and hid behind them. They were building a stupid kid's fort, like they were stupid kids, so Holly broke something else: a mason jar that one of them was using for a water glass. She crushed it, and used the largest piece to assault the fabric fortress. She cut through the sheets, through all the cheap material until it bled stuffing and springs, and she pulled those out, too.

"Did you do it together?" she demanded. "We all wondered if you sat around and jacked in tandem, you fucking creeps!" She'd hacked most of the way through one mattress. The shorter, older prison king kicked it aside and joined his brother behind the cover that remained.

Holly grabbed the other mattress. She wedged her fingers like spikes into the sides, and she pried it away. They were rats, cowering in a corner. The short one covered his eyes, burying his head against his brother. The taller one, the one who looked so much like a dead man, wasn't looking right at her. He was looking over her shoulder—but when she looked, she saw nothing, not even their mother, who must've heard the commotion by now.

She swung the chunk of glass like a sword, and slashed until she hit an artery. The short one's neck blossomed as red as funeral roses, as wet as the gutter snow. It was a marvel of color in this city, where everything churned in grayscale. He slumped, and she loomed triumphantly.

One down. Halfway there.

But. She buried the gore-sticky weapon in the wall. "It shouldn't have been you!" She roared it in the tall one's face. She retrieved the shard and swiped it at his cheek, leaving a thin line of red across his skin. The line was a slim, razor-fine italic. Then it was bold. "Your brother was always a lost cause, but we thought you were better. We thought you would *be* better!"

She wished she could cry, but that didn't happen in the city—so she swung the glass instead, again and again striking the wall and not the cousin because he was wearing Grandpa's face. Or he wasn't, and she knew that, but.

Her cousin sobbed and swore in equal measure. Someone could cry here, after all. She smashed her hand through the bureau mirror, and took a bigger piece of glass, one the size of a plate. It should've cut her hand to hold it. But nothing cut her here. She couldn't bleed and she couldn't cry, and she'd have to come to peace with it.

She held this new, foiled dagger to the tall boy's neck, and let it dig. (It was okay. It wasn't Grandpa's neck.) She let it split the skin in a tender spot that was better suited to a kiss, if you were the kind of mother who did that sort of thing. She let the bead of blood form, and well, and swell, and drip while she wailed the tears she couldn't cry. His frail remaining hairs billowed, and his eyes went dry and pink but he couldn't close them. Could he see her? No, he was still looking behind her. There still was nothing there.

"Accident…" he gasped.

She didn't know if it was a reply, or merely an expression of confusion. "All this time, you should've been in jail. Your mother shouldn't have been stealing Grandpa's life insurance, like there was anything else keeping the lights on except for me, and that shit job at the courthouse."

"Lawyer…" He was digging his own grave, and too stupid to stop.

She remembered it now—pieces of the disbelief, the *murderous* fury she'd felt when Aunt Jean had shown her the statements, where the lump sum pittance was bleeding away, signed over check by check from Grandma to Aunt Patty. In Aunt Patty's handwriting.

"You came to me, at the courthouse. You wanted me to throw it away, to look away. To make it go away."

"Accident," he said again, but that didn't make it true.

She didn't care. She realized it as her hands were going slick, because another half an inch and he'd be right there with her in the city, where no one can see the sky, but no one gets in your way.

Out to her car, he'd followed her that night—trying to stop her. Trying to keep her from filing the complaint that would send his mother to jail. The sky had been so white, and so had the snow on the ground; but on the piles of garbage, it'd all gone brown around the edges. You don't accidentally push someone. You don't accidentally take the paperwork and run while the snow goes red and the sky drops lower and lower by the minute.

But he wasn't looking at her, he was looking behind her. She couldn't hear the voice that was talking so softly, so firmly, so hopelessly in the distance. She could only see this terrible thing that wore someone else's skin, and she pressed the broken glass under that face, against that neck. She could peel that face right off. He didn't deserve to wear it.

Nobody knew what Grandpa would've done.

She fell back. She stood in the wreckage of the room, all broken glass, clotting blood, and tooth-stain yellow foam. The light overhead sputtered, but kept the room a gruesome shade of wet fluorescent lime. All the shadows were too damn hard. She couldn't see anything except the resemblance, and that wasn't fair at all. The city was supposed to be fair. Wasn't that how it worked?

Wasn't that how it worked.

"I still have time," she told him, as he bled and cringed. She held out her hand, and called the fog to bring her something useful. It brought her the envelope with the complaint, signed by herself and Aunt Jean in their own goddamn handwriting. Either Aunt Patty hadn't destroyed it, or the city had seen fit to return it. She clasped it so hard that her knuckles would've turned white, if.

In the other room, her aunt moaned.

To hell with her.

"Good night, preacher's kids. Good night, prison kings." Holly turned her back.

She hated the city, for all its second chances—because she could only scream and she could not cry as she left them behind: one dead, and one who would probably live. She should've reversed the two, if you'd asked anyone. Take the killer, and punish the other to even the score. But the killer wore a dead man's face, a prison king with the preacher's profile.

She left them there, and she left the shitty old building standing in one piece.

She deserved to cry. Both brothers deserved to bleed out slow, all the way, remembering why everything had come to this. Everyone deserved to mourn, on their way out of town.

Didn't they?

DEAR DIARY

by

SCOTT SIGLER

Dear Diary,
Today my foot went through the floor. But nothing broke. It
blended in. Or shifted in. I'm not sure how to explain it. It
felt warm, and nice. My foot wasn't all there. I saw it and
I got scared and I pulled it out and it was fine. Makes no
sense. I had about a bottle of wine, so maybe just drunk.
But the weird thing is when it happened I felt loved. I don't
know why. I wish I could feel love again.

I am so very lonely.

—Carmen

* * *

John stands on the stained WELCOME! mat in the hallway in
front of Apartment 214. The mat was there when he helped his
friend Robert move in three years earlier. John takes a breath,
remembers the things he has promised himself he will *not* say.

Two things: *Is your back any better?*

And the big one: *Are you still reading that goddamned diary?*

John is tired from the long flight. He wants dinner and a
beer. But first, he has to do this. He has to try one last time.

He rings the doorbell. He waits. He rings it again. He waits.
He rings it a third time. Finally, he hears the slow shuffle of

approaching footsteps. Robert opens the door just enough for his body to block the narrow space. He stares out, sunken eyes narrow with… not *hate*, exactly, but more *disdain*.

"What the fuck are you doing here?"

"I flew in to see you," John says.

Robert looks so different now. Gone is the can't-stand-still excitement for anything and everything. Gone is the blonde hair. Gone is the frantic energy that made Robert's eyes dance and dart. Gone is *Robert*—the person who answered the door is just not the same one John went to college with. Robert stands there, in a bathrobe and slippers… the clothes of the old man he has become, not the thirty-year-old he is.

"You shaved your head," John says. He doesn't know what else to say.

"Hair is a pain in the ass. Have to wash it all the time, and it hurts when I shower."

John nods, catches himself doing it. He wasn't nodding because he agrees, he was nodding because he thought what he always thinks when Robert complains about pain, he was thinking *of course it hurts, just like everything else—hurts when you stand, when you sit, when you walk, when you lie down… all part of the mental gymnastics you use to keep you trapped here.*

"That sucks," John says. "Is your back any better?"

The question came out automatically, the way one might say *bless you* when someone sneezes. John cringes inside—he promised himself he wouldn't ask that, but it came out anyway, like a worm forcing its way from a pasty apple.

"No," Robert says. "It's not. I'll ask again—why the fuck are you here?"

John knows how this will end. He has to try anyway. One last time, he has to try.

"You stopped answering my calls," he says. "And my emails."

Robert shrugs. "There's nothing left for us to say, so what's the point?"

John glances past him, into the dark apartment. He can feel the heat pouring out—Robert keeps the temperature ungodly high. John spent enough time there, in the early days after the back injury, to know Robert mostly walks around naked, because the elastic waistband of underwear or boxers—like everything else, it seems—hurts his back.

The apartment... everything was great until Robert moved in here.

"There's plenty to say, Robert. You have to get out of this place."

Robert stares. A look of annoyance, fatigue, and even betrayal.

"And go where? I can't afford anything else in this city, and you know I can't drive."

Or fly. Or take a train or a bus. Because Robert can't sit down without excruciating pain in his back. Half the time John feels so sorry for him—imagine not being able to *sit*, at all—and half the time he thinks Robert is fucking crazy and has set up this crazy construct to keep himself trapped here.

Trapped in this hot, dark apartment.

"I talked to Christine," John says. "You can move in with us."

Finally, Robert smiles. "I wonder what you had to promise her to make that happen."

John doesn't answer. He didn't have to promise anything, he had to *threaten*. Threaten to walk out on her if she was so selfish she wouldn't help his best friend. Oh, that argument. Christine has been telling John for years to wash his hands of Robert, that Robert is the walking dead, that it is Robert's *choice* to write off humanity and live alone, *die* alone. John has defended his friend to his wife for years. Trouble is, it's taken John those same years to realize Christine has been right all along. That's what she does: she gives the hard truth, whether you like it or not.

"John, this is bullshit," Robert says. "You know I can't make a fifteen-hour drive to Wisconsin."

John doesn't want to say the next thing, because he's said it before—he already knows what Robert will say in response. Still, John has to say it.

"It's a five-hour flight, man. Five fucking hours to get out of here, to be with friends."

Robert shakes his head. John has asked Robert to bite the bullet and fly, to live with the pain of the flight and the aftermath, and Robert has his reasons why he won't do that: the pain is too great for five hours of sitting; the landing might jar him and the last two times Robert was "jarred" it resulted in weeks of nine-out-of-ten pain instead of the normal seven-out-of-ten; the airplane seats might cause more damage, making Robert's miserable life even worse. Et cetera, et cetera—no matter what the solution, Robert always has a reason that solution won't work.

Chronic pain is a real motherfucker.

Finally, even though he knew it was coming, John gives up. He feels lower than low. A guy's crew is supposed to be his crew forever. Boys for life. Always down for the gunfight.

If real men don't give up on friends, then it's time for Robert to admit that he's not a real man.

"I can't do this anymore, bro," he says. "This is it. If you won't get out of this apartment, I'm not going to call you or write you. And I'm not coming back."

John is making a threat, not so different from the one he made against Christine.

Robert shrugs. "I already told you not to call me."

"I know I'm the only one left," John says. "I know Sara doesn't talk to you anymore. Neither does your brother. You don't work. You don't leave this place. You're *dying* here."

"Sara is a fucking lying whore," Robert says, in a tone so matter-of-fact he might be listing what kind of soup cans he has in the cupboard. "My brother doesn't care, you know this. And I can't work. I can't sit at all. And I can't even stand up for thirty minutes before I have to lie down for an hour, so who is going to hire me?"

John starts to answer, to offer ideas, to suggest for the thousandth time Robert find a home-based job, do *something*, but the fact is that John is exhausted. He's done all of this before. Robert always has a reason why that solution won't work.

And then, without warning, it slips out.

"Are you still reading that goddamned diary?"

Robert slowly shakes his head, not to say *no*, but as if to say John is the one who is crazy.

Robert shuts the door.

John stares for a moment. He stares at the welcome mat, the filthy, tattered mat.

Then, John leaves.

John feels a weight lift. He did all he could. No exaggeration, no self-congratulating hyperbole—he did all he could. Robert has made this life for himself and won't fight to get out of it.

That's on Robert, not John.

John won't come back. And he won't call. And he won't email.

John is done.

* * *

Dear Diary,
I'm so tired of people using me. I've come to realize that it's better to not talk to some people at all rather than let them walk all over me. Sometimes I think it's better if I don't even bother, if I just stay home.

Maybe being alone is better than being hurt.
But I wish I wasn't alone.

—*Julia*

* * *

"Sweet, a welcome mat," Robert says. "I wonder if they'll let me keep it?"

Sara watches Robert shift the armful of shirts on hangers to his other arm, then fumble for the keys. He doesn't want the shirts to get tossed into a corner like the last time he moved, so they are the first things he brought up from the U-Haul. Sara holds the rest of his hanging clothes.

John reaches out a toe, gives the mat a tiny kick.

"Dude, that mat is nasty with a capital *T*," he says. "Just get a new one."

Robert smiles, shakes his head. His blonde curls—the hair that Sara both loves and is jealous of—shake in time.

"Fully furnished apartment," Robert says. "The mat counts as a *furnishing*."

John leans against the hallway wall, struggling under the weight of a box of canned goods and mismatched, scratched frying pans he schlepped up five narrow flights of steep stairs. The place is a fifth-floor walk-up—no elevator. Robert could have just given his canned goods to a homeless shelter in Cleveland and then made one lousy trip to the grocery store, but no; he packed up everything in his kitchen and brought it with him to Philly.

Sara is excited that Robert is here. *So* excited. Their long-distance affair has gone on for just over a year. They met on a business trip. She should have told him she was married before they had sex that first night, but it had been so long since someone flirted with her, hit on her, told her she was beautiful.

So long since a man made her feel *wanted*. Robert did those things. And after, he wanted to see her again. She told him she was married—he said that was okay, he got it, but he still wanted to see her again.

Sara knows she should have left it as a one-time thing. She did not. Her husband lost interest in fucking her years ago. Didn't she deserve to feel desired? Her business trips had given her the opportunity, her body the motive, and Robert flying to meet her the means.

And now, he'd moved to her city. He'd taken a job here. Robert was smart, very much in-demand and recruited by several companies, but he chose *here*. She could see him every day if she wanted. *Every day*. Thrilling. Terrifying.

"You told us the landlord was coming," Sara says to Robert. "Don't you have to wait for him?"

"Wait for *her*, you sexist pig." Robert waggles his keys. "And, no, we don't have to wait. She mailed me the keys. She'll be here soon, probably."

He adjusts the shirts again, puts the key in the lock and turns. It makes a metallic squealing noise that reminds Sara of a baby bird begging for food. She doesn't like the sound. She'll make sure to oil that lock for him.

They all step inside.

The air seems stale. The windows are covered by heavy curtains. But the look of this living room, the unused feel… she wouldn't have been surprised to see sheets over all the furniture.

Sara is impressed. The word *retro* doesn't do it justice. Maybe *antique* is more like it. The last owner must have had a serious thing for the roaring twenties—the apartment looks like a set from a working-class version of *The Great Gatsby*. Plush chairs of curving, carved wood and faded maroon fabric. A matching couch. End tables with marble tops and three legs ending in carved, clawed feet. Recessed bookshelves complete with leather-bound books. A tarnished brass lamp with strings of beads hanging from a stained-glass lampshade. They don't make furniture like this anymore.

"This place is so cool," she says.

Robert smiles wide. He was obviously hoping she would like the apartment. She does. Very much. She imagines how much fun they will have here together.

"Sorry I'm late," comes a voice from the door.

It's a woman, early thirties, attractive and skinny, with perky hair that screams *I can rock the latest fashion no matter what it is*. Sara is instantly jealous. Instantly worried. Does this woman live in the building?

Robert walks to her, all smiles.

"Hi, Janet—so nice to meet you in person, finally."

She shakes his offered hand, smiles up at him. "You too!"

Does Robert always have to be so charming? Sara wonders if he'll get tired of waiting for her to leave her husband, if he'll hook up with this Janet. She has a ring on her finger, but Sara knows first-hand that Robert doesn't really consider that an obstacle.

Janet spreads her arms, gesturing to the apartment. "Great, right?"

"Amazing," Robert says. "The video didn't do it justice."

John clears his throat.

"Ah, sorry," Robert says. "These are my friends, John and Sara."

His *friend*? Sara is instantly mad—is he just saying that so he can hit on Janet?—then remembers herself and feels stupid. She's made it clear to Robert that he must not acknowledge they have any kind of romantic relationship. She's not ready for her husband to find out. She's just *not*.

John adjusts his box of canned goods—his hands are full,

but he extends his pinky. Janet laughs, gives it a gentle shake.

She offers her hand to Sara, who shakes it automatically. Sara knows she's being weird—this woman has done nothing.

"Pleased to meet you both," Janet says. "I'm the building super." She turns to Robert. "You didn't really need dishes—the kitchen is loaded."

She leads the way. Sara, Robert and John follow.

If the living room is like a time capsule from the twenties, the small kitchen is like warping into 1976. Avocado-green stove/oven, fridge, dishwasher; dark wood cabinets; yellow and green floral-print wallpaper. Everything is worn, but not beat up. The wallpaper has a few seams that are slightly raised, but not so much that Robert will have to worry about tearing it out. At least, not right away—the kitchen is in good shape, sure, but it is hideous.

"This is *awesome*," Robert says.

"No doubt," John adds. "Straight out of *Mad Men*."

Sara doesn't bother to correct him that said TV show took place twenty years before some twisted soul invented this obscene combination of colors and patterns.

"The living room is kind of roaring twenties," Sara says. "Why is the kitchen, um… *not*?"

Janet shrugs. "No accounting for taste, I guess. I've been the super for three years, but Mister Desmond—the previous tenant—moved in six years ago. I think the place was as-is when he moved in, but I really couldn't tell you. Kind of kitschy, no?"

"Kitschy," Sara says. "That's one word for it."

John opens the fridge. It's empty. He wrinkles his nose a moment before a faint waft of mildew hits Janet.

"Stinks a bit," Janet says. "Cleaning crew said fridge would air out, but if you want we'll get you a new one."

John shuts the fridge door, looks at Robert, raises an eyebrow.

"A new fridge," Robert says. "Will it look exactly like this one?"

Janet shakes her head. "Nope. Afraid the building owners won't spring for a vintage appliance. Plain white is your only option."

"Oh, hell no," Robert says. "I'm not changing one *thing* about this kitchen."

"Goddamn right," John says. "This is *classic*."

Sara sighs. John is a perpetual adolescent in a grown man's body who thinks *everything* is "classic." She'll have to subtly work on Robert's taste—she's already taught him how to dress better. Doesn't look like a clown anymore, can't have him living in a clown castle.

She's struck by a sudden thought.

"Mister Desmond just left all of his stuff," she says. "He didn't... *die* here. Did he?"

"Blargh," John says.

Janet shrugs. "No, he didn't die. He was just *gone*. He stopped paying rent three months ago. We couldn't track him down. Cops couldn't, either. We waited to see if anyone came for his things, but no one did. Even his neighbors didn't know him. Kind of a shut-in, I guess. At least he didn't die here—that happens more often than you'd think. People live alone, don't have anyone, they just... *pass on*... and no one knows until the smell spreads."

Robert laughs. "Worse than the smell of this fridge, I imagine."

"Hope I never find out," Janet says. "Well, Robert, you have the key. If you need anything else from me, let me know."

Robert thanks Janet, sees her out.

Sara wonders just what Janet meant by *if you need anything else from me*.

John and Robert head down to the truck. Sara starts unpacking the canned goods. She can't wait to be done—

because when they are, John will leave, and she can finally get her hands on Robert.

He's *here*. She can have him over and over. Every day, if she wants and can pull the right strings.

* * *

Every day.

Samuel has stopped visiting. You know what? I'm glad. That's right, Dear Diary, I AM GLAD! He's not a good man. He's not a good person. Did I tell you that he tried to pin our relationship troubles on ME? He said I was "different." Well, I am different, because I won't be his pushover any more.

It's so funny, Dear Diary, but reading Clyde's words has helped me a lot. I never met him, yet I feel close to him. He understands what I'm going through. I mean, I understand what he was going through. Are those the same thing?

Anyway, I think I'm done dating for awhile. Today's men are not yesterday's men.

—Adele

* * *

Robert is naked, sitting in the chair in his bedroom, reading. The bedroom has a similar feel to the living room, but is more modern—if circa 1950s can be called "modern." He doesn't know how long this furniture has been in here, but it's well-made, built to last a lifetime. As far from IKEA as you can get. No one makes stuff like this anymore. Scuffed up, sure, but still in good shape. Oddly, he loves the bedroom decor because it makes him feel closer to grandparents that all died before he was born: they might have had stuff just like this when they were his age.

And right now, any feeling of family, of connection, is so important.

Sara has tried several times to get him to redecorate. All subliminal stuff, passive-aggressive, trying to get him to suddenly not like what he obviously likes. She doesn't seem to know he knows she's doing that. Sometimes you have to let women spin themselves out… easier than a confrontation. But her efforts are getting annoying—why spend money on new furniture when everything in this apartment is free and perfectly good? The chair he's sitting in isn't really comfortable, for example, but it's not *un*-comfortable, either.

Sara walks out of the bathroom, toweling off her hair. She's naked. Robert loves the way her body looks with the afternoon sun filtering through the bedroom's lace curtains. She smiles at him. He doesn't smile back. Not because he doesn't love her anymore—he does—but his heart is heavy and there is nothing in this world that can cheer him up.

"Oh, baby," she says. "Did it hit you all over again?"

Robert starts to speak, stops. Three weeks now, and he still can't talk about it. He nods.

"She loved you," Sara says. "How could she not?"

Robert says nothing. Sara's comment is stupid, shallow. Of course his mother loved him. Of course. But now she's dead. Losing his father years ago was hard, but it wasn't like this. Now, *both* parents are gone—a sharp, undeniable break from Robert's childhood, adolescence and young adulthood. No one to lean on anymore. He is on his own.

And, because the years keep constricting, he realizes more and more that it's not *if* he will die, but *when*. The logical understanding of that concept has always been easy—feeling mortality finally sink in deep and set up shop is much harder to accept. The time from *now* until *dead* used to feel so forever-far-away that it wasn't real. Not anymore. Now he senses the days flying by so fast, the end—whenever it comes—might as well be tomorrow.

Sara steps closer.

"Do you want to talk about it?" she asks.

His annoyance with her is shifting toward anger. If he wanted to talk about it, wouldn't he have said so? Talking doesn't solve anything. And if she really gave a fuck, she would have come to the funeral. But she couldn't, of course. She couldn't travel to Georgia on such short notice, not without arousing suspicion from her husband. She could fly all over hell and high water to fuck Robert, but she couldn't make up one lie to come with him when he needed her most?

"No," he says. "I don't want to talk about it. Thank you, though."

She gives him a sweet smile. "Okay. I'm here if you need me."

Which is utter bullshit. Robert knows this now. He moved here six months ago. He knew she was married. Maybe he didn't realize it at the time, but he came hoping she would leave her husband. She hasn't. He's beginning to think she isn't going to. Ever.

Sara looks at his book. "What are you reading?"

"The diary of the previous residents. I found it in the bookshelf in the living room."

She holds out her hand, asking for the book. He hesitates— he doesn't want anyone else to touch it; he shouldn't have told her about it, should never even have let her *see* it—then blinks away the irrational thoughts and gives it to her.

Sara looks at the page Robert was looking at. She starts to talk, stops, brings the book closer to her nose and sniffs. She makes a face, like the odor is slightly offensive.

"Leather-bound," Robert says. "Nice, right?"

Sara forces a smile.

"Kind of," she says, then looks at the page. "I thought the previous tenant was some guy named *Desmond*. This is signed by Julia. Who is that?"

Robert shrugs as if he doesn't know. Julia was the tenant before Carmen, who was the tenant before Desmond. Adele came before them, just after Clyde, who has the oldest entries in the diary. Why they all made entries in the same book, Robert doesn't know. Why none of them took it with them, Robert doesn't know. But, the book is *very* cool—almost like the apartment is a time-ship, with the residents chronicling their lives. It's fascinating to think that people older than even his grandparents lived here when they were his age. Somehow, it makes the past more *real*. It's a strange sensation, a… a *connection*… and he likes it.

Sara frowns. She reads out loud: "There is a vibration to this apartment, something I can't explain. I feel so at home here. I need that right now, because Alphonse hasn't written me since I told him about the baby. And I don't want him to write anymore, anyway. A real man would have done the right thing. I don't ever want to see him again. Everything seems so dark in my life right now, so I thank God for this place. Signed, Carmen."

She closes the diary, losing Robert's page. Isn't that just like her? So selfish she doesn't even think of his needs. Sara hands the old book to him.

"That's creepy," she says. "I wonder if that woman had the baby here."

Robert shrugs, as if he doesn't know that fifteen pages later, Carmen's entries stop when she is six months pregnant. Desmond moved in sometime after that.

"It's weird that there's some random diary here," Sara says. "Maybe you shouldn't read it."

"Maybe you should mind your own goddamn business,"

Robert says. "You want to tell someone what to do, what to think? How about you try that out on your nut-less husband."

Sara's eyes widen.

Robert doesn't know why he said that. His sudden burst of anger ebbs.

Sara slowly moves her arms, covering up her nakedness as if they hadn't just fucked like banshees an hour earlier, soaking the sheets with sweat. She doesn't know she's doing it, probably, but the idiocy of that affectation makes his anger return. A crazy thought: *have I really been putting my cock in someone this stupid? Did I really MOVE HERE to be near THIS?*

"I'm going home," Sara says quietly.

"Well, your *home* certainly isn't here."

She blinks.

Is she going to cry? Looks like it. And even *that* makes Robert mad.

He stands. Naked, he takes his diary to the bathroom, shutting the door behind him.

Robert hopes Sara will take the hint and let herself out.

* * *

I've thought about killing myself. I don't have anyone. People walk up and down these halls. No one knocks. Sometimes they see me and nod, or just hurry past without looking at me. I know in the past my appearance was better. It's not my fault I'm sick, even though the doctors told me there's nothing wrong with me. Like they even care.

There was only one neighbor, Mrs. Sheldon in the apartment next to me. She always said "hello" and asked about the weather. But I saw someone else coming out of her apartment this morning. Mrs. Sheldon moved away. I wish someone would have told me.

She was the last person in this building that I knew. Why should I bother meeting more people? They will just move away.

Sometimes this apartment is so silent. I can't hear anyone else in the building. But it's nice here. Kill myself? Maybe I would, but when I'm in here, it's not so bad. It's really bad when I go outside for groceries and see an entire city's worth of people who could give a shit if I live or die. Maybe no one is here with me, but at least this is my home.

I think it's time to give up on the outside world.

I'll just stay in more. At least Daisey loves me.

She's a good dog.

—Clyde

* * *

"Dude, calm down," John says. "Why are you acting like this is a personal attack on you or something?"

John doesn't understand what is happening. He is moving away, starting a new life with Christine, and Robert is being one Grade-A giant douchebag.

"So what am I supposed to do?" Robert asks. "What the fuck am I supposed to do?"

The question depresses John, and also angers him. For a year now, he's been the best friend he could be, catering to Robert's every need since the accident. Isn't a year enough? Hasn't that been plenty of time for Robert to recover?

"I'm not moving for another two months," John says. "Can't you find someone to help you before then? Have you called your brother?"

That is a question John has asked often, with increasing venom over the past twelve months. Robert's brother, Frank, has sat on his fat ass in Sacramento and done *nothing*. Since

Robert's accident, Frank has been to visit—*once*—for a grand total of twelve hours, six of which were spent at the Philadelphia Zoo with his wife and daughter while Robert stayed in his apartment.

In fact, since Robert broke it off with Sara, John is the *only* one who comes to help Robert. Robert should be *grateful* for the help—not be a giant asshole when it's time for John to move on with his own life.

"Look," John says, "you can get groceries delivered. As for stuff around the apartment, can't you ask your neighbors?"

Robert's eyes narrow at the word. He speaks with forced patience, as if John is stupid and needs things explained to him over and over.

"I don't know them, John. I know *you*."

John tries to hold onto his temper, his absolute exasperation. Yes, he understands Robert has chronic pain—or at least thinks he does—but if John were in his shoes he would handle things so differently. John wouldn't *give up*, which Robert seems to have done.

"Have you even *tried* to meet them?" John asks. "Jesus H. Christ on a stick, Rob... are you so helpless you can't even knock on a fucking door?"

"Are *you* so helpless you can't stand up to Christine? Have you even *tried*? You get laid for once in your life and she leads you around by the dick? Does she have your balls in a jar up on the shelf, John?"

The words sting, and not just because of the hate that's laced in them. John's face flushes red. Yes, Christine demanded they move. Yes, she said if John didn't go with her, she would leave him. John is in his thirties now—most single women his age are losers. They are single for a reason, and those reasons won't change as they get older. He loves Christine and is sure he won't find anyone as great as she is. John is a man, yes, but deep down he knows that Christine has all the power in their relationship.

Knowing that is one thing—having your best friend rub your nose in it is another.

"Fuck you," John says.

"Fuck you back," Robert says. "Glad I finally learned what kind of a person you really are. I thought you were my friend."

John's hands clench into fists, and he comes an eye-blink away from throwing a punch. If Robert wasn't so hurt (or *thought* he was so hurt), John would lay him out.

They have known each other since freshman year at college. In all that time, John has never wanted to hit Robert.

"I can come back from time to time," John says. "I can help you find people who can come here, do the things you can't."

Robert shakes his head. There are tears in his eyes.

"Don't bother," he says. "Maybe being alone is better than being hurt."

John's anger vanishes. He knows that phrase, that *exact* phrase.

"That's in the diary," John says.

"So? It doesn't make it any less true."

John doesn't know what to say. Robert seems to read that nasty-smelling old book non-stop. It's *weird*. And Robert isn't just *reading* it, he's *writing* in it. New entries. Robert has changed since he started reading that thing.

Since he came to Philadelphia.

Since… since he started living *here*.

"You need to move out," John says. "This place, Rob… I think this apartment is bad for you."

Robert sneers. "You want me to move somewhere else? *Where?* I can't lift a goddamn thing, and I can't afford a new place. How about I come live with you?"

John's face feels hot all over again. Christine would never go for that—and Robert knows it.

"Just go," Robert says. "If my back wasn't so fucked up, I'd throw you out. Leave me alone."

John has run out of words. Emotions spin through him: anger, frustration, loss, shame.

He walks through the living room he once thought was so cool. When he reaches the front door and opens it, Robert shouts: "Don't bother coming back."

"Don't worry about that," John says.

He slams the door behind him.

* * *

Dear Diary,

Fuck them all. How did I go so wrong choosing the people in my life? I don't know what's harder—seeing them abandon me, or knowing that I am such an utterly poor judge of character. I'm alone now. I don't know what I'm going to do.

I hurt, all the time. No one understands what it's like to spend every minute of every day feeling like there is a spike in my back. I can barely move.

This morning I dropped some pretzels. I can't even bend over to pick them up.

What kind of life is this?

If I was a dog, someone would just put me down.

At least I have my home. I'm so grateful I found this place before my injury. Without this apartment, I'd be completely and utterly fucked, instead of just completely fucked.

—Robert

* * *

Sara doesn't know why she calls. She doesn't know why he answers—it's been so long since he picked up the phone.

"What do you want?" Robert asks.

He doesn't even sound like the same person anymore. His voice is thin, brittle as fine china. The man she adored—maybe even loved—is no longer there. In the two years since he moved to Philly, the twelve months since she last saw him in person, he's *changed*. Chronic pain does that to a person, she's read.

"I… I have something to tell you," Sara says.

"Make it fast."

She wants to ask him how he is, but she knows that won't float. In the few times she's talked to him since they broke up (if "breaking up" is something a married woman can even do), when she asks about his pain or how he's doing for money, he says something awful and hangs up on her. So this time, as bad as it is, she knows she has to get right to the point.

"Robert, I'm pregnant."

The pause is heavy. Thick.

"Whose is it?"

Anger at those words, but it doesn't last. Maybe she deserves that reaction.

Sara has been reading the Bible, and just started going to church for the first time since she left her parents' home. She needs to be tolerant, forgiving. Learning about the miracle inside her has changed her, instantly and permanently. She was sinful before, but that is over. She's not living for just herself anymore.

"My husband's," she says.

The next pause is longer than the first. Can silence be accusatory? This silence is.

"So much for you not fucking him," Robert says. "I get hurt and can't perform for you anymore, and you go back to riding that pony? I guess I really was just a piece of meat for you after all."

Sara literally bites her tongue. Yes, Robert's inability to make love was difficult. It made her try again with her husband. She now knows all of it was God's will, the proof being the new life growing inside her.

"That's not how it went down, and you know it," she says. "You told me to get out and never come back—that was a month before your accident."

"And you ran to your hubby. I guess you didn't have to run far, seeing as the guy sleeps in the same bed you do."

His voice sounds strained. Like he's in pain. He's *always* in pain. Sara doesn't doubt this, but come on—at some point doesn't he have to embrace the pain and get on with it? Make the most of his life?

"I want you to be happy," Sara says. "I really do."

"And I want you to die, you fucking whore."

The phone clicks. He's hung up on her.

Sara feels so sad for him. Maybe if Robert finds God, he will heal. Then he can start his life again.

She has to admit it—she can't help Robert anymore.

It's time to put the Robert phase of her life behind her.

* * *

Robert shakes.

This is impossible, this can't be happening. His hand... it's *dissolving*. Like steam from a cup of tea, but thicker—like white mist wafting off dry ice. His skin bubbles... not *boiling*, exactly, but something else.

How? How can this be?

And why does it feel *good*?

The mist rises up, moves toward the wall on an unfelt breeze. The walls... they seem to be absorbing him, breathing him in.

Robert feels... *loved*. As if the crazy things he's seeing are some kind of giant hug from this room. No one loves him, but this apartment does, he can *feel* it.

It's been so long since he felt loved.

Robert shakes his head. The peaceful feeling in his chest, it's a delusion—he is fucking *evaporating*.

He knows he has to get out.

Robert tries to rise from the old-fashioned couch, the place where he has sat in the few moments per day where he *can* sit. Why he sat down this time, he doesn't know; his back is screaming, feels like someone is dripping acid on his spine, the same way it feels every goddamn minute of every goddamn day... but that doesn't matter right now.

Doesn't matter because he's hallucinating. He's going insane.

Robert looks at his right hand: the skin is spotted with negative spaces. Through those, through the clouds of vapor or mist or gas or *whatever the fuck* is rising off of him, he can see raw muscle—red, glistening, wet.

"Oh, God," he says.

This can't be happening. It can't.

But... didn't something like this happen to Carmen?

In the diary, she wrote that her foot went through the floor, *blended* in. Robert thought she was some crazy, lonely lady, but...

He looks down, at his feet. The left one is fine, but the right one... it's... it's... *sloughing*. Like his bones are slowly liquefying, like his flesh is chocolate melting into the old rug.

"Oh, God," he says.

But he doesn't believe in God. Or he didn't until this very moment.

Robert wobbles... the foot won't support him anymore. He tries to take a step, but he can't—he falls.

The fall is terrifying because he knows the pain is coming, a one-second eternity of dread, then his body hits the floor. The agony that shoots through him crushes his spirit. Feels like a sword just slid into the small of his back, razor edge radiating through his belly, his ass, his legs.

His *hand*—the skin, only a few patches left, slowly drifting away. And now the muscle, the twitching muscle, is misting off in a cloud of pink.

Robert tries to roll to his shoulder, but *the pain*. Jesus Lord he will believe now he will believe in *anything* that makes this all go away.

He fights through the agony, pushes himself to hands and knees in an ultimate effort of will.

Robert shakes his head again, so hard it rattles his brain. He can't give in to this.

"Oh, Gaw..."

He can't make a "D" sound? A strange taste in his mouth, a hotness in the air he breathes. His tongue... turning to gas?

Robert wants to scream, but he can not—his throat doesn't work right.

His body lurches to the left: his left hand is flowing into the rug. Flowing, or being *sucked*... a thick milkshake through a thin straw...

The skin of his face dangles from his head like swinging snot, globs dripping down grayish-red, his life making wet stains on the rug. He sees similar stains, *old* and *dry* stains—how could he not have noticed those before?

He falls flat, the remains of his cheek smacking wetly. He sees things in the rug: dirt that the vacuum missed... bits of popcorn he dropped and was unable to pick up... and is that a dog hair jammed into the rug fibers? Robert doesn't have a dog...

No, but Clyde did.

That dog hair is eight decades old.

Robert can see his skin slowly sloughing into the rug,

melting into the fibers, *through* them, to the hardwood below.

He tries to move, tries hard… but he can't.

Robert gives up. Robert gives in.

He is the only one here.

No one is coming to see him.

His neighbors have never visited.

The people Robert once loved, who once loved him… he chased them away. He burned those bridges with gas and dynamite and even nukes, destroyed them so they could never be fixed.

Robert realizes he is going to *vanish*.

That sensation of love, of belonging, pours through him again, stronger than before. Overwhelming. Placating.

Finally, Robert relaxes. Robert *accepts*.

Will he join Clyde and Adele and Julia? Carmen and Desmond? Are they somehow still here, a part of the furniture and walls and rug and floor?

If he does join them, will it be like a family?

Family… that would be so nice.

WHAT I'VE ALWAYS DONE

by
AMBER BENSON

There's only so much suffering you can endure before you break. Not like a plate that arcs across the room and shatters on the floor—oh, nothing so dramatic as that. More like a hairline fracture you can't see until you hold it up to the light.

That's what happens to the psyche when it bends too far.

One tiny crack and you are never whole again.

Only mended. Maybe.

* * *

Gorgeous George. Double G for short. The nickname was silly—but that's because only the ridiculous ones stick.

He was missing four front teeth and had a nose like a twist tie, all kinds of bent. He kept his head shaved and the immense ripples of fat on the back of his neck were like mountains. He wore size fourteen dress shoes that were old, but well kempt, having never seen a day without polish. The three-piece black undertaker's suit that he put on each and every night was as tight as a tourniquet, the pale ivory buttons glinting like silver dollars in the glow of the streetlight.

"Heya, Double G," I said. I was being nonchalant, hoping the word hadn't trickled down yet.

It had.

"Can't leth you in."

Not a lisp. The missing teeth.

I stopped in front of the door, cocked my head, squinting, wrinkles forming in my brow.

"Can't leth you in," he repeated.

I bit my bottom lip and nodded, eyes switching lazily from side to side. Like I was thinking about what he'd said, understanding his predicament even.

"Okay, I hear that."

His shoulders lowered almost imperceptibly, but I saw it. Saw he wasn't really consciously worried about keeping me out, but still something in his lizard brain had told him to be wary of me. Now that I'd backed down without a fight, he could relax.

I wasn't much to look at. Not the kind of guy a muscle-bound bouncer outside a private club in a rough part of a middle-class city usually had to worry about. Yet the old lizard brain had engaged when I'd stepped up to the door. Double G was more intuitive than he realized.

I started to turn away, but stopped. Spoke with my back to him.

"I'm going to fucking kill you after I kill her."

We were alone. The street was empty, the cold keeping the rabble indoors. My voice carried on the wind and it was cold as a knife sliding into a warm gut.

"Excuth me?" he asked, incredulous.

He was having a hard time believing what he'd heard.

I turned back around and grinned at him.

"You heard me."

He frowned, uncertain now.

"Excuth me?" he repeated. Lizard brain wasn't so quick on the uptake now. If I were him, I'd have slipped inside the club and locked the door behind me. Grabbed the manager, called the police… run for my life.

"You heard what I said. I'm not going to say it again."

It was a Joker's grin. It split my face in two. It was not pleasant to look at. I'd stared at it before, lost hours to my mirrored reflection.

He opened his mouth, but I was too fast. I reached out with my left hand and slid the stiletto into the soft tissue protecting his trachea. It went in without much effort, the blade parting flesh like butter. Blood gurgled around the wound, but no sound came out. He wore a confused expression on his meaty face, his pink tongue darting out from the gap in his teeth, as if it could search out an answer to the age-old question: *Why?*

"You won't die. At least not yet," I said as I rammed my elbow into his midsection and he reeled into the brick exterior wall. "I'll come back and do what I said."

He stared up at me as he slid to the ground, both hands pressed to his throat.

"And this is so you don't disappear while I'm gone."

I slammed the heel of my palm into his nose. Not hard enough to break it and send shards of cartilage and bone up into his brain. Just enough to knock him out.

"Don't move," I said, grinning again.

I stepped over him and pushed open the door.

* * *

The lake was iced over. The cold like a vise squeezing my nuts.

I was outside without proper clothing for the weather. This came from necessity. The jacket I'd been wearing was covered in blood. Not mine. I'd ditched it in the trash bin of a public restroom. I'd kept the sweater because it was made of thick black wool and didn't show the bloodstains.

I walked quickly, the wind blowing strands of dark hair into my eyes. I didn't push them away. Just kept moving forward, not stopping for anything or anyone.

The voice came out of nowhere. So small and feminine I almost didn't notice it, but something about the timbre caught my ear and I turned my head.

"Do you need help?"

She was angelic. Blonde hair whipping around her head, the wind pulling at it in frantic bursts. She had intense aquamarine eyes the color of the Caribbean sea.

"You look lost."

I stared at her mouth. The taut lips, the tiny pearl teeth. Her words were superfluous. She could've been speaking Swedish and I would've been entranced. I shook my head.

"No, ma'am. I'm fine."

Her little forehead furrowed, the pale yellow brows drawing together in a "v."

"You don't look fine."

She was wearing a white winter coat that made her seem even smaller than she was. Her snug boots were clean and unscuffed, a creamy pink clutch caught up in a fluttering hand.

She smiled at me, her skin stretching across delicate features. I smiled back. I couldn't help myself.

"I'm Sandy," she said and offered her hand.

I took it.

I shouldn't have. Because I knew—even then—that we were fucked.

* * *

Monsters don't fall in love.

Correction.

Monsters *shouldn't* fall in love.

* * *

We moved to Portland. Oregon was clean and bright. A place to begin things. It was full of people with the usual human pretensions. I did my job of fixing things—I had always fixed things—and life went on.

Sandy was a dancer. Not the kind that took their clothes off for sweaty men in clubs, raking singles into their G-strings and blotting out their nights with alcohol. Sandy did higher-end work; performance art stuff that went over well in a liberal, arty place like Portland. It required talent. Which she had in spades.

I think we were happy.

I *know* we were happy.

And then Sandy discovered what "fixing things" actually meant.

* * *

I am a fixer. Have been for centuries. I say that and you laugh. Think it's all hyperbole.

It's not.

I'm old. So old that I don't remember where I came from. So many miles of muddy earth have been caked on top of me that the crust is long forgotten. My beginnings are a sludgy mess. But when I think back, rack my brain for the few foggy memories remaining from those bygone days, I know that even then I was a fixer.

I kill with my bare hands and have no remorse. I murder and there is no glee… only the sense that a job has been completed and I can move on to the next. I work for no one… and for anyone who can reach me. I am a fixer of problems, a sorter of details. I am a wolf patrolling a world full of sheep.

* * *

Sandy ran away. She wanted no part of me and something inside me broke. I became unhinged. It was not a feeling I enjoyed.

So I went looking for what I'd lost. Went looking to claim what was mine.

Or to kill it. If I found my ownership null and void.

* * *

It was the kind of place you went when you wanted to impress. Dark interior, Victorian red velvet wallpaper in a fleur-de-lis pattern, banquettes of expensive black leather around dark wood tables.

I caught sight of myself in the antique-mirrored walls. Multiples of me—but all dreamy and surreal with their dark heads of curly hair, their sneering lips and rakish faces. I watched the feral movements of my body as I stalked the room. Past candlelit tables of unsuspecting patrons who'd paid a pretty penny to eat their classy meal and see a classy show.

They had no idea what I meant to do.

I had been here before. I knew where the dressing rooms were. Knew where Sandy would be sitting, lipstick in hand. Like me, she was putting on another kind of face.

* * *

She was expecting me. She might not have known when I would come, but she knew I would appear eventually. Some night I would be there waiting for her. We'd lived together for long enough by then for her to know some things about me. My single-mindedness was one of these things.

She was alone, perched on a tiny wooden stool, a pale rose-pink dressing gown hanging loosely around her shoulders. I could see the oxygen-blue veins running through the translucent skin of her chest, could see the rise and fall of her breath as she fought to remain calm. She was so beautiful that it pained me to look at her.

I closed the door behind me. Locked it. In the brighter light of the dressing room I could see the blood already on my hands. *She* could see the blood already on my hands.

"Just doing what you do," she said, teeth gnashing down on the words like it disgusted her to speak to me.

"I'm a fixer."

She nodded. As if to say she understood it all.

And then I did what I've always done.

GRIT
A Monk Addison Story

by

JONATHAN MABERRY

1

Her name was Betty.

All diners should have a waitress named Betty. Or Babs. Maybe Brenda. Something with a B.

This one was a Betty and she was a classic example of the type. You know what I mean. Lots of hair, combed and sprayed so that it wouldn't get messy in a typhoon. Frosted, too, because that hair color doesn't have a correlation in nature. Not supposed to.

Betties usually have a good rack, nice legs, but there's a little bit of middle age in the rump and the stockings maybe hide some veins. Bra's a pushup because, you know, gravity. Shoes are practical because she's on her feet all goddamn day. Must have fifty extra aprons 'cause hers is always clean. Couple of pins on her uniform. Cats, dragonflies. Like that. Once in a while it's seasonal. Christmas tree or a wreath. Wears a plastic nametag or has her name stitched across one boob. If she has glasses then she has a chain so she can dangle them, and even when she wears them it's halfway down her nose. Lipstick and a perfume that's not expensive but it's nice to smell. You remember that smell, even beneath the scent of coffee, eggs, Salisbury steak, beef stew and regret.

Like I said, you know what I mean.

This Betty was at the diner at the corner of Boundary Street and Tenth. If the place has a name nobody ever bothered to put it up in lights. Everyone I know calls it "the diner," as if there's only one. There are other diners—in this part of town it's diners, bars or pizza joints. Nothing else, not even fast food. Those other diners have names. Lucky Pete's, Stella's, American Dollar. But this one was just The Diner. And it had a really good Betty.

I was at the counter because I don't like booths. Counters are where the action is. Booths are where you sit when you want to talk somebody into something. The farther back the booth the less legal the conversation. I wasn't here for that sort of thing. I mean, sure, I do some pretty questionable stuff, but I skate on this line of the law because when you're a skip tracer you have special dispensations from the Constitution. I can kick doors a cop can't touch without losing a case. I can do all sorts of hinky shit, but it's legal. Kind of. Ethical…? Yeah, not so much. Mostly I work for six or seven bail bondsmen on Boundary Street, though most of my steady gigs come from Scarebaby & Twitch. I'm serious, that's their real names. J. Heron Scarebaby and Iver Twitch. Fucking Addams Family names, but I ran a background check on them and that is their hand-to-God birth names. I guess the fact that they found each other, became friends, and hung out a shingle is some kind of fate. Or maybe it's one of those jokes fate plays on the world but doesn't care whether you ever hear or understand the punch line. Whatever.

Scarebaby is a lawyer and Twitch is his investigator. They do criminal law, and talk about truth in advertising. I'm pretty sure all of their clients, even the ones they got acquitted, are actually criminals. Guilty as sin, and either too desperate or too stupid to get better representation. If Scarebaby gets you acquitted you will owe him a lot of whatever you make for the rest of your life.

He owns you. I know for a fact that a lot of his clients do more crimes after being let out of jail because they need to pay off those legal fees. When someone's either crazy or sane enough to want to try and run farther than they can grab, I get a call. The job blows, but the pay isn't bad, they give me really good bottles of bourbon for Christmas, and they don't need me to like them. The real perk of the job is the certain knowledge that no one I chase down for them is an innocent schnook being unfairly charged. So, I can do what I need to do to close the assignment out.

Today, though, I was off the clock. I wasn't here to meet them or to get a tip on a bail skip. I was here for coffee, the sports section of the paper, a grease-burger with cheese and chili, and my own thoughts. Didn't mind at all looking at Betty. She didn't mind being looked at, but I knew that was as far as it went. Little bit of banter that was on the PG-13 side of flirty and never, ever went any further.

It was a Tuesday night in that gap between Thanksgiving and Christmas. People who gave a shit were out shopping. The whole city was full of them. Walking over here from my office was like a salmon swimming upstream, except I wasn't going to get laid or, hopefully, eaten by a bear. I let the shoppers flow around me, and I guess I'm about as big, solid, ugly and conversational as a rock, so they swirled past and let me be. Which was fine. Every once in a while one of them would take a closer look. I'm bigger and wider than most and no one's called me handsome since a hooker in Shanghai and she pretty much had to. I don't look evil but I do look mean. People get that and they don't stop to engage, and only the complete maniacs wish me a "Happy" anything.

The Diner was a refuge for anyone who wanted a quiet night. Sure, people sometimes found me there, but never for idle chatter. Betty could even tell when I wanted to shoot the shit and when I didn't. She always smiled, though, and even on a cold night on a dark street like this one, that smile was usually the warmest part of the day.

Except today.

I was tired and didn't catch it right away, but when she refilled my cup and turned away I saw her smile change. It slipped, like a mask that wasn't tied in place very tightly. In the act of turning away to return the coffee carafe to the heater her smile changed from Betty's normal no-problems red lips and white teeth, to something unhappy and even a little unhealthy. And she was quick, because she saw me see the change and instantly upped the wattage. She could fake it the way a lot of lonely women looking close at the fine print of middle age could fake it. And maybe if I wasn't used to studying people and getting a read on them I might have bought the con.

When I continued to look at her for a few seconds too long, she realized that I wasn't going to pretend I hadn't seen something. I mean, sure, I didn't know *what* I'd seen, but it was something. There'd been some pain there. Some sadness, too. And something else. Shame? No. Fear. Sometimes they look the same. It's a wince, a flinching away from a thought.

I picked up my paper and my coffee cup and walked over to a booth. Halfway back, on the quiet side of the diner. And waited.

2

In a couple of minutes Betty showed up at my table and set the plate down. New burger and a side of fries. I'd left half my burger on the plate at the counter. She had a tuna melt with chips on a plate for herself.

"Join you?" she asked, as if that was a question.

Sometimes the formalities matter. I folded my paper and dropped it on the bench seat next to me and watched as she slid in. She didn't launch immediately into an unburdening of her soul. Some people will, but most have to work up to it, even when they come to me. This was me kind of letting her know that I knew something was up. Betty knew me, knew what I did for a living. Not just the gigs I did for Scarebaby and Twitch, but the other stuff. Some people know about that. They see the tattoos I have inked onto my skin and they hear stories around this part of town. This is the part of town where stories like that get told.

We ate.

The short order cook had on a station that was playing Christmas songs. I don't do Christmas and I don't pay much attention to Christmas songs. But there was one song they kept playing at least once an hour, so now I *did* know it. Enough to be really fucking tired of Mommy kissing Santa and instilling in her child the belief that his mom was cheating on his dad with some fat fuck from the North Pole. There's a therapy bill waiting to happen.

I caught Betty's eyes flicking over to the tats visible on my forearms. I usually wear a leather jacket, but it was warm inside the diner, and I even had my sleeves rolled up. I watched her eyes move from one face to another. That's what they are. Faces. All over my body. Not every inch, though. Not yet. I knew that there would be more faces I'd need to add. It's like that, and Betty knew it. That was obvious.

"How many?" she asked. First thing she'd said in five minutes.

"I don't count them."

"A lot?"

I shrugged.

"Does it…" she began, faltered, took a breath and tried again. "Does it hurt?"

Another shrug. What's the point of going into that part of it? The tats hurt when the ink's being drilled into me. But that wasn't what she was asking. That kind of pain doesn't mean shit. People get tattoos for fun. No, she was asking about whether having those particular tats hurt *me*. Because of what they are.

She looked away out the window. Even down here on Boundary the streets swirled with people. Stores had colored lights up, stoplights and cop car lights kept it all moving. Big Smalls was across the street dressed in a Salvation Army coat, ringing a bell. You had to be legally blind to believe he was anything but what he looked like, which was a crackhead trying to work the rubes for small change. There were real people down here, but most of them had stopped being rubes after they'd already been conned. If you lived or worked on Boundary Street you understood the game. Even so, a few of the locals tossed coins into his bucket. After all, Big Smalls was one of us.

Without turning to look at me, Betty said, "I wasn't going to bother you with it. I suppose this really isn't your kind of thing."

"I do a lot of things," I said.

"No… I mean, the kind of *special* things you do."

Special. Interesting word for it. I know people talk about me, and a few of them even know the deal. Or some of the deal. Nobody knows all of it except my tattoo artist, Patty Cakes, who has a little skin art place just off Boundary, right between a glam bar called Pornstash and a deli called Open All Night, which, to my knowledge, has never been open. Apart from Patty, the other people who know only have a bit of the story. They know I have the faces of certain clients inked onto my skin. I do that when I'm looking for a killer, and a little bit of the victim's blood is mixed in with the ink. It does something, creates a bond. I can't see everything but I see enough. Sherlock Holmes would call them clues, but it feels more like I'm actually there with the vic, feeling the bullets or blades or beatings. Feeling and seeing the last few seconds of their lives. Dying with them. If they saw—or in some cases, *knew*, their killers—then that would give me a starting place. If they didn't know who killed them and never saw the perp's face, then I'd have to start from scratch. So far I only have a few cases of that kind in my 'open' file.

Some of the perps I'm able to track go to trial. Not with me on the witness stand, let's be real. But, remember, I'm a bounty hunter and I know how to get the goods on people. I don't play by any rules but my own. And, sure, I've had to sometimes drop anonymous dimes on the bad guys, or blind-mail evidence, or even spook them into confessions once or twice.

Not all of the bad guys go to trial. Not even half. Sometimes there's no way the system is going to be able to touch them. I *can* touch them. So to speak.

But, like I said, those are special cases, and it's usually the victim who reaches out to me. Read that any way you want and you'll get close to how it works. Not nice, not pleasant, not fun. And once the case is over those vics are with me for the long haul. Their blood's in my skin. People talk about being haunted, but they don't know what that really means. No fucking way.

I said nothing. Ate a few fries. Waited for Betty.

"People say you know stuff. They say that you understand what people are going through."

I dipped a fry in ketchup, ate it, looked at her.

"I think you said something just now," she said. "When you looked at me."

"Something," I said.

We sat for a bit. The other waitress was handling the few customers. New kid. Her name was Kristen. Not really a diner waitress name, so I figured she wouldn't last.

"It's my nephew," said Betty. "He died last week."

"How?"

Her eyes clicked toward mine, held for a microsecond, then fell away. "You probably heard about it. Over by the projects?"

Sure, I'd heard about it. Everyone around here had. The William Lloyd Garrison Community Housing Project was the official name, but I doubt anyone's called it that since they broke ground back in the seventies. It was 'the projects.' Nine five-story drab brick buildings erected around a playground and common area that was probably a needle park before the first tenants moved in. Poor white, poor black, poor Latino, and poor melting pot all shoved into cheap apartments with flimsy doors, suck-ass security, sub-standard plumbing, and no hope at all. Over the years a few lucky souls managed to get the hell out, but you couldn't call it a majority. Not even close. A lot of people grew old and died there. Of the nine buildings, only three are in moderately decent shape, and by that I mean they aren't active crack houses or simply falling down. Two are condemned; one's a burned-out shell.

But what Betty was talking about was the kid who got so high in one of the crack pads that he thought he could fly. Or something. Witnesses say he fell right out of the fifth-floor window on one of the buildings. Did a turn and a half on the way down and landed in the pile position. Which is a smartass way of saying he took a header onto the concrete. Smashed his head, snapped his spine and probably never knew what he hit.

"He was your nephew?" I asked.

She nodded. "Jimmy. James O'Neill. He was only nineteen." Betty sniffed. "Jimmy was my little sister's only kid. Sherrie doesn't live here in the city; she's out in the suburbs. Got a nice house with her second husband. She's a teller at a Wells Fargo out there."

"Uh huh."

"Jimmy was a good kid until sophomore year. He went out drinking with some other kids—first time for him, I think—

and they got really drunk. Sick drunk. One of the kids was a senior and had his parents' car. They… well, there was an accident. The papers said that the car never even tried to brake when it went through the red light over on the main drag that goes through Japantown. Their car hit an SUV." She sniffed and shook her head. "Oh, god, it was horrible. There was a woman in the other car bringing her daughter home from dance class. They were both killed. And the little girl was only nine."

"Jesus. What about the kids Jimmy was with?"

"There were two others and they… well, the boy who was driving wasn't wearing a seatbelt. He went partway through the window. They said he died on impact. The other one was Jimmy's best friend. He was on life support for seventeen months before the family had him disconnected."

I nodded. That was on the news, too. Kid was a straight-A student.

"Jimmy was the only one who survived the crash," said Betty. "And he was awake the whole time. He saw everything. Saw all that blood. Saw his friends… and the woman and her…"

I touched her wrist to let her know that she didn't need to jam broken glass into her own skin by telling me the rest.

"What happened to Jimmy after that?"

"He was expelled and there were charges, but because he was the youngest and was in the backseat the judge went easy on him. The husband of the dead woman sued his family, though, and my sister had to cash in her 401k, all of their stocks, their savings, and sell their house to pay the legal bills. They bought this little one-bedroom place and Jimmy had to sleep on the couch because there was no room, you know?"

I sighed, getting the picture. Horror, followed by general guilt and survivor's guilt. That's a witches' brew few adults could handle, let alone a kid.

"When did he start in on the drugs?" I asked.

She dug a tissue out of her uniform pocket and dabbed at her eyes. I have always found it interesting, and kind of sexy, that women will be careful of their eye makeup no matter how much their heart is breaking. "His folks tried to get him into other schools, but no one really wanted him. They tried homeschooling, but that was a mess. My sister and her husband had to work all the time to pay their bills, you know?"

"Sure."

"Sherrie doesn't know when Jimmy started using. Or, maybe she did because she told me later that money was always missing from her purse. And some stuff around the house."

"Stuff a kid could pawn?" I suggested.

"Yes. But when Jimmy was arrested, the cops told Sherrie that he was a junkie." She picked her shoulders up and dropped them as she sighed, long and heavy. "They couldn't afford rehab or counseling. Not a good shrink, anyway. They made him go to N.A. meetings, but you know how that is. You have to want to work the program."

"And Jimmy didn't?"

"No," she said, "I think by then he was already lost."

I've heard a lot of sad shit in my life. More than most people. But sitting there with this woman, hearing the echoes of the deep grief in her voice, seeing the brave little smile she kept hoisting up so I didn't have to see her pain… fuck, man. That was one of the saddest things I ever heard.

I leaned forward and took her hands. It was a liberty, a line that she hadn't invited me to cross, but I trusted her to know that it wasn't any kind of come on. She looked at my big, knuckly, scarred hands, and then she curled her fingers around mine and held on for dear life.

3

"So how do you think I can help," I asked. "I don't mean to be a prick, but I've heard this story a thousand times. Kid loses his hold on the world, bottoms out, and then decides leaving is better than staying." There was a song lyric about life being bigger than the strength he had to get up off his knees. Something like that, but it wasn't the time to quote a song to her, not even a country and western song.

"The cops and the news people all said that he killed himself," said Betty.

"But—?"

She chewed her lip for a moment and then nodded as if she had come to a decision. Then she dug her cell phone out of her pocket. An Apple model that has been out of style so long I'd be surprised if they were still updating the operating system. Small, with a tiny screen. But she brought up her messages, scrolled through, sighed again, then turned the phone around and slid it across to me. I bent to read the screen display, and then used my forefinger to scroll up a bit so I could see more of the conversation. It was a short series of texts between Jimmy and his aunt. Jimmy had written to ask her for some cash and she was pretty blunt in her response.

BETTY: U know I won't give U $ for that.

JIMMY: Not 4 that.

BETTY: ??

JIMMY: Need 2 get out.
All weird here now.

BETTY: What do U mean?

BETTY: What's wrong?

The time code said that it was over ten minutes before Jimmy answered that post.

> JIMMY: The stuff's all wrong.
>
> BETTY: What stuff.
>
> JIMMY: U know. Grit.

I glanced at Betty. Grit was one of the street names for crack cocaine. There were a lot of cute names for it. Cloud, gravel, nuggets, piece, raw, 24-7, bad-rock, scrabble, sleet. Like that. Maybe it makes it taste better. Who the fuck knows and, more to the point, who the fuck cares?

> BETTY: What do U mean 'wrong'?
>
> JIMMY: He knows I know it's bad. But he's selling it anyway. Says there's no more til this is gone.
>
> JIMMY: A girl I knew got sick. They took her away. Other kids, too.
>
> JIMMY: Couple of kids in the
>
> JIMMY: My friend Rix ran right into traffic. He was all wrong. I'm scared.
>
> BETTY: U need help.
>
> JIMMY: He's crazy. He knows it's bad. He doesn't care.

There was no more.

I looked up at Betty and there were fresh tears in her bright eyes.

"He wrote that to me at 5:21 that afternoon," she said. "The police report says he went out of the window at 5:30."

I sat back. "Who is 'he'? Who's the cat Jimmy was talking about? You know his name? Know anything about him?"

Her eyes darkened. "Jimmy talked about him a lot, but all he ever told me was his nickname. His street name, I guess. Dill."

"Ah," I said.

She frowned. "You know him?"

"*Of* him. Marcus Dillman," I corrected. "I work for bail bondsmen and we always hear shit. What do *you* know about him?"

"I know he's a dealer."

"Yeah, he is. What else?"

"Not much, but I believe that Jimmy was telling me the truth," she said, and when I didn't comment, she added, "He never lies to me. To his folks, sure. To everyone else. Never to me."

"Okay," I said. "What else do you have other than Jimmy's word?"

"Nothing," said Betty. "I tried asking around, but nobody wants to talk about anything. They're afraid to. Somebody's always listening, you know?"

"Sure. There's no percentage in diming the bad guys when they live there and the cops don't."

She nodded. "I was there this morning, but when I pulled up to the building where Jimmy was staying—squatting, I guess, though he called it crashing—there were two guys leaning against the wall. Like they were watching for me to come back because as soon as I parked they pushed off the wall and started walking right toward my car."

"What'd you do?"

"What could I do? I left and I'm afraid to go back."

"Smart. Don't go back. Don't even think about it."

"But the cops aren't even looking into it. They marked Jimmy as a suicide and because of his record they don't even care that he died."

I nodded. "They *don't* care. They don't have a reason to care and they don't have the time or manpower to care. That's how it is, especially in this part of town. Nobody much cares."

"I care," she said fiercely. She balled her fists and pounded the table. Not loud enough for anyone else to hear, but loud enough for me to see the fire inside her. "If no one else will help then I *will* go back. Jimmy knew something and he wanted out. He was scared of this guy, Dill, and he knew something, and that got him killed."

"Killed? You're saying he didn't fall out of the window?"

"Jimmy didn't commit suicide, if that's what you're asking," she snapped.

"It's what I'm asking."

"Well... he didn't."

"Maybe he got stoned and didn't know what he was doing. Or maybe Dill was selling some bad junk and Jimmy took a bad high," I said, then before she could say anything I said, "No."

The timing was all wrong for that. He wouldn't have been firing up a crack pipe while he was texting his aunt for runaway money. I couldn't sell that to myself anymore than Betty could.

How had Jimmy put it? *My friend Rix ran right into traffic. He was all wrong. I'm scared.*

Jesus.

I took a small bite of the burger, chewed it, didn't taste it at all, put it down, looked across at her. "What do you want me to do?"

It took her a moment to actually say it. If she really had known about how the tattoos worked and what it cost me to go as far as getting one inked onto my skin, then maybe she wouldn't have asked. Jimmy was her nephew, sure, and clearly she loved the kid, but he was dead long before he went out that window. He probably died in that car crash, and maybe should have. I don't know. I'm not a therapist and I'm not a saint. But I've seen people who have tried to live past their own expiration date, and I've seen the tortured ghosts they became, haunting their own lives. Sure, some of them can be saved, but coming back to life is a lot like working the Twelve Steps—you have to want to do the work. Some people don't. Some people want to be dead and are simply taking the long way around. And some people—and my guess is that Jimmy was one of them—needed to do some penance. Being alive was exactly the same as being in hell for their sins, and they had just enough self-respect to not want to dodge that responsibility. It's fucked up and it's miles past sad, but there it is.

It took Betty a lot to ask. It took all of her love for her nephew; it took compassion for anyone else this Dill cocksucker might hurt; it took her personal courage and it took every atom of her battered pride.

"Can you find out who killed Jimmy?" she asked, her voice rough with emotion. "Can you find out why?"

The clock on the wall above the door was one of those big, industrial battery-operated clunkers that ticked very loudly. The jukebox was between songs and the Christmas noise from the street seemed muted. I listened to a lot of seconds being chopped off by the sharp blade of the ticking hand of that ugly clock.

"Yeah," I said. "I'll find out."

4

Here's the thing.

I wasn't taking a case to do a full-blown investigation. Because I'm a skip tracer in this town it means I had to get a P.I. license, but Betty wasn't hiring me to collect evidence and build a case that we could take to the local police. She was too much of a decent person to ask what she really wanted.

Not sure the word 'revenge' is the right word. And 'justice' is too corny.

Maybe the word is 'payback', but that's pretty trite, too.

Whatever it was, she asked and I said yes.

It was getting late, and if this was a normal gig I'd wait for daylight and maybe even put on a sports coat and try to look normal.

Instead I left the diner and walked the five blocks to the projects. The holiday shoppers were thinning out because nice people don't go out in the dark in this part of town. Not twice. Because the later it gets the more the neighborhood looks like what it is.

The streets were dry and we hadn't had any rain in weeks. That was good, because I was able to find the spot outside of the building where Jimmy stuck the landing. In nicer neighborhoods someone—the cops or the building super—hoses down the pavement so there's nothing horrible to see. This isn't one of those neighborhoods, so the red splotch was still there. It didn't look like anything. Just a mess. A central impact point and tendrils of blood spatter going out as far as the blacktop. He'd fallen five stories, so he'd had time to build up some speed.

There were people around, but no thugs leaning on the wall, so I knelt and used the blade of a Boy Scout knife to scrape some dried flakes of blood into a little glass vial. I keep a couple of those in my jacket pocket for this kind of thing. They look like crack vials. The next step would be to take the vial over to Patty Cake and have her mix it with ink. Sometimes she'd roll a blunt and we'd both get baked before she set to work. Sometimes it was Kentucky whiskey. Sometimes we did it just on nerves. A lot of it depended on what kind of vibe we were getting from just being on the fringes of a new case. Or, maybe the ghosts would be breathing cold air on the back of our necks and freaking us out. Even I don't know which.

I straightened, listening to the creak and pop of my knees, looking around at the desolation of this place. It looked like a demilitarized zone but people lived there. Lights burned in a few of the windows of the other buildings and in one I saw the silhouette of a Christmas tree and as I stared at it the little twinkly lights came on. Nobody here had an extra dime, but there was someone who'd bought a tree and was willing to pay the bump in electricity bill to let it shine. That kind of optimism made me want to cry.

As I turned to go, I saw that there was someone standing by a burned-out shell of a stripped car. A skinny young man wearing a hoodie and stained jeans. Sneakers with graffiti on them, hands jammed into his pants pockets, shoulders hunched against the cold. It wasn't actually too bad out, but he didn't have an ounce of meat on his bones.

I walked over and stopped in front of him. His face was almost invisible inside the shadows of his hood.

"Hey, Jimmy," I said.

He said nothing. Just looked at me. One eye was all red, the other was blue. He wasn't a good-looking kid, and maybe some of the guilt of what happened a few years ago was his, but not as much as I saw haunting his eyes.

"You know why I'm here?" I asked.

He nodded.

"Your Aunt Betty loves you," I said. "You know that, right?"

Another nod. His face was covered with blood and bits of brain and bone. He looked fucking awful. I saw tears rolling through all that muck.

"Tell me something straight, kid," I said. "Did you get wasted and walk out the window?"

He didn't move.

"Or did Dill do something to you?"

A fresh set of tears rolled down.

"Why?" I asked. "Was it something you saw?"

He looked at me. I knew he wanted to talk, but he couldn't. They can't until I have their faces inked onto me, and after that they're stuck with me. And me with them. This wasn't about justice, and somehow Jimmy knew it the same way they all knew it. If I inked his face onto my flesh then, sure, I'd be able to know how he died. Know it for sure, but it meant that Jimmy would join the parade of other pale ghosts that were always with me. Nobody could see them but me, but they were always there. At night, when I tried to sleep, they stood around my bed. Some of them were silent, and maybe Jimmy would be one of those. Some were screamers. They screamed and screamed and screamed. They would scream until my heart finally stopped beating. And none of us—not them or me—knew if that would put an end to it. If I died, would they move on? Or would we all be in that purgatory together forever?

Yeah. It's like that for me. Pretty sure Betty didn't know all of it. She'd never have asked me. She wasn't one of the cruel ones. If she'd known, she'd have either kept poking around until someone scraped her up off the pavement, or she'd have eaten her pain like a piece of poison, knowing full well that it would kill her one of these days. Sooner than her time.

I waited for something from Jimmy. A sign, a sense of what he wanted. If he needed revenge of some kind, then it would be up to me to make a call. I'd given my word to his aunt, but all I promised in words was to look into it. I hadn't promised to go any deeper than that.

No, I'd made that promise to myself.

God damn it.

Jimmy turned and looked past me, and I followed his gaze to see two figures approach a small metal utility door on the side of the building. Two girls. Maybe minors or maybe emaciated adults. Put them both together and I outweigh them by eighty pounds. As the door opened I caught a brief image of a man's face in the doorway. Older, not wasted, shaved head, dark eyes, hard mouth. He also wore a hoodie, but he looked clean and fit.

Without turning to Jimmy, I said, "Dill?"

I didn't need him to answer. It's why Jimmy was here right now.

We watched the two girls go inside. Dill leaned out and looked around. He saw me. I don't look like a cop. I don't even look like an undercover cop. I'm big, square, ugly, and anyone can tell there's something not right about me. People like Betty see one kind of thing. People like Dill see something else. He gave me five full seconds of a hard, flat stare, and then he closed the metal door.

"You know those girls?" I asked Jimmy.

His hood moved indecisively. Could have been a nod, could have been a shake. Not sure it mattered. He knew Dill. He knew something about Dill that made him willing to risk coming to me.

And that put us both out on the edge of the cliff.

I had three options. One was go home, watch some TV shit

with the sound turned up and drink myself to sleep. Typical day for me.

Option two was go over to Patty Cake's and give her the vial. Let her do her thing. Light the fuse.

Or...

Or, maybe this wasn't that complicated. Maybe it didn't have to be.

I looked around at the buildings here in the projects. There's not a lot of life here and there's fuck-all when it comes to grace, or hope, or luck.

Except every once in a while.

I looked at the vial, held it up so that I could see those little Christmas lights through the curved glass. They made the flakes of dried blood look like dust. Jimmy came around and stood in front of me. I could still see the lights through him. Ghosts, you know?

I held the vial out to him and he frowned at me, not getting it. Then, he tentatively reached out his hand, palm upward. I dropped the vial. It fell through his hand, hit the ground, and cracked apart.

"This one's on the house," I told him as I began walking toward the building. Then I paused and turned to look at him. "Your Aunt Betty never gave up on you, kid. Never. Use that. Let it pull you in."

He said nothing.

I nodded and kept walking.

The door was metal but the lock was Mickey Mouse. I jimmied it open and I stepped inside. It smelled like shit and piss and bad decisions. Nothing unexpected.

I stood at the bottom of the fire stairs and listened. I could hear some voices talking. Muffled, wordless noise from several stories up. I began to climb. I'm big but I learned long ago to move quietly when getting shot wasn't on my Day-planner. Rubber-soled shoes and some skills acquired in places that were even worse than this.

The lookout guy on the second floor didn't even know I was there. He was too busy texting on his cell. Had no clue at all I was there until I hooked an arm around his throat, braced my other hand against the back of his head and squeezed. There are two versions of that choke. With the judo version you put the guy out in about eight seconds—sixteen if you cut off only one of the carotids—and then you lower him down and let him sleep it off. The jujutsu version is a lot older and less civilized. With that version you quiet him with the choke, and then you shift your arm and use the long forearm bones like a paper cutter to crush the windpipe and the hyoid bone.

I didn't know this cat. He might have been every bit as bad as Dill or he might have been some kid who couldn't find work and this looked easy. Whatever. No reason to kill him. So he got the judo choke.

People try to fight it, but if it's done right and you mean it, they've got to be pretty well trained to get out. He wasn't. He was meat and muscle and then he was a slack weight. I laid him down, patted his pockets and found a cheap nine mil and a knife. Took those. Debated stomping on his knee to make sure he wasn't going to be an issue later. Didn't.

Moved up the stairs.

The second guard was on the fifth-floor landing. He *did* hear me coming and tried real hard to do something about it. A lot of street kids are tough and experienced, but there's street tough and there's Special Forces tough. I wasn't always a big city skip tracer, and I'd fought tougher men than these on four continents. He managed to get his gun out of his waistband, but I took it away from him and pistol-whipped him into two years' worth of orthodontia. He spun around, spitting bloody teeth, and went right down. I caught him and gave him a little shove so he'd go all bumpity-bump down the stairs. Should not have pulled a gun on me.

Dill's voice came yelling out of one of the rooms down the hall.

"The fuck was that, Gogo?"

When Gogo didn't answer, Dill came out of the room with one arm wrapped around a girl's throat and a pistol in his other hand. She was naked from the waist up. Sixteen, seventeen, maybe. Almost no tits, ribs showing, some sores on her that let me know she'd been sucking rock for at least a couple of years. Probably came here with her friend to blow Dill and his goons in exchange for a pipe.

That's some sad, sad shit right there.

Dill had his arm resting on the girl's shoulder to steady his aim, but I was a shadow in a dark hallway.

"Gogo…?" he called.

"Gogo's off the clock," I said and fired the gun I'd taken from the kid downstairs. The girl was a stick figure, Dill was a bull. She didn't offer protection worth a damn. My bullet caught Dill in the hip and the impact of lead hitting all that bone jerked him backward and spun him. Most shots won't do that. Most pass right through, but the hip's a nice, solid target. He screamed and the girl screamed and his gun went off. She fell into a ball, screeching, slapping at her body because she probably thought she'd been shot. The other girl, still inside the room, started screaming, too. But Dill screamed louder than both of them. He tried to shoot again, but by now I was running. I kicked his wrist and then stomped it flat onto the floor. I liked how that felt so I did it again until bones broke and the gun went flying. Then I knelt on him, my knee on his chest, my left hand braced against the wall, the barrel of the stolen gun jammed against his forehead.

"Shut. The. Fuck. Up," I said and tapped him hard with the barrel on each word. He did shut up, but the screams were boiling right behind his gritted teeth. I turned to the screaming girl. "Get dressed and get the fuck out of here."

She was hysterical and probably out of her mind even before this, but she still had her animal instincts. She was up and running in a second. Topless. Without her friend.

I bellowed for the other girl to get out, and she ran past me. A little older, but just as wasted. I saw that she had her friend's shirt clutched in one small fist. That tiny bit of courtesy, that little display of presence of mind, was somehow touching. I listened for them as they pounded down the stairs.

That left me and Dill.

"You got one chance, asshole," I said. "Tell me about the kid."

"What... kid...?" he gasped.

"Jimmy," I said, though I thought he already knew. "He said there was something wrong with the grit."

"No... it's—"

I banged his forehead with the gun butt. "No, no. I'm not a cop, I'm not wearing a wire and this isn't a time to get cute. What's wrong with the grit?"

When he didn't answer fast enough I swung the gun back and hit him in what was left of his hip. More screaming. It took a little more effort to calm him down this time.

"What was wrong with the grit?" I asked when he was able to hear me.

He said two words. Not a real explanation, but enough of one. "Bad... cook."

"Why'd you sell it if it was bad? Your fucking customers are dying, dumbass."

Dill looked at me as if I was an idiot. "Always more where they came from."

It was enough. It was too much, really. It showed the scope of what he was as a person, just as it told me exactly how much the penal system would ever fix him. Or rehabilitate him.

It made me feel old and tired.

It made me feel sick.

It made me wish that I could do one thing to him that would stop this kind of thing from happening everywhere. But that was just plain stupid. Who was I? God?

I felt a coldness in the hall and turned to see Jimmy standing there. Silent and bloody. He didn't say anything to me. Probably wouldn't if he could. All he did was watch me as I dragged Dill into the room where he'd been having sex with the girls. There was a soiled mattress on the floor, a chair, a gym bag open and a pipe sitting on a folding chair.

If I was into the drama of it, I'd have made Dill smoke a whole bowl of the tainted shit he was selling. But Jimmy was watching me and somehow I don't think he was mean enough to want that. The kid had been willing to join me in purgatory to save other junkies like him from dying. Heroism comes in some funny damn shapes and sizes.

Instead I hauled Dill to his feet and chucked the son of a bitch out the window. Five floors down. I didn't lean out to watch him hit. I'm a motherfucker but I'm not a sick motherfucker.

I walked out into the hall right behind Jimmy, but as I left the room somehow Jimmy was already down the far end and vanishing into the fire stairs. I stood for a moment and watched him go. There was no way to catch up to him. Not anymore. He was going somewhere else. In happier moments I like to think that maybe when it's Betty's time to go—decades from now, I hope—a clean and healthy Jimmy will be waiting for her.

I'd love to sell that to myself. Booze helps.

The truth is that aside from seeing ghosts like him, and the ghosts that haunt me, I have no fucking idea what's on the other side. Maybe the only thing on the other side of that big light is a big black nothing. I've talked to a lot of strange people along the way. Mystics, you might call them. Everybody has a theory, but none of us know. Not for sure.

Not really.

I took my time getting out of there. No doubt someone had seen Dill fall, or heard him. And maybe someone would make a call, but police response in this part of town was always reluctant, always slow.

The air was colder than it had been a few minutes ago, and there was a tingle to it. I felt something on my cheek and when I brushed it away I realized it was a snowflake. I looked up to see a few flakes drifting down on the night breeze.

Corny as shit.

I shoved my hands in my pockets, took a deep breath of the night sky, turned and headed home. The ghosts would still be there, but at least there wouldn't be a new one.

That's something, right?

DARK HILL RUN

by

KASEY LANSDALE AND JOE R. LANSDALE

Johnny ran fast, and it ran faster, catching up rapidly. There was barely enough time between labored breaths for him to reach into his coat pocket and pour salt into his hair and onto his clothes. He hoped he wasn't providing seasoning.

As he passed a wide store window, slightly dark, but reflective, he saw his reflection in it, saw the street lights and cars at the curb, but the one who was following him did not appear in the glass.

No reason it would.

It wasn't human.

He could feel the warm breath on his neck, the reek of the rotting dead flesh, and there was a slight brush at his salt-covered coat collar, a sizzling sound and a puff of smoke, and still he ran, trembling, making good time along the oddly abandoned sidewalk, moving rapidly uphill.

* * *

Johnny wanted to quit smoking. That's how it began.

"I know a hypnotist. Well, he's also a therapist," Darla said.

They were sitting in a café off one of the less busy city streets, but still, horns were honking, people were yelling and talking, sirens constantly blared and the beat of traffic helicopters flying overhead was disconcerting. Johnny, being from a small town, had never gotten accustomed to that. But you couldn't work as a book editor in a small community. He missed the simple backstreets and the skyline and the pinpricks of stars against the black velvet sky, the silence of a summer night. He was glad he had been able to buy an old home here in the city, nestled next to what had once been a country trail, the Camino Real, over a hundred years ago. His house and those on his street, Dark Hill Run, were the last of a forgotten era, when drovers hustled cows along what was then a dusty trail to the market that had existed at the bottom of the hill.

He had arrived a few years before the gentrification of the neighborhood, before the wealthy had moved in and turned old businesses into new boutiques and coffee shops frequented by self-important hipsters.

Darla pushed her short brown hair behind one ear, and said, "He's hypnotized a number of people into stopping smoking, including me."

"You never smoked that much," Johnny said.

"No, but one a day is one too many. You smoke three packs a day. You won't be long for this world you keep that up."

"I'm a runner. Run through this city dodging people, climbing hills, you get pretty strong."

"You can improve yourself, but you can't beat the nicotine in the end by just blowing it out. You have to quit."

"Dang it," Johnny said, and grinned. "I knew that part would come up. It makes me want a cigarette."

"I got his card," Darla said, and pulled a wallet from her purse and opened it and took out the card. "I was just about to clean this thing out. I keep all manner of cards until I don't even remember why I took them in the first place."

Johnny looked at the card.

"You want to quit," Darla said. "This is your guy. Doctor Anderson. He's not fancy, but he gets the job done. Of course, on Tuesday I dance like a chicken and on Thursday I bark like a dog."

"That's funny," Johnny said. "But, not really."

* * *

Johnny left Darla with her promising to drop by and see him sometime in the week after work, and thought about the therapist she had suggested.

On the street outside the entryway of Dr. Anderson's building, staring at the doctor's name on the door, Johnny paused to light a cigarette. He looked at his watch. Good. It was still early. He could have two.

He smoked one slowly, the other more quickly, coughed out some smoke, and trekked past a homeless man wearing a bright red jacket and a big fluffy lint-filled beard, bounded up some steps, and headed inside.

When the elevator opened the office was small and there was a reception desk but no receptionist. Behind the desk there was a pebbled glass window and a door next to it. The door was mostly pebbled glass as well.

Johnny decided to beard the lion in his den. Provided the lion was home.

He tapped on the pebbled glass door. There was the sound of a chair scooting on tile, and then the door opened.

The man standing there was short and fat and bald. He had on a suit with wide lapels that had to go back to the seventies, and wore a tie with a hula girl on it. He looked himself to be in his seventies.

"Do you have an appointment?" Dr. Anderson asked.

"No. Sorry. Actually, I came here to make one, but your receptionist is out—"

"She's been out for ten years. I'm mostly retired. I was thinking you might have an appointment and I had forgotten. I was thinking of taking the day off."

"May I make an appointment?"

"Consider yourself appointed right now, you got the time."

Johnny nodded and came inside. Dr. Anderson left the door open and sat down behind his cluttered desk. There was a worn couch, and Johnny sat there. He glanced about. All manner of odd knick-knacks were positioned on shelves about the room and on Dr. Anderson's desk. Looked like the kind of stuff children give their grandma, things they can buy cheap to fulfill a birthday or grandmother's day debt. There was one wall of bookshelves and they were filled to overflowing.

"You're here to quit smoking," Dr. Anderson said.

"How'd you guess?"

"That's about all I do. I'm a psychologist, not a mind reader, Mr…"

"Johnny Cole."

"How bad do you want to quit?"

"Bad. Yet, I don't know how much smoking is bothering me. I'm a runner. I can't tell the cigarettes are slowing me at all."

"You're young. They catch up. Lots of things catch up to you as you age, and sometimes before you age. We lie to ourselves a lot."

"A lady I know, Darla Snider, used you to stop smoking."

"Ah."

He tilted back slightly in his chair, mentally scanning through his rolodex. "Well, in Ms. Snider's case, she smoked one or two cigarettes a day and was ready to quit on her own. She wasn't really a problem case. Frankly, she'd have quit without me. But you?"

"Three packs a day."

"That's a lot of cigarettes, but if you really want to quit, I can help. Sometimes, you quit smoking you have other problems. Overeating. I'm an example. I can't hypnotize myself, but I was once hypnotized to quit smoking by someone else. It worked. I've been hypnotized to lose weight. That didn't work. So even I know there are limitations. You see, I wanted to quit smoking, but I didn't want to quit eating, and to modify a behavior based on an existing necessity is much harder. Eating is a necessity. Smoking is not. Some other problems here and there might pop up. Our psyches deplore a vacuum, so we give ourselves problems. It can be like whack-a-mole. Solve this one, there's a new one. Solve that one, and so on. What I specialize in is stopping smoking."

"How long will it take?"

"We can do a session now. Might need another. I'm a doctor, not a magician, but I'm pretty good at this."

"Darla said something about dancing like a chicken one day of the week, and barking like a dog another."

"She stole my joke. I tell that because people think things like that about being hypnotized and I want them to know it's silly. But I do need to warn you, sometimes going deep reveals uncomfortable memories unrelated to smoking. Things you might not want to explore."

"I haven't got any skeletons in my closet," Johnny said. "Good family. Good life. No problems."

"Most of us have at least a few bones, some we may have forgotten about. I mention this because the method I use, well, it's truly deep hypnosis. Deeper than the sort I received. I've perfected it over the years. It involves a mild sedative of sorts. It's a drug made from rare herbs. Not widely known, and not everyone in the medical community adheres to it or respects it."

"But it's safe?"

"Yes. I had one client that found they were digging deeper

into memories they would rather not have recalled, but that's been the worst of it."

"Maybe we should talk price?"

"Trust me," Dr. Anderson said, "I'm affordable. Now, settle in the chair, close your eyes, and…"

* * *

Incense was lit and placed in a little ceramic elephant incense burner and pushed close to Johnny. It smelled like sewage, but at the same time it was very relaxing.

"The drug is in the incense," Dr. Anderson said. "Take a deep breath."

There wasn't much to it, and the session was about an hour, and he felt he had slept through most of it. The price was indeed reasonable, but when Johnny left the office he had the similar feeling he had after leaving a carnival palm reader.

Johnny drove home, and then went for his run. As he trotted up Dark Hill, which was named that because in the old days it had been a place for public hangings, he slowed as he reached the summit of the sidewalk, crossed over and entered the edge of the park. Beyond was a great lake. Cool air was blowing off of it. He stood on the rise of the hill and felt its full gusty force. The night had come down, and on the other side of the great lake were more tall buildings suddenly ablaze with what appeared to be a fog of brilliant lights; red, blue and yellow.

The hanging tree had been a massive oak, and it had grown where a Starbucks now stood. There was a plaque on the wall of the Starbucks that told all about it. He had read it several times in the past. In one of the local guide books he had seen photos of the hanging tree, which had lived until the mid-nineteen hundreds. Rumor was it had been poisoned so as to eliminate resistance to future construction.

The park was across the street from the Starbucks, like an island in a sea of sounds and hustling humanity, and there was a large oak amongst smaller trees, not the original hanging oak, but many thought it was, for it was old and large. Some of the guide books even pointed it out as the famous tree.

Before you reached the Starbucks there was a row of hedges, and then a wide alley. Johnny had almost learned the hard way the alley was an exit for a famous bakery.

Delivery trucks came through there regularly, and one of them had nearly wiped him out on several occasions. It had come upon him swift and silent and it was only by accident that he had noticed it in time. Next time out he had forgotten all about it, was concentrating on the evenness of his run, when it happened again. The truck had slammed on its brakes, the front of it almost touching him. He had nearly crapped a shit-shaped Jesus. The driver paused long enough to roll down his window and yell at him, even though it was the driver who was in the wrong.

Both times the near accident happened dead on six p.m.; probably the bakery's last run for the day, and almost his last run for all eternity. From that point on when he came to the edge of the hedge, which was always about six p.m., he slowed and checked before moving across the alley mouth. That truck was always on time and the driver was always in a hurry, and so it was a wise decision to be careful.

As he ran, he looked at his watch. He was five minutes ahead of his usual time, and when he checked, no truck. He kept running up the hill, and then he crossed at the crosswalk and started back down on the opposite side.

On his way down the hill, running swiftly, he realized something. He hadn't even thought about a cigarette.

* * *

At home he took a carton of cigarettes, as well as the two packs by his nightstand, the ashtrays, bagged them up and took them out and put them in the garbage. He wondered if come midnight he'd be rooting around in that can like a raccoon, in need of a smoke.

But it didn't happen.

He went to bed that night and slept well, and in the morning when he had his coffee, which was also when he had his first smoke of the day, he realized he didn't have the urge. After a couple weeks went by he didn't think of smoking at all, not even during his breaks at work.

However, there had been something after his first few nights of good sleep and no need for nicotine. He found himself waking up to pee, or at least that was it at first, but in time he realized something else was causing him to wake up.

He couldn't quite put his finger on it, but it seemed to him that it had to be something he was thinking about in his sleep, something he was dreaming. He'd thought at first it was his long to-do list hanging over him. Making copies for work he had forgotten, reading the stack of manuscripts on his nightstand, the upcoming meeting that usually ended in more work being thrust upon him and no mention of higher pay.

But one night, after waking up with tears streaming down his face, he understood it was something more.

Rolling out of bed, he made his way to the kitchen, opened the door to the refrigerator and pulled out a pitcher of water. Very much awake now, he placed the pitcher on the counter and fumbled through the cabinets for a glass. He was shaking, cold, but not from the temperature.

He stood for a moment, collecting himself. Breathing the same way he might after one of his hard runs.

After a few minutes, his heart rate slowed and he began to calm down. He reached for the glass of water, drank it down in one gulp, and returned to bed and slept soundly.

After work, as usual, Johnny slipped on his running shoes, grabbed his keys, and headed out for his run, jogging into the descending dark. Today the weather had improved and the cool air that kissed his skin the day before was nothing but damp heat. His face was pink from exertion, but he liked the way the sun felt against his body.

He rarely stopped on his run, but today, on his way back, he paused at the false hanging tree, pulled the drinking bottle from its holster on his hip, and sipped at the well-lit park.

When he turned his attention to the tree, he could see clearly by the safety lights in the park. He saw a thick trail of ants marching up the tree. After watching them for a moment, for a reason unbeknown to him, he pressed his palm into the leading troops, smashing them, feeling the little pops of the ants beneath his hand, and then his wrist and lower arm began to burn. Lightly at first, and then with an intensity so severe he wished he could remove it and beat the offending ants to death with it. The living ants had attacked their attacker.

Johnny yanked back his arm and shook it, brushing it off with the opposite hand and wondering why he had done what he did. They were ants, not humans, but there hadn't been any need to do such a thing. It wasn't like him. And that was when he first realized he was nursing some deep anxiety that frightened and frustrated him and manifested itself in something as simple as ant murder.

Something was loose inside his head.

* * *

Johnny sat down on Dr. Anderson's worn couch, said, "Something's happening, Doctor. I'm having trouble sleeping. Bad dreams."

"You just quit smoking. Restlessness could be a side-result. I warned you, you quit one thing, another replaces it, but you should be sleeping well pretty soon. Most things are easier to beat than nicotine. Even cocaine is said to be easier to beat than nicotine addiction, and beating any drug, including nicotine, could result in withdrawal symptoms, even bad dreams."

"It's more than that," Johnny said, sinking deeper into the corner of the couch. "Can you completely forget something, and then suddenly remember it? I don't mean a little thing, but a big thing, a series of events?"

"Depends on the circumstances, how old you were when it happened, how traumatic it was, how much you wanted to forget. Why don't you tell me about it?"

"You are bound by law to keep things secret, right?" Johnny said.

"If you tell me you have plans to blow up a building or murder someone, I'm not bound by law or ethics."

"What if it was in the past? When I was a child?"

"Stretch out on the couch, relax, close your eyes, find your center, and then tell me about it."

Johnny closed his eyes, and as the doctor suggested, he tried to find his center. Somewhere in the back of his mind he heard a sound like a door opening, and then it was as if a cold wind blew across his brain. The door slammed, something moved amongst the shadows of his mind, and then he began to talk.

"When I was fifteen I killed someone. I don't mean I pulled a gun on them or cut their throat or beat them to death, anything like that, but I think it was my deep-seated intention to kill them, and in a way I did."

Anderson leaned back in his chair. "Okay. Let's decide together. Keep talking."

"I had forgotten it until the other night. Oh, now and again, I'd feel a bit of something, a memory, but I swear to you, I didn't truly remember it. It was as if it had never happened, until after you hypnotized me."

"It's called suppression. It's even possible it's a false memory."

Johnny shook his head. "No. It's not a false memory. I grew up in a small southern town, and there was this kid, Ronnie. He was older, maybe sixteen or seventeen. Had been held back in school a couple times, and he's the reason I'm a runner. Health, sure, but he's the real reason. It's so clear to me now. I can't believe I forgot it—"

"Suppressed it. Just tell me, Johnny."

* * *

Long before Dark Hill Run there was Swamp Road, where he practiced running in his old home town. It was a shortcut not far from the school, a twisting path through the woods with swamp water glimmering between the trunks of the trees. He ran home through there because it was a quicker path than going around the woods, walking through a residential area. And another reason he ran there was Ronnie Fischer.

Ronnie was his nemesis. Since the eighth grade the guy had it in for him. Ronnie pretty much hated everyone. Word was he was beat at home and had become a fuck toy for his older brother who was even meaner.

Shit rolled downhill, and rumor was, before he set his sights on Johnny, he had poured gasoline over the family cat, set it on fire, swung it by its tail, blazing into a pit of charred cans and family garbage.

Johnny didn't care about his reasons, why he had become

what he had become. He cared that every day in the halls, and after school, Ronnie was waiting for him, greasy as if his head had been used to mop out toilet bowls, his leather jacket worn thin at the elbows and around the collar. Ronnie had been wearing that jacket for two years now, summer and winter, always a thin tee-shirt under it; wore jeans and sneakers and a sour expression along with it, and always had a toothpick between his lips. And though he hated everyone, for whatever reason, he had chosen Johnny as his main focus. Ronnie looked across the classroom one day, and his eyes fell on Johnny like bricks, and from then on tormenting Johnny was his main purpose in life.

Sometimes it was taunts, but most of the time, in the halls, it was shoving, a short punch to the shoulder, and then outside of school, when classes were done, he chased Johnny.

Johnny told his father about it, and his father gave him advice. Stand up to him, son. You don't, it'll get worse.

So Johnny stood up to him. It was a short and painful experience. He was knocked down behind the gym, kicked, and then Ronnie jumped on top of him and pounded him, and then, as he stood up, tired and bored from beating Johnny, he spat on him. As Johnny told Dr. Anderson about it, he could feel the warm spit running down his forehead.

That was it for standing up to the bully. From that point on, he ran.

Every goddamn day, he ran. And that was one thing he was good at, and now that it was all coming back to him, the fact he had been so good in track he not only owed to his coach and his training, but to Ronnie. That bastard was a frightful incentive. Johnny could always outrun him, but just by a bit. He could hear Ronnie breathing behind him, and once, when he looked back over his shoulder, Ronnie was almost on him, reaching, about to grab him. Johnny put on a burst of speed and left him staggering behind. From then on, it was as if he had been given a jet-propelled ass, because he learned in that moment he could really pour it on when he had to. It was his only defense against Ronnie.

In time it got a little better. His and Ronnie's classes didn't match up the same way as the years went on, so there were fewer encounters in the halls. Ronnie was on the other side of the building, in wood shop, building a crooked bird house, or in metal class, making a chisel or some such, preparing for his career as an asshole. But still, after school, it was the same. Johnny prayed for the day he would have his driver's license and a car. That could change things.

But things changed well before the time Johnny got his license.

The memory washed in on Johnny as he talked, like a tide bringing in debris. He remembered it clearly. It was the last day of school, and he had slipped out a side door and started for home. Ronnie wasn't waiting for a change. Johnny was well ahead of him, running toward Swamp Road, his books shuffling about in his backpack as he ran.

He could hardly believe his fortune. The last day of school and the bastard had been too slow, or hadn't bothered to come to school. And why should he? He'd pretty soon be out in the world without even a G.E.D., looking for a job hosing down grease and oil at a filling station.

And then, Johnny saw him. He was coming out of the woods. Might have gotten out of school early or skipped for just this moment; a last day of school pounding. Had hidden out, waiting to cut Johnny off at the pass, so to speak.

Johnny broke off the road and started through the woods, splashing through the shallow water. And then he saw a rise of clay and trees. Johnny scrambled up that, and Ronnie grabbed his ankle as he did, the weight of the pack on Johnny's back almost pulling him back into the fiend's grasp.

Johnny was barely able to shake his foot loose, scuttle to the summit of the hill. When he stood up and moved forward a few feet he came to a thirty-foot drop through scraggly pines, and down below to a major highway. Cars and trucks whistled and moaned along, riding on a ribbon of concrete cut through the hill.

Johnny turned. He was trapped with his back against a pine, the drop and the highway behind him, and in front of him, Ronnie, scrambling up the rise.

Ronnie stood and looked at him. Johnny could now remember his smile. Like a wolf that's cornered a rabbit in its den, the fangs wet with anticipation. Ronnie turned his head and studied him, and then his head nodded back into position, and he came on slowly, that wolf-grin widening.

"Step by step," Ronnie said.

Johnny put his fists up the way he thought a boxer might. Ronnie laughed, and rushed him, and in that moment Johnny saw something in Ronnie's face that sent chills down his spine. Ronnie had crossed over from being a bully and abuser, to being a killer. Murder blazed in Ronnie's eyes like hot coals in a furnace. Today Ronnie had made the decision, and Johnny knew it as surely as you could feel a change in the weather. Ronnie planned to finish their daily race forever, something he probably could have done at any time. Johnny had replaced that poor cat as an outlet for Ronnie's anger. He understood that now.

As Ronnie charged him, Johnny's will to fight failed; he knew how that would turn out. He screamed and cowered, dropped into a little ball at the base of the tree, and—

Ronnie tripped over him, the inertia of his speed sent

him flying forward. His punch meeting nothing but air as his foot caught on Johnny's backpack. It had been so quick and unexpected that Ronnie tumbled over Johnny's back and went down the hill, and Johnny was knocked after him.

Johnny grabbed at a root jutting out of the clay, clung to it, but Ronnie, he had been launched too far out to grab anything.

Johnny turned and looked down as Ronnie smashed through pine boughs and hit the highway on his head, a one point landing, and then a semi pulling a long trailer full of cattle blared its horn, and the big truck hit Ronnie. There was screeching and smoking tires and a sound like someone dropping a hog carcass out of a helicopter.

There was an explosion of blood and Johnny saw Ronnie's head flying off toward the side of the road like a lost basketball rebound. Johnny was so shaken, he almost let go of the pine root, but instead managed to grab another root, and then another, and reach the summit of the hill, and—

After that he remembered nothing. Somehow he wandered home and took a shower and did what he always did, felt odd and tired, and nothing more.

Next day he heard that Ronnie had died. He was secretly glad of that, remembering the bullying and what an asshole Ronnie was. But he realized now that he had actually disassociated himself from the events moments after, had put up a wall between himself and the memory; a memory that he felt scratching at the back of his mind from time to time, but nothing he could understand or relate to, until the other night when he heard that door open and slam.

When he had gone to search for the source of the sound, at the top of the stairs, looking down on him, for a brief moment, he thought he saw the hulking shape of Ronnie, and though the light was dim, he thought he could see cold, flat, black eyes in that shadowed face. Johnny was overcome with childhood fear, and then, the shape was gone, a collapsing shadow among other shadows, and then the memory he had forgotten for so long was suddenly bright and clear and frightening, all the more for having been dredged up from the dark silt of his memory.

* * *

When Johnny finished his story, his face was wet with flop sweat and he felt exhausted, as if he had been running and Ronnie had been pursuing him.

"Interesting," Dr. Anderson said.

"That's it?" Johnny said. "Interesting? You can do better than that, I hope. Is there a way to stop dreaming about this? Maybe I should come forward, tell the police what happened all those years ago. I'm responsible."

"It was an accident."

"Whatever you call it, if I explain what happened, perhaps I can get it off my conscience. You have no idea how real that dream felt. It was as if Ronnie was actually at the top of the stairs."

"You absolutely believe this was more than a dream?" Dr. Anderson asked.

"I do. I'm scared. I feel that Ronnie has come back from the grave, and he won't be done until he finishes doing what he started out to do so long ago."

Dr. Anderson nodded. "If your life is truly in danger, as you think, it may be my fault."

"Now you've really got me scared," Johnny said.

Dr. Anderson was silent for a long moment, and then he cleared his throat and spoke.

"I am not what you call an average therapist. Well, I may be average, but I'm not the run-of-the-mill therapist. Wrong again. I am not an everyday therapist."

"What the hell does that mean?" Johnny said, and sat up on the couch, leaned toward the desk behind which Dr. Anderson was sitting.

"The incense I had you sniff is rare, and between you and me, illegal. It's associated with supernatural and metaphysical activity."

"What?"

"Yep. I'm into that. It opens the mind to hypnotic suggestion. For whatever reason, it works really well on smoking problems, but if something dark is hidden inside your memories, the results are different."

"So you've been through this before, and you didn't warn me? You're like a goddamn witch doctor."

"I sort of did warn you, and yeah, I suppose the title of witch doctor might be fitting. Witch doctors used to be considered healers." Dr. Anderson stared off into space for a moment, as if to remember the good old days. "Most people's skeletons are a lot smaller than yours. The death of Ronnie, you tucking it back into your memory for so many years. It has grown back there, Johnny, and it wants out, and might stay out until it finishes what it needs to finish. The sound you heard, the doors opening and slamming, that's frequently associated with metaphysical activity. Certain ghosts are called door slammers, and the reason is they use our actual doors to enter in from other dimensions."

"No shit?"

"No shit. We can create living monsters out of our thoughts, especially ones that have been blocked, held under a kind of mental lock and key. It's like a kettle that can't let off steam. Finally it will burn up or explode. You are on the verge of exploding."

"Can you stop it? I mean, surely you've got a trick or two."

"I practice a bit of this and that not found in the psychological text books. But I only had this kind of thing go bad once before. Minor, not worth talking about. Easily fixed with suggestion."

"Then suggest it out of me."

"I think your situation might be considerably less simple than that."

* * *

Dr. Anderson went home to get supplies, and the plan was to meet at Johnny's home. Johnny sat out on the porch, nervously awaiting his arrival, the day dying.

Dr. Anderson arrived carrying a rumpled black satchel. Johnny let him in. The doctor opened the satchel on the couch and took out the goods.

A box of salt. Silver pellets, he said. A variety of amulets, tokens, and herbs. A bit of a nasty-looking liquid in a small bottle with a cork.

"This is what, witchcraft?" Johnny said.

"Therapy is actually a kind of witchcraft. More an art than a science, no matter what anyone tells you. A therapist is probing and guessing. It's mainly about someone talking themselves out of the bad things they're thinking and feeling, and about the therapist making a nice chunk of change per hour. I on the other hand, do not make a nice chunk of change, but there will be a bill. And yeah, this is hoodoo shit. According to what I read off the Internet—"

"The Internet."

"You have to know what you're looking for. Your man, Ronnie, he's becoming stronger with each entry into this world. He comes when your mind is at its most relaxed."

"When I'm sleeping?"

"Correct. According to what I read, in time, he'll become solid. He won't leave then. He won't go back in your head behind doors and barriers. He'll be flesh and bone, at least in appearance. He'll be able to lay hands on you, but he's a revenant just the same. He won't go back into the ether, so to speak, until he finishes what he started. There has to be a finale. He left the world unfulfilled, so he will either fulfill his plans, or they will be thwarted for good. I've always wanted to use the word thwarted."

"You mean I have to kill him all over again?"

"You didn't kill him in the first place, and you can't kill something that's already dead. Okay. Technically, I guess that's exactly what we're hoping to do. Let's say you're sending him into nothingness, and if you're able to do that, he won't bother you again. I'm not suggesting your memories will go back into hiding, like before, but Ronnie the Revenant, he'll be gone from your mind and your life and you'll be able to deal with what happened, and move on. And remember, Johnny. It was an accident. He may not see it that way, but you should."

"What if I stay awake?"

"That'll work for a while, but eventually you have to sleep. I'll stay awake and let you get some sleep, and when he comes you'll wake up, and we'll be waiting for him."

The doctor poured salt from the box into a leather bag he pulled from the satchel and gave it to Johnny.

"Revenants hate this shit," the doctor said. "You can pour it out and toss it at them."

Now the doctor placed the silver beads in another bag, along with a batch of foul-smelling roots and herbs. He gave those to Johnny as well.

"These are supposed to ward off evil," Dr. Anderson said.

"Supposed to?"

"Yep. Can't say for sure."

Dr. Anderson uncorked the bottle and poured some of the

nasty-looking liquid in a circle around the couch and armchair where he would be sitting, and then he poured salt in a circle around both.

"Might as well sleep, Johnny. Ronnie has to be faced some-time."

"With salt? That doesn't exactly inspire confidence," Johnny said.

"Tell me about it," Dr. Anderson said.

Before they settled in, the doctor gave him a mild sedative to help him sleep, but he assured Johnny that he would snap awake in a moment if the need should arise.

Johnny slept on the couch and Dr. Anderson sat in a chair nearby, reading from his Kindle. As Johnny drifted off, one foot dangling from the couch, touching the floor, he hoped what the good doctor was reading was an excellent text on witchcraft. Johnny had a packet of salt in his coat pocket, and he had a bag of herbs and silver pellets, same as Dr. Anderson. He felt he was going to a ghost fight with a wish and a half-assed promise.

* * *

Fear alighted like a locust swarm and gnawed into his memory. Everything that had been pushed down that day came back to him. He heard a door slam upstairs, and then he experienced a spine-nibbling sensation that something was in the house. In due time he heard the stairs creak with heavy footsteps, and Johnny could smell as well as sense the presence; it had a stench like garbage, dead animals and offal. The skin along his neck crawled, and every fiber of his being was calling for him to wake up.

The doctor said he would be able to come out of his drug-induced sleep easily, but Johnny discovered this was less than true. He had an all-consuming feeling that something ghastly was inching toward him, and yet he was unable to surface from the dark waters of sleep.

"Step by step," he heard a voice say, the same words Ronnie had used that day on the hill overlooking the highway.

And though he could only sense the presence, he knew that was exactly what Ronnie was doing, coming step by step toward him. He couldn't wake up, and then Johnny felt icy fat fingers around his throat and a knee on his chest, pushing him deeper into the couch cushions.

Johnny tried to yell, but all he could do was make a sound so soft it could have been cancelled out by a rat breaking wind. The weight had grown heavier. He flailed about, trying to claw at whatever was atop him, but it just leaned in further. Johnny's fingers touched cold, slippery flesh. Hands. Strong hands. He couldn't pull them from his neck. He smelled the sticky warmth of foul breath. His own breath grew jagged and weaker by the moment.

"Go away. Go away!"

Johnny strained and finally opened his eyes.

It was Dr. Anderson yelling.

And there was Ronnie, looking down on him. There was something fish-like about his mouth, like a hook belonged in it. It was stretched beyond reason, revealing teeth and gums dripping saliva, and then the sunlight dappled through the patterned curtains and lay across Ronnie like camouflage netting. His eyes were sunken and dark like shiny balls of coal. Breathing his stench was like eating something rank and solid. Ronnie's head nodded on its neck, as if on a precarious peg.

Beyond him he could see Dr. Anderson screaming, "Go away," and stringing salt from the box through the air, some of it raining down on Ronnie, causing his head and face to sizzle and pop. Then the light outside grew brighter and the camouflage lightened in the dark spots and brightened in the light spots, and Ronnie became a whiff of smoke and shadow, and was gone.

Dr. Anderson was staring down on Johnny, the box of salt in his trembling hand, a look on his face that gave the impression that something cold and sharp had been shoved up his ass.

* * *

Later at the coffee shop down the street, Dr. Anderson said, "As of this moment, I'm retired."

"So you never thought what I was telling you was real?"

"Would you believe that shit? Think about it. I was humoring you. It was a form of therapy. Enter into your belief system, play it out to the end, and the end would be you having a good night's sleep and no revenants. I really do know a bit about the occult. Stuff I told you I got from books and the Internet, but it's a life-long curiosity, not a belief. Until now. After we talked in the office, I went home, found some things I thought fit the materials listed in the occult books, and put them in a satchel. The silver pellets are actually soap beads. I was hoping you wouldn't look too close. I don't think soap is supposed to do anything. But the salt I sprinkled on it actually seemed to work. As for the salt circle around the couch, I noticed you had broken it with your foot dangling off. That may be why it was able to get through to you. According to the books, the circle has to be complete; any lapse in it, and things can get through. Listen to me. I'm talking now like I know what the hell I'm talking about."

"Ronnie giving up may have had as much to do with daylight as salt," Johnny said.

"Fair enough. Listen, kid. Don't go back there. You can't sleep in that house."

"I doubt it matters where I go," Johnny said. "I think Ronnie goes with me."

"Sorry I can't actually do anything to help you. I have to wish you the best and say don't come see me again. It might come with you. What a smell. Holy Mother of Shit."

Johnny touched his throat. "You should have been on my end of the deal."

Johnny had a ring of bruises around his throat, finger marks and thumb prints. The bloodshot look in his eyes was not from a lack of sleep, but evidence of hemorrhaging from attempted strangulation.

Johnny noticed Dr. Anderson staring at the damage, said, "You should have seen the other guy."

"I did, and he looked rough all right, but I don't think it's anything you did to him."

"If you count that time back in high school…"

"Good point."

Dr. Anderson raised the cup of black coffee to his lips, his hand shaking. "I keep thinking I'll wake up."

"I kept thinking that too, but wait, someone gave me a goddamn down in the well sedative."

"Sorry. Here's my last bit of advice…"

"I'm not sure I want to hear it," Johnny said.

"Take it or leave it, but the books I have, stuff I have always considered a hobby, it suggests that the more this thing comes back, the more flesh-and-blood-like it becomes. It's still a monster, but it begins to have more human traits, in appearance anyway. That's why it was able to choke you."

"I figured that part out," Johnny said.

Dr. Anderson stood up, reached in his wallet and took out a few bills and put them on the table. "The least I can do."

Johnny watched as Dr. Anderson hurried away.

* * *

Johnny had two more cups of coffee and walked to the park where the false hanging tree stood. He sat near it, on a bench in the sunlight. Now that he had remembered what had happened those long years ago, he began to lose his guilt. Ronnie had meant to kill him that day up on the hill, and he had only been lucky he had not. Still, that day with the ants made Johnny realize that inside of him was a potential killer, not only of insects, but of most anything. For the moment, he embraced that.

When his courage was built up, he walked to a nearby grocery store, and then home. He looked at the salt circle around the couch, saw where his foot had broken it down. He placed the plastic bag from the grocery store on the floor, removed one of the several boxes of salt he had bought. He widened the salt circle to include not only the couch, but circled it up to the front door. Then he went to his bedroom, dug about in his chest of drawers for a jogging suit and socks. He dressed and put on his best tennis shoes. The jogging top had deep pockets; he filled those with salt and sat on the couch in his living room. He looked through the satchel Anderson had left. The doctor said, except for the beads, the other stuff was supposed to deter the supernatural, but so far Johnny only knew two things had affected Ronnie. Salt and daylight.

That caused Johnny to look out the window. It was still fully light.

Then he saw the electronic reader in the chair where Dr. Anderson had been sitting, grabbed it, sat down on the couch again, and turned it on, hoping it would be a text on the supernatural. What Dr. Anderson had been reading was a self-help book to strengthen the personality.

Shit, Johnny thought. My therapist needed therapy.

Johnny dropped the reader into the satchel, tossed it aside, took a deep breath, said aloud, "Okay. I got nothing."

* * *

Johnny had to sleep for Ronnie to open the door and come into the realm of the living, and as Dr. Anderson had said, there was no avoiding that. Eventually he would sleep. Presumably, he was safe on the couch inside the circle of salt, and since he had made the circle wide and thick, there was no chance of him accidentally breaking the salt line with a dangling foot, as he had done before.

Still, Johnny was not anxious to sleep, not anxious to invite Ronnie into this realm and test the salt circle. The answer might be to sleep during the day, and stay awake nights, safely inside a circle of salt, just in case he should nod off.

Of course, that was impossible. He had a job, something of a life.

Daylight had become shadowed, and Johnny looked at his watch. Five p.m. The sun set early this time of year; another hour and the sky would be gray, and within minutes after that it would be dark. Exhausted, Johnny leaned sideways and lay on the couch, with the intention of resting, not sleeping. He found himself nodding off, popping awake from time to time.

But after the night before, he was exhausted.

I'm in the circle, he thought. I'll be fine.

* * *

He heard the door open and slam and smelled the smell, and then he heard a voice say, "Johnny. It's Darla. Open the door."

This time he was able to awaken more easily, sit up on the couch. Through the glass panel on the front door he saw Darla's shadowed face. She had her hands cupped to the glass panel, and her face pushed close to the glass, looking in. He remembered she said she would come by later in the week after work, and here she was, and at the same time, Johnny could sense Ronnie without seeing him; he had fallen asleep, the door to the other world had been opened, and Ronnie was in the house with him, and poor, sweet Darla was at the door.

"Oh, the door's open," Darla said, and turned the knob, and as she did Johnny saw a dark shadow vibrate rapidly toward the door, and then the vibrations seemed to gather themselves and solidify into Ronnie's leather-jacketed form, his head hanging at that odd angle on his neck. He was moving just outside the salt circle toward the gap between salt and the doorway.

Johnny sprang from the couch, and as he did Darla stepped into the house. Ronnie reached out and grabbed at her light coat. Johnny, still inside the circle, clutched at her coat lapels, and lifted her over the line of salt, tried to pull her into the circle, but Ronnie had her, and Ronnie, as he had been in life, was much stronger.

Darla screamed and Johnny tugged, and suddenly the coat she was wearing was snatched backwards over her shoulders, and then it was jerked free of her arms and of Johnny's grasp. Johnny staggered back with her and fell onto the couch.

"My god," Darla said.

Ronnie rushed about the circle, his head shaking from side to side like a little bobble-head toy.

"What's going on? Who is that?" Darla said, and she sounded a way Johnny had never heard before.

"No one you want to know," Johnny said.

Ronnie began to make a noise that was somewhere between a moan and a screech, a noise that made the skin on his back want to tear away from his spine, and then it hit him, he knew what he had to do; the only thing he could do, the thing he had always done before. He had to run, lead Ronnie away from Darla.

"Stay on the couch," Johnny yelled, and then he was up,

darting toward the door. Johnny knew what Darla was thinking: I need to run too, and she probably would, would probably call the police, but at this moment he had to lead Ronnie away from her. He had to pay for what he had done, and make sure the innocent did not pay with him.

Johnny leaped out of the protection of the salt circle, through the open door, across the concrete porch, bounded over the steps, hit the walkway running, and behind him he heard the pounding of heavy feet.

Glancing back, he saw his ruse had worked. Ronnie had left Darla alone and was pursuing him, and what a sight Ronnie was in the glow of the streetlight that had only in that moment turned on. Ronnie's head swung from side to side, threatening to come off and roll away, and yet, somehow it clung, and his mouth seemed far too wide, and it didn't seem real that he could see Ronnie's eyes from that distance, but he could; dark and yet somehow glowing. He could hear a sound like bare bones rubbing together as Ronnie ran, and the wind was blowing past Johnny, bringing Ronnie's horrid stench with it.

The other thing was Ronnie was gaining, and much more easily than when he pursued so many years ago. The reason was simple, Johnny realized. The dead don't tire.

But Johnny did. The fear he felt had already caused him to burn more energy and adrenaline than he thought possible. He tried not to look back and see Ronnie gaining, tried to concentrate on running, one foot after another, lengthening his strides, bringing his breathing into check.

As Johnny started up the rise that was Dark Hill Run, he saw the traffic thickening on the road next to him. He wondered what the riders would think if they saw him and Ronnie. Two guys, one really odd with a sagging head, out for their evening run.

Good god, surely not. No one could look at Ronnie and think what they were seeing was just a messed-up human being. But if anyone was looking at Ronnie with surprise or curiosity, there was no way Johnny could be aware of it. The cars went by as they did every evening at the top of Dark Hill Run, buzzing like a beehive, people coming off of work, or going out to eat, and here he was with a dead thug running after him, forcing him to run for his life up Dark Hill Run right in the midst of all that normalcy and a symbol of witchcraft at the summit.

Finally Johnny had to look because he could hear that barebone grinding sound, the swishing of Ronnie's jacket as the monster swung his arms and it rubbed against his sides. Johnny glanced back, his heart sank. Ronnie was reaching out for him, his fingers were about to grasp his collar.

Johnny pushed harder, and then he remembered the salt. Reached in his pocket, pulled the bag out and shook it open, flipped salt onto his hair and jacket, and some of the salt sailed over his shoulder, striking Ronnie in the face. There was a sound like grease popping in a hot skillet, and a noise like the one Ronnie had made before, a groaning sound that turned into a banshee-like screech. Ronnie's fingers brushed the back of Johnny's jacket, but failed to gain purchase. Ronnie pulled them back, rotten flesh falling off of them in hissing wads.

Johnny, without meaning to, screamed and began to pant and stumble, gaining his balance just as the hill leveled off. He could see the lights of the Starbucks in the distance. But even if he ran there, it would follow, and it wasn't like the monster had a sense of decorum, would sit down and order a cup of coffee. Ronnie would do what he intended to do anywhere.

There was nothing for it. Johnny realized he would eventually run out of salt and energy, and Ronnie would catch him.

Johnny raced past stores, some of them closed for the day,

others still open, lights glowing inside, the street lights falling over him and his pursuer. In those dark store windows he saw a reflection of himself, but not Ronnie. Ronnie might be solid, but he held no reflection, obviously a by-product of being a revenant.

Feeling his legs start to tire, having expended far more energy than on his usual runs, Johnny stumbled past a row of hedges, felt his feet slip out from under him. He hit the sidewalk sliding, rolling onto his back. And there came Ronnie.

Out of the gap between the hedges and Starbucks, missing Johnny by inches, the six p.m. bread truck came barreling, striking Ronnie hard, knocking him winding over a patch of grass and into the road beside it, and then he was hit by a truck, and then a car, and then pieces of him were hit by several cars.

Honking, screeching tires, burning brakes, cars slamming into the backs of one another, and in a moment, the road was silent as cars pulled to the side and people seemed to pour out of them.

Ronnie was all over the concrete in pieces and smears.

As Johnny watched, Ronnie's head rolled slowly back across the freeway toward him, and bounced up against the curb. The driver of the bread truck was outside of it now, leaning against the grill work, stunned, observing the slow disintegration of Ronnie's head, the flesh peeling into smelly strips off the skull, the skull collapsing like wet cardboard, a crowd starting to gather.

Johnny could see Ronnie's leather jacket lying in the highway, his torso collapsing into a puddle of dark goo beneath it, and then the jacket itself shredding as a wind picked at it and carried it away like confetti.

Johnny sat up, leaned his back against the stone wall of the Starbucks and began to laugh. He laughed hysterically. Even with all the oddness in the street, people turned to look at him, he was so out of control. Salt and spells couldn't compare with a repeat of what had killed Ronnie in the first place. An accident.

Johnny could see Darla walking toward him. She was trembling violently. Her mouth hung open and her arms dangled at her sides, useless. Sirens were screaming their way toward the site of what would surely be thought of as an extraordinary and inexplicable accident.

A man climbed out of one of the cars that had smashed into the curb, came over and put his hand on Johnny's shoulder as Darla arrived and collapsed on the sidewalk next to Johnny.

The man said, "I'm a doctor. Can I help you in any way?"

Johnny, between bouts of laughter, said, "Yeah, buddy. You can. You got a cigarette?"

HAPPY FOREVER

by

SIMON R. GREEN

Everyone knows a street that doesn't feel right. Where the light from the street lamps feels sour and spoiled, like bitter honey. Where the shadows are too deep and too dark, and creep up on you when you're not looking. Everyone knows a house it's not safe to approach, or turn your back on. Where dim silhouetted figures linger at brightly lit windows, and their movements make no sense at all. And you wonder who these people are, and what they're doing. And if you've got any sense at all you keep on walking until you're back in some part of the world you recognise, and understand.

The problem with cities is that they're just too big. People's needs and ambitions expand to fill the space available, and all the sick hidden secrets in their hearts break loose and rise to the surface. Until in the endless back streets and cul-de-sacs, in the private members-only clubs and lonely bed-sitting rooms, people start to realise they can do anything. Anything at all.

* * *

There is a house where Time stands still. Where nothing moves and nothing changes, no-one enters and no-one ever leaves. A house where what is happening will always happen, as long as someone pays the price.

* * *

My name is Gideon Sable, these days. I'm a professional thief, specialising in acquiring the kind of notable items that can't normally be stolen. Like a ghost's clothes, or a photograph of an event that hasn't happened yet. A ventriloquist's dummy that speaks in tongues, or a stamp from a country that never existed. Collectors will buy anything. There was a time I could steal your shadow or your reputation, your self-esteem, your favourite memory, or the life you might have known. There was nothing you could have that I couldn't take from you; and you'd never even notice till it was far too late. It used to be my proud boast that I could steal anything. Until I went after the one thing I shouldn't have, the only thing that ever meant anything to me.

* * *

It was a cold night in a colder city, and someone was looking for me. In those days I drifted from address to address, and went out of my way not to have any regular habits or close acquaintances, because that was the kind of thing people could use to track you down. Given what I did, there were always going to be certain aggrieved individuals who wanted very much to get their hands on me. But I did leave my card in various places, so potential clients could leave their contact details. So I could decide whether or not I wanted to meet them.

On that particular night, I hovered just inside the doorway to a reasonably out of the way public house, The Three Bells. As though I'd merely stepped inside on a whim, in passing. I looked around casually, checking the place out, ready to disappear back into the night if anything didn't feel right. But it was just the usual crowd, sitting at their usual tables, minding their own business. I spotted the client immediately, standing by the bar with a drink in his hand that he didn't seem very interested in drinking. They all have the same look: a need, a hunger for something they believe only I can get for them.

No other new faces, nothing out of place, so I made my way to the bar. The client turned to face me, and I got my first surprise of the evening. I knew him. Daniel Lennox, small-time solicitor. A faded, middle-aged man with tired, defeated eyes. I used to go out with his daughter, a long time ago. He didn't recognise me at first. Back then, I used to change my appearance as often as my hideouts. But after a moment he nodded to me, and I nodded back.

"Been a while, Andrew."

"I don't use that name any more," I said.

"Of course," said Lennox. "You're the infamous Gideon Sable, now. The man who can get you anything, for a price. It's been years since I last saw you. Ten years since my daughter Julia disappeared."

"What do you want, Lennox?" I said patiently. "Why track me down, after all this time?"

"Because I finally found her. She's trapped, in a place she can't get out of. I want her back. I want you to steal her back."

Lennox's words put a chill in my heart. Julia… I kept my face professionally calm and unmoved, and met Lennox's gaze steadily.

"Why come to me?"

"Oh, you weren't my first choice. I have my pride. I sent others to bring Julia home."

"What happened?"

"I don't know. They never came back. But they were good men, ready to help just because it was the right thing to do. It seems the place I sent them is too much for heroes. I'm hoping a professional thief might do better. I asked around, and your name kept coming up. There are a lot of stories about Gideon Sable.

Did you really steal the Hand of Eibon, and the Box of Beyond?"

"I never talk about what I do," I said. "That's part of what you're paying me for."

"I understand you only steal things to order," he said. "Never anything for yourself."

"I don't care about things."

"Or people?"

"I haven't cared about anyone since Julia walked out on me. All I care about now is cash. With enough money, you can buy whatever things or people you think you need."

"Did you ever really love my daughter?" said Lennox. He seemed honestly interested in my answer.

"Yes," I said. "You know where she is, now?"

"She's being held in a house where the doors never open. Where no-one can reach her. But maybe you can, if you're as good as everyone says." He looked thoughtfully at me for a long moment, and then handed me a card. "Go to this address. She'll be there."

I took the card, looked at it, and then at him. "What's the catch? Why can't Julia leave?"

"Because Time itself has come to a halt, at that house. The people inside are trapped in a moment carved out of Time. Like insects preserved in amber."

"How the hell am I supposed to get her out of that?" I said.

"I'm sure a uniquely experienced thief such as yourself will think of something," he said, smiling faintly. "What's your price, Mister Sable?"

"No price," I said. "Not this time. It's Julia."

He nodded slowly. "I did hope… she might still mean something to you."

"You should have asked me first," I said. "How much has this cost you, so far?"

"She's my daughter," said Lennox. "I'd do anything for her."

"She walked out on me," I said. "She said I could never make her happy. But still, there hasn't been a day in these past ten years when I haven't thought about her. I have to rescue her. If only to prove to Julia that she was wrong about me."

"I have no doubt… that you are what she needs, now," said Lennox.

"What about all the other people trapped in the house?" I said. "Am I supposed to steal them, too?"

"This is all about Julia," Lennox said steadily. "I don't know any of the others. And I have been told that just maybe the house will let one of its victims go, when it would fight to keep all of them."

"What is this house?" I said. "How is it doing… what it's doing?"

He shrugged briefly. "Every jungle has its predators. All we can ever really do is try and save the ones we love."

He finished his drink, and left. Didn't look back at me once. I studied the address on the card he'd given me. *The house where Time stands still…*

* * *

Julia. Sometimes I think she was my last chance to be someone else, someone better. When I think of her, it's always the small important things I remember. Walking hand in hand, shoulders pressed together, laughing quietly at some private joke. Slow dancing to a favourite song, lost in the music and the moment. Lying beside her in bed, in the night, watching her sleep. Watching over her.

I tried not to think about how happy we were. About the life we were going to have, and the promises we made to each other. I tried not to remember the look on her face when she told me it was over. Because she knew there was no room for her in the life of a professional thief. Because I wanted us to be rich, more than I wanted her to be happy. She turned her back on me and walked away, and I was left alone. I tried not to remember Julia, because then I wondered what my life might have been like if we hadn't argued. If I might have been happy, instead of merely successful.

* * *

The address on the card was easy enough to find, just a house on a street in one of the more comfortable areas of the city. Not rich, or fashionable, but comfortable. The house before me seemed pleasant enough and perfectly respectable. Nothing out of place, nothing to draw the attention. But I only had to look at the house to know something was wrong. The placid exterior and calm facade were just that little bit too ordinary. Like the false face the monster wears, to fool you into thinking it's just like you. I looked at the house, and I could feel it looking back.

The few people out taking the air that evening passed on by without even glancing at the house. As though it wasn't there; and perhaps for them it wasn't. The house was protecting itself with a *nothing to see here* glamour. But I could see it, and know it for what it was. Because I had trained myself to see what was really in front of me, instead of what I expected.

The secret to any good theft is to do your research. I found a great many references to this particular house, in the kind of books that tell true stories, as opposed to the ones that make it into history books. Like the hidden horrors of Undertowen, the world below; the subterranean galleries and forgotten enclaves where the unwanted people go. The ghost parades of murdered children, stumbling forever through the early hours, weeping silently. The streets that don't go anywhere, and the signposts to places that might have been. The taxi cabs that pick up people who are never seen again. Cities attract people; and people attract predators.

The house where Time stands still was a recent addition. Nothing had moved inside that house since everyone inside was caught between the tick and tock of a stopped clock. No-one knew why. Various people had tried to get in, just on general principle, to see if they might be missing out on something. But how do you force an entrance into a moment of Time that has been taken out of the world?

Well, it helps if you have a key. I hefted it in my hand. Just a simple metal key, with engravings in a language no human being has ever spoken. It was able to undo any lock, open any door, give entrance to any place. The secret of my success. How did I come by such a fantastically useful thing? I stole it, of course.

I walked up the path to the house. All the lights were on, every curtain drawn back, but no sign of anyone. I could feel a tension on the air, and the pressure of unseen watching eyes. My key opened the front door, and I went inside.

* * *

There was a party going on, in absolute silence. The living room was full of men and women standing perfectly still, like living statues. Dressed in their best, like peacocks on parade, smiling happy smiles, posed for a photograph that would never end. Everyone having the best of times, forever. I walked slowly forward, and it was like moving underwater; struggling against the resistance of a constant pressure. Time clung to me like a dead man's hands, trying to hold me back; but as long as I had my key nowhere was closed to me. I moved among the guests and none of them could see me.

They were all frozen in a particular moment, enjoying what pleased them most. Bright young things drank expensive wines, glasses forever tilted against open mouths. Couples danced together, elegantly poised, caught between one step and the next. Several were laughing, heads tilted back to enjoy a joke told ten years ago. All through the house it was the same. In every room unblinking eyes enjoyed the best party ever. No-one stood alone. It was couples everywhere. In the bedrooms, they were having sex. Forever. And when I pressed a cautious fingertip against a bare back, it felt cold and unyielding as stone.

The perfect party, seen from the outside. Joy and laughter, caught in a bottle.

I went back downstairs, and moved among the guests like a ghost at the feast. Staring into one frozen face after another. Until finally I found Julia. Embracing a man I didn't know. She'd been here ten years, holding him close, the two of them lost in each other's eyes.

I'd already worked out what was happening. The house wasn't a prison, and none of these people were trapped here. They'd done this to themselves. Stopped the passing of Time at a moment of their choosing, when they were at their happiest, so they could enjoy it forever. Heaven is a place on earth. But none of that mattered to me. I hadn't come to this house to solve a mystery, I was there to steal one of the guests. I looked at Julia for a long moment. Tall and slender, raven-haired and heart-stoppingly lovely, just as I remembered her. I'd changed, but she hadn't. All the years I'd spent filling my life with things I didn't care about, because I couldn't have the one person I did care about... she'd spent here, in the arms of a tall dark stranger. Did I have the right to destroy a moment of such perfect happiness?

Of course I did. That was what I was being paid to do. I

specialised in taking away the things that other people cared about. And it wasn't as though Julia had given a damn about the happiness she took with her when she walked out on me.

I put a hand on her arm; and then stumbled backwards as she turned her head to look at me. Still smiling. I hadn't done anything to free her; something had changed, in the house. I could feel it. Time was no longer still. Julia let go of her perfect man, and turned to face me. He turned to smile at me as well. People all around stopping drinking and dancing and laughing, and moved to surround me, cutting me off.

"Hello, Andrew," said Julia. "We've been waiting for you. Oh look at you; you got old."

"You look just the same," I said numbly. I nodded to the man she'd been embracing so closely just a moment before. "Who's he?"

"This is Peter. Isn't he lovely? He makes me happy. Unlike you."

"We were happy," I said.

"We were always arguing. That's what drove me away. You never really cared for me. Only for what you wanted me to be."

"I came here to save you!"

"No you didn't," said Julia. "You came here to steal me. Like all the other things you wanted, but couldn't get honestly. You're here because Daddy sent you. Just like he sent all the others, down the years. Because he wants me to be happy. Because he'd do anything for his daughter." She laughed softly. "Did he tell you I was trapped, and needed rescuing? I'm not the maiden in distress, sweetie; I'm the wolf in Granny's clothing. I'm the bait in the trap."

"I don't understand," I said.

"No. You never did; that was the problem. You never listened to me before; but you will now. This house stopped

Time for all of us, so we could be happy forever. Cut free from the tyranny of Time's progress, living constantly in the moment and savouring it. But that takes its toll on the house; so it must be fed. A living sacrifice, once a year. The destruction of one man's happiness, so we can continue to enjoy ours. I'm glad Daddy finally found you. I wouldn't be here, if it hadn't been for you."

"You loved me," I said. "I know you did. Let me take you out of here. You could learn to love me again."

"Love? Why should I want the complications of love, when I can be happy here with Peter, forever and ever?"

I looked desperately around me, and the party guests smiled back. People will do anything in pursuit of happiness. They put back their heads and cried out all at once, and the house answered them. A huge overpowering sound filled the room, like some great mechanism slowing down and grinding to a halt, as the house took all the years of my life, and all the years I might have had. Eating them up, like the predator it was. So Time could stop in the house again, for another year. The guests went back to what they'd been doing, and froze into place. And everyone was happy.

* * *

I've been here ever since. Just a bodiless presence, drifting from room to room. A ghost at the feast. Watching everyone else be happy. I don't know where they found the house, or if it found them. Perhaps one predator can always sense another. Julia was right. I know that now. This was all my fault. Because I stole her heart instead of winning it, and tried to keep it for myself. Now my life has been stolen from me, so everyone else can be happy forever.

I try to be happy for Julia. It's all I've got.

THE SOCIETY OF THE MONSTERHOOD

by

PAUL TREMBLAY

AN EXPLANATION FOR THE READER

You do not speak the languages of our city, certainly not of our neighborhood. You don't because you don't want to. You are as purposefully deaf as you are blind and have been so for so long no one remembers it being any different. This isn't that kind of story.

Nah, fuck that, every story is that kind of story. I want you to know that we know. You may have difficulty understanding the actions of The Society of the Monsterhood, and those difficulties are all yours.

THEY USED TO BE THE NOT-SO-FANTASTIC FOUR

They are our neighbors. They live in the same tenement buildings stacked and leaning against each other like the empty pizza boxes all piled up in that Greek place on Norton Street. They are four of our children; three girls, one boy. Every school-day morning a little white van, a lame school crest with some bullshit Latin motto stenciled on the side in red and black, tiptoes in and picks them up at the corner of North Prospect and Downey. 5:30 AM; too late for trouble, too early for everyone else. When the van picks them up, the sky is dark and metal grates are still pulled down over our storefronts like drawbridges on castles.

Like those *shoppes* with their radioactive orange chips, shit-filled spongey-ass snack cakes, corn syrup sodas, and the cheap (capital *chee*) beer and wine in boxes (a fine vintage for boxing) are our treasures, our lost arks of the covenant.

Look at them in their school uniforms; the girls in blue and green plaid skirts, regimented hems at the kneecaps, blue socks covering up the rest of their legs, white button-down shirts, blue blazers; the boy in too-skinny khaki pants graffitied with stray pencil slashes, the same blue blazer, green tie fastidiously tied, dark hair plastered to his forehead. The van drops them back at the same corner at 6 PM normally, sometimes as late as 8 PM if they are participating in extracurriculars, which they call their "dontwantas," as in their don't-want-to-come-homes. Two of them play sports (even if they aren't very good at them) and one of them is in the drama club (fucking drama club, right?) and the fourth doesn't do anything but read. They are now two months into their freshman year at their K through 12 private school with a tuition more than most of us take home in one year. They won the life-lottery back in fifth grade and go to Our Lady of the Saint Suburb Day School for free. Some of us are happy for them and support them and we are in their ears reminding them of the opportunity they're being given, to not blow it, to not let what everyone (both at their school and here back home) calls them, says to them, does to them, keep them from graduating and getting the hot fuck out of here. Some of us think that hand-picking four kids and only four kids from the neighborhood is bullshit, a slap in the already battered face, a reminder of the exclusion practiced on us unwashed masses every day. Some of us take it out on those four kids. It's not fair and we're not proud of it, but it's something we have to do, are moved to do, as though there is no other way. Kids their age, and the younger ones too, and yeah, the older teens, the dropouts, and sure, the adults who hate them for having the chance they never had, we all make it hard for them. We treat them like traitors; the worst kind of enemy. We say the worst things to them. We sabotage. We punch and kick and steal and cut up their shit.

When they started seventh grade they called themselves the Not-So-Fantastic Four, (one of them reads comics—typical, yeah?) a lame-ass lifeline of self-deprecation that didn't do shit for them. If anything, that bogus nickname made things worse for them, made it sound like they thought they were separate from us, not of us, that they were better than us and they deserved their free education and by proxy, none of us deserved it but them four. So yeah, that nickname thing didn't work out so well for them.

And then they changed their name this year, freshman year. Everything changed this year.

WHAT THEY TOLD US

Early September, and the four of them were starting to look not like shitty-ass kids but gangly, meta-morphin' teenagers; and like all teens they were bigger, louder, stronger, smarter and stupider at the same time, and more dangerous. But how dangerous can you be in that Catholic school uniform, yeah? Still they were now old enough, and more importantly, big enough (attitude, street smarts only get one so far; size matters in these situations) to take out their frustrations on the younger kids who'd follow them around and taunt them (no need to recount exactly what was said; we all heard it when they said it and only some of us would try and make them stop saying it).

The four of them told those little kids (and their not-so-little insults) that they had a new name and no one was going to fuck with them anymore. Then they told those kids they had a new name because they found a monster. They said that on their first day of high school they were waiting for the van in the morning and it was late and the empty 9 bus came blasting through the square and one of them, the tall one, the one who will be beautiful someday to someone, saw it hanging off the rear of the bus, curled up and around the bumper. When the 9 turned the corner that thing fell off and rolled across the street and into the side of the Brazilian market, denting the brick wall. (There is a dent in the wall, down at its base, close to where brick meets sidewalk. No one else knows why that dent is there; or no one else can prove they know why. We check it every day.) One of them said it was a like a giant sloth with arms long as fire hoses. One of them said it had spaghetti-long white hair, like some inner-city Yeti, but that wasn't quite right and didn't explain how it moved like it was made of something other than thick bones. One of them said its fur wasn't really fur and looked more like filaments, tendrils, thin tentacles that were alive and could move and pick up anything it wanted, and she said it wasn't white either; dingy, dirty, slightly changing color to match the sidewalk. The four of them weren't scared so they went to it, and it was just lying there making noises none of them could really describe (though each tried describing and it made less sense than their group attempt at physical description) and without saying a word to each other they helped it up, and when it stood, it was massive, taller than the market, which put it over ten feet. You know, they weren't ever clear on whether or not they actually touched it; they said "helped it up" but didn't detail how they helped it, and they never said what touching it felt like, not from a lack of our asking. Anyway, they directed the fucking thing into that little u-shaped, dead-end alley behind the market and Mr. Chef's and the Dollar Store with dumpsters and trash bags and tied-up corrugated boxes that never get recycled and rats the size of dogs. They said they built it a nest, a home, and they visit it each morning before school to make sure it's okay and they can talk to it without having to talk and one of them always sneaks out at night too, to make sure it's okay, keep it company, feed it. They said if anyone gives them anymore shit about going to school where they go to school, they'll feed their asses to the monster.

And they said they had a new name; they're The Society of the Monsterhood now, which is a dumb-ass name, yeah. Drama geek came up with it. One of them said (as an afterthought, because the story was more weird than threatening at this point) the monster was big, mean, and always hungry.

K.G.: WHAT WE KNOW AND DON'T KNOW HAPPENED TO HIM

K. G. was a big-ass fifteen-year-old, mustache and muscles and attitude. He went to school two, maybe three days a week. He wasn't all that coordinated but he was strong, could take a punch and then give more than he got. The kids said his temper wasn't a temper, it was who he was. He also liked to sing to himself when he didn't think anyone was paying attention to him. He wasn't a very good singer. His dad worked third shift at the electrical plant and while I don't like saying ill of the ill, his mom didn't come home sometimes. A lot of times. K. G. didn't come home all the time either, which was why when he went missing, no one thought it was a big deal for a day or two. Or three.

We know that he called big-time bullshit on the Society's monster story when his little brother came home crying with it, or a version of it. None of us really believed the Society's story and we ignored it. If we didn't ignore it, it was more like we were waiting to see what the repercussions of the story and new group name would be. K. G. was such a repercussion. The morning after the unveiling of the Society, K. G. didn't go to school and he sat at the corner all afternoon and into the early evening, waiting for the white school van to drop the Society off, which it did eventually, and like a sigh of exhaustion. Those four got off with their heads down, not looking at anyone or anything, like playing hide-and-seek with a baby, like if they didn't look then you couldn't see them. How could we not see them? We always saw them.

K. G. didn't even wait for them to get off the van. He started yelling and threatening and he punched the van in its side before it pulled out into traffic. He dented a panel, swear to God. There is a dent in the panel and it looks like the dent in a soda can and the dent in the Brazilian market. We don't know if there's some sort of coincidence or connection there, like there's a special power to the Society's story, like the act of telling it makes things fit, but after, we always talked about K. G. denting the van first like this was where it really started, that the dent was where the monster came from. The van limped away and the rest of us were either laughing or shaking our heads as K. G. yelled at the Society some more and knocked book bags off their shoulders and kicked their feet into each other as they tried to ignore him and walk away, and then he had his thick arm around the boy (who had gotten bigger, but not K. G. big, not even close), squeezing him tight, sneaking in quick gut punches and one oops-my-fault-didn't-mean-it-but-I-did-mean-it head butt. That abuse, it all happened in the short trip from the corner past the dented market to the alley. They stopped at the alley, stood there like acolytes, and stared into it. We don't know if K. G. saw anything. He didn't say. The Society told him to meet them there, same spot, later that night. They told him to come alone. Maybe because he saw it, saw something, sensed something, or maybe it was such a fucked-up weird unexpected request that sounded like a threat (he had to be thinking *did the four of them think they could jump me in the alley and take me?*) so he must not have known what to do or say right then because K. G. only said, "All right," and he let them walk away while he still stood there in front of the alley and not in it.

Some of us saw K. G. walk home after that and some of us saw him milling around the streets. Some of us saw him with friends getting a burrito at the Taqueria and some of us saw him by himself stalking the corner at the Brazilian market that night. I saw him feeling that dent in the wall. I did. No one saw him go into the alley. No one saw him come out. No one from our neighborhood has seen him since. Sure, there are some of us who say that he got in trouble and couldn't get out (so many different kinds of trouble to choose from, you know?) or that he ran away because so many of our teens and kids run away or go missing (monsters or no monsters). Some of us say he's living in another part of the city with his cousins. There's almost anything that could've happened to him.

This is what we know: No one has seen him.

WHAT THEY SAID HAPPENED TO K.G.

The Society said that they didn't do anything. They only met him in the alley that night and watched him with the monster. They said that K. G. walked over to the monster of his own accord (their own words) and he kept saying, "What is it?" and first he got close but not too close; he didn't want to touch it, make contact. If he wasn't full-on afraid, to his credit, he had the proper sense of awe. Then he started acting tough, saying it was nothing but a sick dog, or a couple of sick dogs, and he pushed all the kids away from him. The drama geek bounced off the back wall of Mr. Chef and she later showed us a scab on the back of her head from the bouncing. The Society said it was all over once he did that and there was nothing they could do to protect him, save him. There was no turning back. They said he had his chance. The monster filled the alley and grabbed K. G. with two monster hands at the end of two monster arms and it pulled him into its mouth. Its mouth was open wider than a freeway and took up more than half its body, then its whole body; it became all mouth. And teeth. There were teeth, they said. Big, jagged triangles that dripped saliva and digestive juices. They told everyone that the monster ate K. G., and that the eating wasn't clean, wasn't a sit-down restaurant eating. It was messy. It tore him apart, literally. Biting and pulling him into twitching, quivering pieces. They said it was the worst thing you could ever see. The Society said they were forced to read *Beowulf* at school and what happened to K. G. was way worse than what Grendel ever did. They said they named their monster Grendel too, and the alley was now Grendel's Den, (too-smart-for-their-own-good assholes always naming everything, right?). The Society said they don't want to see it do what it did to K. G. ever again, so please do not pick on us anymore.

WHAT WE FOUND

Nothing.

After K. G. was missing for a fourth day, a whole bunch of us went into the alley and couldn't find anything other than what was supposed to be in an alley. No evidence of a nest, never mind a Grendel's Den. No signs of a great struggle. Certainly no blood or spit-up bones and clothes and sneakers, no ooze or ick that would be expected leave-behinds from a ravenous monster. And no monster. It was an alley damp with garbage and stink, and it rumbled and echoed with the buses, trucks, and cars that needed new mufflers. Just an alley, right? But it wasn't just an alley. Something had happened there. We could sense it. There was the unease of the aftermath, aftereffects, afterimages of violence. It's like a presence and the lack of a presence at the same time; the feeling you get when you stare at a broken window, you know? We had that feeling and that's all we had, and we argued about it and then we got angry because, come on now, the monster was bullshit.

We went to the Society's apartments and we banged on their doors. We demanded they address us, answer our questions. We confronted them with all the nothing we found (including K. G. in that nothing—where was he? where did he go?).

Each one of the Society, with their solemn and mummified parents standing behind them, eyeing us, told us that K. G. deserved what he got and if we got it too well then we deserved it (and maybe they were right about some of us, but fuck them for saying it). They told us the story of K. G. and the monster again, and ended the story with, "Leave us alone. Or else." They all said the same thing, like they were giving out a practiced statement.

They didn't really say the *or else* part out loud but it was there if you were listening. We heard it. All four times.

THERE ARE MANY MORE WHO WENT MISSING

Every school night after we confronted the Society there was someone else there at the corner to meet them when the van dropped them off. It became the new normal, which is to say it was like this goddamn ritual; it was something that just happened and we were supposed to accept, deal with, like everything else shitty we were supposed to accept, deal with, and to our immense shame we followed the unspoken rules. But don't think you are any different. You would simply follow the rules too. That's the truth.

The van and the Society weren't overrun by a wave of angry and righteous humanity. There'd be just one kid, barely taller than a fire hydrant, or one teen who was confused about everything, confused about why things were the way they were, or one adult who'd given up on trying to figure out why things were the way they were. There'd be a *whoever* there every night and whoever would punch the van in the same spot K. G. punched the van and then whoever would be led over to the alley, the empty fucking alley. (We'd checked that alley, remember? Empty. And we would check it again and it would still be empty the next day after another whoever would go missing.) And then at night, again inexplicably following the inexplicable rules, whoever would come back and go into that alley with the Society and whoever would disappear.

It's late October now and I want to make some comparison to fallen leaves, because, you know, it's fucking autumn, but comparing our missing persons to leaves is wrong, so wrong that you almost don't notice how wrong it is.

Anyway, in the early evening, we would also go back to the Society's apartments. (Our little group was growing larger as the number of people, mostly kids, who went missing also grew larger.) We would knock on their doors just like we did for K. G. We wouldn't expect answers or satisfactory conclusion, and our demands of action were more feckless and desperate. The Society wouldn't lose patience with us, they would repeat the same story each night and tell us to leave them alone.

YOU AND I GO INTO THE ALLEY AND THEN LEAVE IT

The youngest kid yet is there, sitting on the corner. He can't be more than eight or nine. He sits on the curb, hands on knees, rolling an empty bottle between his feet. I don't know his name. I ask him what it is when I walk by and he doesn't answer me.

I ask where his parents are or his grandparents, a grandmother? You got to have a grandmother around here, I say, and then I ask why isn't he in school and he doesn't tell me shit. I walk up and reconnect my ass with the front stairs of my building, only a few doors down from the corner. I watch the kid watching for the van. I imagine the monster, if there is one (how can there be one? how can there not be one?), wouldn't have to open its mouth all that much to eat him. I don't know about you and everyone else, but I can't abide by this anymore. Something has to change. We have to change it.

The van rolls in. Kid doesn't move from the curb and makes the van stick out into the street. Cabs and cars beep at it lazily as they swerve by. The Society gets out of the van. They look older. In two months how did they get so much older? They're still just kids, we need to remind ourselves. The other kid, the little one, sitting on the corner, he stands up and throws that glass bottle off the side of the van. The bottle explodes into glittering shards. It's almost beautiful. The van doesn't stop and drunkenly waddles off on its christened voyage. I stay on my stairs, on my stoop, and I don't do anything. Not yet. It's too early. I can see what I need to see from here, for now. The Society doesn't say anything to the kid and the kid doesn't say anything to them and together they walk over to the mouth of the alley. Yeah, it's an obvious mouth, isn't it. They stand and stare and nothing special seems to happen, not that I can see. Time doesn't slow down, the city doesn't stop doing its city thing, and we know the city is a monster too and we're already inside of it.

The Society walks away first, like they always do, but they'll come back. The kid stays there. He sits down, right on the sidewalk, a period placed in the middle of a sentence. When we walk by (because we have shit to do, city being city, like I said) he doesn't move and we have to go around him. I walk by him three times and each time I pass I tell him to go home, to forget about it, go eat dinner. He doesn't do anything. Fucking kid is so small and thin; hands and feet like a puppy's. I get him one of those sports drinks and a protein bar. Not much of a dinner but it's better than nothing. To my surprise, the kid takes it from me and drinks and eats. He tells me in his hardest voice (still little, still small, and it breaks our already broken hearts) that he's K. G.'s brother. (We should've known that.) He tells me to go back to my stoop. I tell him that I'll be back later.

I'm watching him and watching for the Society as the street lamps flicker on and the temperature drops, and it drops fast now as the sun flees behind the building tops. Hours go by and I keep watch. I don't get distracted. The rest of us walk by the kid and the alley like nothing is going to happen there, like we're not supposed to look.

Later. The Society of the Monsterhood shows up, and they show up one at a time, each from a different direction. The kid doesn't get up off the sidewalk until the four of them are there.

I yell out at them. That's all I have to do to stop it, right? Dumb-ass that I am hoping it's that easy to stop whatever it is that's going to happen. The Society ignores my rants from the stoop and walk into the alley first, one at a time, single file, a progression. I'm off my stairs and running (I can't run that fast, not anymore, and it's less a run and more a fast limp), and I need to get there to stop the kid from going into the alley. He's too young (would him being two years older, five, ten, make a difference?). He's too everything. This isn't right. We've all had enough of the monster, and yeah we all believe there is a monster, we always did.

The city is still the city. It doesn't stop for this, or for us; it never has and never will. I'm not quite sure how I manage to do it, but I must be faster than I think because I get to the alley before K. G.'s brother goes in. I grab his shirt, the back of his collar, and he yells and hits my arms. He squirms out of my grasp but had to go backwards, away from the alley to do so. I'm not fast or strong or tough, or that kind of tough, anymore, but I'm big enough to block the entry to the alley. K. G.'s brother is full-on crying now and he tries to scoot by me, to scramble under my legs, but I stop him. He yells at me and says things a kid his age shouldn't know how to say so well. I tell him in a quiet voice to go home. He doesn't give, and he's wearing me down. I'm breathing hard enough that there's a stitch, a little knife in my chest. He rams into my stomach, shoulder-first, but I push back, harder than I should, and he goes flying backwards and lands on his butt on the sidewalk. I say, "Please." Maybe the please does it. Or maybe he just gives up. I don't know. I don't exactly see him go away because I take the opportunity with him stunned and on his ass to turn and run into the alley ahead of him. Only one of us can go in, right? That's the rule.

And it's still just a fucking alley. That's it. Garbage cans and dumpsters and bins all spray-painted different colors. Black skeletons of fire escapes dripping high up from the back walls. There's no monster.

The Society of the Monsterhood stand up against the back of the Brazilian market. If they're surprised to see me come in and not the little kid, they don't say it or show it. The Society holds a chair leg, a piece of rebar, a folded-in-half NO PARKING sign, a metal rod that might've had a bike seat on its end once. They stare at me. They stare at me and hold those things like weapons.

I yell at them, ask them what the hell they think they're doing, some half-assed gang, ready to, what, beat down that little fucking kid out there who doesn't know any better, and now me, instead? They don't react. I lose it and I'm yelling all the terrible and unfair things that have been said to them by some of us and I yell the stuff that I know they've been hearing at their rich white school too; I make sure to say those things, to say everything. And then I hear it behind me, coming up from underneath the garbage bags, growing from out of nothing. It knocks over the barrels and even flips one of the dumpsters and black, garbage-smelling dumpster water rushes over the tops of my sneakers. It's bigger than I am, so much bigger, and it's humanoid for an instant and then it's not, and how it moves, like a movie with frames missing, and it's kind of white, then it's dark, and has two arms, then more, then none, and it grows and shrinks, expands, retracts, and it's coming toward me. I turn away and the Society are walking toward me too, and I'm shaking and my legs won't work anymore, so I bend down, a dead-battery robot; one knee crash lands on the dampened alley floor. The Society all raise their weapons over their heads and over my head for their mightiest swings and smashes but they sail right by me and attack the monster. And I mean they fucking attack it, wildly swinging their weapons. I scuttle away and don't get too far, sitting on my butt like that little kid was, and I watch. At first I'm thinking that I got through to the Society, showed them how wrong this all is; yes, I got through to them and now this will be the end. I watch them hit the thing, bashing it like a piñata, and opening holes in it, and there is blood, and then they lose their weapons but they beat it with their bare hands and they snap its arms and legs over their knees and stab and pry with their fingers and tear open deep gashes in its hide, in its skin, and the sounds the monster makes, so awful, I can hear it without my ears. I know that this isn't happening because of what I said or did; this is what happens every time they take a whoever into the alley and to the monster. They do this every time.

I'm crying and I can't help it because they won't stop and the monster looks like a toy with everything twisted and warped into unnatural directions, and it twitches, painfully trying to correct itself, and it's the worst thing I've ever seen. The beating goes on for hours but they don't kill it. I can still hear it and see it breathing.

The Society does stop, finally. They stop. And they stumble out of the alley without saying anything to me or to each other. The monster is still there, smaller than it was before, or maybe it's always been that size and what I remembered from before is a trick, you know? I'm already not sure what I just saw earlier or even what I'm seeing now. But what I do know is that I'm going to disappear from this neighborhood too. I'm going to get up and walk down to the Downey St. Metro stop and get on the train and take it to somewhere else and I'll never come back. How can I come back here after all we did and didn't do, and then seeing this? How can any of us? This isn't to say I know where the rest of us went when we disappeared because I don't. We just go.

It's cold out but I'm not cold. I stand up and the stitch in my chest is gone and my legs work again. Maybe I won't take the Metro and I'll just walk. And then I get this idea. Shit, it's the best idea that I've ever had: I'm going to take the monster with me. I am. It's that simple. I can save everyone else in the neighborhood from this continuing madness. I can save us and you and take away this poor, terrible thing that's blighted our neighborhood for two months, has always blighted our neighborhood.

I go over to the monster and I'm not sure how to pick it up, how to get my arms around it and its ripped and rented pelt, broken and bent corners, holes leaking blood and fluids, mouth somewhere leaking pitiful cries. Its fur feels mealy, like the hair (is it hair? something else entirely?) will slough off at my touch, but it doesn't. It stays together. I feel it straining to stay together for me and it allows me to compact it gently, a collection of untied, loose sticks. I sling some of it over my shoulder and hold the rest of it to my chest with both arms. I try not to gag at its smell and then one step, two steps, and I'm walking out of the alley.

Concentrating on walking away, going away, disappearing, and as I'm walking out of my neighborhood and into the next and then the next and then the next my biggest fear is not that the monster will heal and subsequently attack my sorry ass (this thing will never heal, it'll be broken forever). No, my biggest fear is that my best-idea-ever isn't so best, you know?

What if all those who went missing before me are walking around in their somewhere-else carrying their own busted-up monster too?

THE MAW

by
NATHAN BALLINGRUD

1

Mix was about ready to ditch the weird old bastard already. Too slow, too clumsy, too loud. Not even a block into Hollow City and already they'd captured the attention of one of the wagoneers, and in her experience you could almost clap your hands in front of their faces and they wouldn't know it. Experience, though; that was the key word. She had it and he didn't, and it was probably going to get him killed. But she'd be goddamned if she'd let it get her killed too.

She pulled him into an alcove and they waited quietly until the thing had passed.

"You need to rest?" she said.

"No I don't need to rest," he snapped. "Keep going."

Mix was seventeen years old, and anybody on the far side of fifty seemed inexcusably ancient to her, but she reckoned this man to be pretty old even by those standards. He was spry enough to walk through streets cluttered with the detritus and the debris of long abandonment without too much difficulty, but she could see the strain in his face, the sheen of sweat on his forehead. And a respectable pace for an old man was still just a fraction of the speed she preferred to move at while in Hollow

City. She'd been stupid to take his money, but she'd always been a stupid girl. Just ask anybody.

They turned a corner and the last checkpoint, a little wooden shack with a lantern gleaming in a window, disappeared from view. It might as well have been a hundred miles away. The buildings hulked into the cloudy sky around them, windows shattered and bellied with darkness. The doors of little shops gaped like open mouths. Glass pebbled the sidewalk. Rags of newspapers, torn and scattered clothing, and tangles of bloody meat lay strewn across the pavement. Cars lined the sidewalks in their final repose. Life still prospered here, to be sure: rats, roaches, feral cats and dogs; she'd even seen a mother bear and her train of cubs once, moving through the ruined neighborhood like a fragment of a better dream. The place seethed with it. But there weren't any people anymore. At least, not the way she used to think of people.

"Dear God," the man said, and she stopped. He shuffled into the middle of the street, shoulders slouched, his face slack as a dead man's. His eyes roved over the place, taking it all in. He looked frail, and lonely, and scared; which, she supposed, is exactly what he was. Despite herself, she felt a twinge of sympathy for him. She followed him, took his elbow, and pulled him back into the relative shadow of the sidewalk.

"Hard to believe this is all just a few blocks away from where you live, huh?"

He swallowed, nodded.

"But listen to me, okay? You gotta listen to me, and do what I say. No walking out in the middle of the street. We stay quiet, we keep moving, we don't draw attention. Don't think I won't leave your ass if you get us in trouble. Do you understand me?"

He disengaged his elbow from her hand. At least he had the decency to look embarrassed. "Sorry," he said. "This is just my

first time seeing it since I left. At the time it was just, it was…
it was just chaos. Everything was so confused."

"Yeah, I get it." She didn't want to hear his story. Everybody
had one. Tragedy gets boring after a while.

Hollow City was not a city at all, but a series of city blocks
that used to be part of the Fleming and South Kensington
neighborhoods, and had acquired its own peculiar identity over
the last few months. Its informal name came from its emptiness:
each building a shell, scoured of life, whether through evacuation
or the attentions of the surgeons. The atmosphere had long
turned an ashy gray, as though under perpetual cloud cover,
even around the city beyond the afflicted neighborhood. Lamps
burned all the time, but not in here. Electricity had been cut off
weeks ago. Nevertheless, light still swelled from isolated pockets,
as though furnaces were being stoked to facilitate some awful
labor transpiring beyond the sight of the surrounding populace.

"There's things coming up that're gonna be hard to see," she
said. "You ready for that?"

The old man looked disgusted. "I don't need to be lectured
on what's hard to see by a child," he said. "You have no idea
what I've seen."

"Yeah, well, whatever. Just don't freak out. And hustle it up."

Mix did not want to be here after the sun went down. She
figured they had five good hours. Plenty of time for the old
bastard to find who he was looking for, or—more likely—
realize there was no one left to find.

They continued along the sidewalk, walking quickly but
quietly. The rhythmic squeaking of unoiled wheels came
from around a corner ahead, accompanied by the sound of
several small voices holding a single high note in unison, like a
miniature boys' choir. Mix put out her hand to stop him. He
must not have been paying attention, because he walked right

into it before stuttering to a halt. She felt the thinness of his chest, the sparrow-like brittleness of his bones. Guilt welled up from some long-buried spring in her gut: she had no business bringing him here on his stupid errand. It was doomed, and he was doomed right along with it. She should have told him no. There were other ways to make money. Another client would have come along eventually. Except that fewer and fewer people were paying to be escorted through Hollow City, and those that were tended to be adrenaline junkies, who were likely to get you killed, or—worse—religious nuts and artists, who felt entitled to bear witness to what was happening here due to some perceived calling. It was a species of narcissism that offended her on an obscure, inarticulate level. A few weeks ago she had guided a poet out to the center of the place and almost slipped away while he scribbled furiously, self-importantly, in his notebook. The temptation was stronger than she would have believed possible; she'd fantasized about how long she'd hear him calling out for her before the surgeons stopped his tongue for good, or turned it to other purposes.

She didn't leave the poet, but she learned that there was an animal living inside her, something that celebrated when nature did its work upon the weak. She came to value that animal. She knew it would keep her alive.

This sudden guilt, then, was both unexpected and unwelcome. She set her jaw and waited for it to subside.

The prow of a wheelbarrow emerged from beyond the corner of the building, followed by its laden body, the wooden wheels turning in slow, wobbling rotations. The barrow was filled with the gray, hacked torsos of children, some sprouting both arms, most with less, but all still wearing their heads, eyes rolled back to reveal the whites with little exploded capillaries standing in bright contrast to the gray pallor, each mouth rounded into an ellipse from which emitted that single, perfect note, as heartbreakingly beautiful as anything heard in one of God's cathedrals. Then the wagoneer hoved into view, its naked body blackened and wasted, comprised of just enough gristle and bone to render it ambulatory. The skin on its face was shrunken around its skull, and a withered crown of long black hair rustled like straw in the breeze. It turned its head, and for the second time that day they found themselves speared into place by a wagoneer's stare. This one actually stopped its movement and leaned closer, as if committing their faces to memory, or transferring the sight of them via some infernal channel to a more distant intelligence, which might answer their intrusion with punishment.

Her gaze still fixed on the wagoneer, Mix reached behind and grabbed the old man's wrist. "We have to run," she said.

2

The dog was gone. Carlos realized it at once, and a gravity took him, a feeling of aging so suddenly and so completely that he half expected to die right there. He looked at the kitchen floor and wondered if he would hurt himself in the fall. Instead, he pulled a chair from the kitchen table and collapsed into it, settling his head onto the table, his arms dangling at his sides. A great sadness moved inside him, turning in his chest, too big to be voiced. It threatened to break him in half.

Maria had been with him for fifteen years. A scruffy tan mutt, her muzzle gone gray and her eyes rheumy, they were walking life's last mile together. Carlos had never married; he'd become so acclimated to his loneliness that eventually the very idea of human companionship just made him antsy and tired.

It was not as though he'd had to fight for his independence; his demeanor had grown cold and mean as he aged, not from any ill feeling toward other people, but simply from an unwillingness to endure their eccentricities. He had a theory that people warped as they aged, like old records left out in the sun, and unless you did it together and warped in conformity to each other, you eventually became incapable of aligning with anybody else.

Well, he'd grown old with Maria, that grand old dame, and she was all he needed or wanted.

When the tremors had started in Fleming, and the nights started filling with the screams of neighbors and strangers alike, he and Maria had huddled together in his apartment. He'd kept his baseball bat clutched in his thin, spotted hands while Maria bristled and growled at his side. She'd always been a gentle dog, frightened by visitors, scurrying under the bed at a loud knock, but now she had found a core of steel within herself and she stood between him and the door, her lips peeled from her yellowed teeth, prepared to hurl her frail old body against whatever might come through it. That, even more than the screaming outside, convinced him that whatever was out there was something to fear.

On the second night, the door was kicked in and bright flashlights sprayed into his apartment, the commanding voices of men piling into the room like something physical. Maria's whole body shook and snapped with fear and rage, her own hoarse barking pushing back at them, but when Carlos recognized what they were saying, he wrapped his arms around his dog and held her tight, whispering in her ear. "It's okay, baby, it's okay, little mama, calm down, calm down. Calm down."

And she did, though she still trembled. The police, one of them sobbing unashamedly, loaded them both into a van parked at the bottom of the apartment building, not giving him any grief about taking the dog, thank God. He cast a quick glance down the street before a hand shoved him inside with a few of his terrified neighbors, huddled in their pajamas, and slammed the door behind him. What he saw was impossible. A man, eight feet tall or more, skinny as a handful of sticks, crossing a street only a block away with eerie, doe-like grace. He was a shape in the sodium lights, featureless and indistinct, like a child's drawing of a nightmare. He was stretching what looked like thin, bloody parchment from one streetlight to another; suspended from one end of the parchment was a human arm, flexing at the elbow again and again, like an animal in distress.

He looked at his neighbors, but he didn't know any of their names. They weren't talking, anyway.

Then the van surged to life, moving with ferocious speed to a location only a mile distant, behind a battery of checkpoints and blockades, and rings of armed officers.

Carlos and his dog were provided with a small apartment—even smaller than the one they'd been living in—in tenement housing, with as many of the other residents of the besieged neighborhood as could be evacuated. The building was overcrowded, and the previous residents received these newcomers with a gamut of reactions ranging from sympathy to resentment to outright anger. The refugees greeted their new hosts in kind.

No one knew exactly what was happening in South Kensington and Fleming. Rumors spread that a tribe of kids, homeless or in gangs or God knows what, had started charging people to go in looking for people or items of value left behind, or sometimes even chaperoning people to their old homes. Though some minor effort had been made to quell these activities, the little industry managed to thrive. It disgusted Carlos; someone was always ready to make a dollar, no matter what the circumstance.

It was thanks to them, though, that news bled back of the old neighborhood transformed, stalked by weird figures pushing wheelbarrows or hauling huge carts of human wreckage, strange music drifting from empty streets, the tall figures—surgeons, some called them—knitting people together in grotesque configurations. Buildings were empty, some completely hollowed out, as though cored from within, leaving nothing but their outer shells. The kids sneaking back inside starting calling it Hollow City, and the name stuck. Which was just one more thing Carlos hated. The old place had a name. Two names, in fact. There was a history there, lives had been lived there. It didn't deserve some stupid comic-book tag. It had belonged to humanity once.

A gray pallor hung over the place, slowly expanding until most of the real city was covered. Carlos believed it was responsible for the way people acclimated too quickly to the transformation of the old neighborhoods. Apathy took root like a weed. Police kept up the blockades, but they were indifferently manned, and the kids' scouting efforts grew in proportion. The Army never came in. No one in the tenements knew whether or not they were even called. There was nothing about this on the news. It was as though the city suffered its own private nightmare, which would continue unobserved until it could wake up and talk about it, or until it died in its sleep.

Carlos was resigned to let it play out in the background. He was nothing if not adaptive, and it did not take long for him to accept his reduced surroundings. It was noisy, chaotic, the walls were thin, but these things had been true of his old apartment, too. Sound was a comfort to him; he might not have friends, but his spirit was eased by the human commotion. He would have died there, as close to contentment as he might get, if only Maria had stayed with him.

He knew Maria was gone almost instantly, well before he hobbled out of bed and saw the apartment door ajar. He could feel her absence, like a pocket of airlessness. And he knew immediately that she'd gone back to her old home. What he didn't know was why. Was there something there that called her? Was she confused? Did the place mean more to her than he did? Her absence almost felt like a betrayal, like a spade digging into his heart.

But she was Maria. He would go and get her. He would bring her home.

* * *

Everything had gone lax at the border to the old neighborhood. The checkpoints seemed to be devoid of the police altogether; only these kids now, living in makeshift shacks, sleeping on mattresses harvested from local housing or perhaps from the afflicted area, living out of boxes and suitcases and school backpacks. Carlos knew he ought to be grateful for it, because it would only help him get back inside, but a part of him couldn't help but despair for the continued decline of responsibilities and standards in the hands of this privileged youth. It's good to be old, he thought. I'll be dead before they've finished their work on this world.

It took a while to find anybody willing to give him the time of day. He knew they considered him too risky: old, slow, fragile. But eventually he found one who would: a girl with a shaved head, dressed in a dark blue hoodie and jeans, who called herself Mix. Ridiculous name; why did they do that? Why couldn't they just be who they were? She considered the three crumpled twenties he offered her, and accepted them with poor grace. She turned her back to him, reaching into a box she kept by her sleeping bag and jamming it with bottles of water, a first aid kit, and what looked like a folded knife. She interrogated him as she packed.

"What are we looking for?"

"Maria," he said.

She stopped, turned and looked at him with something like contempt. "You know she's dead, right?"

"No. I don't know that at all."

"Do you know anything about what's going on in there?"

He flashed back to the tall man—one of the surgeons, he supposed—stretching the twitching human parchment between streetlights. "Sure," he said. "It's Hell."

"Who knows what the fuck it is, but there's no one left alive in there. At least, no one that can be saved."

A swell of impatience threatened to overwhelm him. He would go in alone if he had to. What he would not do was stand here being condescended to by an infant. "Do you want my money or not?"

"Yeah I want it. But you have to follow my rules, okay? Stay quiet and stay moving. Keep to the sidewalks at all times, and close to the walls when you can. They mostly ignore stragglers, unless they're traveling in big groups or making some kinda scene. If one of them notices you, stay still. Usually they just move on."

"What if they don't?"

"Then I make it up on the fly. And you do exactly what I fucking say." She waited until he acknowledged this before continuing. "And whenever we realize this Maria or whoever is dead, we get the fuck out again. Like, immediately."

"She's not dead."

Mix zipped up her backpack and slung it over her shoulder. "Yeah, okay. Maybe you think you're the hero in a movie or something. You're not. You're just some old guy making a bad choice. So listen to me. Once *I'm* sure she's dead, I am leaving. If you come with me I'll make sure you get back out safe. If you stay behind, that's on you."

"Fine. Can we go?"

"Yeah, let's go. Where are we looking?"

"Home. She'll have gone home." He gave her the address.

She sighed. "Old man, that building has been cored. There's nothing inside."

"That's where she is."

Mix nodded, already turning away from him. Already, in some sense, finished. "Whatever you say."

3

She yanked him around, as close to panic as she'd been in weeks, and they walked briskly back in the direction they'd come. She wanted to run, but either he couldn't or he wouldn't. It wasn't until he wrenched his wrist free of her grip, though, that she considered leaving him there. The animal inside her started to pace.

He stood resolutely in place, rubbing the place she'd grabbed him. Behind him, in the dense gray air, the wagoneer still watched, its lidless eyes shedding a dim yellow light. The thin choir of dismembered bodies held their sustained note. She'd been glanced at before, but none had ever stopped and stared until now. She thought about the knife in her backpack. An affectation. So stupid. Unless she gutted this old man right here and ran while the things fell upon him instead.

"Where are you going?" he said. He wasn't even trying to be quiet anymore. His voice bounced down the empty street, came back at them like a strange reflection of itself.

Out, she wanted to say. We're getting out. But instead, she said, "We'll go around. A detour. Hurry." She wasn't a dumb kid. She had a job. She would do it. She could handle this.

"Okay," he said, showing her a little deference for the first time. He joined her, even picking up his pace. "I thought you were going to leave me."

"Fuck you, I'm not leaving." She could hear the tears in her voice and she hated herself for it. Stupid girl. That's what they called her. They were right all along.

They doubled back, turned a corner, pursuing a longer route to the address. Mix glanced behind her often, sure they were being followed, but the wagoneer was nowhere to be seen.

The streets had continued to transform since last she'd been here. The wagoneers hauled their cartloads of human remains, coming from some central location and depositing them in moldering piles throughout Hollow City, where the surgeons continued to stitch them together into grotesque, seemingly meaningless configurations: there were more torsos like the ones they had just seen strung like bunting from one side of the street to the other, each one tuned to a different pitch; great kites of skin flapped tautly in similar fashion, punched through with holes of varying sizes and patterns, as though a kind of Morse code had been pierced into them with an awl; skeletal structures made from the combined parts of a hundred rendered people loomed between the buildings in great, stilled wheels, fitting together like cogs in some grotesque engine. The bone wheels had been hastily assembled, still wet with blood and dripping with rags of meat. The eyes of the workers boiled with furnace-light as they toiled, and the air grew steadily colder.

Mix stopped, hugging the corner of what had once been a 24-hour drug store. Blood splashed the interior of the picture window now, obscuring whatever was inside. She plotted their course in her head, and realized with a buckle of disbelief that the address they were going to—the building she knew from reports of the others had been cored from the inside—seemed to be the center of the wagoneers' activity.

If Carlos was impatient with her stopping, he gave no sign. He was leaning against the wall too, breathing heavily. His eyes were unfocused, and she wondered how much of this he was taking in.

"You still alive back there?" she said.

"I think so. Hard to tell anymore." He made a vague gesture. "What is all this?"

"Shit, you're asking me? It's just another bad dream, I guess. You're the one with all the life experience, you ought to recognize one by now." When he didn't respond, she said, "So, you seen enough now?"

"What do you mean?"

She pointed ahead, to where his old apartment building hulked into the sky a little over a block away. The desiccated bodies of the wagoneers came and went from inside with a clockwork regularity. "There's no one left in there, old man. That's fucking grand central station."

"No. She's in there."

For a moment, Mix couldn't speak through the rage. The degree of obliviousness he was displaying, the absolute blind faith in an impossible outcome, had just crossed the border from desperate hope to outright derangement. He was crazy, probably had been for some time, and now he was going to get them both killed. Or worse than killed. The thing inside her paced and growled. She was ready to let it out at last.

She felt a curious dread about it. Not at his fate—he'd bought that for himself—but at the simple act of walking away, and at the border she would be crossing within herself by doing it. It was one she had always taken pride in being ready to cross, but now that the moment had come, she was afraid of it, and afraid of the world that waited for her on the other side. She pressed her forehead against the wall, closed her eyes, and listened to the strange sounds the new architecture of flesh created around her: the gorgeous notes, the flag-like snapping, the hollow tone of bones clattering in the wind. It reminded her of the various instruments in her school band tuning themselves before a concert. She heard him breathing beside her, too, heavily and quickly, as he expended what she knew were his final energies on this suicidal quest.

"So who is she, anyway? Your wife? Your daughter?"

"No. She's my dog."

It was as though he had said something in a foreign language. She needed a moment to translate it into something she could understand. When it happened, the last beleaguered rank of resistance inside her folded, and she started to laugh. It was quiet, almost despairing, and she couldn't stop it. She pressed her face into the stone wall and laughed through her clenched teeth.

The absurdity of it all.

"She's my dog," Carlos said, a little defensively. "She's my only friend. I'm going to bring her home."

"Your home is gone," she said, the thin stream of giggles reaching its end, giving way instead to a huge sadness, the kind that did not seem to visit her but instead emerged from within, as much a part of her body as a liver or a spleen. She wanted to hate the old man but what she felt for him wasn't hate. It was something complicated and awful and unknown to her, but hate was too simple a word to describe it. If she had ever loved a child still innocent of its first heartbreak, she might have known the feeling. But she wasn't a parent; and anyway, she couldn't remember love.

"A dog," she said.

Carlos stood beside her, the aesthetic of Hell manifested around him, an abyssal acoustic being built by its wretched servants, and he looked like what he was: a slumped, fading old man, lonely in the world but for one simple animal, and fully aware of the impossibility of retrieving it. His speech was defiant but his mind had already recognized the truth, and she could see it erode him even as she watched, like a sand dune in a strong wind.

Somewhere in this bloody tangle of bone and flesh, maybe even some still-muttering faces affixed to a wall with an unguent excreted from the lungs of the surgeons, were her parents, their cold anger still seeping from their tongues, their self-loathing and their resentment still animating the flayed muscles in their peeled faces. She could hear them as clearly as ever.

Stupid girl.

God damn them anyway.

"All right," she said. "Let's go get your dog."

4

The girl was careful, but there was no need to sneak. What could they do to him? Death wasn't shit. Carlos knew he should tell her to leave—it was obvious he wasn't going to be coming back, with or without Maria—but it was her choice to make. Life was long or short, and it meant something or it didn't. It wasn't his business to tell her how to measure hers.

The walls of his old apartment building bowed slightly, as though some great pressure grew from within. The doors had been torn off and the windows broken, though, and he could see nothing inside but shadow. Pacing the perimeter of the building were three dark-robed figures, their heads encased in black iron boxes. They exuded a monastic patience, moving slowly and with obvious precision. The lead figure held an open book in his left hand, scribbling busily into it with his right. The one in the middle swung a censer, a black orb from which spilled a heavy yellow smoke. The scent of marigolds carried over to him. The figure in the back held aloft a severed head on a pole, which emitted a beam of light from its wrenched mouth.

Carlos waited for these figures to pass before approaching the doors as casually as if he belonged there. Mix made a sound of protest, but he ignored her. A surgeon emerged from the doors just as he reached them, stooping low to fit, but though it cast him a curious glance, it did not interfere with him, or even break its stride. It stretched itself to its full height and walked away, thin hands trailing long needles of bone and bloody thread. It moved slowly and languidly, like something walking underwater.

He moved to enter the building, but Mix restrained him from behind and edged in front of him instead. She held her left arm across his chest, protectively, as they crept forward; in her right she held the knife she'd stashed in her backpack, unfolded into an ugly silver talon. He didn't know what had changed her mind about him, but he was grateful for it.

Though barely enough light intruded into the building to see anything by, it was immediately obvious that the girl had been right: the building's expansive interior had been scooped clean, leaving nothing but the outer walls, like the husk of an insect following a spider's feast. A great, wet hole had opened in the earth beneath it, almost as deep as the building's foundation. The hole looked like a gaping wound, raw and bloody, its walls sloping inward and meeting a hundred feet down in a moist, clutching glottis. Above it, the walls and ceiling had been sprayed with its meaty exhalations, red organic matter pasted over them so that they resembled the underside of a tongue.

Bodies of residents who'd been unable to evacuate were glued to the far wall with a thick yellow resin; even as they watched, one Carlos recognized as a young cashier at a local take-out was peeled from his perch and subjected to the attentions of a cleaver-wielding surgeon, who quickly quartered him with a series of heavy and efficient chops. The cashier's limbs quivered yet, and his mouth gaped in wonderment at his own butchering. But instead of a cry or a scream, what emerged from him was a pure note, as clean and undiluted as anything heard on Earth. Tears sprang to Carlos's eyes at the beauty of it, and ahead of him Mix put her hand over her lowered face, the curved knife glinting dully by her ear, a gesture of humility or of supplication.

"Maria," Carlos said, and there she was, snuffling through piled offal in a far corner, her snout filthy, her hair matted and sticky. The laborers of Hell walked around her without concern, and she seemed undisturbed by them as well. When she heard Carlos call her name, she answered with a happy bark and bounded over to him, spry for the moment, slamming the side of her body into his legs and lifting her head in grateful joy as he ran his gnarled fingers through her fur. Carlos dropped to his knees, heedless of the bright pain, of how difficult it would be to rise again. His dog sprawled into his lap. For a moment, they were happy.

And then Carlos thought, *You left me. You left me in the end. Why?* He hugged his dog close, burying his nose in her fur. He knew there was no answer beyond the obvious, constant imbalance in any transaction of the heart. *You don't love me the way I love you.*

He forgave her for it. There really wasn't anything else he could do.

5

Mix watched them from a few feet away, the knife forgotten in her hand. She knew why the dog had come here. She could feel it; if the old man would leave the animal alone for a moment, he would too. The sound coming through that great, open throat in the ground, barely heard but thrumming in her blood, had called it here. She felt it like a density in the air, a gravity in the heart. She felt it in the way the earth called her to itself, with its promise of loam and worms, so that she sat down too, beside them but apart, unwelcome in their reunion.

Stupid girl. You weren't invited. You don't belong. You never did.

The sound from the hole grew in volume. It was an answer to loneliness, and a call to the forgotten. It was Hell's lullaby, and as the long tone blew from the abyss it filtered out through the windows and the doors and it caught in the reedlike parchments of skin and set them to keening, it powered the wheels of bone so they clamored and rattled and chimed, and it blended with the chorus of notes from the suspended bodies until the whole of the city became as the bell of a great trumpet, spilling a mournful beauty into the world. Every yearning for love rang like a bell in the chest, every lonely fear found its justification.

The clangor of the song kept rising, until it filled the sky. Their ache stretched them until their bodies sang. In dark fathoms, something turned its vast head, and found it beautiful.

FIELD TRIP

by

TANANARIVE DUE

Tonya counted the bouncing heads as her sixth graders raced into the subway car.

Nine... ten... eleven... twelve. She finished just as the door shooshed shut behind her, and the car was already lurching while she did her second count, trying to pick them out from the office refugees hoping to beat rush hour. Most of her kids had worn red, or tried to, as per the letter she'd sent home to all of the parents: *Red T-shirts will both instill school pride and make them more visible in a crowd.* She hoped they hadn't inferred what she'd left unspoken: *This will make it more difficult for me to lose your children, or for someone to snatch them on the street.* Only three of the twelve were wearing the requested red shirt—the girls always stuck at the hip—but most had made a gesture: a red scarf, a red belt, a red baseball cap. (Red *sneakers*, one of them—Kai, the group smart-ass. Of course.)

"Kai, nobody's going to notice your feet," she'd said before they left.

"My mama said she can't afford no red shirt."

And that, she knew, was true: she'd made another middle-class assumption, one of a string since she'd been hired as a permanent sub at Ida B. Wells Middle School deep in the heart of the inner city, worlds away from the suburban science magnet school she'd attended back when she thought she wanted to be an astronaut. For these kids, a future in aeronautics was just as unlikely as new clothes on a whim because the clueless sub sent home a note.

On their ride downtown to the theater, the kids had followed her instructions to stay close enough to link arms, and with no crowd at mid-morning, she'd felt only relief when the doors closed and sealed out any complications. Now, the kids had scattered: the Red Shirts near the back, giggling as they'd been all day, Kai showing off for them by hanging on a strap as if he were doing a trapeze act, Diego and Jaxon wrangling over best hand positioning at a center pole, and the other six invisible in the crowd of at least twenty other riders.

A flash of red scarf near the window: *Good*. Sharmanita had found a seat. That was Sharmanita: quiet, off to herself. Police had mistakenly shot her brother dead at a playground over the summer and she barely spoke a word. Tonya had begged Sharmanita to come on the field trip. Sharmanita hadn't submitted a five-sentence essay, one of the requirements, but screw it. That kid needed a field trip from her whole life.

Tonya eyed the unshaven thirtyish man sitting beside Sharmanita, a bear in a mountainous coat, and quickly wished she were closer to the girl. Maybe profiling by size was wrong, but this guy worried her. His coat practically swallowed Sharmanita; he could carry her off under one arm. *Just because he's big doesn't mean he isn't a sweetheart.* This was the reasonable voice that had guided her through her day, talking down her various panic attacks. A kid about to cross a street too soon, in a bus's path. A too-long visit to the bathroom that conjured fantasies of abduction. All fine, in the end. But Sharmanita was a special case: her photo at her brother's funeral had gone viral. Strangers might recognize and harass her.

"Diego—Jaxon—go stand by Sharmanita. I told you guys to stay together."

Diego cupped his ear like he hadn't heard, mouthing *What?* Jaxon copied him.

They tested her every day, never letting her forget how much more they loved their sainted Mrs. Lopez, who was recovering from a hysterectomy with her sister in the country.

Tonya gestured to direct the boys, firmly. "*Go on.*" By now, she was hoarse.

The field trip was blackmail, plain and simple. The biggest troublemakers in her class were also her brightest students, mostly—those with enough creativity and curiosity to write an essay to win a chance to go see *The Lion King* at the Regal movie theater downtown. Most of them had seen *The Lion King*, but none had seen it on the big screen. The movie barely mattered. The breadth of it—the hours off from school, a cafeteria-packed lunch, a ride on the subway, a trip downtown—was enormous to sixth graders from the projects. Tonya was constantly amazed that they lived in one of the biggest cities in the country and rarely saw the world beyond their school bus routes. They had squealed, giggled and pointed the whole day like tourists.

Both parent volunteers who'd signed up had canceled at the last minute because they had to work, so that morning Tonya had stood with twelve students outside of the school and realized it was up to her alone to create this memory that might breathe life into one of these kids in the harder times to come. But how could she handle it alone?

Almost there. Almost finished.

The train speaker exploded gibberish.

"*What?*" Jaxon and Diego yelled in unison, as they had following every previous indecipherable announcement. Other students laughed. Was that Blake she'd heard? Good.

"We get off on Fifteenth!" Tonya called. "I'll warn you at the stop before." She held up three fingers high above her head for all to see. "We have *three* more stops."

Tonya scanned the car for signs of red or nodding heads. The Red Shirts had ended their conference, paying close attention as they felt the subway car slowing. Diego and Jaxon were no longer jostling, hovering close to Sharmanita. Where were the others? Check: Yoshi in a red jacket in the corner, buddied with Kateisha, whose braided scalp swarmed with red butterfly barrettes. Amir chewing gum, wearing no red, but it was impossible to miss his woven white skullcap. Amir's buddy was... who? Tonya began her frantic count again.

Five... six... seven... eight...

The train entered a tunnel, all light wiped away. "Movie Club—you need to move closer together. I can't see all of you!"

The brakes screamed over her in the tunnel as the train car rattled around a corner, slowing. Ahead, light from the tunnel's mouth allowed her to make out Jonah, Kofi, Marisol. (Or was it? Marisol was tall for her age, and the girl Tonya thought was her might be a teenager. Hadn't Marisol worn something red?) The train shuddered as it struggled to slow. Kai led the laughing at the train car's jittering, pretending he might fly free.

Tonya heard a deafening clank beneath her and felt an impact beneath her feet, as if a piece of the machinery had fallen free and had knocked against the subway car's underbelly. The errant piece rattled down the length of the car beneath the wheels. *Hope that wasn't the brakes.*

"No one get out here!" Tonya shouted, and strangers glanced over their shoulders to see if she held authority over them. A few gaunt faces were streaked with grit, as if they were fresh from a coal mine. The strangers' plaintive, bottomless eyes startled her. These faces might have stared at her from a prison cell. And the car was more crowded than she'd thought at first glance—not twenty people, more like thirty-five.

"Movie Club—we're in *three stops*."

What had she been thinking to propose a field trip, expecting help from parents who couldn't take time off from work? The principal, Mr. Johanssen, was always flirting with her, but he should have known this field trip was too ambitious for a sub. *Your enthusiasm is so refreshing*, he'd said, and warned her again to stay clear of the "moaners" in the teachers' lounge who would counsel against it. Oh, plenty had warned her, but she'd written their warnings off as resentment, since most of her colleagues were suspicious of do-gooders.

Here today, gone tomorrow, someone had muttered to her in the hall.

Tonya was trying to save the world, as her mother put it: if not for Tonya's vow to spend two years teaching in the city, she would be in law school by now. Her grandmother's Selma activism gene had skipped a generation and left Tonya making up for lost ground. Tonya *would* go to law school, but not before she did *something*. Grandma Pat had lain down in front of garbage trucks and gone to jail. How hard should it be to teach a couple years? Plan a field trip?

The train finally slid to a stop, and the doors opened to a crowded platform. Tonya had hoped to lose riders, but everyone stepped back to let new ones on. Passengers crowded the doors, jostling with their elbows. They showered each other with expletives. An aged woman swung her hip to dart in front of a man as if she were half her age. One man's beard was so full that Tonya could only see his glowering eyes.

"My kids, remember—*no one get off here*. Only get off when I get off!"

"Miss Stephens!"

The thin, reedy voice seemed to come from everywhere, laced with panic. Behind her, in front of her. Tonya didn't know the voice—couldn't say for sure if it was a boy or girl, or even one of her students—but she stood on her toes to try to see who was calling her. No red in sight.

Tonya almost missed the worn sign on the platform as the doors closed: MARKET, it read. *What?* She peered through the dust-coated window: Market Avenue. Where was that? She had never heard of a Market Avenue on this side of town. She'd taken the train a dozen times since she moved to her dreary one-bedroom with bars across the windows to be close to the school. She loved the Regal theater's old opera-style seats, and she rode out at least once a week to see a movie and remember sushi and bagels. She *couldn't* have taken the wrong train.

"Miss Steeeeeeeephens!"

"Who is that?" Tonya said, but her eyes searched for the subway route map above her.

On the map, the top line was red for eastbound, the bottom blue for westbound. But that was all she could make out. The writing was illegible, the words blurry, just out of focus. She inched closer, brushing past the screaming B.O. from an impossibly thin woman in yoga clothes, but the words were no less blurry. The closer she got to the sign, the more obvious the blurriness, like a dirty camera lens.

The sign's blurriness looked and felt utterly wrong—like knowing she had brought the kids to the *westbound* platform, which had no Market Avenue on its route. Like the possibility that the voice calling for her was *not* one of her kids—that she was just losing her mind.

The train was gaining speed, but it didn't sound the way it had before, gears grinding.

The car rocked back and forth, also a new development.

Did she smell something burning? Maybe a necessary piece had dropped off before the stop and no one had noticed. When the train jolted so hard that it seemed to jump from the tracks, a child screamed. Tonya's heart raced.

One of her kids playing? Or as scared as she was?

And there was no red. No red in sight.

"Movie Club, call out your last names in alphabetical order!" Tonya shouted. "Then say 'It's me' if you were calling for me just now."

The loudspeaker belched nonsense above her. A blink of clarity—"Next stop…"—and then formless ranting, an intercom system glitch that sounded half man, half machine.

Tonya could not hear if any children were trying to say their names. The faster the train sped, the louder the gale in the car. Had it been this loud before? Had someone opened windows? She craned her ears for the frightened voice that had called out at the platform, but the *chunk-chunk-chunk* of the train drowned everything.

Yes, something was wrong.

She had to find the children. She had to count them again. Then they had to get off of this train. Tonya knew these things, but the wall of flesh around her bloated when she thought about moving. She could see only pieces of people: a briefcase, an engagement ring, a neatly pressed lapel, another briefcase— the promise of her future. *Her* future, not her students'. No red.

"Movie Club! Come to me right—"

Tonya gasped and nearly fell when a sudden clamp pinned her knees. When she looked down, two moon-sized, teary eyes were staring up: Sharmanita was on the floor as if she'd crawled there, holding her tightly.

"I wet," Sharmanita said, or maybe Tonya only read her lips. Tonya made out the large splotch of moisture between the girl's kneeling legs, like spilled coffee. Sharmanita was twelve, but she'd started having daytime accidents after she saw her brother shot down at the park. She had run to him when it happened, staining her clothes with his dying blood. Today, her eyes looked the same way they had looked in her close-up during his funeral on the front page of *The New York Times*, full of the centuries-old question: *Why?* Several of Tonya's undergrad activist friends had changed their social media profile photos to her slain brother Jamal's school photo in homage, for a time. Tonya never told them she was Sharmanita's teacher now, and that those photos had done nothing to keep dead Jamal's sister from wetting herself in public.

The train car careened, and Tonya's weight lurched against sharp shoulders. No straps or support bars were within her reach. If Sharmanita didn't let go of her, she would fall.

"Don't worry, we'll be back soon," Tonya lied, because she had no idea how far they were from home. Thank God Mrs. Lopez would be back soon. Tonya raised her tattered voice to try to be heard. "It's OK, Sharmanita! Have you seen the others? Were you calling me?"

Lights flickered in the train car. Pitch black, then overbrightness. One time. Twice.

The vise around her legs vanished as the lights returned, sickly and dim, ready to be extinguished by the wind howling through the car.

Sharmanita and her bright red scarf were gone from sight, as if she had never been.

THE REVELERS

by

CHRISTOPHER GOLDEN

We've all had a friend like that.

Jon was mine.

Jonathan Vincent Carver showed up in my class halfway through seventh grade, something to do with his dad's job. Like a military brat, he'd been moved from state to state his whole life and he had the combination of feigned arrogance and desperate yearning that often goes along with that kind of upbringing. Translate that to mean that he lied a lot, said whatever he had to say to be accepted. To be liked. They were little white lies, mostly, so my buddies and I didn't mind much. Jon was usually good company, and by high school, he'd become one of my closest friends.

If you're lucky, you gather a small tribe together when you're young, people you believe will have your back in the dark times. But even the lucky don't usually stay that lucky. College comes and people drift and change. Jon put on a mask of arrogance and faux-charm in his quest to enter the business world, the kind of thing he believed would make him a lot of money after graduation. He recognized the process, pursued it with an admirable single-mindedness, but at the same time, he held on to his high school friends and the tangible truth of our tribe, the people we'd been. It was only later that I'd realize he needed the reminder of who he'd been because he was finding it harder and harder to remember that the grinning salesman face was only a mask.

The first clue came our junior year in college. He'd been going to Fordham down in New York and come back to Boston for a long weekend right at the beginning of baseball season and he wanted to catch up. I was his touchstone, you see. That reminder he needed. He could only do Sunday night—he had no classes on Mondays that semester, but I did, and my political science professor had scheduled a test at 8:50 a.m. The test had me worried, but Jon had always been so persuasive.

We met early for dinner. He told the waitress all about our high school glory days, and then he sprang it on me—he had tickets to the Red Sox game. Could we eat in a hurry and head over to Fenway Park? I insisted that I couldn't, offered to let him out of dinner and he could shanghai someone else into going with him. He let it go… until we'd eaten, and then somehow I let him talk me into it, but only because he promised to drive me back to campus as soon as the game let out. I still needed to study and the clock was ticking, but him driving me back would save me three quarters of an hour or so.

What he hadn't told me was that he had a couple of pals from Fordham meeting us there—guys I'd met before, guys who only saw Jon's mask and who had fashioned their own façades of smug assholery. He hadn't told me, because he knew I'd never have gone along to hang out with these two.

When the game ended, the Fordham boys wanted to go out drinking. Jon extolled the virtues of this plan, trying to persuade me, but I had an early exam I wasn't ready for, remember, Jon? And you promised to drive me back to campus?

He gave me a sour look, pulled a twenty out of his wallet, and tucked it into the pocket of my jacket like I'd just given him a sloppy back-alley blowjob and this was my reward. "Sorry, man. You're right. Take a taxi on me. I owe you."

I couldn't even argue. All of the abuse I wanted to hurl his way just sat in my throat, lodged there like something I'd need the Heimlich to choke up. The Fordham boys went off, having quite a laugh.

Have you ever tried to get a taxi within a mile of Fenway Park right after a Red Sox game?

Yeah. It's like that.

The moment stuck with me. I ran into Jon's father in a restaurant a few months later and I couldn't help myself. I told him that story. The elder Carver seemed disgusted but unsurprised, and that was when I realized that even his parents thought their son was a bit of a prick.

We saw each other less and less. We graduated. He came back to Boston for work, while my fortunes took me to New York, to a magazine publisher where I'd been working for a couple of years by the time I got that phone call from Jon. The phone call that led to meeting Mollie and Leigh and the party in this girl's apartment.

"Tim Donovan," I announced as I answered the phone.

"Timmy! You don't need your dancing shoes, but put your motherfucking drinking hat on!"

I laughed, sat back in my chair. "What the hell do you want, Carver?"

"What time can you kick off work?"

My cubicle had a great view of Times Square. Rent would drive the company out of there a few years later, but those were halcyon days, so even a little punk like me had a view. I poked my head up to see who might overhear, but the three other staffers who shared the office were all elsewhere—coffee break, cigarette break, or running errands for the higher-ups.

"I usually get out of here around seven. The boss is out of town, though, so I figure six o'clock sharp," I said. "From the question, I assume you're in town."

"I have meetings till three-ish," Jon said. "Then I'll hit up my local office for a few hours and meet you at six-thirty. Wherever you want, provided there's a bar with women in it."

* * *

We met at Dooley's Tavern, an Irish pub at the corner of 57th Street and 7th Avenue. It was the kind of place we'd always frequented in college, all brass railings and dark wood soaked in decades' worth of spilled ale, so the whole place had the stale-beer stink of fraternity basements. In those days, to me, that was the scent of nostalgia.

I slipped through the door at quarter past six and sat at the bar to wait, ordered a pint of Guinness and chatted up the bartender for half an hour until Jon arrived. The bartender's name was Leigh, a tall brunette with wildly curly hair and mischief sparkling in her dark eyes. Smart and funny, she kept the conversation going, kept the counter clean, kept the drinks coming, managed to take care of everyone without making anyone else feel left out.

"Maybe your friend's not coming," she said at one point.

"Nah," I said, "he'll be here. He's what you call 'mercurial.'"

"Meaning he thinks his time is more important than yours," Leigh observed. She cocked an eyebrow, maybe realizing that had been a little more honest than it was smart for a bartender to be if she wanted decent tips.

I smiled. "Oh, there's no doubt that's what he thinks."

And you let him? She didn't ask the question, but I could see it in her eyes.

Half a second later, Jon pressed himself against my back,

reaching around me to start caressing my chest through my shirt. I spilled a couple of ounces of my beer onto my pants and laughed, twisting out of his grasp before he could tweak my nipples.

I swore at him, setting my beer down, but I was laughing as we embraced. We'd had a lot of good times together. Despite the way our friendship had withered, I was happy to see him. His eyes were glassy from the several beers he'd doubtless already had while he spent the afternoon at his "local office," which was a stool at a strip club half a dozen blocks from our present location.

"So this is the infamous Jon," Leigh said, placing a coaster on the bar. "What'll you have?"

Jon grinned, studying her like she was the menu. "Is that an open-ended question, or are we just talking alcohol here?"

Leigh arched an eyebrow. "Why don't we start with alcohol and see where that takes us?"

It might have been a bartender's diplomacy, a way to sidestep the come-on, or she might've been flirting with him. I wasn't sure at the time and I'm not really sure now, regardless of where it went. It always astonished me how successful Jon was at seducing women. He wasn't the best-looking guy in a room. Too short, too cynical, too many damn teeth in that shark smile. The pickup lines he used should have been comedy gold. *Sorry about last Christmas; Santa forgot to pick me up.* That shit should not have worked, and yet somehow he'd figured out the formula, the perfect ratio of cockiness to charm, to move things from conversation to copulation.

He flirted with Leigh. As I downed my second Guinness, I did the same. We told stories about our high school and college days, trying to amuse her but mostly just amusing ourselves. It felt good to reminisce.

"This guy and I grew up together," Jon told Leigh, brow furrowed. "Hung out at each other's houses after school, drank in the woods together, did our stupid science project together. Life goes on, right? But if you have a couple of friends you can hang onto from when you were a kid, it means something, y'know? There's always someone who knows who you really are."

Leigh cocked her head, her lips pursed together, pert with attitude. "You're either sweeter than you look, or drunker than you sound."

He laughed. "Maybe both."

I put a hand on his back. "All right, brother. Time to get a table and order something to eat."

He made a pistol out of his thumb and forefinger. "Excellent idea."

Jon picked up the bar bill. I worked in publishing and he worked in sales. The guy could have sold ice to Eskimos, so needless to say he was making a shitload more money than I was. I offered to pay, but he rolled his eyes. He knew my salary.

Leigh waved over a waitress and introduced us. "Sit in Mollie's section. She'll take good care of you."

Mollie looked me up and down the same way Jon had looked at Leigh. Almost elfin, she was a tiny redhead with a spray of freckles across the bridge of her nose, and she wore a black skirt so short it might as well have been called a sash. Mollie started to lead us over to a table.

"Hey," Leigh said as I turned away from the bar.

I glanced at her.

"He's everything you said he was."

"Is that good or bad?"

She smiled. "Probably both, don't you think?"

I returned her smile and carried my third Guinness with me to the table.

* * *

In the interest of honest reporting, I must say we were drunk as fuck. We'd had our dinner and talked for hours about old times and new times. Being with Jon had reminded me why we had been such close friends in high school and college. He might have been a bullshitter of the highest order, but he knew me better than almost anyone and I knew him, and one of the first things I'd realized about post-college life was that those kinds of intimacies were hard to come by. I had started to wonder if maybe I still loved him a little more than I hated him.

We had pulled other patrons into our conversation, but most of them had left after a while, and come last call, there were about a dozen customers left in Dooley's. Mollie had closed out her station half an hour before and sat at one of the many empty tables around us, tallying her tips for the night and making sure all of her math had been correct. In the midst of that, she'd said something nice about my eyes, and Jon had taken that as his cue to play matchmaker. He spent some time extolling my virtues, and when Mollie had taken off her apron and grabbed her coat, instead of leaving she took a seat with us and got a beer of her own. We were seven or eight drinks ahead of her.

"You know the drill, amigos," Leigh called from behind the bar. "You don't have to go home—"

"—But you can't stay here!" the chorus of people with nowhere better to go chimed in.

Mollie had just said something funny and I realized I'd smiled a little too long at the joke. Smiling at her was easy. She confessed to being an actress and a dancer and that she had been writing a musical about a cocktail waitress in 1940s Los Angeles who spent her nights serving stars of the silver screen and dreamed of being discovered, but who felt invisible every moment of her life, except when she went to the movies. Sitting in the theater with the lights down, Mollie said, the waitress could always feel like she lived amongst those stars.

I fell in love a little, I think. Drunk as I was.

Jon said he'd produce her show after he made his first million, but only if he got to help with casting, so he could see if all of the stories about hungry young actresses were true. Maybe once I would've laughed, but you couldn't hear Mollie talk about her dreams and think that line was funny. Unless you were Jon.

Mollie laughed politely as she finished her beer. Last call had come and gone, so I offered her the rest of mine. The staff were getting their coats on when Leigh came and stood beside Jon's chair, hands thrust into the pockets of her ratty old pea coat, a bright raspberry scarf around her neck. Out from behind the bar, she seemed taller than ever.

"Where are you guys going from here?" she asked.

I blinked in surprise and glanced at Jon, who grinned. To him, it didn't seem at all unusual that Leigh might want to spend more time with him, no matter that she was stone-cold sober and we'd been drinking for hours. We weren't incoherent— we'd been drinking all night, but we'd had a meal and hours had passed—but we were drunk enough to irritate sober people.

"We have no plans," I said.

"We do now," Jon corrected me, sliding back his chair and standing to look up at Leigh. "We're going wherever you're going."

Mollie downed the last of my beer and stood as well. "Leigh and I are headed to a party, if you guys want to come."

"Might be we've partied enough," I found myself saying. Then I saw the disappointment on Mollie's pixie features and wondered what the hell was wrong with me. "You guys don't mind us being so far ahead of you?"

"Mollie's got a little packet of something to help us catch up," Leigh said.

The mischief in her eyes made Jon very happy. Mollie took my hand and guided me away from the table, and suddenly we were leaving the restaurant and walking the streets of New York, and pretty soon I wasn't sure where we were, which was quite a feat when you consider that most of Manhattan is comprised of numbered streets and avenues. It's hard to get lost there. I wondered if I'd lost count of my drinks at some point during the night.

Then Mollie slid her arm through mine and started to sing a wordless tune, softly but beautifully, and I stopped worrying. I worried too much, Jon had always told me. I felt sure, in that moment, that he had been right.

Mollie took a little plastic bag out of her pocket, tapped a couple of pills into her palm and swallowed them dry. She offered them around. Leigh took two, but cautioned Jon and me to start with one each, given we were already slightly hammered. I followed their advice. Always the cautious one. But not so cautious I wouldn't take a pill a pretty girl gave me out of a plastic bag from her pocket.

"Where's the party?" he asked Leigh.

"This girl's apartment."

"That's all you know?" I asked.

Mollie bumped me with her hip. "It's supposed to be a massive bash. Late night party, past the witching hour in New York City. What else do you really need to know?"

I smiled, recognizing truth when I heard it. "This girl's apartment" really was all I needed to know.

* * *

We never met the girl. Or at least, I never did. The party raged on the third floor of an old brownstone jammed between two modern structures, like a piece of an earlier New York had been somehow passed over by the passage of time. Forgotten. I hoped for one of those great, claustrophobic elevators with the accordion gates, but the place was a walk-up. Whatever Mollie had given us had kicked in on the way up the stairs, so as the thump of blaring hip-hop drifted down from above, Jon started bopping to the music. He took Leigh by the hands and danced up the last flight of steps. At the landing there were cases of empty beer bottles, neatly set out for return and redemption.

"Empty!" Leigh said, laughing in frustration, as if she'd really thought they might be full cases of beer. Her pills had kicked in, too, and her eyes were wide and hypnotic. That's mostly what I remember of her from that night, those kaleidoscopic eyes. I might have dreamed them, I don't know. It's been a long time since then.

"Fucking empty!" Jon echoed.

He picked up a case of the empty bottles, turned and hurled it down the steps. The cardboard box dulled the thump and the sound of glass shattering inside, but it was loud enough to make us all flush with guilty amusement.

The drugs racing through me, I shoved the nearest stack of cases over, toppling them onto the stairs.

Jon and Leigh looked at me in shock, then started whooping. Jon patted me on the back and yelled something about getting fucked up. Or maybe that was me doing the yelling.

They led the way out of the stairwell and into the hall. Mollie took my hand again. She cocked her head and even soaring on whatever she'd given me, I could see she was looking at me differently. What I couldn't tell was whether or not it was good differently or bad differently.

She kissed me, and from the hunger in it, I had my answer.

* * *

The room thumped with the music. The walls breathed with it. The lights were dim and though all of the windows were wide open, the gyrating bodies were sheened with glistening sweat. Side tables were laden with top-shelf booze and clean glasses that seemed to appear without being replenished by anyone I noticed. Coolers full of beer on ice stood in corners. The drugs, though… they were never on display. They manifested in people's hands as if summoned from the ether. I saw one girl, maybe seventeen, pull a small vial of cocaine from the unruly bun of her hair.

"This is fucking amazing," Mollie said, dancing with me. Holding my hands and gazing into my eyes.

The apartment had seemed like one big room with a bathroom and small bedroom off to one side, but as we burned up the small hours of the night and we kept dancing and drinking, I realized we'd moved into a different room, and that the place must be larger than I'd first imagined. The sweaty little box we'd started in had given way to a much bigger space, and the music kept shifting styles, sometimes improbably as hell. Somebody put on Frank Sinatra, and then something older, a heartbreak ballad from the 1920s or 1930s, followed by a screaming bit of party blues from the sixties. Whoever had been picking the music had to be on even better drugs than we were. Mixing it up like that only ever worked with a group of people as wasted as we all had gotten by then.

I had no idea of the time. Once in a while I'd glance out the window, expecting to see the edge of dawn creeping into the sky, but the old building had been swallowed by modern New York, so I wasn't sure if we'd even notice the sun come up.

Whiskey burned my throat. I blinked, coming to my senses for half a second, wondering how much time I'd lost. How much of that whiskey I'd had to drink. Feminine hands caressed my stomach, fingers stroked the front of my pants, nails scratching, stirring the most familiar of all urges. Blond hair whipped around her face as she danced, but Mollie wasn't blond.

Frowning, I stumbled back from her, glancing around in search of Mollie. I spotted Jon and the bartender. *Leigh*, I reminded myself, though I forgot her name again a moment later. So fucked up by that time.

The dancing bodies made strange shadows on the wall, undulating darkness. The music had shifted and I stumbled amongst the dancers, shoved a couple aside. The woman wore flowers in her hair and a gypsy skirt. Her partner wore a suit with thin stripes and a wide lapel, a long sloped hat. I turned to stare but the hat had vanished. The lights flickered and I turned to glance at the walls, where gaslight burned inside sconces, little flames casting odd shadows of their own.

I spotted Mollie with another guy, tall and dapper. Bow tie undone. They had taken a small mirror off the wall and were snorting lines of something off the silver glass. Coke, maybe. I had no way to know.

"Hey," I said into her ear as I moved up beside her and took her by the hand.

Her eyes were glassy, her pupils dilated so large they were nearly all black. She kissed me, pushed her fingers through my hair and pulled me close so she could deepen that kiss. She ground herself against me and I flushed with the best of hungers. Kissed her back, put a hand on her ass and pressed my hard cock into her so she could feel what she had done to me.

Then she was kissing the other guy. Dapper fucking Dan. His hand slipped down her pants and I saw her shudder with pleasure. She reached for my hand as if she wanted me to stay, but I'd never been good at sharing. I started to back away and she paused Dapper Dan and shot me a disappointed look.

"I should go," I mumbled. Blinking. Unsteady on my feet. I shook my head to clear it but was unsuccessful. "Come with me?"

She seemed to be considering it. Took one step toward me. Then she stopped and swayed, nearly fell over. Dapper Dan caught her.

"I don't think I can," Mollie said, a look of surprise on her face.

Hammered and high, stung by her, I staggered away. In the haze, I tried to focus on the room around me, searching for an exit. I didn't recognize the art on the walls and for a few seconds it seemed to me that the music filling the apartment had strings and horns, some baroque composition that these people would never have chosen as their evening's dance soundtrack. These people, men in black tie and women in elaborate gowns.

Bile burned up the back of my throat and I bent for a second, leaning against the wall, feeling the texture of the wallpaper under my hand. I blinked, trying to breathe, and looked around. What the fuck had Mollie given me? I'd never had hallucinations before, but now… what else could that have been?

I weaved amongst the dancers and the drinkers, all of them just as trashed as I was by now. Their eyes looked hollow to me, their smiles false masks. Were they all so shallow, or was I just pissed at myself for being lulled by nostalgia into forgetting how much Jon had changed over the years? This wasn't the life I wanted, but should I hold it against these others, who had never been my friends?

I just wanted out. The party around me seemed like it might go on forever, and that was all the revelers wanted. There seemed so many of them now—impossibly many—the room impossibly large, people crushing against me as I tried to find my way out, searching for Jon along the way. Bitter as I was, I needed to tell him I was leaving.

What room was I in? How had I made my way there?

Girls dressed like flappers did the Charleston in the center of the crowd. I spotted them for a second and then they were gone, my view obstructed by human flesh. By a strange masquerade of unfettered joy and depravity in equal measure.

I found myself in another room. Then another. Each seemed new to me. I bumped into a table laden with champagne flutes, spilled several glasses and saw that there was confetti on the floor, as if tonight had been New Year's Eve and I had somehow missed it, though months had passed since then.

A dancing couple collided with me and herded me into a narrow corridor, thick with other human flesh. A doorway presented itself, the door hanging half open, and thus I discovered Jon and Leigh by accident in a bathroom complete with brass fittings and clawfoot tub. She snorted a line of cocaine off the sink while he worked her panties down, reaching for his own zipper.

The temptation to close the door, to just go, dragged at me. Instead I knocked hard, slid into the bathroom, and turned my back so as not to get a glimpse of them. In my peripheral vision I could see their faces in the mirror above the sink.

"Timmy, what the fuck?" Jon barked. "Give us a minute, okay?"

"Take all night, man. I just wanted you to know I was leaving."

Leigh didn't care. She didn't know me. She did another line.

"You fucking pussy!" Jon cried in dismay. "This is the best party ever! I'm never leaving this goddamn place!"

I hesitated. Wrecked as I was, unable to focus my vision, I still managed to worry about him. I shook my head to clear my thoughts, wondering if he'd be all right.

He sneered at me. "What do you want, *cab money*?"

I went cold. We'd never talked about the night of that Red

Sox game, but apparently he remembered it as well as I had.

"Fuck yourself," I spat.

I reeled out of there, stumbled down the corridor and into another room. My vision blurred again and I saw those gaslight sconces flickering on the walls. They couldn't have been there. The building might be old, but surely such things were not legal now. I went to my knees and someone stepped on my hand. My head pounded as dancers swirled past me. Some of them wore masks, as if I had accidentally stepped into some nineteenth-century masquerade ball.

Darkness edged in at the corners of my vision and my head lolled forward, dreadfully heavy even as the rest of me seemed to lighten, to drift and float. Someone shoved me and I managed to crawl enough to find a wall. A window. I sucked in the cold air breezing in from outside and then I glanced out at a city that could not have been, a Manhattan without skyscrapers.

I puked out the window, body rigid as vomit poured out of me. I heaved a second time, and then a third before I could catch my breath. The cold air felt good but did not clear my head. With the back of my hand, I swiped a sleeve across my mouth and then the world turned to shadow again.

Someone slapped my face, more than once.

I tried to focus, barely managed, and saw it was Mollie. She hadn't poured all of the beer and whiskey down my throat and she hadn't made me take the damn pill from her little plastic baggie, but she had been the one to give it to me.

I was on the floor again. My hand closed around her wrist and I dragged her down there with me. "What the hell did you give me?"

I slurred the question, but she understood.

"It was just Ex!" she said, extricating herself from me. "Just Ecstasy. But there's something else… something…"

Mollie took my face in her hands and shook my skull, forced me to meet her terrified gaze. "We have to leave."

Upon that we could agree. But her eyes held something other than urgency. They were full of fear.

"What... what's happened?"

Mollie slapped me hard. "Look around, Tim. Jesus, look!"

She slapped me again and my mind sharpened just a little, the fog clearing. I slid my back up the wall beside the window and blinked, sucking air into my lungs. What I was seeing could not be. I tell myself even now that it had to be the drugs, that there must have been something in that pill, or in the whiskey I'd been drinking at the party. Some of the revelers were as I'd seen them before, wasted shells, club kids or young professionals blind drunk, having the party of their lives. Others were true husks, barely shadows of people. They might have been ghosts, but in that moment I felt sure they had begun just like the rest... like me and Jon and Mollie and Leigh, young and searching for meaning and identity in a city that denied both, desperate to feel something other than the uncertainty of new adulthood. They'd found this party just like we had, and they'd surrendered themselves to it.

Mollie took my hand. "Come on. I've got to find Leigh."

I flashed on the bathroom. The lines of coke on the sink. The sneer on Jon's face. *What do you want, cab money?* Fuck them.

"We have to go," I said, echoing Mollie's own words.

She'd taken my hand, but now it was me dragging her. Mollie protested, but not much. Fear became her engine. I kept shaking my head, forcing the fog to clear from my thoughts, keeping my vision from fading. And yet it did. Whatever moment of crisp clarity Mollie had given me, I lost it quickly. The husks had their masks on again, looked just like the rest of the revelers, but I had seen them now. All around us were faces from other eras, clothing from decades past. The music shifted with the décor as we shoved through dancers and drinkers and people smoking all manner of things.

Fear suffocated me. It felt like a kind of madness, seizing me, building up in me like steam in a kettle. Just when I thought I might scream, Mollie and I pushed our way through the throng and into the room where we had first entered. I recognized the door. Seeing we meant to leave, several of the dancers reached for us, snagging our clothing. One girl kissed me, her mouth tasting of burnt smoke and herbs. We yanked ourselves free, and I felt so grateful that I could no longer see which of the revelers were new arrivals and which were only shadows.

The door resisted at first, but Mollie put her hand over mine and something about that moment of contact, the warmth of her touch, must have given us both a bit more clarity. The knob turned, the door opened, and we stumbled into the hall. As the door slammed behind us, muffling the thumping hip-hop we'd heard on our arrival, Mollie pulled me into the stairwell and we picked our way carefully past the cases of empty beer bottles we'd knocked over earlier. She'd given up on Leigh, no longer determined to go back for her.

Until we reached the street.

The sky had lightened slightly, deep indigo to the west but to the east I could see the soft glow of impending dawn. I glanced around, grateful that the street seemed the same as the one we'd left behind. The modern buildings dwarfing the ugly brownstone.

"We have to go back in," Mollie said, standing beside me. She'd let go of my hand at some point and I hadn't noticed.

"Are you out of your mind?"

"Tim, we have to. I can't leave Leigh in there. And what about Jon?"

What do you want, cab money?

I shook my head and staggered across the street. Whatever clarity I'd achieved had started to wear off and now the alcohol and drugs crashed back into my system like adrenaline had built a dam and now it had let go.

Some time later—I don't know how long, but there were people out jogging and walking their dogs and the yellow edge of the sunrise had just touched the eastern edge of the city— Mollie shook me awake. I'd passed out in a shoe store doorway across from the brownstone.

There were tears on her face.

"She's gone," Mollie said. "I went up and I knew it the second I got to the top of the stairs. The cases were gone, the ones you guys smashed. Just gone. No broken glass, no boxes, nothing. And the music had stopped."

"That's…" I started to say *impossible*, but bit down on the word.

Mollie had knocked on the door, hammered on it, until she heard someone swearing on the other side. She'd pleaded for it to be opened and when at last her pleas were answered, she found herself confronted by an old man holding his stained robe closed with one hand while he cussed her out and threatened to call the police.

"It's over," I said.

"It can't… where have they gone, Tim?" Mollie asked, wiping at her tears, afraid for her friend.

I thought about all of those different rooms, the view from the window, the shifting music and clothing I had seen.

"The party's moved on. Go home, Mollie."

"But Leigh and Jon…"

"They got what they wanted. They moved on, too. So should you."

Mollie stared at me, frowning at first in shock and then in revulsion. She took a step back, moved off the curb and then froze at the blaring horn of a taxi. She waited while it slid by, the cabbie stabbing his middle finger out his window as he passed. Then she hurried off.

I watched her until she reached the end of the block, where she turned a corner, shoulders hunched, and disappeared. I never saw Mollie again, but the memory of her face is vivid in my mind. Her eyes, especially. The disappointment that shaded them in that last instant, when she glanced at me while the taxi drove past. I had not turned out to be the person she thought I was.

As for Jon, I took my own advice. I let him go. The city had claimed him. Changed him. So fuck that guy, y'know?

But.

I'd let him go.

Which meant it had claimed me, too.

Maybe it gets us all, in the end.

THE STILLNESS

by

RAMSEY CAMPBELL

At first Donald thought only the man was familiar—just another of the street performers who would keep up a pose until somebody dropped them a coin. Last week he'd played a businessman arrested in the act of dashing somewhere with a briefcase as dead white as himself, and now he was portraying a dignitary painted just as pale. A robe or at any rate a sheet was draped over his shoulders, and he held a book of which not only the pages were white in front of his stern set face. Even his eyes looked excessively colourless. Donald was watching him between two books in the shop window when Mildred jangled hangers on a rack of dresses. "What's so interesting out there?"

"I was trying to think what that fellow is supposed to be."

"A statue, I imagine," Mildred said like the teacher Donald was often reminded she'd been, and tramped across the bare boards to plant her hands on her wide hips. She might almost have been squeezing out the perfume that her capacious russet one-piece costume exuded. "The one they moved," she said.

Now Donald knew what he'd been struggling to recognise. The street had featured an actual statue until the town centre was redeveloped. He went to the bookshelves and found an outsize dog-eared paperback of local photographs. "Here he is," he said, squinting at the inscription on the plinth, which showed that the subject had died almost a century ago. "Samuel Huntley, educator and mayor."

Mildred kept her hands on her hips to mime patience as he took the paperback to the window. While the photograph was frontal, the man in the street had his left side to the shop, but Donald thought the pose was exactly the same. He was trying to identify some detail that seemed odd when Mildred said "Are those books in order? That's how books ought to be."

He supposed his wife might have told him not to let Mildred talk to him like that, if he'd had a wife to tell about his day. He'd had his fair share of liaisons, but by now he was too fond of his own ways to become involved with anyone else, and his relationship with Mildred quite amused him. As an accountant he'd observed how some of his colleagues would create work in order to seem busy, but he'd never met another one like Mildred. He assumed she meant to convince herself she was still active, though he suspected she wouldn't own up to the trick. He took his time over restoring order to the bookshelves while he watched to see the human statue perform its routine, but while people loitered until Donald felt like urging them to throw a coin, nobody paid.

The November night had fallen by the time Mildred locked Pre-Treasured Prizes and hurried away to the car park. The colourless glare of the streetlamps turned the painted man even paler. His white breaths lingered in front of his face, and Donald saw how few and how measured they were, presumably in aid of the performance. Donald was about to move on, having grown shivery from dallying, when he realised what he'd failed to notice. Street performers always left coins in a receptacle to encourage people to donate, but this fellow had nothing of the kind, despite having used the ploy when he'd played the headlong businessman. "Don't you want to earn anything?"

Donald murmured, but the whitened face didn't twitch.

The evening crowds thinned out and vanished before he reached his apartment, on the ground floor of a converted warehouse in a side street that was becoming overrun with nightclubs. He changed his clothes and jogged to the gym, where he cycled and ran for a couple of hours. He didn't mean to slow down while he had the energy to outdistance it, and he returned home with more of an appetite. His chicken casserole and half a bottle of wine kept him company for the duration of a Sinatra album, and then he was ready for bed, where he dealt with several chapters of this month's choice for the reading group. At least the nightclubs were relatively dormant during the week, and he slept without much trouble until dawn.

He was on his way to the Pre-Treasured shop well before opening time. He preferred to be with people whenever he had the chance, but he wasn't expecting to see the human statue so early in the day, or to find the man facing the shop. There was still no sign of money, not even the man's own. Donald hitched up his quilted overcoat to extract a lukewarm pound, which he dropped at the man's feet. He could only assume the performer didn't think much of the amount, because he didn't even twitch.

In the overcast winter light the pale eyes looked dull, unpleasantly close to lifeless. Donald felt as if they'd fixed him in the act of willing them to blink. He stared at them until he began to feel not much less cold than stone, and revived himself with an uneasy laugh. He was heading for the shop when he heard a rustle of activity behind him, but when he looked the statue seemed not to have stirred. "What did you just do?" he said. "You have to let people see what they paid for."

He saw the man ignore him, which was too much. He came close to sprawling on his face as he crouched to recover the coin. "Last chance to show me," he said without result, and pocketed the pound as he made for the shop.

As Mildred locked the door she said "You didn't need to encourage him."

"Why, what's he been up to?"

"Nothing I'm aware of. I'm simply saying money paid to him may be income lost to us."

"You should be glad I took mine back, then."

"I hope nobody saw. That won't do our image any good." As if she was extending Donald an opportunity to redeem himself she said "We've had a box of books for you to price. Ninety-five for the paperbacks except one ninety-five for the big ones, and three ninety-five for the hardbacks unless they're big enough for seven."

"Ninety-five," Donald added so wryly that he kept it under his breath. He was already aware of the prices and how she used them to embarrass customers, saying "Will you want your change? It'll help to fight cancer." His task took up the morning, not least because the books reminded him of the one the human statue held. Had Donald drawn the man's attention by retrieving the coin? He had to keep glancing towards the window, but couldn't tell whether the man was watching him across the book; indeed, the fellow never even seemed to blink. The spectacle had begun to unnerve Donald by the time he set about making space for the new books, and then he had a thought. "Hang on," he said to nobody in particular as he found the book of local photographs.

While the lower floors of all the buildings on both sides of the street had been altered beyond recognition, the roofs and the architectural details beneath them hadn't changed. Stone faces peered out below the eaves behind the statue in the photograph, but there was no sign of them across the road. The November chill fastened on Donald as he stepped outside to look for them. On his way past the human statue he glanced at the book—a ledger with its pages painted even whiter and then covered with names and dates, which had been dug into the surface so as to look carved. There was no sign of the architectural features anywhere in the street. "Excuse me," he said, "you're in the wrong place."

Several bystanders stared at him as if he might be mad for talking to a statue. They weren't behaving too impressively themselves, having already hung around so long that Donald could have thought the performer was infecting them with stillness. This close to the statue Donald saw that the eyes must be shut, the lids painted an unrelieved white, though he had to fend off the notion that the eyes had no pupils or colour, any more than they had lashes—that they were set like pebbles in the sockets. "You shouldn't be here if you want to be real," he said and retreated into the shop.

Mildred was transferring the book of old photographs to the window display. "What were you saying to him?"

"I was trying to move him. I thought you wanted him to go away."

"I hope you didn't say you were acting on my behalf. Did anyone else hear you?"

"I don't think anyone was very interested. Maybe not even him."

While that had to be part of the man's act, he looked set to maintain his pose all day if not longer. As Donald made room for the latest lot of books by adding to the window display he tried to see the white eyes blink, but they never did. They must be the lids, because otherwise they would have pupils. All the same, he was glad to leave the sight behind when he went for his break.

The cramped back room smelled of stewed tea and Mildred's

fierce perfume, both of which might have infiltrated the drab brown wallpaper. Donald dangled a teabag in his Can That Cancer mug and lingered over sipping until he began to wonder if the statue might have shifted in his absence. He poured the remains of his tea into the thunderous metal sink and used the venerable toilet before hurrying out to rejoin Mildred, only to demand "Where's he gone?"

Mildred glanced none too instantly towards the window. "He must have listened to you after all."

"Yes, but did you see where he went?"

She gave Donald just as delayed a glance. "I was dealing with a customer."

Why should Donald wish he'd seen the performer move? Surely all that mattered was his having moved, and now he was nowhere to be seen. On his way home Donald caught himself looking out for the statue, but everyone in sight was moving— at least, apart from a distant group of people halted by whatever they could see. Donald had to peer hard along the side street to be sure that they were queuing for a bus, though why should their inactivity have bothered him? He put on speed, not just to prove he could. Tonight was the meeting of the dining club.

This month they met at Crabracadabra, the new seafood restaurant across town. Some were couples, and all of them were at least Donald's age. Quite a few of the topics of conversation— political failings, familial ailments—felt close to growing too familiar. As he tried to bring more vigour to the dialogue Donald was distracted by a waiter who loomed over him to serve wine. Even once he grasped that he'd been reminded how the human statue had towered over him while Donald recaptured the coin, he had to wait for his heart to steady and slow down.

Strolling home, he realised he was surrounded by statues— dummies in the store windows. He thought he'd left the lifeless shapes behind until he saw a figure down a side street. The man had no cause to move while he was waiting for a bus, of course, and perhaps he was a slow reader. A nearby streetlamp seemed to turn him as pale as the cover of the book in his hand.

Donald slept well enough. In the morning he had to flex his arms and legs to help wake up his heavy eyes. As he trotted to work he noticed that the bus stop wasn't visible along the street where he'd seen the man reading, though why should it matter? He was more disconcerted to see someone in the doorway of the shop, standing absolutely still with an object in his hands. Then the man turned to face him, revealing that the item was a jigsaw in a box. When Mildred let Donald in, the customer tried to follow him. "We're open in ten minutes," Mildred said.

"I'm just returning this. Since you're a charity I won't ask for my money back."

Mildred sounded not far from affronted. "Why would you?"

"Half of it is missing. I'm surprised you offered it for sale."

"Then I hope you'll accept our apologies." Once the door was locked she said more accusingly to Donald than he thought was called for "You'll need to check this."

As he sat behind the counter to count jigsaw pieces out of the box into the lid he felt like a schoolboy in detention. The stone eyes of a Roman statue gazed up from the midst of the cardboard chaos, and Donald could have imagined they were willing him to reassemble their body. "I'm afraid the customer was right," he said. "A lot of it isn't here."

"Well, I don't know how that could have happened." This sounded like an indictment in search of a culprit. "You'd better see all the others are complete," Mildred said.

Donald only just succeeded in staying amused by her attitude. People chose how they behaved, and he could. He felt he was back in detention, and perhaps defiance made him count the pieces of the jigsaws as slowly as he was able to bear, until he seemed to be in danger of dawdling to a standstill. People at the window didn't help, though he needn't think that the motionless folk were watching him, and in any case they couldn't know that he was being penalised. In time he grasped why they were troubling him. While people generally halted when they were looking in shop windows, he'd begun to feel as if their stillness was both an imitation and a symptom of an unseen presence. Each time he established that a jigsaw was complete he stepped out of the shop on the pretext of taking a breather, but he could never be sure that the crowds weren't concealing someone too pale and still.

That night the reading group met in the town's solitary bookshop. Nearly all the members had chosen the month's book, but very few had finished the novel, which was narrated in this year's slang if not in a future lingo. Donald had made himself understand it so as not to feel left behind, but everyone else was more interested in regretting the present and yearning for the past it had dislodged. So tardily that he felt slowed down Donald realised this was his cue to ask "Does anyone remember where Samuel Huntley's statue used to be?"

"Who?" more than one listener said, and the most historically inclined of them answered for Donald. "He was meant to be something of an educational pioneer."

"In what way?" Donald felt inexplicably anxious to learn.

"He was supposed to have developed a method of calming his pupils, for one thing, but I don't know how."

"He mightn't be too calm about having his statue knocked down," another woman said.

Donald didn't need the comment, surely only because it was a distraction. "But do you know where he," he asked his informant, "that's to say where it was?"

"Somewhere near here." She shut her eyes, reminding him unnecessarily of the human statue, and opened them without having found more of a memory. "I should be able to tell you next month," she said.

Donald had to suppress a ridiculous inkling that in some way this would be too late. As he returned to his apartment he was dogged by a notion that the plastic sculptures in the shops weren't the only static figures he ought to notice. He was almost home when he saw one along a side street—somebody not quite as distant as last night's loiterer had been. Perhaps he should feel heartened to observe that people still read books, although the man might just be consulting a street map by the light of the streetlamp that turned him unnaturally pale. He was certainly taking his time over the book, and Donald felt equally immobilised by trying to identify it without venturing closer. He didn't stir until his efforts or the glare of the streetlamp began to make his eyes smart, and he had to jerk his body out of its torpor before he was able to hasten home.

That night he didn't sleep a great deal. Drifting off felt too much like a threat of growing excessively still. Whenever he floundered awake he had to reconfirm that he could move his limbs and to ward off the idea that his plight was being watched or wished upon him. Of course he was alone in the ground-floor bedroom, where the curtains were too thoroughly shut for anyone to be able to peer in. A trace of streetlight surmounted the curtains, and having convinced himself yet again that he was alone in the dim room he made himself risk sleep.

As he trudged to work he found his panic hadn't altogether left him. Might it catch up with him if he didn't put on speed? He was panting by the time he reached the shop, and the sight of his winter breaths brought to mind a child's portrayal of a steam train. He hadn't seen a train like that since he was very young, and he didn't want to dwell on the past in case it slowed him down.

Mildred was waiting to greet him. "What are we going to do today?" she said as though to a child.

"Stand around looking important." Accusing her of that would hardly improve the situation. "What's there to keep us busy?" Donald asked instead.

"The discs could do with checking. See all the cases match."

Donald tried to lend the task more animation by tramping back and forth between the counter, where the discs were stored, and the shelves. He felt driven to behave yet more strenuously once Mildred started watching him, until she said "Haven't you ever heard of time and motion, Donald?"

"I hope I've got plenty of both left." When this went nowhere near amusing her he said "I just need to keep moving. You may find you do when you get to my age."

"You're making me feel idle, like your friend who was outside." As various rejoinders clamoured in Donald's head— the man was anything but his friend, she deserved to feel inert compared with Donald, he wasn't causing it, surely nobody else could be—Mildred said "Take a few at a time to the counter. You'll be tiring yourself out if you aren't careful."

The prospect of slowing to a standstill daunted him enough that he followed her suggestion. Instead of sitting at the counter he marched on the spot while he found the discs their cases, even after Mildred gave him a lengthy frown. Several cases for bands he'd never heard of—Chorus of Snails, the Devastating Artichokes, the Nostrils, the Complicit Eggs—had been stolen, presumably to house pirate copies. "We need less wandering about," Mildred declared, "and more vigilance."

Donald already felt unwillingly vigilant, watching out even when they had no customers, though he never caught anyone watching him. The compulsion accompanied him home and out again for his weekly meeting with friends in a downtown pub. He mightn't have ventured into the streets overlooked by posturing plastic figures if he hadn't wanted to question somebody who worked near the town hall. "Do you know if they've moved Samuel Huntley up your end of town?"

"I've really no idea, I'm glad to say." Whatever the solicitor found objectionable, he said no more except "We can do without him."

Another drinker was a doctor, and Donald turned to her. "Isn't it quite common to wake in the night thinking someone's there and you can't move?"

"I wouldn't say common." As if taking pity on him she said "That's what nightmares meant originally, waking up paralysed with the idea someone was causing it. Has that been happening to you?"

"It nearly may have. I won't let it," Donald vowed.

When he left the pub he found he'd had quite a lot to drink. The figures in the windows might almost have been mocking his bids to walk straight or stand still. He managed to laugh at his erratic progress until he was nearly home, when he caught sight of a man loitering in the middle of a side street. "Stay out of the road," Donald managed mostly to pronounce, "before you get yourself run over."

Perhaps this was unnecessary, since he couldn't hear any traffic or even anybody else. Donald's eyes weren't focusing too well, so that he might have taken the man to be holding a portable computer, but although the object was as dead white as its owner he couldn't avoid recognising that it was a book. "Are you following me?" he blurted and tried to laugh. "You can't if you can't move."

At least the blurred sight of the man let Donald stand still;

in fact, he might almost have been forgetting how to behave otherwise. The thought overwhelmed him with a panic worse than any he'd experienced last night in bed. It seemed to rob him of speech, even of breath. With an effort that made his chest ache he sucked in a lungful of air, which released him. He staggered forward without meaning to and then without desiring it at all. "Go where you're wanted," he shouted, "and that isn't here." He'd already turned his back on the fellow, and was able to stumble home.

His conversation with the doctor didn't help him sleep. It simply left him conscious that his experience wasn't quite like the one she'd described, because he felt as if lying there in the dark could attract a watcher, unless his confrontation in the street had done so. Eventually he struggled out of bed and reeled across the room to fumble the curtains apart. The street was deserted except for an ill-defined face—his own dim reflection. After that he made himself lie still in bed, though this felt like a threat of paralysis. Sleep caught up with him at last, although never for very long, and he rose none too steadily before dawn.

By the time he left the apartment the streetlamps had shut down. Mist turned the ends of streets into charcoal sketches, imperfectly erased. Donald found he welcomed the vicious chill, which was bound to have driven the loiterer away. He felt like celebrating the absence as he reached the junction, but the man was still in the side street. He might not have stirred since Donald had last seen him, except that he was hundreds of yards closer. "Have you been like that all night?" Donald cried. "Are you completely mad?"

The white face held as still as the marble carving it resembled altogether too much. He couldn't tell whether the empty eyes were gazing at him or the book, if they could see at all. He found he was desperate to provoke a response, any response. "Don't you like being talked to? Better make yourself scarce before I call someone."

He very much hoped this would do the trick, but the figure stayed lifeless, not even displaying a breath. Its defiant inertia and his failure to shift it enraged him, and he strode at it, hardly knowing what he meant to do. He grabbed its left hand to jerk it into some kind of life, but let go at once and fell back. However cold the day was, the man's hand felt dismayingly colder, and as hard as stone.

Donald could have thought the fellow had frozen to death overnight, except that as he made for the junction he heard a surreptitious rustling behind him. He'd heard that sound before, and now he recognised the turning of a page. He swung around to catch the statue in the act, but its stance was challenging him to prove it had moved. "I warned you," Donald shouted and strode furiously to work.

Mildred blinked at him. "Aren't you feeling well? Do you want to go home?"

"There's nothing wrong with me. I need to be here," Donald protested and thought of a reason he could say aloud. "Two of us can keep twice as much of an eye out for pilfering."

That needn't entail staying still whenever a customer came in. Donald followed them about, enquiring whether he could help. Perhaps he shouldn't have asked quite so often, since it visibly irritated Mildred. He tried varying the question, not least because it had started to feel like a threat of stagnation. "Can we show you anything?" he said, and "Anything we can find for you?" as well as "Are you after anything in particular?" until at last it was time for his lunch.

There were human statues in the streets, but not the one he'd touched. Ten minutes of dodging through the crowds brought him to the town hall. While a number of stone statues occupied the square in front of the colonnaded entrance, none of them depicted Samuel Huntley. The girl inside an enquiry booth in the marble foyer sent Donald into an enormous hall where a roped-off zigzag queue brought him at last to a clerk behind a window. "Do you authorise street performers?" Donald said.

The greying man peered at him as if trying to decide what manner of performance Donald might put on. "They need to get a permit from us, yes."

"And if they don't behave you'll deal with them." When the clerk raised his face to prompt more information Donald said "I'd like to report the man who's being a statue of Samuel Huntley."

"We don't tell them who they have to be. You'd need to give us his name." The man squinted at Donald before adding "A statue, you said. What's your complaint?"

"He's been following me home. I believe that's called harassment. Yes, I said a statue. I can see that may sound a bit ridiculous."

The clerk's face wasn't owning up to an opinion. "Any reason he should do that?"

"I took back my money when he didn't move. Maybe this is his revenge."

The clerk's lack of an expression was an answer in itself. "It wouldn't be our business," he said. "You'd want the police."

"And I'll get them if I need to, believe me." Donald's fury at the scepticism he sensed made him almost unable to say "Perhaps you can tell me where the actual statue has gone."

"Mayor Huntley, did you say? He's gone all right, for good."

Donald wouldn't have expected the clerk to sound so openly gratified. "Why, what happened?"

The clerk leaned towards the aperture beneath the window and lowered his voice. "The contractors weren't too careful about moving him, and someone here didn't think he was worth sticking back together."

"I thought he had a reputation. Didn't he pioneer some way of calming children down?"

"That's the tale his friends put about." Lower still the clerk said "There's some families that know what he used to do to our grandparents. Made them stand for hours and Christ help anyone who moved an inch."

Donald found he preferred not to hear any more, let alone to ponder what he'd heard. He hadn't time to go to the police now, and he rather hoped he'd already done enough. Mightn't the confrontation have sent the street performer on his way? Donald hurried back to the shop, which was less of a refuge than he would have liked, even from his thoughts. Whenever a customer lingered to examine an item he was seized by an urge to budge them, so that he felt compelled to point out other articles to them—anything he could find that seemed even remotely appropriate. "You need to calm yourself down, Donald," Mildred said after he'd tried to sell a book of cartoons to a man who was deliberating over a comedy film. "Make sure you get some rest tonight. You're disturbing people."

Better that, Donald almost retorted, than leaving them so undisturbed that they mightn't be able to move. Besides, dealing with customers felt like postponing his return home. All too soon he had to make his way through the crowds that might be hiding somebody less active than they were, although why should that be so threatening? As the streets grew emptier he began to hope for company or else to see nobody at all. When he reached the side street where he'd seen the frozen man, he almost couldn't look. But the street was deserted, and so was everywhere closer to home.

He'd been secretly afraid that if he was the first to touch the statue, that might have brought it after him. Suppose the woman at the book group was right, and Samuel Huntley had been roused somehow by the destruction of his image? If Huntley had regarded stillness as power, how determined might he have been to exert it? Although Donald was able to conclude none of this was true—the part about Huntley, at any rate—he found his thoughts distressingly irrational. However dull tonight's meeting might be, at least it would make sense.

The tenants met in Miss Hart's apartment on the top floor. Until now Donald had quite liked the figurines in her living-room, miniature sculptures collected from around the world, and why should he change his mind? Everyone agreed that the apartment committee should campaign against the proliferation of nightclubs in the neighbourhood and involve the local councillor. As Donald wondered why agreement had taken several sluggish hours, Miss Hart said "There are too many people lurking round here as it is."

"You've seen him?" Donald blurted. "Where is he now?"

"I don't mean anyone specific, Mr Curtis. I was referring to the types who loiter near the clubs."

Donald couldn't let this reassure him until he looked out of her window. As far as he could see, the street below and all those in sight were deserted. He very much hoped that the Huntley imitator hadn't merely gone away but had found a new role or reverted to his previous persona. "We all need to deal with any undesirables in the locality," he said as he left Miss Hart's, and didn't mind sounding pompous.

He walked down three floors to his apartment without feeling any need to put on speed. He took his time over preparing for bed and promised himself he would sleep. He was taken aback to find he'd been so nervous earlier that he hadn't opened the bedroom curtains. They looked untidy from his fumbling at them in the night, and he made to adjust them. Taking hold of them let him glimpse a man outside the window—waiting for a friend, no doubt, or else a taxi, or simply having halted to talk on the phone. But the figure was silent, and the object in its pallid hand wasn't a phone. When Donald snatched the curtains apart he saw that the statue was staring at him.

The wide blank white eyes were directed at him, at any rate, and so was the colourless face. The statue had altered its posture, so that the head was turned towards him. In a moment he realised that Samuel Huntley was waiting for him to read the book. A solitary name was etched at the top of the left-hand page—Donald's name.

He had evidence of harassment now. He had a reason to contact the police. Should he let the man hear him calling them, or would that warn the fellow off? Better to make certain he stayed there to be arrested, and Donald made to turn his back, except perhaps he should keep his persecutor in sight to ensure he didn't escape. Donald needn't leave the window; he had only to take out his phone. Or perhaps he should summon witnesses first, in which case he would have to shout loud enough to be heard all the way upstairs, although how would he let anybody in when he was having trouble even reaching in his pocket for the phone? The struggle seemed to be interfering with his vision, filling his eyes with the glare of the streetlamps or with some other pallor. In another moment unrelieved white was all he could see, though it wasn't quite like seeing. With an effort that stopped his breath Donald wrenched his arms up so that he could find his eyes, but when he groped at them he didn't know which felt more like stone: his fingertips or the globes beneath the unblinking lids. Then the distinction ceased to matter, any more than it applied to the rest of him, though he felt anything but calm. Indeed, his panic felt as though it was set in stone.

SANCTUARY

by
KEALAN PATRICK BURKE

"Go get your father," Mother said, and the spoon froze a half-inch from Liam's milk-sodden lips. His gaze moved from the daydream he'd been projecting upon the wall above the scarred kitchen table, to his left, where his mother was laboring over the stove. The bacon and eggs were burning. He could smell them as they hissed and popped. His mother, almost skeletally thin beneath her threadbare robe, stabbed at them as a blue plume of smoke rose around her, or maybe *from* her. It was hard to say. It was, after all, Sunday morning, and he couldn't remember the last time he'd seen her be anything but angry on a Sunday.

Between his mother and the table stood an empty chair, where on any other morning, his father would have been sitting, face buried in a newspaper and communicating in mumbles. But as the sacristan, Father was required to go to church on Sunday, both services. Afterward, he celebrated spirits of a different kind.

With difficulty, Liam swallowed his cereal and lowered the spoon. His mother's request made him feel sick. He didn't want to get dressed, didn't want to walk through the snow down the narrow crumbling street. Lately it had begun to feel like a throat eager to ingest him. And most of all, he didn't want to go to

McMahon's, the corner bar where he knew he'd find his father. He just wanted to finish his breakfast and go back upstairs to his room, to his sanctuary, where he spent most of his time reading and writing and drawing. It was safe there, surrounded by the portraits he had drawn to keep him company, portraits he wished were real so that they could take the place of the real world. Down here where the adults existed, there was nothing but raised voices and hurt feelings, infrequently punctuated by unexpected bursts of violence from which not even he was immune. Like the smell of those burning eggs, he felt the sourness and uncertainty of the world outside his room trying to attach itself to him like a second skin, trying to induct him into the same misery that had assimilated his parents.

"Won't he be back soon?" he asked his mother, quietly.

"Do what you're told," she snapped without turning to look at him, and that was good because he felt as long as the coldness of her gaze was not on him, he could be brave, continue to make his case. As soon as she looked at him, she would kill the words in his mouth and he would know he was doomed.

"The weather's really bad," he said, and glanced out the window. Beyond the frosted glass, thick snowflakes fell like feathers from a ruptured pillow. "He'll probably want to get home before it gets any worse."

He jumped as the spatula made a sharp clang against the side of the frying pan. "For fuck *sake*, Liam," she said in a dangerous voice. "If I have to ask you again, I'll put your head through the wall."

He rose quickly, careful not to let the legs of his chair scrape against the stone floor. His parents hated that. He didn't like it much either, but it's not like it was ever intentional. He cast a longing glance at the half-eaten bowl of soggy cornflakes and the slice of cold toast and marmalade sitting untouched next to it, and went to get his coat and boots on. At the doorway, he looked back at his mother. Although he was only ten years old, he could remember a time when she didn't look so pale and faded, like a photograph left too long in the sun. There were still memories of her lit from within by the light of summer. He remembered her smile and the color in her cheeks, the twinkle in her eyes. He remembered her love. Now, as he looked upon a lank-haired witch glaring down into a frying pan full of blackened, twisted things, he feared he would never know that love again.

"And tell him if he doesn't come home, he can stay with whatever whore will have him," she said through an ugly sneer that made her face look like a cheap mask melting in the heat from the stove.

Silently, Liam exited the room.

* * *

Winter had made a monochrome gradient of the world, broken here and there by dark strips where the snow had fallen like flesh from the withered arms of the trees and the twisted remains of broken streetlights, which bent over the street like the ribcage of some long-dead giant. Liam was bundled up in a thick woolen jacket, but the holes he'd worn in the elbows allowed the icy wind to creep in, chilling him where he stood. Over his scarf, the wet wool sent bolts of discomfort through him whenever it brushed against his teeth.

He looked down at the path. The snow had all but erased his father's footprints, leaving only faint impressions behind.

A series of muffled thumps behind him. Liam turned around. The house was an old Cape Cod, as dilapidated as everything else in this part of the city: a squat dispirited structure, the gaps in the once-white siding so stained with green mold, it looked like the side of an old boat. The inverted triangle of his mother's vulpine face, contorted in anger, filled the kitchen window. Mercifully, the thick glass and the soughing of the wind immunized him from the poison of her words, but the jab of her finger made the message clear enough: *Get moving.*

Breath held, shivering for reasons other than the cold, he did as instructed and stepped off the stoop.

The snow reached his knees, which made traversing the short path to the street all that more difficult, but he was thankful for the delay. The world on this side of the chain-link gate may not have been a paradise, but it was still home and home was where his sanctuary was: up the stairs and down the end of the hall. It may as well have been another country. That's where dreams were allowed; the nightmares stayed downstairs.

Aware without looking that his mother's eyes were on him, he trudged onward toward the gate.

* * *

The street was too narrow to allow the passage of vehicles, even if such a thing were possible, and the snow made it narrower still, which did nothing to alleviate Liam's impression of it as a gullet that would feed him into the ugly belly of the neighborhood. Once upon a time, this part of the city had thrived, an extension of the bustling metropolis that had long ago been rendered inaccessible by a wall of kudzu vines and weeds, which, almost unnoticed, had sprouted from the earth from between the remains of the old steel and grain mills before tearing them down and fortifying the wall. Before nature had reclaimed it, this had been a vital industrial outpost on the outskirts of the city, but with the death of industry and the departure of men whose aspirations ran further than drink, drugs, and murder, it had become a dead zone, a literal wrong side of the tracks, themselves buried beneath the tangles of blackened vine and twisted steel.

To Liam's left stood a rank of dead blank-faced houses, their eyes lightless, the caps of their porch roofs pulled low as if in shame, open maws empty of anything but dust and dark. Discarded toys half buried by the snow made an incongruously colorful cemetery of the yards, rusted swing sets like shriveled scale models of all that remained of the mills which had once served as the district's thriving heart.

To the right, a sharp decline led down to all that remained of the train tracks, the veins through which life had coursed through this outpost. In places some unknown force had ripped the tracks up and twisted them back in on themselves. The gravel had long been scattered. Beyond, the land fell away, became an industrial wasteland masked by the drifts. Here there were no children building snowmen or throwing snowballs or sledding. Everything was quiet, everything was buried. This did not surprise Liam. It was, after all, a Sunday, and in places such as these, places in which all that's left is faith, Sundays meant reverence. Outward signs of joy not directly affiliated with the gods would have been considered an affront.

Liam shivered, the cold now deep within his bones, his hands chilled beneath the gloves. He welcomed the discomfort, however, for it kept him from thinking about what he had seen the last time his mother had forced him to fetch his father.

Open your mouth about this, Liam, and it'll be the last time you'll be able to.

The houses drifted silently by and his school hove into view. Liam hated the school almost as much as he hated church (though he would die before he'd admit such a thing out loud), the tavern, and the neighborhood itself. School was prison, the walls speckled with some foul-smelling mineral deposit that glowed blue in the halflight. The hallway floors were bowed upward as if they'd built it atop the back of a sleeping giant. Few of the classroom lights worked and the teachers all appeared as if they'd been raised from the dead: pallid, drawn, their voices those of people who have found themselves in some terrible dream. The bathrooms smelled of brine; the chalkboards appeared to ripple when written upon, as if made of tar. To anyone else, it would have been a thing from nightmares. To Liam, it was the place of his education, though as he grew older, he had started to question the catechisms and syllabi to which he was being exposed. They seemed antiquated and decidedly cruel.

The school was an enormous Italianate Victorian, the structure much too big for the two dozen or so students who went there, an anachronism whose façade seemed to suggest a smug awareness of its own incongruity. The upper floors had been sealed off with strict warnings to all students not to trespass, which of course Liam had, and though he had found nothing but an endless series of faltering rooms stacked full of ancient books, he hadn't felt quite the same since. "The dust found its way inside me," he'd written on his sketchpad after returning home that day, but he had no idea what that was supposed to mean. He didn't even remember writing it, or drawing the picture of the janitor with the arms growing out of his mouth. In one of the old man's hands, he had drawn an alarm clock.

Liam looked away from the school. At the far end of the neighborhood, barely visible through the blizzard, stood the church. Even from here it looked like a face with hollow, admonishing eyes and a gaping mouth, the head atop the body he was now traversing like a tick. As much as he feared the school, the church absolutely terrified him, for surely if this part of the city had a black heart, a source of all its hated life, it was there within the unnaturally thick walls of the crumbling church. His parents had raised him to pray, to revere the gods that dwelled inside that place, and, as he was a good child and afraid of parents and gods alike, he had obeyed, might have continued to do so if not for his mother.

It was a day he would never forget. The Day of Leaves. He had been sitting in his room, daydreaming, the pencil in his hand moving of its own accord, sketching. His mother had burst into the room and slammed the door behind her, startling him. Her nose was bleeding and her eyes were wide. She looked like a wild thing, feral. It was the first time he had seen her look this way, but it wouldn't be the last. On that day, his body had tensed as she rushed toward him, but rather than strike or admonish the boy, she had grabbed him by the shoulders and brought her face close to his. Her breath had smelled sour, toxic, alien.

"You must listen to me, Liam," she'd said in a tone he wasn't sure he had ever heard before. Pleading, almost whining. "You must listen to your mother now, do you understand?"

Confused and frightened, he'd somehow managed a nod.

"Good, good. That's a good boy." She sat down next to him, her skin reeking of smoke and ash. Her hair was tangled, the edges singed. She kept pulling at it as she spoke. "I don't want you going to church anymore. I don't want you going anywhere your father goes, okay?"

"Okay," he'd said, because there was nothing else he could say.

"Promise me."

"I promise." Given his feelings on the subject, it was not a difficult promise to make. He appeared to be the only child not enthused by the prospect of further visits to a monstrous building that made his head hurt. He could have gone forever never smelling that sulfur smell again, or sitting on those mildewed pews, or looking upon the strange upside-down effigy with the goat's head someone had hung above the altar. He would be happy to never again hear the organ that only played tunes better suited to old ice cream trucks even when nobody was playing it. No, he would be perfectly happy to never set foot inside such a place again. Up until that moment, the only thing that had kept him from obeying his instincts in that regard had been his parents' intervention.

"You don't know what it is. What they're doing to us. What they've already done to your father. You must stay away from there and you must stay away from *him*. Do you understand?"

"Yes."

"You'll be safer in your room where nothing has to change."

"Okay."

She had shaken him one more time to be sure the words had reached him and then, satisfied, she did something she would never do again: she kissed him lightly on his brow. It burned where her lips had touched his skin. Then she was gone.

He thought that day might have been the last one in which his mother was capable of showing him any love. Though there had been far better days in the beginning before they reopened the church and tore the light from the sky and the color from the world, he still considered the Day of Leaves a good one because she had still cared. She had even kissed him!

But soon the poison got to her too, changed her, and while she continued to resist—sometimes so much he could *feel* it radiating in warm waves from her skin—she was no longer the same woman now. It was only a matter of time before she started going to church again, and then she'd make him go too. And gods only knew how they would be made to pay for straying.

The school lurched away from him, an explosion of vines

separating supposed innocence from the world of the adults. Here, propped up atop cracked concrete sidewalks, was McMahon's, the town hall, The Elder's House, the police station, and finally Ned's Grocery Store. Stone facades leaked viscous fluid from the cracks; fungus hemmed the bottoms. The roofs had sunken in the middle as if under the weight of something enormous and unseen. The breeze tore wisps of smoke from the slanted chimneys. On the opposite side of the road, a six-foot high stone fence topped by wrought iron railings blocked the view of the marsh but not the turbulent motion of the phosphorescent air above it. Green and yellow lights pulsated within the miasma. Tall withered trees that had grown up through the muck only to die looked like the masts of shipwrecks. And perhaps some of them were. The history of all but the marsh was known. Nobody in the neighborhood was permitted to know more, or worse, to venture beyond the fence, and nobody had ever tried. At least, that was the official story. Liam had heard whispers about foolish souls who had braved the marsh, their inevitable demise accompanied by the sound of something immense and soggy shifting itself to accommodate the induction of more life to be processed into nutrients. Others said that a contributing factor to the death and decay of this part of the city had been the derailment of a train ferrying toxic materials, which Liam supposed might explain the presence of a marsh within the confines of a city, the strange fog, and the things rumored to live in its depths.

All Liam knew is that it smelled like wet dog and saltwater.

Against the wall stood a row of scarecrows, or rather the remains of them. On the Day of Leaves, these creatures had their burlap chests stuffed with dead vegetation before they were set alight. Now all that remained were the charred crosses and twisted shreds of material that called to mind the burnt bacon and eggs on his mother's stove. The scarecrow's hoods, though blackened by the flames, retained their shape. The sheep skulls that had been placed inside those hoods would be there for always. Only the straw bodies would be replaced.

And at the north end of the neighborhood, a twelve-foot wall of dead, twisted trees and vines at its back like some kind of cape, sat the church, watching him with stained-glass eyes. The longer he stared, the more it seemed to tip its steepled hat at him, as if in acknowledgment. Lights flickered within as the last lingering penitents made their way through the aisles.

Without transition, it grew dark in an instant, long shadows yawning toward him from the open maw of the church.

Liam quickly averted his gaze and battled his way through the drifts to the pub.

* * *

There were half a dozen men inside, all of them clustered around the bar, all of them hunched over pints of whatever heady brown slop passed as ale. They fell silent as he entered, as if whatever they'd been discussing before his arrival was something not meant for his ears. He recognized them all as his neighbors, but if they recognized him, it didn't show. All he saw were wary deep-set eyes over pale faces and stained beards. A fire crackled in a large open hearth in the corner, but the heat was occluded by a trio of men who were watching their shadows dance upon the wall.

McMahon's head rose like a gray egg above the cluster of men at the bar. His face was a mass of lines, his eyes like black pebbles in a stream. Tattoos of mermaids crawled up both arms as he braced them on the mahogany bar and scowled at Liam. "This is no place for you."

Feeling as if the attention of the whole room was on him,

though only McMahon was looking directly at him, Liam swallowed and cast a hurried glance around at the men, hoping he might locate his father among them and therefore avoid having to engage McMahon in conversation. But his father wasn't here.

"I'm looking for—"

"I know who you're looking for. He'll be home when he's ready, and you can tell your mother that too. Haven't you learned your lesson by now?"

Again, Liam looked around. Clearly his father was here, somewhere, but he had already scanned the faces, or, when not made available for his study, the coats, and had come up empty. Where, then, was he? He put this question to McMahon, whose ruddy face seemed to darken with every second measured by the raven-faced clock above the bar.

"I told you to go home," he snapped. "And you'd better do it before you cause us any more trouble."

Liam stood immobile, helpless. If he returned home without his father, his mother would beat him to within an inch of his life. If he stayed, there was every chance McMahon would do the same. So he said the only thing he could think of to buy him some time.

"I need to use the bathroom."

"Go outside in the snow," said McMahon.

Then, rather unexpectedly, a voice piped up from beneath the smoky glow of the amber lamps. Liam thought he recognized it as that of Mr. Wyman, his maritime studies teacher, but couldn't be sure because Wyman's voice had a tendency to change depending on the weather.

"Let him look. None of this is our business anyway."

Though visibly displeased, McMahon threw up his hands and went back to scrubbing mildew from the beer taps. "As you like," he grumbled. "But it won't be on me. You can explain it to them when it all goes to hell."

Wyman—if that was indeed who had spoken from beneath the shelter of his tattered tweed jacket—breathed laughter that sounded like the snow huffing beneath the door. "We're all headed there anyway, McMahon. Doesn't matter in what order it takes us."

On the wall directly opposite where Liam stood was a cupboard with a missing door, inside which he could see an old dartboard. There were no numbers on the board, only symbols made of wire, symbols he recognized from his schoolbooks and the placard set into the stone block by the church door. The darts were made of boiled leather wrapped around shards of sharpened rat bones. Next to the board was a half rotted oak door that looked as if it had been designed for dwarves, but Liam knew it only appeared that way because time had forced it, like the rest of the building, to sink so that one had to step down into the adjacent room.

Eager to be free of the atmosphere his presence seemed to have generated among the gathering, Liam hurried to the door, grabbed the metal ring and shoved. Too large for its frame, the door resisted, the wood scraping against the stone lintel, the resultant sound monstrously loud in the confines of the small bar. Even the shadows seemed to shrink away from it. And then he was inside and forcing the door shut behind him.

He found himself in a narrow room with no windows and a ceiling so low he could touch it without fully extending his arm. Chaotic explosions of fungus gave the impression that the walls and ceiling were cushioned, or had been painted black, red, and gray. Broken chairs and tables had been stacked to the ceiling and back to the far wall so that there was little room to move. Liam had to skirt around them to reach the door in the far wall. When he did, he stopped, one hand on the ring, his heart in his throat.

Going beyond this point meant reliving his previous nightmare. The door led outside to an open-air bathroom covered only by a faltering tin roof, beneath which a single ceramic trough served as the place for men to relieve themselves. There were no facilities for women, because women never came here. There were no stalls. It was little more than a back alley with access blocked from the street by an avalanche of empty gas canisters and pulverized furniture.

Liam considered opening the door just a crack and calling his father's name, but he knew the howl of the wind and snow would likely make it inaudible. He lingered on the threshold, heart ramming against his ribs, until yet another voice entered the fray, this one more comforting than any other: *You can undo it. It will hurt at first like it always does, but you can take the pain. Later, when you're all alone, you can revise it and make it yours.* He had come to think of this soothing voice as echoes of his adult self, sent back through the mildewing pathways in his brain from some incomprehensible future, or a dream of one. And thus far, it had always steered him right.

Bracing himself, he yanked open the door and immediately recoiled at the stench of piss the icy breeze blasted into his face. Grimacing, he wiped his nose on his glove and stepped out into the alley.

The single naked bulb suspended from the tin roof threw little light. The cobblestones out here were greasy and uneven and missing in places. With the warmth of the bar shut behind him, Liam wrapped his coat tighter around himself and squinted into the poor light. The trough where men did their business was empty of all but stains, discarded cigarette butts, and a half-inch of dark brown water, which bubbled and gurgled as if alive. Liam avoided looking too long at it as he made his way past the "toilet" and out into the area of yard unprotected by the sagging roof.

The snow buffeted his face like gravel as he surveyed the dark expanse before him. He stood still for a moment beside the calamity of gas cans and furniture blocking the exit until he detected a sound to his right, from the area next to the old tin shed where the darkness was thickest.

Last time he'd come here on such a mission, he had not needed to venture so far into the yard. On that occasion, he'd found his father sitting in the trough, pants around his ankles, face raised to the tin roof in ecstasy as the violin woman worked on him.

Yes, no women came to McMahon's Bar, but these visitors had been women in shape only. Nothing else about them suggested femininity. Nothing about them was remotely human. And of course there wouldn't be. The church had sent them.

Liam dreaded coming upon such a scene again. It had taken him the better part of six months to recover from the last time, and only then because he had drawn sanity back into his head through his pictures. He knew he could do the same thing again now, no matter what he found, but he didn't want to have to experience it again first.

Unbidden, a small pulse of anger warmed the base of his throat and he frowned. Why had his mother made him come here again, knowing what he was likely to find? The answer, when it found him, was startling in its simplicity: they *wanted* him to see, *wanted* him to be driven mad, maybe in the hope that this time, it would take and they'd finally be rid of him.

Incensed now, the anger spreading downward, setting fires throughout his chest and down into the pit of his stomach, he forgot his fear and made his way over to that suffocating swatch of darkness beside the old tin shed in which McMahon kept the spare barrels of beer, the moonshine, and the mason jars full of animals he had never had the heart to let go.

The sounds were louder here. Sounds he recognized despite being too young to know them. He stood there for some indeterminate amount of time until his eyes adjusted to the gloom and he could see the shapes, the nakedness, hear the passion as his father had his way with another one of *them*.

The violin lady was suspended above his father via her broken, twisted arms, her long-fingered hands clamped to the roof of the shed on one side, the wall on the other. She had no legs to speak of. Instead, her ragged torso ended in violin strings that started somewhere in her throat. Made taut by the concrete block suspended at the other end of the strings where the rest of her body should have been, the wind played a haunting tune she controlled by moving her mouth and working her throat. His father knelt before her, her bare breasts clamped in his dirty hands, his mouth working feverishly over her erect nipples. When she moaned, it was music; when he gasped, it was an ugly, hungry, desperate sound. His manhood was erect, stabbing pitifully at the empty air beneath the concrete block as she weaved from side to side.

The woman became aware of Liam first. She did not panic—they never did—instead she released one hand and then the other and dropped down into the darkness of the rubble until she was out of sight, the faint twanging of the violin strings the only indication that she was still there, hidden, as she alerted his father to their visitor.

The old man still had his hands before his face where the violin woman's breasts had been only a moment before. Slowly, as if surfacing from a dream, he dropped them and looked dazedly at the boy standing before him. The confusion quickly turned to rage as he rose like a wraith, tugging up his pants as he readied a hand to strike the boy.

"I fucking *told* you, I told *her* not to bother me," he said, a string of drool dangling from his lower lip. Even in the gloom, Liam could see the red glare in his eyes. He was drunk on more than just the beer.

Liam braced himself for the blow, his head turned slightly to the side, eyes shut tight.

It didn't come.

When next he opened his eyes, his father was staring uncertainly at him, something like fear on his long haggard face, both of them shivering from the cold.

"I'm allowed to do whatever I want here," his father said. "That's how it is now."

Discordant music as the violin woman skittered away down through a rent in the rubble. The old man looked over his shoulder with something like sadness before turning his attention back to his son. "I'm not coming home. I don't belong there anymore. But you know that already."

The snow whipped itself into a frenzy around them.

"I'll stay here and die with the rest of them. That's what was going to happen anyway. We all knew it. We just didn't expect it so soon. The gods can have us. I'm sure they won't turn us away. But whatever happens, this place can't last forever. Not like this. The city is dead."

Despite the anger, Liam shared his father's sadness. It didn't have to be this way. *Revise*, advised the voice he kept secret inside him, but he knew even if he did it would do nothing to erase the horror that lived on this side of things. All was darkness here, because it belonged here, and if it didn't stay contained in places such as these, it would corrupt everything.

"I'll go then," Liam said. "What should I tell Mother?"

His father shrugged on his coat, tied up his shirt and looked grimly at his son. "Whatever you want. It hardly matters now. She's lost, I'm lost. So are you." Then he walked by his son and went back inside the bar.

After a few moments of staring at the rubble and the life that was no longer hiding within the shadows, Liam turned and followed.

When he went inside, the crowd of men had doubled. Everyone in the neighborhood seemed to be there, with the exception of the women, of course, all of whom would be at home tending to their sons and waiting for the end.

* * *

His mother was still standing by the stove when he returned with the bad news, but when she failed to answer him, he realized the blackening of the bacon and eggs had spread up to her elbows.

"I tried," he told her through the tears. "I always try. Sometimes it's just bigger than me and I can't make it any better."

She turned to look at him and he saw the grease sizzling in her eye sockets. Her hair fell out in clumps and landed in the frying pan, where it shriveled and died. When she opened her mouth to respond, he saw that it was full of straw, and as he looked on, the tears coming freely now, she collapsed in a heap on the floor. A sheep skull skittered across the stone and bumped against the leg of his chair, making it shriek.

Despondent at his failure, he went upstairs to his sanctuary and shut the door behind him.

Then he withdrew his sketchpad from beneath the bed.

His limited talents, which would not reach their full potential for years yet, perhaps ever, frustrated him as he erased and replaced and scratched and scribbled, but never got it right.

* * *

"Mr. Thompson, did you hear a word I said?"

Groggily, Liam raised his head from the protective darkness of his arms. When the other children saw that he'd been sleeping, a fine thread of drool connecting his lips to his desk, they giggled nervously. Nobody would outright laugh at him. They knew his history, knew what he'd done, and that only the fact that he was so young had kept him from being stuck in a white room with rubber walls somewhere.

Blinking away the confusion, Liam looked up at his teacher. Dressed bat-like in the professorial robes typical of teachers in Catholic boys' schools, Mr. Wyman clucked his tongue and grabbed the sketchpad from the desk. "More of this macabre doodling? Mr. Thompson, I daresay if you put half as much effort into your language studies as you did these... these..." He gestured helplessly at the peculiar, morbid rendition of their church and the school and the myriad monsters his subconscious suggested could inhabit them, and tossed the pad aside. It hit the desk with a bang.

"Focus, child," the teacher said, and headed back to the top of the class.

Bright autumn sunshine turned the windows to gold and flooded the room with light, illuminating the dust. At Wyman's request, the other children gradually tore their attention away from Liam, from the weird kid, and returned their attention to the scrawl of French on the chalkboard.

"*Je m'appelle* John," Wyman instructed, his patrician smile aimed at every child in turn as he punctuated the air with a wizened finger as if it were a conductor's baton. "*Je m'appelle* Rebecca."

Liam tried to return his focus to the classroom, to the fraudulent construct his mind had created to protect himself from the wrath of the gods. Even though Wyman had moved away and let him be, he knew there would be consequences. Lately he was falling asleep more often, found it almost impossible to concentrate. His grades were dropping and the few friends who didn't hold his past against him had drifted away. He was stared at in the halls, mocked in gym, bullied in the bathroom. And then home, the most dreaded place of all, where his mother did her best to make it seem as if the divorce was not tearing her asunder. She too had quit the pretense of being a loving mother, confining him to his room with his books and his drawings. Sometimes late at night he could hear her weeping through the wall. Sometimes early in the morning he heard her talking on the phone and screaming about her "loser husband" and that "musician whore he shacked up with."

None of it meant anything to Liam. He was safe in his sanctuary where everything was under his control. He could exist between these two worlds, but not forever. Sooner or later he would have to find a way to tie them together so some kind of balance could be restored.

He glanced out the window through the glorious fraudulent day and saw the church on the horizon. Pristine, uncorrupted, normal. Dead leaves fell silently through the amber haze as the trees began to reveal their true selves. The city was like a held breath. Soon it would be time again to fill the scarecrows.

"Mr. Thompson?"

He snapped to attention and looked at Mr. Wyman, with his sweeping gray hair and rosy cheeks. "Yes, sir?"

"Eyes up here, please."

"Yes, sir."

"*Comment allez vous?*"

"*Je m'appelle Liam.*"

"*Très bon.*" He began to pace, his focus moving to another child. "Alex? *Comment t'allez vous?*"

Liam went back to pretending, but not before checking the ceiling behind him where in the corner nearest the door, the mold was starting to spread.

MATTER OF LIFE AND DEATH

by

SHERRILYN KENYON

"Ding dong, the bitch is dead."

Elliott Lawson looked up from her email to laugh at her assistant Lesley Dane. "And there is much rejoicing."

Dressed in a pink sweater and floral skirt, Lesley flounced around Elliott's tiny office with a wide smile before she added yet another bulging manuscript to the top of the mountain of manuscripts in Elliott's inbox. Was it just her or did that thing grow higher by the heartbeat? It was like some bad horror movie. *The Stack That Wouldn't Die.*

"Just think," Lesley continued, "no more emails with her calling us names and complaining about everything from title to synopsis to... you know, everything."

That was the upside.

The downside? "And no more selling three million copies the opening day either." While Helga East had been the biggest pain in the ass to ever write a book, her thrillers had set so many records for sales that her unexpected death left a huge hole in their publishing program. One that would take twenty or more authors to fill.

Elliott's stomach cramped at that reality and at the fact that she'd just lost her star pony in the publishing race. "What are we going to do?"

"We'll build another blockbuster."

She scoffed at her assistant. "You say that like it's an easy thing. Trust me, if it was, every book we published would be one." And that didn't happen by a longshot. They didn't even break even on ninety percent of them.

"Yeah, but still the bitch *is* dead."

It was probably wrong to be happy about that, but like Lesley, she couldn't help feeling a little relief. Helga had been a handful.

Oh who was she fooling? Helga had been the biggest bitch on the planet. A chronic thorn who had given Elliott two ulcers and a permanent migraine for four solid months around the release of any of Helga's books. In fact, Helga had been screaming at her over the phone when she'd had a heart attack and keeled over. It was creepy really. One second she'd been calling Elliott's intelligence and parentage into question and the next...

Dead.

Life was so fragile and *tragedies* like this rammed that home.

Lesley's phone rang. She left to answer it while Elliott stared out her tiny window at the red brick building next door where another drone like her worked a sixty-hours-a-week job at the bank. She didn't know his name and yet she knew a lot about him. He brought his lunch to work, preferred a brown tweed jacket, and he tugged at his hair whenever he was frustrated. It made her wonder what unconscious habits she had that he'd pegged about her. They'd never waved or acknowledged each other in any way, yet she could see enough personal details about him that she'd know him anywhere.

Not wanting to think about that depressing fact, she returned her attention to the cover proofs piled in front of her. One was for Helga's next book—the one she'd been working on when she'd died.

Her phone dinged, letting her know she had a new email. Sighing, she picked up her phone and looked at it.

For a full minute she couldn't breathe as she saw the last name she'd ever expected to see again.

Helga East.

Relax. It's just an old email that was forwarded by someone else or one that'd gotten lost in cyberspace for a couple of days. No need to panic or be concerned in the least. It was nothing.

Still, her stomach habitually knotted as she opened it.

Tell me honestly, Elliott, does it hurt to be that stupid? Really? What part of that heinous, godawful cover did you think I'd approve of? I hate green. How many times do we have to have this argument? Get that bimbo off the cover and take that stupid font and tell creative to stick it on the cover of someone too moronic to know better.

H.

PS the title, Nymphos Abroad, is disgusting, demeaning and insulting. Change it or I'll have another talk with your boss about how incompetent you are.

She sucked her breath in sharply as she realized the email pertained to the cover on her desk.

A cover Helga had never seen. It'd only arrived that morning. Two days after Helga's funeral.

Yeah, there was no way it was Helga. Anger whipped through her as she hit reply to the email. "Okay, Les, stop messing with me. I'm not in the mood."

A second later, a response came back.

Les? Are you on drugs? Surely you can't afford them on your measly salary. I've seen the cheap shoes you wear and that sorry excuse for a designer handbag that you think no one will know you bought in Times Square for five dollars. Now quit stalling, stop reading your email and call down to art and get me a cover worthy of my status.

She looked out her door to see Lesley on the phone, her back to her computer. Definitely not her pretending to be Helga.

But someone was. And they were doing a good job of it, too. They sounded *just* like her.

Who is this? she typed.

Helga, you nincompoop. Who did you think it was? Your mother? I swear, is there no one up there with a single brain cell in their head?

It couldn't be. Yet the return address in the header was Helga's. It was an email addy she knew all too well. Numberonewriter@ heast.com.

Maybe one of Helga's heirs was messing with her. But why would they do such a thing? Surely they wouldn't be as cruel as Helga had been?

Then again, maybe it was genetic. Meanness like Helga's had seemed to be hardwired into her DNA. Venomous cruelty was what the lonely old woman had lived and breathed.

Her heirs wouldn't be able to see that cover. They'd have no way of knowing what was on it.

There was that. No one outside of their publishing house had seen it.

Another email appeared.

Why are you still sitting at your desk, staring into space? I told you what to do. Get me a decent cover, you twit.

A chill went down her spine. One so deep that she actually jumped when her cell phone went off, signaling her that she had a new voice mail message. Weird, she hadn't heard it ring.

Reaching down, she pulled it up and accessed her box.

"I will not stand for that tawdry, disgusting cover. Do you hear me, Elliott? I want it gone, right now. Hit delete."

Her heart pounded at a voice she'd know anywhere.

Helga.

"You all right?"

She looked up at Lesley who was staring at her from the doorway. "I... I..." Pulling the phone down, she hit the four button to make it repeat. "Tell me what you hear?"

Lesley put it up to her ear. After a few seconds, she scowled. "Man, I hate those pocket dials where all you get is background noise. What kind of imbecile doesn't lock their phone?" She handed it back.

Baffled, Elliott replayed it and held it up to her ear to listen. It was still Helga, plain as the desk in front of her. "It's not a butt dial. Can't you hear her?" She held it back out to Lesley.

Again, Lesley listened. "There's no voice, El. Just a lot of background sounds like trucks on the highway or something, and someone laughing. You okay?"

Apparently not. How could they listen to the same thing and yet hear such radically different messages?

She hung up her phone and gave Leslie a forced smile. "Fine. Stressed. Tired."

Crazy...

Clearing her throat, she put the phone on her desk. "Did you need something?"

"Just reminding you about the marketing meeting in five minutes."

"Thanks." Elliott gathered her notes for the meeting while she tried her best not to think about the phone call and emails from a writer who was dead. It wasn't Helga. Some sick psycho was messing with her head.

Or it was a friend with a sorry excuse for a sense of humor. Yeah, that would be her luck.

It's not funny, folks. But the one thing she knew from being an editor was that humor was subjective. How many times had Helga written something that she'd rolled her eyes over only to have the billions of readers out there find it hysterical?

Maybe I'm being Punk'd.

Could happen… If only she was lucky enough for some hot celeb to pop out of a closet.

But there was no hot cheese in the meeting. Only mind-numbing details about books they'd already gone over a million times that left her attention free to contemplate who was being highly cruel and unusual to her.

Maybe it's someone in this meeting.

She looked around her coworkers, most of whom appeared as stressed out and bored as she was. No, they were too involved with their own lives to care about harassing her.

Why is this meeting taking so long?

It was hellacious.

Subversively, she glanced down at her watch and did a double take. Was it just her or was the second hand making a thirty-second pause between each tick?

By the time the meeting was out, she felt like she'd been stretched on the rack. Oh good Lord, why did they have to have these time-sucking wastes all the time? What Torquemada SOB thought this was a good idea?

But at least it was finally over. She breathed a sigh in relief as she gathered her things and headed back to her personal space.

The moment she was back in her office, she checked her email. There were ninety, n-i-n-e-t-y, messages from her wannabe Helga stalker.

She deleted them without reading.

Trying to put it out of her mind, she turned around in her chair to look at her "friend" in the other building. For once his office was dark. How strange. He never left early. But her attention was quickly drawn to something that was being reflected in the darkness of her glass. Something someone had attached to her cork bulletin board that she'd hung next to her door.

With a gasp, she turned around to see if her mind was playing tricks.

It wasn't.

Her heart in her throat, she got up and went to it. As she reached for it, her hand shook.

Someone had taken the mechanical printout of Helga's cover and pinned it with a blood-red tack to the board. It had nasty comments written all over it with a black magic marker. Worse? The handwriting looked just like Helga's.

Terror filled her as she ripped it down, then made her way to Lesley's desk. Lesley paused mid stroke on the keyboard to look up at her.

"Who did you let into my office while I was at the meeting?"

"No one."

"Someone went in there." She held the marked-up printout toward Lesley.

She frowned. "Why are you showing me that?"

"I want you to tell me who wrote on it."

Her scowl deepened. "You did, Elliott."

What? She snatched it back and turned it over.

All of Helga's writing was gone from it. Now the only pen marks were where someone had approved the art by placing Elliott's initials in the margins. "I didn't do this."

Lesley looked at it carefully. "It's your handwriting, hon. Believe me, I know."

But Elliott hadn't written on it. Not even a little bit.

How was this possible? How?

Her head started throbbing. Without another word, she returned to her office and sat down to stare at the mechanical of the cover sans the nastiness.

"I'm losing my mind." She had to be. There was no other explanation for what was going on.

The skin on the back of her neck tingled as if someone was watching her. She turned around in her chair to inspect her office.

She was alone.

Still the feeling persisted. And even more concerning was the prickly sensation that something wasn't right.

I'm being haunted…

Yeah, that's what it felt like. That uneasy feeling in the pit of her stomach. Something evil was in the room with her. It was all but breathing down her neck.

Panicked, she shot back to Lesley's desk. She needed to feel connected to someone alive.

Lesley gave her an arch stare. "You're pale. Is something wrong?"

If not for the fear of Lesley thinking her insane, she'd confide in her. But no one needed to know her suspicion. "Doing research for a book on my desk. You know anything about the paranormal?"

"Not really, but…"

"What?"

"I have an exorcist on speed dial."

Elliott burst into nervous laughter. Until she realized Lesley wasn't joking. "You're serious?"

"Absolutely. My best friend in the world is an exorcist and demonologist."

"Who in the world has a friend who's an exorcist?"

She held her phone up and grinned. "Me. Whatcha want me to check?"

"Um… do you think I could speak with your friend?"

Her grin returned to a frown. "Sure. Her name's Trisha Yates. You want me to email it to you?"

"Please." Even though she was still skittish about her office, Elliott returned and closed her door. There was no need in Lesley overhearing this particular conversation.

Out of habit, she glanced to the office across the way to see her "friend."

Her heart stopped beating.

He was hanging from the ceiling, swinging in front of his desk.

No! It wasn't possible. She closed her eyes and covered them with her hands. *It's not real. It's not real…*

But it was. As soon as she opened her eyes, she saw him across the way. Medics were swarming his office, cutting him down.

He was dead. Her unknown partner across the way was gone.

All of a sudden, both of her phones started ringing. Gasping, she jumped. She grabbed her cell phone. "Hello?"

No one was there.

Same for the office phone. All she heard was a dial tone.

"It doesn't hurt, you know."

She spun at the sound of a male voice behind her. It was the ghostly image of the man from the other building. "W-w-what doesn't hurt?" It was like someone else had control of her body. She was strangely calm and yet inwardly she was freaking out.

"Death. We all die." He walked through her.

Breathless, scared and shaking, she watched as he continued past her, to the wall. He went through it and walked back to his cubicle in the other building.

No… No…

No!

As soon as the ghost was over there, the corpse which was now lying on the floor turned its head toward her and smiled.

She stumbled back into the door. Terrified, she spun around and clawed at the handle until she was able to open it.

Lesley met her on the other side. "Okay, you are seriously starting to freak me out. What's going on?"

I'm locked in a horror movie.

She didn't dare say that out loud. Les would never understand. Without a word, she headed for the bathroom with her phone. She pulled up the email and then dialed the number.

"Hello?"

Wow, the exorcist sounded remarkably normal. Even friendly. "Is this Trisha?"

"Yes. You are…" She paused as if searching the cosmos for an answer. "Elliott Lawson."

"How did you know that?"

"I'm psychic, sweetie. I know many things."

Elliott wasn't so sure she liked the sound of that. But before she could comment, the phone went dead. She growled in frustration as she tried to dial it again.

Nothing went through.

Instead, her email filled up with more postings from Helga…

And other authors, too—some of whom she hadn't worked with for several years.

"Why did you refuse to renew my contract?"

Elliott shrieked at the mousy voice that came out of a stall near her. A woman in her mid-thirties came out. Her skin had a grayish cast to it and her eyes were dark and soulless.

"Emily? What are you doing here?" Emily had been one of her first authors she'd bought as a new hire. They'd had a good ten-book run before Elliott had made the decision to cut her from their schedule. While Emily's numbers had held steady, they hadn't grown. Every editor was held accountable for their bottom line and Emily had been hurting her chances for advancement. So Elliott had decided to move on to another author.

"Why did you do it? I was in the middle of a series. I had fans and was growing. I don't understand."

"It was business."

Emily shook her head. "It wasn't business. I can count off three dozen other authors who don't sell as well as I did who you've kept on all these years."

"Not true." She always cut anyone who couldn't pull their weight.

Emily looked down at her arms, then held them up for Elliott to see. "I killed myself over it. After five years of us talking on the phone and working together, you didn't even send over a card for my funeral. Not one stinking, lousy card."

"I didn't know."

"You didn't care."

Elliott struggled to dial her phone. "You're not dead. This is a nightmare."

"I'm dead. Damned to hell for my suicide because of *you*!" Her eyes turned a bright, evil red as the skin on her face evaporated to that of a leather-fleshed ghoul. She rushed at Elliott.

Screaming, Elliott ran for the door.

The handle was no longer there. She was trapped inside.

With Emily.

Terrified and shaking, she pounded on the door with her

fist. "Help me! Please! Someone help me!"

Emily grabbed her from behind and yanked on her hair. "That's what I begged for. Night, after night, after night. But no one answered my pleas either. I spent two years trying to get another contract and no one would touch me because of the lies you told about me. All I ever dreamed about was being an author. I didn't want much. Just enough to live on. Two books a year. But you couldn't allow me to have that, could you? You ruined me."

"I'm sorry, Emily."

"It's too late for sorry." Emily slung her through the door.

Elliott pulled up short as she found herself back in her office. Only it was hot in here. Unbearable. She went to the window to open it.

She couldn't.

When she tried to turn the furnace down, it burned her hand. It whined before it spewed steam all over her.

She turned to run only to find more hateful notes from Helga.

Suddenly laughter rang out. It filled the room and echoed in her ears.

She spun around, doing her best to locate the source. At first there was no one there. No one until Lesley appeared in the corner.

Elliott ran to her and grabbed her close, holding on to her like a lifeline. "I need to go home, Les. Right now."

"You are home, Elliott. This is where you spend all of your time. This is what you love. It's all you love." Lesley pulled out her chair and held it for her. "Go ahead. Reject those books. Crush more writers' dreams. You're famous for not pulling punches. For telling it like it is. Go on. I know how much you relish giving your honest, unvarnished opinion."

A thousand crying voices rang out in a harsh, cacophonous symphony.

Your writing is amateurish and pedestrian. Do not waste my time with any further submissions. I only give one per customer and your number is up.

If you can't take my criticism, then you've no business being a writer. Trust me. I'm a lot kinder than your readers, if you ever have any, will be.

While I found the idea intriguing, your writing was such that I couldn't get past the second page. I suggest you learn a modicum of grammar or better yet, stick to blog posts and Twitter feeds for your creative outlet.

Over and over, she was inundated with rejections and comments she'd written to authors.

And for once, she realized just how harsh they were.

Elliott shook her head, trying to clear it. "Helga! Why are you haunting me? Why can't you leave me in peace?"

Lesley tsked at her. "Oh, honey, Helga isn't haunting you."

"Yes, she is. I know I should have gone to her funeral, but—"

"Elliott, Helga didn't die." Lesley gestured toward her computer monitor. Her email vanished to show an image of Helga happily at work in her office. "You did."

"I don't understand."

Laughing, Lesley transformed into the image of a red demon with glowing yellow eyes. "Welcome to hell, my dear. From this day forward and throughout all eternity, you will get to be Helga's editor. Oh and I should mention, she's now doing a book a week."

GRAFFITI OF THE LOST AND DYING PLACES

by

SEANAN MCGUIRE

The Financial District was a corpse in the twilight. The streets lay empty, gutters choked with trash from the dearly departed workday. Sidewalks that had been crowded and vital only a few hours before seemed cracked and long-deserted, like no one had walked them in a hundred years. The faint smell of decaying food, human urine, and despair hung over everything like a shroud.

A few stores at the district's edge were still illuminated, flickering neon signs hanging in their windows to lure weary travelers and overtime wage slaves into the comfortingly stale air inside. The shelves in those stores were always too close together, forcing all but the slimmest consumers to walk awkwardly sideways, eyes scanning the array of stale crackers and aging chocolate until they found something that looked, if not nutritious, at least palatable; some small morsel of fat and empty carbohydrates to get them home.

Lindy drooped at the counter of one such nameless convenience store, chin propped on her hand and her eyes fixed on the security monitor. It was split into four quadrants, one for each of the two aisles, one for the register, and one for the street outside. Nothing had moved on any of them for over an hour, not since she'd watched the last businessman run for the subway entrance, coat flapping behind him like the wings of some great and bewildered moth. She hoped, in a vague way, that he'd managed to catch his train home. This was no place to be stranded.

She glanced at the clock. *She* was only going to be stranded for another four hours and twenty-six minutes.

"Piece of cake," she mumbled, letting her head fall forward until it hit the counter with a gentle "bonk." She left it there. The wood was cool against her forehead, and besides, she hadn't had a customer since before the businessman ran by. She was alone. She could take a breather.

The bell over the door chimed gently, and was still.

Lindy sat upright, suddenly so stiff that her shoulders felt as if they'd been wrenched back by an invisible hand. She scanned the aisles, and when that didn't reveal a customer, she looked to the monitor, searching for signs of movement. Nothing moved. Nothing failed to move, either: there were no strange shadows or unexplained silhouettes reported by her cameras. She was as alone now as she'd been since the start of her shift, when Zack had fled for the door with a quickly muttered "the bathroom's out of order again" and a wave as perfunctory as it was insincere. For the most part, she didn't mind the fact that her interactions with her coworkers never amounted to anything of substance. It hurt less that way.

This store had been standing for sixty years, successful in the beginning, when the neighborhood around it had thrived, then aging and becoming more run-down as the neighborhood around it fell into decline. Now, with the Financial District doing so much *better* than those little Mom-and-Pop businesses that used to fill the streets, with its tall towers lighting up the sky every time the sun rose, with its well-groomed worshippers flooding the sidewalks every morning on their way to their sweet and soulless church, it would have made sense for the store's business to boom. It didn't. It was dying, an inch at a time, snubbed by those same worshippers, who saw neon signs and cluttered shelves as signs of shabbiness, and not proof that this was a place that knew the city better than any of their workplaces, which still smelled faintly of sawdust and fresh paint.

Lindy had been nine years old the first time she heard the word "gentrification," still ten years out from her job at the edge of the Financial District, but she'd recognized it for the venomous thing it was the moment its syllables were loosed into the air. Gentrification slithered and struck, sapping the good things from the places it hunted until all that remained was an empty shell that had once been a healthy community. Gentrification raised prices until the folks who'd lived and died in a neighborhood couldn't even afford to haunt it anymore.

It had started small here. A new high-rise in a vacant lot, the sort of thing no one could object to: the space had been going wanting, after all, and didn't that tower sparkle pretty in the sun? The people who came to work there shopped at the local stores and ate at the local restaurants, and it wasn't a bad thing, no, not at all. It brought money to the neighborhood. Everyone liked money.

Especially the landlords, who'd seen the potential for more money and started raising rents at a rate no one could keep up with. Half the little stores the new businesspeople had been shopping at were closed within the year, soaped-up windows looking in on empty, dusty rooms. Only a few of them found new tenants. The rest were sold, demolished, replaced with more high-rises, this time with built-in retail space at their foundations, perfect little boxes waiting for perfect little franchise locations with familiar logos and comforting designs. Some people objected. Some people always objected. The rest said look, isn't this just capitalism in action? The businesses that closed were old, tired, ready to be replaced by something new and vital and capable of contributing to the neighborhood. It was still mostly the same as it had ever been, right? Let change come. Let revitalization happen.

Change came. Revitalization happened, if revitalization meant new money and more money and all the old neighbors leaving and all the old stores closing, until it was just the Financial District, nothing more; until the history was fading, a footnote in the story of the city. Until the whole neighborhood became a vampire in reverse, dying when the sun went down, springing back to life every morning.

It was only a matter of time before the Financial District got hungry again, before the landlord who owned this building heard the siren song of revitalization and raised the rent past what the owners could afford. When that happened, Lindy would be out of a job, and would go looking for something else to keep body and soul together. And odds were that she'd find it at the blasted outer edge of the revitalization zone, where the people with any prospects at all had already seen the writing on the wall and moved on.

Sometimes she envied them for having that kind of foresight, for being flexible enough to trade no-name Mom-and-Pop convenience stores for the security of 7-11 or Quiznos or whatever the hot new thing to cram into prefab retail space was these days. Lindy couldn't do it. She loved the weird little hole-in-the-wall places that paid her rent, loved the uniqueness of each one, the way they all had their own characters and personalities. Buildings could be people: she'd decided that a long time ago. So could businesses. These little stores lived, in their way, until gentrification and revitalization came along and drained them dry.

She couldn't save them. She couldn't even save herself. But she could stand witness as they died, and maybe that wasn't enough, but it was more than most people seemed willing to do.

The bell above the door jingled again. Lindy looked up. The monitors were empty.

"Fucking earthquakes," she muttered, and went back to her long, quiet vigil, while the Financial District slept outside, and the last living pieces of the great beast that had been the old neighborhood trembled, waiting for their hour to come.

* * *

Her shift ended when it was supposed to end: no surprises there, not tonight, not tomorrow, not the next night, or the night after, as her tenure as clerk for this inconvenience store inched toward its close. She counted out the register, put the night's proceeds—such as they were—into the safe, made the little notes that made the owners happy, and locked the door. They used to be open twenty-four hours a day. Now they closed at midnight. There was a hand-written apology taped to the inside of the door, explaining to their long-time customers—the five or six who remained—that this was a cost-cutting measure and would only last until business improved. Business wasn't going to improve. Lindy knew it; the owners knew it; the customers knew it. This was last call. Chairs on the tables, please clean up behind yourself on the way out the door.

She had run into one of their regulars a week ago, when some imp of the perverse had driven her into the 7-11 down the block to buy a gallon of milk. She felt bad about being unfaithful to the ghost of the old neighborhood, but she also worked for minimum wage, and she felt good about paying two bucks less for her dairy. Carl had been standing at the counter, waiting to pay for his coffee. He hadn't been by the store in

353

almost a month, and he'd reddened when he saw her, like she'd caught him cheating. In a way, perhaps she had. But then, in a way, she was cheating too, so she'd simply given him a genial nod and gone about her business. By the time she'd reached the counter with her milk, he'd been gone.

She locked the door, shoved her hands into her pockets for warmth, and turned her back on the silent, pristine monstrosity that was the Financial District. She'd be miles away when it shambled back to life, in the room she was subletting on the other side of the city, in a neighborhood that wasn't her own, that would never be home. The apartment building she'd grown up in had been right at the heart of the gentrification. It was still there, unlike so many others, rebuilt and improved and turned into live/work spaces for people who thought it was just *so great* to live in the *city* where so many things had *happened*, where now *they* could start happening. She'd managed to hold out through three rent increases, but like so many others, in the end, she just couldn't hold on.

No one could, when money came to town.

The further Lindy walked from the Financial District, the more the gangrene of gentrification appeared around her. There was always graffiti in the city—she knew some of the artists personally, admired their work, loved the way they could make a political statement in freehand spray paint—but the graffiti here was crude, angry, more swear words, more enormous painted genitalia, none of the finesse or subtlety she'd seen in the murals that still sprang up in healthier neighborhoods. FUCK THE RICH said one wall, and THEY'VE ALREADY FUCKED US said another, and she didn't disagree.

The stores here were still small, still varied: no chains or outlets, not yet. *Give it time*, she thought. The tendrils of the Financial District were ever-reaching and ever-hungry, searching for their next victim even as they twined around their current one. Money would come here, as it had come everywhere else, and these sickening streets would succumb to an infection they didn't even know they had.

There were footsteps behind her. Lindy tensed but didn't turn. She'd found that money had a way of behaving like a tsunami: once it began concentrating in one place, everyone swore it would trickle down into the local economy, but it didn't. Instead, it pulled itself out, one dollar and one dime at a time, leaving people starving and desperate. Poverty didn't make people cruel. Money did, she sometimes thought. And hunger could make anyone a monster.

She walked all the way home, ten blocks of after-midnight streets and silence, and the footsteps were with her almost to the end.

* * *

The next night, it all repeated itself. The corpse of the Financial District sat glittering in the sunset, like a beautiful, expertly embalmed movie star preparing for her final audience, and Lindy sat alone in the store, her chin cupped in her hand, watching the monitors for signs that she was actually going to earn her paycheck for a change. Technically, she earned it just by showing up, not shoplifting, and not stealing anything from the register when she had the opportunity, but technicalities didn't make her feel good about her work ethic. She wanted to *work*. She wanted to *engage*. And she wanted to stay in this job until it went away, no matter how incompatible that was with everything else that she desired. Sometimes humanity was a complicated thing to hold onto.

The bell over the door rang twice over the course of her shift, both times when there was no one on the monitors and everything about the store said that she was alone. Again, the footsteps followed her home, through a night gone chilly with despair.

On the third night, the door actually opened. Lindy took her chin out of her hand and sat up straight, watching as Mr. Wallace, the owner, came into view. He was in his eighties, and when she'd taken the job, he had walked like a much younger man, chest puffed out with a pride that she had envied, even as she'd scurried behind him, trying to memorize the ins and outs of the store in a single training session. Now he shuffled, shoulders bowed, head low, eyes red with either drinking or crying or some combination of the two. He didn't normally come to the shop in the evening unless there was some sort of emergency.

Oh, no, thought Lindy, with dull resignation. Aloud, she said, "Hello, sir."

"Lindy, isn't it?" He walked in her direction. "You've been a good employee. No one has a bad word to say about you, not even some of my regulars who, well… they haven't had good things to say about many of the people who've worked here. People can get set in their ways, you understand, when they spend too much time in one place. I suppose that's why change is so important. We need to… go new places, do new things, if we want to keep growing."

Lindy's heart sank. "The rent went up again, didn't it?"

His smile was mirthless. "By sixty percent. The lease allows it, if the increase brings the unit into alignment with comparable local properties."

The only comparable local properties were the ones nestled in the bodies of the high-rises, the chains and the franchise outlets, which sold the same things, and were technically the same type of store. Only technically. Worlds could rise and fall on a technicality.

"How long do we have?"

"I can keep the doors open until the end of the month. Maybe a few months longer, if I want to cannibalize my retirement fund."

Lindy looked at him and couldn't imagine that he'd have much of a retirement fund to cannibalize. "Maybe it's best if we don't draw it out," she said, as gently as she could.

Mr. Wallace looked at her with tears in his eyes, and nodded. "That was my thought as well. I just... I can't bear to let this old girl go. She's been with me for sixty years, did you know that? I kept these doors open through earthquakes, civil unrest, rain like you wouldn't believe, and all so the people who live around here would know they could always get a loaf of bread and a gallon of milk at a fair price, no matter how bad things got. But no one lives around here anymore. The homeless folks can't afford to pay a fair price—they take what they can get from the dumpsters, and they buy fast food with the money they beg for, because a cheeseburger is a better deal than a bunch of bread that's going to go off before you have a chance to eat it all. The suits don't shop in places like mine. I should have been smart enough to get out months ago."

Maybe that was true. Lindy still shook her head and said, "I think staying was the right thing to do."

"I'll understand if you need to quit. Finding a new job can't be easy."

"It's not," she admitted. "But I like this one. If you don't mind, I'll stick it out until we close."

Mr. Wallace smiled at her, looking quietly, profoundly relieved. "If you're sure."

She wasn't, but how could she tell him that? She was losing a boring dead-end job. He was losing his livelihood, and sixty years of toil. It didn't seem right. It didn't seem fair. Something like this shouldn't have been happening to someone like him, who had never done anything wrong. Sadly, right and wrong had never had much to say when it came to this sort of thing.

"Thank you, Lindy," he said, and left, and Lindy was alone again.

That night, the footsteps followed almost to her door.

* * *

Zack quit on the fourth night. He had already been gone when Lindy showed up for her shift; she found the door locked and the lights on, which would have frustrated any customers who actually wanted to *buy* something. When she let herself in, she found a third thing: Zack's note of resignation taped to the register, where she'd be sure to see it. Lindy yanked it down with a muttered curse, crumpling it into a ball and throwing it into the corner. Let it be forgotten. Everything else was going to be.

There'd been some hope that business might pick up when people realized another neighborhood institution was about to disappear. Maybe that would have worked before everything else had closed and vanished, but here, now, there was no one left to come. The aisles stayed empty and the shelves stayed full. Lindy wondered what would happen to the stock when the doors closed for the last time. It wasn't like Mr. Wallace was selling the place to a new owner who really wanted a convenience store: the doors would be locked, the windows would be soaped over, and one day the wrecking ball would come crashing through, and the day after that the high-rise would start going up.

It would be easy to start shoplifting, just take home sacks of soda and snack cakes and stale Saltines. Mr. Wallace probably wasn't checking the security tapes anymore, and even if he was, what was he going to do? Fire her? She was already working on borrowed time.

Lindy sighed and shifted positions at the counter. Maybe he'd let her give all the food that was left on the day they closed to the local homeless population. Do a good deed and spit in the face of the Financial District at the same time. The rising rents were closing shelters and shutting down halfway houses every day, but the suits who worked in those shiny new buildings still got angry about the "homeless problem" in the city, as if all those inconvenient people should have just disappeared as soon as something *important* started happening.

The bell above the door chimed. Lindy raised her head and frowned. There was no one there. There was never anyone there.

That night, she locked up, dropped the key into her pocket, and turned away, feeling like it was the last time, even though they had another two weeks of openings and closings to go before the doors were shut forever. She turned to glare at the glittering towers of the Financial District with real hatred.

"This is all your fault," she told them, and they didn't hear her, and they didn't care. But she felt better for having said it out loud, putting the words out into the world, where there was a slim chance that they might make a difference.

Turning on her heel, Lindy began the long walk home.

The band of decay surrounding the Financial District had spread again, blighting another half-block of local business and Mom-and-Pop stores. Homeless people dressed in gray and brown—it didn't matter what color their clothes were in the beginning; they always wound up gray and brown—slept in recessed doorways, backs pressed against retractable grates, their worldly possessions cradled in their arms. It wouldn't be long before the police started coming down this block too, rousing the homeless, telling them to move along and find another place to sleep.

Three of the local shelters had closed in the last six months.

There was no other place. But still the cops said move along, move along; mustn't offend the delicate sensibilities of the ones who pay the bills and keep the lights on. They would rather have a beautiful tomb than a living city.

The graffiti had gotten even more vulgar and even angrier over the past few weeks. FUCK THE RICH was still there, but it had been joined by MAKE CAPITALIST BACON and SQUEAL PIGGIES SQUEAL and other, far more graphic suggestions about what could be done to take back the city for the people who had built it, loved it, and were now losing it, one block at a time. Lindy's eyes skirted over the walls, and she shivered, even though the night was warm. None of the violence on the walls was directed at her, but that didn't make it any more reassuring. She had been walking these streets all her life. She'd never felt unsafe until the gentrification came and stirred up all the silt that had been lying, silent and still, at the bottom of things.

It was almost a comfort when the footsteps started up behind her, like they did every night, escorting her through the dark. And as she did every night, she looked back, trying to see who was trailing her. Maybe it was another late-shift worker, making their way home through the gloom, needing a friend as much as she did. Maybe it was a serial killer, looking for their next victim. Whoever owned those footsteps, she couldn't see them. Frowning to herself, Lindy turned to face forward—

—and nearly ran straight into a brick wall. She took a stumbling step back, staring at the graffitied image of a headless businessman, complete with spurting cartoon blood. The caption read BANKERS GET WHAT THEY DESERVE— WITH INTEREST!

She must have made a wrong turn. There wasn't supposed to be a wall there, and the image was faded enough that it had obviously been there for weeks; something new would have been brighter, fresher, with the distinct chemical smell of fresh spray paint. She must have made a wrong turn. She took another step back, unwilling to put the image to her back until there was some space between her and the wall, and turned around, to face a street she had never seen before.

It was a part of her city: the architecture was correct, the patterns in the stones, the construction of the buildings. There was a certain symmetry to a healthy city, and hers had been healthy, once, before the cold rot of revitalization set in; walls grew in predictable ways, bricks were laid according to local fashions. This *was* her city. It couldn't be anything else. She could even see the skeleton spires of the Financial District in the distance, like obelisks standing guard at the mouth of a graveyard. Those, at least, looked familiar. But this...

The sidewalks were cracked and pitted, even further down the road to complete disrepair than the ones she walked along every night. The businesses were shuttered, some with broken windows, all with empty displays. Not one of them looked as if it had been opened in the last five years. Several had plywood nailed over their doorways, like sheets pulled over the faces of the dead. There was graffiti there as well, suggesting more things that could be done to the invading rich. Lindy tore her eyes away.

How could she have gone so far wrong? It made no sense at all. This was the route she always took, the way she always walked... but here she was, on an unfamiliar street, where nothing moved, nothing walked, nothing seemed to breathe. Heart hitching in her chest, she began walking briskly back the way she had come, scanning constantly for something familiar. The spires of the Financial District would be her lighthouse, guiding her back to her home ground. She could start again. She could find the right path, and leave this blighted, broken neighborhood behind.

The footsteps started up again as soon as she started moving.

Lindy stopped, balling her hands into fists at her sides. The footsteps stopped at the same time.

"Who *are* you?" she demanded, harshly, her voice sounding loud and tinny in her own ears. "Why are you following me? Do you know… do you know how to get back to the store?"

There was no response. Lindy closed her eyes, counted to four, and turned to look behind herself.

Again, the street was gone. Again, there was a wall, this one blazoned with the image of a woman in a stylish lilac business suit, slit from throat to navel, with worms squirming out of the cavernous gash that had been her torso. It was almost photorealistic. Lindy slapped a hand over her mouth, trying to swallow back the hot tide of vomit that threatened to rise up and overwhelm her. This wasn't possible. This couldn't be happening. Walls didn't just suddenly *appear*.

Lindy whirled, focusing on the distant spires of the Financial District. For the first time, that sterile corpse of a neighborhood looked like something more than gentrification. It looked like safety.

Eyes on the skyline, Lindy began to run.

Running down a pitted, broken sidewalk was dangerous even when she was watching her feet. With no attention left for where she was going, it was only a matter of time before her foot hooked on a thin place in the pavement and she went sprawling, landing hard, her chin and elbow both slamming into the concrete. Pain flared up, followed by blackness, and everything was gone.

* * *

Lindy woke to find herself lying on her back, looking up at a sky bright with stars. The taste of blood was in her mouth. She tried to sit up. Her body refused to listen. She made a small whimpering sound, and a face appeared in her frame of vision, leaning forward and looking at her with cold, concrete-colored eyes. It was androgynous, fine-boned, topped with a mop of shaggy hair the color of dust on windowsills. Lindy blinked. The face blinked back.

"Are you who's been following me?" she asked, in a whisper.

"Who's been following me," said the stranger.

"Please," said Lindy.

"Please," said the stranger, almost gently. It reached out a long-fingered hand and caressed her cheek.

Its skin felt like brick walls and empty rooms. Lindy sat up with a gasp, whipping around to face the stranger, and was somehow dully unsurprised to find that there was no one there. The sidewalk was empty. The buildings around her had broken windows and empty doorways, their walls ripe with poisonous graffiti. The Financial District still glittered in the distance, as far away as ever, an unreachable oasis of sterile, empty streets and silence. Lindy clambered to her feet, feeling the new tenderness in her joints, and started walking.

The footsteps started up behind her immediately. She did not look back.

What felt like hours later, she was still walking, and the Financial District was no closer, and the footsteps were still there. The graffiti around her was continuing to worsen, becoming more graphic and more terrifying every time she dared to look. A few times, she'd seen what she thought might be her face, rendered in spray paint and marker and agony. She hadn't taken the time to find out for sure. She was too afraid of what she'd find.

The sun had to rise eventually. The buses had to start running, or some midnight janitor had to finish their shift and emerge onto the street where she could see them, and go to them, and be saved. The world *worked*, and as long as she could count on that, she was going to make it home.

Her feet were starting to hurt. Her head ached from where she'd hit it when she fell. She was hungry, and tired, and somehow, the idea that the world worked was getting harder and harder to hold onto. None of this made sense, and all of this made sense, and it was never going to end.

Finally she stopped, head hanging, arms going limp by her sides.

"Why me?" she asked. "I didn't do anything. I stayed as long as I could. I've never done anything to hurt you."

"Hurt you," said the voice from before, next to her ear.

Lindy didn't lift her head. She knew that there would be nothing there for her to see if she did. "I stayed," she said. "Shouldn't that count for something?"

"Hurt you," said the voice again.

A dog will bite its master if it's in enough pain; sickness can drive even the sweetest creatures to violence and cruelty. Lindy loved her city as she had loved little in her life. That was why she'd always put her faith in it, always believed it would treat her well. That was why she'd stayed, even as gentrification and revitalization sunk into its bones like a cancer, killing its flesh and replacing it with sterile desolation. It was no wonder that the city was beginning to lash out, to bite, to devour what it couldn't bear to live without.

"Please," said Lindy again.

"Hurt you," said the voice of the dying city, and pulled her close, and she said nothing more.

* * *

The next morning, when Mr. Wallace came to open the store, he found a new piece of graffiti scrawled across the window, paint clinging to glass like a veil. It was a portrait of a girl who looked like one of his employees, her mouth open in a silent scream, her palms toward the viewer, like she was trying to break through into three-dimensional space. Like she was trying to break free.

He looked at it for a moment, drinking it in, before he shook his head and unlocked the door, stepping inside. On the next block, the corpse of the Financial District slowly woke and lumbered back into terrible vitality, looking out with blind and mirrored eyes at the city dying all around it.

THE CRACK

by

NICK CUTTER

My son will not stop crying.

I'm lying in bed. The red numbers on the digital clock read 3:09 AM. My kid is screaming.

He's been at it three hours tonight. It's been the same every night since we put him in the nursery. He screams himself to sleep when we put him down, then wakes up in the witching hours for another round. His screams possess a tempo; they crest and ebb and taper to sniffling sobs, then to whimpery moans and just when you think he's cried himself to sleep, there he goes again at a lung-splintering octave. I've come to realize that those lulls are only rest periods, where he's recharging his batteries to launch into another fit. He never cheats us, always gives full measure.

Right this minute, my entire body is knotted with anger. I could strangle him.

I understand how parents can kill their kids—I have great sympathy for them. Just shaking some sense into the little turds. Shaking a bit too hard. It's a thin fucking cut, man.

Ben, my kid's name. Benny. A set of lungs on him. He's a precision-engineered mutant made to do one thing, and do it at a paint-peeling pitch. The kid cries. Only at night. During the day he's an angel. He makes me proud to be a father. But as soon as the lights go off the nightly screamfest begins. And then I sort of hate him.

John Goggins. That's my name. Thirty-four years old. Foreman at the Kirkland Construction Co. Rosa, my wife, she's a mess. Ben cries until he pukes. Rosa's washing the sour sick off his pajamas daily. The dumb kid—Christ, he's old enough to know better—shrieks until his vocal cords fray. I go into his room in the morning and there's blood on his pillow from *screaming*, if you can believe it. He practically rips his throat out.

Rosa's a softie. Me? Hard as a millstone.

He's going to learn, though. The hard way, if that's how he wants it.

That's what parenting is, right? A battle of wills. Give an inch, they take a mile. So you hold onto that fucking inch like hoary old death. Ben can take that inch from me when I'm old and gray. Take it from my cold, dead hands. He's our first kid. I wanted a brood, six or seven, but Rosa's not built for it. She's got the hips, but not the mind. There are some things you only discover about your partner when you're chucked into the meat-grinder together. Those things aren't always cheery.

At first, I let his crying slide. Hell, he even slept in our room the first month or so. It wasn't a problem then. I swaddled him in a blanket and he slept between us. The sleep of the damned, too, let me tell you. But you can't get in the habit of letting a kid sleep in your bed. He'll grow up to be a mealy-mouthed little wiener. No son of John Goggins is gonna be *that kid*, understand? So into his own room he went.

Rosa breastfed the boy. When he screeched from the nursery in the dead of night, her milk let down. An instinctual thing. These two wet blotches on the front of her nightgown, her tits leaking like drippy faucets. Plus a kid's supposed to eat every few hours in the early months, so no use in him starving. But he'd scream when she put him back in the crib, even with a bellyful of milk. She tried to stay in there with him. Nope. Not happening. I went in there and dragged her out—not by the hair or anything, mind you, but she knew I wasn't fucking around. You've got to be that way with women or children. An asshole, basically. Suits me fine. And did Benny shriek like a banshee? You bet! And did Rosa cry into her pillow? You can take that to the bank! Me? I slept. I had a job to do in the morning. You think those freehold townhouses build themselves?

After three months of this Rosa suggested we get a sleep doula. A doula—the *fuck*? What are we, vegan mystics? Mona, the doula's name. A white chick with dreadlocks who smelled of alfalfa or something. I just about threw her out of the house on her ear as soon as she showed up, but I'd promised Rosa. Mona told us to keep to our room while she stayed with Benny at night. I said she ought to make breakfast in the morning with what she was charging. It was a quiet week, sure. But Mona slept on the floor curled up beside Benny's crib. I'd have the same success if I lied there like an Irish setter. But I'm not doing that because I'm not a flake.

Mona left after five days. We paid her for a week but she refunded us for the final two days. Her eyes were bloodshot. She mentioned a draft in Benny's room. Inconstant but very cold, coming from the wall beside the crib.

"A draft, huh?" I said.

"That's what I said," went ole Crazypants.

"The walls are double insulated. I supervised the insulation myself."

"I'm telling you what I felt, Mr. Goggins."

"You goddamn shyster," I said, highly pissed. "When you fail, just admit it. Go peddle your snake oil someplace else."

The next night Benny was screaming before the lights

switched off. Rosa started to sob, too. *Christ.* I wanted to walk out the door, to the bar, get drunk and hop a bus somewhere. Anywhere that didn't involve me sitting in the basement while my wife blubbered on the main floor and my son's screeches traveled down the vents to my ears.

He screamed himself to sleep the next week, the next, the next. He wasn't swaddled anymore by then; you could hear him shaking the bars of his crib as his squeals shot through the house and mainlined straight to my nerves.

"Those are scared screams," Rosa would say. "Not angry ones or hungry ones, but *scared*. A mother can tell."

"I don't give a shit." I was tired of indulging her. "We're not coddling him. A child sleeps in his room, in his bed. That's natural. You want to breastfeed him until he's eighteen?"

One night I got pissed. I mean, *really* pissed. It was gone past eleven and he was still screeching. Five straight hours! A new record. Rosa was out late at some therapy group. Was I going to some touchy-feely session where everyone braided marigolds into each other's hair after spilling their guts? Like fuck I was! I didn't need help. I wasn't broken. My kid was. But I'd fix his wagon.

I went into his room. It was dark, shadows stretching over the walls. Benny stood in his crib clutching the rails. Screaming holy hell. A wave of rage crashed over me. A blanketing sheet of red. He was my kid, blood of my blood, but in that moment all I saw was some little *freak*, a fat disgusting grub with a soupy mouth whose sole function was to make life hell for everyone around it.

I grabbed him and lifted him up. He weighed next to nothing. My fingers dug into his arms. Snot was webbed down his face. I squeezed. I felt the heat of him, the flush of his face, the spasms of his little heart. He kept crying. *Even louder*, by

Christ. He reached towards me even though I had his arms manacled. As if to hug me—to keep me there with him. I shook him. I shouldn't have, I know that, but my rage was redlined.

"Shut *up*!" I said. "*SHHHHHH!*"

His skull snapped back and forth. A rope of drool whipped out of his mouth. My heart was hammering in my own chest. It was something I could go to jail for if Rosa had put a fiber-optic video camera in one of Benny's teddy bears. He started to gag like he'd swallowed his tongue. I stopped rattling him around. His face was pink and swollen like a fleshy balloon set to burst.

Oh, Jesus. Oh, God. What had I done? My world came thundering down around me in that moment. I'd hurt him real bad. My boy. I visualized him in an electric wheelchair blowing on a tube to pilot his sagging body around.

Then his eyes focused and his gagging quit. He looked at me with that wretched look only a child can get—this *why are you doing this?* look, as if the world had been drastically reformatted in a way that terrified him.

Predictably, he started to scream. My teeth *snicked* together. I put him back in bed as he grasped desperately for me. I shut the door on his agonized shrieks. He would *learn*, goddamn it. The same way my daddy taught me and his daddy taught him. Hard lessons, sure, but needful ones.

The next morning I noticed a crack in the nursery wall. A hairline fucker. It started at the top of the wall where it met the ceiling and ran five inches down. A spidery crack. Just the one.

Cracks piss me off. I'm a foreman. A crack is a sign of shoddy workmanship. It means the walls don't line up true. But I supervised the build of my house. Me. Every detail. I centered the bubble on my level on these very walls. So it couldn't be *my* fuckup. Who the hell did the drywall? I'd check the work order and fire the prick if he still worked on my crew.

I put my hand over the crack. Cold. A draft traveling down the fireplace flue? A rupture in the bathroom vent running behind the wall? Was Crazypants right? Christ. Heads would roll.

I put my ear to the wall. Nothing but the low hum of the furnace drifting up from the basement…

But behind that sound was something else.

I couldn't put a finger on it. Weird, inconstant, like… like bugs? Beetles or crickets or mealworms maybe?—thousands of them, tens of thousands—crawling over each other, the dry rubbing of their bodies making this chittering, vaguely metallic burr that almost sounded like whispers. I pressed my ear to the wall, straining to catch a different register of that sound; my eyes rolled upwards and my chin, too, my neck muscles tensed with strain. There was something gross about that noise—*lewd*, was the word that fit. You get roaches in your walls and man, they're a bitch to get out. But we didn't have insects in the walls; I knew that to a certainty. Foam insulation with a protective mesh wraparound—there's no fucking way.

I patched the crack with drywall filler and sanded it smooth. Then I painted over it. I didn't tell Rosa. What she didn't know wouldn't hurt her.

And Ben kept screaming.

Night after night. Two, three hours. By this point, I spanked him pretty regularly. Some people would say a twelve-month-old is too young for a big league ass-paddling. I'm not one of them. I'd pull his sleeper off, tug down his diaper and spank his bare ass. It made a nice, meaty smack. His body juddered over my knee. He screamed louder, sure, but there was some pleasure in that for me.

One night it got pretty serious. Rosa was screaming herself, pleading for me to stop. Nope. We're doing this, babe. *I'll give you something to cry about, me bucko!* His little butt went red as a beet. My hand stung. I stood him on my knees. His eyes bulged out, his nose leaked snot. Calmly, I said: "If you don't stop crying, Benny, I'll come back and do it again. And again, and again." He kept shrieking and blubbering, completely hysterical. I pulled his diaper up and put him back in his crib. His screams intensified. He pressed himself to the bars, clawing through them as he tried to clutch at me. You'd think he'd prefer I was in the room, even if it meant I was spanking him, rather than sleep on his own. Then he puked—of *course* he puked. All over the mattress, the sweet pablum-y ralf of a baby. "Rosa!" I yelled, storming out.

He'd learn, goddammit. He *would*.

Later that month, he got real sick. His eyes went yellow. He stopped eating or drinking much. His stools had a sour acidic smell. His skin had this greasy feel to it, like he'd been spritzed with cooking oil. He lost three pounds almost overnight, which was like twenty percent of his body weight.

We took him to the ER. Was I scared? Yeah, I'll cop to that. I mean, I love the kid, damn it. What father wants to see his boy in pain, right?

The doctors did bloodwork, turning the poor kid into a pincushion. They tied a bag around his penis to collect his pee and stuck a cold thermometer up his caboose. Benny didn't even cry. He just gazed at me with wide bewildered eyes. Took it like a champ! The docs had figured maybe uremic poisoning, but they couldn't find anything. Tickety-boo, according to them. Fucking morons. My kid was *yellow*. How was that *fine*? They put him on IVs and gave us drops for his eyes. We spent the night in the hospital. Benny slept as peacefully as any baby ever has, I'd say. Why wouldn't he do the same in his comfy crib?

When we brought Benny home, Rosa wanted him to sleep in our bed. I caved. We were both pretty raw. Dodged a bullet, maybe, although we never got a good look at it. Benny was doing better. His color came back. He slept with us three nights. And slept well. We had to wake him up every morning because he slept so deeply, kind of like a prisoner subjected to sleep deprivation finally getting a few nights of shut-eye. There was plenty of room in our bed—we've got a California king, so Rosa and I can spread out like starfish and still not touch each other. But that's not the point, is it? The point is that a boy's got to sleep in his own bed—unless that boy's father wants a pansy on his hands.

On the fourth night, I put him back in his crib. Rosa pleaded with me not to, but the grace period was over. Back to business! Did he scream? Does a bear shit in the woods? Did that stop me? Not for one hot minute!

I could have soundproofed his room—I refurbished a recording studio one time; I could get the honeycomb panels at discount—but Rosa would have had a bird. I bought a fan at the hardware store instead. With it running full blast and the door shut, we could barely hear him in our bedroom.

A few days later, he fell out of his crib and broke his arm.

I don't know how he managed it. It happened at night. We didn't hear. An arm-break scream sounds the same as every other scream, apparently. The next morning, Rosa found him curled up next to the door, his body packed into the corner and his arm tucked under him at a funny angle. She screamed. First with horror, then at me. Did I feel a little bad? Okay, sure. But I didn't make him fall out of the damn crib, did I? He's a fucking willful child. Sometimes you've got to pay a price for that stubborn streak.

We took him to the ER again. A doctor set the break and put a cast on. It's sad to see your baby in a cast. That perfection's been ruined just a little, y'know? The world had left its first real mark on him. Rosa said we weren't going to switch the fan on anymore. Okay, fine. But he wasn't sleeping with us. I went out and bought some mosquito-netting-type stuff at the baby store, which I draped over his crib to stop him from clambering out.

It was later that same week that Rosa came downstairs while I was packing my lunchbox and said, "There's a crack in the wall in Benny's room."

A wave of unfocused anger washed through me. Anger at the house for falling apart around us; anger at Rosa for bringing this shit to me when I was set to head out the door; anger at my son for crying all night and leaving my nerve endings raw. And there was something else behind that anger, nibbling away at the edges of my mind. I couldn't tell you what that was.

The crack was bigger this time. A lot bigger. A foot-and-a-half. And wider: a jagged split in the wall, this narrow "V" of darkness. I didn't have to put a hand up to feel the cold this time: it was obvious even a few feet away. A meat-locker chill that pebbled the flesh on my forearms. Fucking *Christ*! I pounded my fist on the wall harder than I meant to—as if I was trying to frighten away something on the other side. Which was silly because there wasn't a damn thing there. Not a god*damn* thing.

There was an odor, too, almost too faint to credit. It was like… well, my son has a smell. *New baby*, you might call it. All babies have it. You put your nose right on their heads and smell their scalp. It's a wonderful scent. The *best*. Kind of sweet, sort of milky, a bit summery. The smell of a factory-fresh, showroom-mint human. The smell of youth, of innocence. It makes the world feel a little less grim. They should figure out a way to bottle it.

The smell coming from the crack had a hint of that new-baby smell, but corrupted somehow. I can't describe it except to say… think of the smell that permeates an old-folks' home:

a mixture of ointments and iodine and the yellowing sick smell of bodies rotting from the inside out. That smell terrifies a lot of us. It makes us not want to visit our great-aunt Gertie at Shady Acres, because it's the smell of death. Living death. Now imagine a person even *older* than anyone you'd find at one of those homes—so old that their certificate, the one they get for making it to their hundredth birthday, has gone ancient as old parchment. Unnaturally old—I'm talking two hundred, three hundred years old. So old that this person, whoever it is, maybe isn't fully *human* anymore; they've lived so long, seen so much with their egg-yolky eyes, that they've surrendered the fundamentals of humanity… or maybe they were never human in the first place. Now imagine such a creature with its ancient pruney body and the face of a baby. Its face has undergone the same ravages as the rest of it—but there's still that trace of an infant in its toothless smile, in its high-pitched giggle. Now imagine this corrupted thing giving off a scent, and that scent having some remnant of the new-baby smell, except remade to suit its age. Rancid and mealy, infused with that burnt-dust stink you get when you turn on the furnace for the first time in the winter. The perverted stench of youth that some wizened old *thing* might give off, if such a thing were to exist.

That was what I pictured, only for a moment: an ineffably ancient creature, some twisted goblin with the leering wrinkled face of a baby squatting behind my wall, in the dark chasm between the drywall and brick. Tapping with one black-nailed finger, tap-tap-tap-tap-tap, until the wall cracked and its revolting stink wafted up to perfume my son's room.

Which was the stupidest fucking thing in the world. Which is why I slammed my fist into the wall, pissed at myself.

I put my eyeball to the crack. I couldn't see or hear anything. No movement. Not the rustle of animals that had built a nest, not the whistling of wind. Maybe the attic was the culprit—had something up there caused the crack? I didn't hear any dripping water and the drywall wasn't water-fattened. Plus the attic was only a few feet high and packed with pink fiberglass insulation.

I filled the crack, sanded and painted it. I went downstairs where Rosa sat in the kitchen with Benny, who was doodling on his cast with a crayon. "I took care of it," I said, and left. That night I came back with flowers for Rosa and a wooden train for Benny. No reason. Just, I love them both.

Then I started having a hard time sleeping.

Living with Benny at night was like living with a grenade with the pin pulled—you never knew when it was going to go off. So even when it *was* quiet, you couldn't trust that silence to last. I'd lay in bed, acidly awake at 4:00 AM. Sometimes I'd get up while he shrieked and pace the main floor... sometimes I put my ear to the wall directly below the nursery and listened. Nothing but Benny's hoarse screams traveling through the vents.

One time, when Benny fell into an exhausted sleep, I stood outside his room. The house was utterly dark. I could hear him breathing... and—this is idiotic, but here it is—I swear I heard *someone else* breathing as well. This doubled breathing, a breath taken after my son's own nasally inhale. The other breath was lower, more subtle, a weird echo of my son's. I opened the door to check, which was stupid for many reasons, but primarily because Benny is such a light sleeper that I swear he can be awoken by air pressure shifts, such as the subtle one that registers when you open his door. He was wedged at the edge of his crib in the same uncomfortable position he always falls asleep in... one that puts him furthest away from the wall.

There was nothing else in the room. Of course there wasn't. Just my wonderful, challenging son.

Sleep deprivation is a classic form of torture—did you know

that? You stop a guy from sleeping for a few days, blasting loud music or screaming at him whenever he closes his eyes, and he enters this weird la-la-land where nothing's quite real. His brain unkinks or something, smoothing out until he loses all sense of balance and reason. You can ask him anything; he'll tell you whatever you want. The moon's made of green cheese. The Bolsheviks are poisoning the groundwater. Whatever! What-the-*fuck EVER*! Just let me sleep, you merciless pricks!

* * *

Two days ago, Rosa and I got into a fight. A doozy, as the old salts say. Busted crockery, angry curses. It got a little physical. That's on me. She pushed me, though. Pushed my buttons. She knows better. She threatened to take Benny and leave. I said it would be over her dead body. I'm not monstrous but any man, pushed to it, can do monstrous things I guess. Like I said, buttons. We both said things we didn't mean. But I knew what it was. We were tired. The household situation was tearing us apart. Lack of sleep, plain and simple.

I told her to give me two nights. Like detox. We were going to put this whole nightmare to bed once and for all. I wasn't going to hurt the kid—*I swear, Rosa, I won't harm a hair on his head*—but it would be best if she wasn't around for it. I was worried about Benny, too, I told her. He was smaller than kids his age. His growth factors were screwy because he never *slept*. More than good food or vitamins or any other shit, sleep was the biggest determiner for his health. A child who slept well was a shipshape child. So we needed to help him *be* healthy, right?

She packed a bag. Reluctantly. I told her to stay two doors down, with our neighbors. She's close with the woman. I wasn't shipping her off to a Siberian gulag, for fuck's sake.

The first night—just last night—I put him down before the

sun went down. I wanted him to feel it going dark around him. Night closing in. I was going to break him, you see. That's what it had come to. The world can be a scary place, sure. But we all have to cope with it. And once you walk through the fire, whatever that may be—well, you come out purified.

Around seven o'clock, he began to scream. I let him. Game on. I stood outside his room and in a calm and steady voice repeated: "Go to bed, Benjamin. Daddy is here. You are safe. Go to bed." He kept screaming. For hours, it seemed, I stood outside the fucking door. He *never stopped*. At some point, I guess I got frustrated and began to mock his croaky shrieks: "*Waaaaah! Waaaaaaaah!*"

Round about midnight, he began to let out these shrill doglike yelps, the purest fear-struck sounds I'd ever heard.

I imagined him standing straight up in his crib, spine stiff as a board, his eyes bugged out in terror.

I didn't open the door.

This was the heat of it, I figured. He was in the crucible. The fever was going to break and we'd be shut of this nonsense forevermore. Twenty months old is a little young to have to walk through that fire, I grant you, but every one of us has to be tested. I was, and my dad, and his dad before him. And look how we turned out.

It's strange, but after hearing a person scream for that long—being that close to it, separated only by a door—you start to hear other noises behind the screams. It's just that you're starved for different sounds, nothing more, but your ears can play funny tricks. Like you might hear something that sounds a bit splintery, like ice cubes fracturing in a glass. Or squishy and kind of sluglike. Or what may sound like the hiss of a snake, or whispers in a tongue you've never heard before. All this stuff you might hear but it's nothing. Just… like I said, tricks.

It was one o'clock when his shrieks quit out. All at once, too, like a radio snapped off. Stone silence for a full minute. Hallelujah! Then… talking. My son talking. He hardly had two words to rub together. *Mamma* and *Dadda* and *truck* and *owie* and *Do you want a smack?* and *Are you sorry?* which he picked up Lord knows where.

But I swear I heard him talking to someone. His voice warbly and raw but flat, too, like something had been pounded out of it.

I went to bed. I didn't hear a damn thing from him the rest of the night.

This morning, I go in and he's still asleep. He was shivering. He woke up screaming, but then he saw me or maybe the sunlight and simmered down. There was this crusty white foam at the edges of his mouth. Like a rabid dog! And his diapers were just *sopping* with piss. Like he'd pissed himself in fear a few times. His skin was clammy and a touch cold. I felt a little bad for putting him through it. But kids are tough and we don't remember shit from our first few years on earth, anyway. I mean, do we?

I took him out today. To the park, and for ice cream. He usually loves that stuff. We've got this petting zoo at the park and he likes feeding the llamas and sitting with a chicken in his lap, petting it gently. He's a softie, my boy. Probably grow up to be a florist or something. But today he was zoned out and distant. I don't know that he spoke two words. Usually he's a chatterbug, even if it's the same five words in a different order. He shivered a lot and threw up his ice cream, which he didn't eat much of anyway. *It's like some part of his brain has burnt out*, was the stupid thought that ran through my head—so stupid that I dismissed it, naturally.

Tonight I put him back in his room to sleep. He started

wailing before I'd gotten his pajamas on, but there was something defeated to it, like he'd given up trying to fight back. Which was good. *Finally!* I win. But then when I hugged him roughly before setting him in his crib, he grabbed my hair, twin handfuls, and held on like grim death. I had to pull him off my scalp like tenacious Velcro. He took a few strands in each of his little, white-clenched fists. He stared at me with the most pleading, wretched look. There is something about the way a child expresses themselves—there's a nakedness to it, just one-hundred percent bald emotion—that is unlike anything else. I *almost* decided against it, based on that look. Give him the night off and let him sleep with me. But the pity was short-lived. The world doesn't have much use for pity. The world eats up the pitied.

He started with those doglike shrieks when I set him down. I actually watched his pajama bottoms bulge out as he peed himself in what I can only imagine was fright. I put him down as he squealed and reached desperately for me. Nope. *Sorry, sport. We're close. We're almost through.*

I shut the door and went to my room and ran the fan. I slept for a few hours then woke at midnight to him screaming.

That was three hours ago. Right now, my anger could be charitably termed as fucking *epic*.

The clock reads 3:12 AM. A loud *crack* from Benny's room—a shuddery, fibrous sound. I'm thinking he's fallen out of bed again but no, he'd get tangled up in the netting and anyway, that didn't sound like the crack of a broken bone.

I'll check on him. Damn it! I'm breaking the first rule.

The hallway is dark in a way that is different than usual. Like the walls have dissolved and I'm walking through deep space. Benny's door is open. Just a hair. How the hell did that happen?

I walk into his room. Benny's not in his crib—I can tell

without really seeing, because it's dark in the room and my eyes haven't adjusted. A dad just *knows*, okay?

That's the first thing I notice. The second is the crack.

It's enormous. It starts at the ceiling and forks down six feet, ending two feet above the baseboards. An inconceivable crack, really. It's two feet wide at the top, winnowing down to a quarter inch at its base.

"Benny?"

My voice is strangled and tinny. A wedge of ice splits up my spine. It's so damn cold in the nursery.

I can hear something. It's coming from the crack.

These weird guttural noises. Sucking, *slurping* sounds.

"Ben, buddy?"

A powerful numbness blows through me—it's like a Novocain wind has blown through the room, numbing the surface of my skin. My heart is hammering against my breastbone so heavily that I can feel the pounding of blood in my ears.

That smell again, heavier now. The smell of a new baby ripped open and stuffed full of dust. The smell of an ancient, cavernous room filled with taxidermied infants.

"Benny—oh, Benny, oh, buddy…"

I'm at the crack. My whole skull can fit through—but I don't *want* to put it through. Terror seeps into me slowly, an IV drip pumping in slow poison. That smell, the terrible darkness that sears my eyeballs… those horrible sucking sounds.

My boy. Oh my God. My only son, my most precious possession—

"Are you sorry?"

I turn and see him in his bed. Jesus. Oh God oh thank Christ. I can't see him well—only his shape squatting in the crib. My boy my boy my sweet sweet baby—

I cross to the crib. One big step gets me there. My heart

floods with love and joy. He will sleep with me the rest of the night. He will sleep with me until he's ten if he fucking wants to. I was stupid. A man must admit when he's stupid or he's not a man at all. Benny buddy oh thank Christ we're going to patch that crack I'm going to rip the whole fucking wall down and level it to the ground and build it up safe and strong and you'll never ever—

He's in my arms. My boy! As I pull him up his scalp slides under my nose and I inhale that wondrous new baby smell—

...no, not exactly. There's something off about that smell.

I'm raising him up now, in a crisp and fluid movement fueled by fear and concern—I just want to look into my son's eyes and show him how much I love him and how sorry I am for... for...

It's difficult to see. The room is so dark it's almost funereal.

But I do see the wrinkles. Oh Christ yes. Deep as the bark on an ancient tree, each line trenched with darkness. And the eyes. Old and piss-colored, with a perfect coin of darkness in the center of each.

I'm holding him out at the ends of my arms. My boy. My precious Benny.

Something gurgles at the pit of the crack. Clotted and sludgy, the laughter of something terribly and incomprehensibly old.

My son... it reaches for me. Its arms are very long indeed.

"Daddy," it says.

ABOUT THE CONTRIBUTORS

NATHAN BALLINGRUD is the author of the novella *The Visible Filth* and the acclaimed short story collection *North American Lake Monsters*. Several of the stories have been chosen for Year's Best anthologies, including the Shirley Jackson Award-winning tale "The Monsters of Heaven." The collection itself has also won the Shirley Jackson Award, and has been nominated for this year's World Fantasy Award.

AMBER BENSON is a writer, director, actor, and maker of things. She wrote the five-book Calliope Reaper-Jones urban fantasy series and the middle grade book, *Among the Ghosts*. She co-directed the Slamdance feature *Drones* and co-wrote and directed the BBC animated series, *Ghosts of Albion*. She also spent three years as Tara Maclay on the television series *Buffy the Vampire Slayer*. Her latest book is *The Last Dream Keeper*.

KEALAN PATRICK BURKE is the Bram Stoker Award-winning author of *The Turtle Boy, Kin*, and *Sour Candy*. Visit him on the web at www.kealanpatrickburke.com and find him on Twitter @kealanburke

RAMSEY CAMPBELL is described in *The Oxford Companion to English Literature* as "Britain's most respected living horror writer." He has been given more awards than any other writer in the field, including the Grand Master Award of the World Horror Convention, the Lifetime Achievement Award of the Horror Writers Association, the Living Legend Award of the International Horror Guild and the World Fantasy Lifetime Achievement Award. In 2015 he was made an Honorary Fellow of Liverpool John Moores University for outstanding services to literature. Among his novels are *The Face That Must Die*, *Incarnate*, *Midnight Sun*, *The Count of Eleven*, *Silent Children*, *The Darkest Part of the Woods*, *The Overnight*, *Secret Story*, *The Grin of the Dark*, *Thieving Fear*, *Creatures of the Pool*, *The Seven Days of Cain*, *Ghosts Know*, *The Kind Folk*, *Think Yourself Lucky* and *Thirteen Days by Sunset Beach*. He is presently working on a trilogy, *The Three Births of Daoloth* – the first volume, *The Searching Dead*, was published in 2016, and *Born to the Dark* is forthcoming. His collections include *Waking Nightmares*, *Alone with the Horrors, Ghosts and Grisly Things*, *Told by the Dead*, *Just Behind You* and *Holes for Faces*, and his non-fiction is collected as *Ramsey Campbell, Probably*. *Limericks of the Alarming and Phantasmal* are what they sound like. His novels *The Nameless* and *Pact of the Fathers* have been filmed in Spain. He is the President of the Society of Fantastic Films.

Ramsey Campbell lives on Merseyside with his wife Jenny. His pleasures include classical music, good food and wine, and whatever's in that pipe. His website is at www.ramseycampbell.com.

M.R. CAREY is a writer who is equally at home in a wide range of media. His latest novel, *Fellside*, is a ghost story set in a women's prison. Its predecessor *The Girl with all the Gifts* was a word-of-mouth bestseller and a movie based on his own screenplay has just had its UK release. He has written for both DC and Marvel, including critically acclaimed runs on *X-Men* and *Fantastic Four*, Marvel's flagship superhero titles. His creator-owned books regularly appear in the *New York Times* graphic fiction bestseller list. He also has several previous novels, two radio plays and a number of TV and movie screenplays to his credit.

NICK CUTTER is a pseudonym for a Canadian author of novels and short stories. He has written *The Troop, The Deep, The Acolyte*, and *Little Heaven*. He lives in Toronto, Canada.

TANANARIVE DUE is the author of *The Living Blood, The Black Rose,* and *My Soul to Keep*, among others. Her short fiction was included in the groundbreaking *Dark Matter,* an anthology of African-American science fiction and fantasy. A two-time finalist for the Bram Stoker Award, the former *Miami Herald* columnist is the Cosby Chair in the Humanities at Spelman College, where she teaches screenwriting and journalism. The American Book Award winner and NAACP Image Award recipient is the author of twelve novels and a civil rights memoir, *Freedom in the Family: A Mother-Daughter Memoir of the Fight for Civil Rights*, which she co-authored with her mother, the late civil rights activist Patricia Stephens Due.

CHRISTOPHER GOLDEN is the *New York Times* bestselling author of *Snowblind, Ararat, Of Saints and Shadows*, and many other novels. A winner of the Bram Stoker Award, he has also been a finalist for the Stoker on multiple occasions, a three-time finalist for the Shirley Jackson Award, and a finalist for the British Fantasy Award and the Eisner Award, among others. With Mike Mignola, Golden co-created two cult favorite comics series, *Baltimore* and *Joe Golem: Occult Detective*. As editor, his anthologies include *Seize the Night, Dark Duets*, and *The New*

Dead. He is one third of the popular Three Guys with Beards podcast and is a frequent speaker at conferences, libraries, and schools. He is also a screenwriter, video game writer, workshop instructor, and chocolate enthusiast. Please visit him at www. christophergolden.com

SIMON R. GREEN has written fifty-eight novels, two collections of short stories and one film, and he's going to have a little lie down any time now. His best known series are the *Deathstalker* books (space opera), the *Nightside* books (a private eye who operates in the Twilight Zone solving cases of the weird and uncanny), the *Secret Histories* (Shaman Bond, the very secret agent), and the *Ishmael Jones* mysteries (Agatha Christie style mysteries with very weird elements). He rides motorcycles, appears in open air Shakespeare productions, and once punched a swan.

SHERRILYN KENYON is a regular at the #1 spot on the *New York Times* bestseller list. Since 2003, she has placed more than seventy-five novels on the list in all formats including manga and graphic novels. Current series are: *Dark-Hunter®, Chronicles of Nick®, Deadman's Cross™, Lords of Avalon®* and *The League®*. Her books are available in over one hundred countries where eager fans impatiently wait for the next release. *The Chronicles of Nick®* and *Dark-Hunter®* series are soon to be major motion pictures while *Dark-Hunter®, Lords of Avalon®* and *The League®* are being developed for television. Join her and her Menyons online at SherrilynKenyon.com and www.facebook.com/ AuthorSherrilynKenyon

JOE R. LANSDALE is the author of forty-five novels and numerous short stories, articles, essays and reviews. He has received numerous recognitions for his work, including the Edgar, the Spur, and ten

Bram Stoker Awards, eleven including Lifetime Achievement. He has written for comics, film, and television. A number of his works have been filmed, including *Bubba Ho-Tep, Cold in July*, and the *Hap and Leonard* television series for Sundance Channel. He lives with his wife in Nacogdoches, Texas.

KASEY LANSDALE was first published at the tender age of eight by Random House and is the author of several short stories and a novella, as well as the editor of several anthologies collections including Subterranean Press' *Impossible Monsters*. She is best known as a singer/songwriter whose music has appeared on Animal Planet, the Sundance Channel, and in the film *Cold in July*.

TIM LEBBON is a *New York Times*-bestselling writer from South Wales. He's had over thirty novels published to date, as well as hundreds of novellas and short stories. His latest novel is the dark supernatural thriller *Relics*, and other recent releases include *The Silence, The Hunt,* and the *Rage War* trilogy. He has won four British Fantasy Awards, a Bram Stoker Award, and a Scribe Award, and has been a finalist for World Fantasy, International Horror Guild and Shirley Jackson Awards. The movie of his story *Pay the Ghost*, starring Nicolas Cage, was released on Halloween 2015, and several other novels and screenplays are in development. Find out more about Tim at his website www.timlebbon.net

JONATHAN MABERRY is a *New York Times* bestselling novelist, five-time Bram Stoker Award winner, and comic book writer. He writes the Joe Ledger thrillers, the *Rot & Ruin* series, the *Nightsiders* series, the *Dead of Night* series, as well as standalone novels in multiple genres. His YA space travel novel, *Mars One*, is in development for film, as are the Joe Ledger novels, and his

V-Wars shared-world vampire apocalypse series. He is the editor of many anthologies including *The X-Files, Scary Out There, Out of Tune, Aliens: Bug Hunt,* and *Nights of the Living Dead,* co-edited with zombie genre creator George A. Romero. His comic book works include, among others, *Captain America,* the Bram Stoker Award-winning *Bad Blood, Rot & Ruin,* the *New York Times* best-selling *Marvel Zombies Return,* and others. A board game version of *V-Wars* was released in early 2016. He is the founder of the Writers Coffeehouse, and the co-founder of The Liars Club. Prior to becoming a full-time novelist, Jonathan spent twenty-five years as a magazine feature writer, martial arts instructor and playwright. He was a featured expert on the History Channel documentary, *Zombies: A Living History* and a regular expert on the TV series, *True Monsters.* He is one third of the very popular and mildly weird Three Guys with Beards pop-culture podcast. Jonathan lives in Del Mar, California with his wife, Sara Jo. www.jonathanmaberry.com

SEANAN McGUIRE lives in the Pacific Northwest with an assortment of felines, reptiles, and stranger things (some of them are even human). When not writing, she hunts for the perfect swamp, reads more books than is really reasonable, and watches an abnormal number of horror movies. Keep up with her at www.seananmcguire.com, or on Twitter as @seananmcguire. Seanan is the author of more than twenty books, including the *October Daye* series, the *Newsflesh* series (as Mira Grant), and *Every Heart a Doorway,* first book in *Eleanor West's Home for Wayward Children.*

HELEN MARSHALL is a Lecturer of Creative Writing and Publishing at Anglia Ruskin University in Cambridge, England. Her first collection of fiction *Hair Side, Flesh Side* won the

Sydney J. Bounds Award in 2013, and *Gifts for the One Who Comes After*, her second collection, won the World Fantasy Award and the Shirley Jackson Award in 2015. She is currently editing *The Year's Best Weird Fiction* to be released in 2017, and her debut novel *Everything that is Born* will be published by Random House Canada in 2018.

CHERIE PRIEST is the author of twenty books and novellas, most recently *The Family Plot, I Am Princess X, Chapelwood*, and the Philip K. Dick Award nominee *Maplecroft*; but she is perhaps best known for the steampunk pulp adventures of the *Clockwork Century*, beginning with *Boneshaker*. Her works have been nominated for the Hugo and Nebula awards for science fiction, and have won the Locus Award (among others) – and over the years, they've been translated into nine languages in eleven countries. Cherie lives in Chattanooga, Tennessee, with her husband and a menagerie of exceedingly photogenic pets.

SCOTT SIGLER is a #1 New York Times bestselling author the creator of fifteen novels, six novellas and dozens of short stories. His works are available from Crown Publishing and Del Rey Books. He is also a co-founder of Empty Set Entertainment, which publishes his young-adult Galactic Football League series. In 2005, Scott built a large online following by releasing his audiobooks as serialized podcasts. A decade later, he still gives his stories away—for free—every Sunday at scottsigler.com. His loyal fans, who named themselves "Junkies," have downloaded over thirty-five million individual episodes. Scott lives in San Diego, CA.

SCOTT SMITH is the author of two novels, *A Simple Plan* and *The Ruins*.

PAUL TREMBLAY is the author of the novels *Disappearance at Devil's Rock*, the award winning *A Head Full of Ghosts*, and *The Little Sleep*. His fiction and essays have appeared in *The Los Angeles Times*, *Supernatural Noir*, and numerous Year's Best anthologies. Paul is currently on the board of directors for the Shirley Jackson Awards and he hates pickles. www.paultremblay.net